Praise for Jonathan Tropper's Novels

EVERYTHING CHANGES

"Women: Want to know how men think? Here's a smart, funny, brutally honest, much-needed guy's point of view on how messy love can be. Jonathan Tropper makes me laugh and breaks my heart at the same time."
—Lolly Winston, author of *Good Grief*

"*Everything Changes* is funny, smart and touching, it made me laugh, it made me think, I teared up more than once while reading it. It's an excellent book, Tropper's an excellent writer, I highly, highly, highly recommend it."
—James Frey, author of *A Million Little Pieces*

"By turns funny and moving, Tropper's warm, winning tale will appeal to both male and female readers and may draw comparisons to Nick Hornby."
—*Booklist* (starred review)

"Reading *Everything Changes* felt like diving headfirst into a man's brain—a bit scary at first, certainly outrageous, and ultimately both hilarious and very sweet. A wild ride not to be missed."
—Claire Cook, author of *Multiple Choice*

"Funny, sensitive and occasionally over-the-top ... Tropper continues to display a fine feel for romantic comedy in this enjoyable follow-up to *The Book of Joe*."
—*Publishers Weekly*

THE BOOK OF JOE

"A beautifully crafted book of enormous heart, humility, wit, honesty and vulnerability. You want to call your friends at 3 a.m. and read whole passages out loud. You want to press it into the hands of strangers. You cannot stop thinking about it because it has rearranged your very molecules. You know that kind of book? This is that kind of book. *The Book of Joe* is utterly magnificent. I wish I'd written it myself."
—Augusten Burroughs,
author of *Running with Scissors* and *Dry*

"An elegiac, wickedly observant look at a small town and its secrets. In Jonathan Tropper's highly readable novel, the problem isn't that you can't go home again, it's that eventually you have to, whether you like it or not."
—Tom Perrotta, author of *Little Children*

"Jonathan Tropper's hilarious and heartbreaking novel *The Book of Joe* ... [is] eloquent and meaningful ... a worthwhile offering from an author who has the talent and market insight to pen a bestseller."
—bookreporter.com

"*The Book of Joe* is a sweet, deft and sentimental coming-of-age-at-34 story.... [Tropper's] humor keeps his tale buoyant as Joe stumbles into maturity."
—*New York Daily News*

"Witty, tender and beautifully written. You really fall in love with Joe. By the end I wanted to have his babies!"
—Sue Margolis, author of *Original Cyn*

"There is so much to praise in this winner of a book about a loser of a man that I won't waste my words. Read *The Book of Joe* and you too will laugh and cry (and cringe) as you watch Joe Goffman return to his hometown to make things right, only to make more and more of a mess for his family and friends—and more of a loveable jerk of himself. Like Richard Russo or Michael Chabon at their best."
—Rita Ciresi, author of
Remind Me Again Why I Married You

"The novel skillfully illustrates the tenderness and difficulties of first love and friendship.... Fans of Tom Perrotta's sarcastic humor will appreciate Tropper's evocation of both the allure and hypocrisy of small-town American life." —*Publishers Weekly*

"In the marvelously funny and self-deprecating voice of Joe, Tropper fully realizes his characters and tells their stories with poignancy, wit, and charm. This coming-of-age story is a keeper; fans of Tom Perrotta and Nick Hornby will enjoy. Highly recommended."
—*Library Journal*

"Moving, funny and compulsively readable ... Tropper leads Joe through a quest for a better self that is wise, honest and often downright hilarious. He erects a story of emotional truth that leaves you with a lump in your throat and a smile on your face."
—*BookPage*

"Fantastically funny ... A first-rate tale of a thirtysomething's belated coming-of-age." —*Booklist*

Also by Jonathan Tropper

The Book of Joe

everything changes

jonathan tropper

delta trade paperbacks

EVERYTHING CHANGES
A Delta Book

PUBLISHING HISTORY
Delacorte Press hardcover edition published April 2005
Delta trade paperback edition / April 2006

Published by
Bantam Dell
A Division of Random House, Inc.
New York, New York

Cover design by Royce M. Becker

Book design by Carol Malcolm Russo

Library of Congress Catalog Card Number: 200456110

ISBN-10: 0-385-33742-6
ISBN-13: 978-0-385-33742-7

Printed in the United States of America
Published simultaneously in Canada

www.bantamdell.com

BVG 10 9 8 7 6 5 4 3 2 1

For my brothers, Elisha and Amram,
and my baby sister, Dassi,
with love

acknowledgments

Thank you.

To my family: My wife Lizzie, who tolerates my often erratic behavior, and who deals so gracefully with the occasionally uncomfortable social implications of my "artistic temperament." And to my wonderful kids, Spencer and Emma, whose constant laughter and perfect affection make it impossible to brood for any extended length of time.

To Simon Lipskar, my fantastic agent, who pours gasoline on the fire under my ass whenever it starts to die down, and even when it doesn't, because he's just one of those people who likes to burn your ass from time to time. Thanks also to Dan Lazar, Maja Nikolica, and all the other great people at Writers House.

To Kassie Evashevski, my equally savvy West Coast agent, who can generate a buzz faster than Jell-O shots, and who always seems to know at least thirty players who are just going to love it.

To Jackie Cantor, my effervescent and loving editor, whose zany brilliance makes her a pleasure to work with. If Diane Keaton swallowed Woody Allen whole at the end of *Annie Hall,* the result would be someone like Jackie, the only person I know who can spend ten minutes coherently debating a point with my voice mail.

To Irwyn, Nita, Barb, Susan, Cynthia, Betsy, and everyone else at Bantam who worked so hard to get you to read this book.

To Ethan Benovitz, who unwittingly planted the first seed from which this book would grow. I'll never tell, but you, my friend, will no doubt have some explaining to do.

To Robert Feiler, for your friendship and inspiration, which, no matter how many times you say it, still doesn't entitle you to any royalties.

To my fantastically screwed up friends, and my normal friends with fantastically screwed up families, for feeding my insatiable imagination on a daily basis.

one one one one one one one one one one one
one one one one one one one one one one one
one one one one one one one one one one one
one **one** one one one one one one one one one
one one one one one one one one one one one

one

The night before everything changes, an earthquake jolts me out of my sleep and I instinctively reach over for Tamara, but it isn't Tamara, of course, it's Hope. There was never even a time when it might have been Tamara. And yet, lately, whenever I wake up, my first, dazed instinct, before real life comes back into focus, is to assume it's Tamara in the bed beside me. I suppose that in my dreams, not the one or two that I can recall, but the millions that vanish into oblivion like flies when you've barely even begun to move your cupped, ready hand in their direction, in those dreams, she must be mine, over and over again. So there's always this vaguely troubling notion when I wake up like this, this sense that I've somehow been transported to an alternate universe where my life took a left instead of a right because of some seemingly insignificant yet cosmically crucial choice I made, about a girl or a kiss or a date or a job or which Starbucks I went into . . . something.

Meanwhile, back in real life, the Upper West Side of Manhattan trembles like a subway platform, rattling windows and uprooting corner trash cans, the shrill wail of multiple car alarms rising up over Broadway, piercing the night at its stillest, in the hour just preceding dawn.

"Zack!" Hope shouts, reaching out urgently for me, the volume of her voice almost as startling as the quake, her manicured nails slicing painfully into my shoulder. *Hope, not Tamara. That's right. Beautiful Hope.* I open my eyes and say, "What the hell?" It's the best I can manage under the circumstances. We look up at the ceiling as the bed shimmies lightly under us, and then quickly climb out of bed. My trusty Felix the Cat boxers and her satin Brooks Brothers pajamas belie the postcoital nature of our broken slumber. The tremors have stopped by the time we run downstairs to the living room, where we find Jed, my housemate, standing naked and peering out the window with mild curiosity.

"What happened?" I say.

"I don't know," Jed says, rubbing his toned abdomen absently. "I think it was an earthquake." He turns from the window and moves lazily toward the couch.

"Oh my God!" Hope cries, simultaneously spinning around and covering her eyes.

"Oh," Jed says, first noticing her. "Hi, Hope."

"Can you put that thing away for a minute?" I say on Hope's behalf.

"I didn't know she was here," Jed says, making no move to conceal his kinetic nakedness.

"Well, you do now," Hope says in that high, aristocratic whine that never fails to bug me.

I love Jed, but he's been pulling this naked shit more and more lately. I can't recall the last time I saw him wearing a shirt. One of the few downsides to living with an unemployed millionaire is that he has nothing to do but watch television and cultivate eccentricities. On the other hand, I live in a newly renovated brownstone on the Upper West Side and haven't paid rent in over three years. In Manhattan, this makes me nothing less than fortune's son. When you do the math, I am being highly compensated to tolerate the occasional flapping phallus. I grab a pillow off the giant leather sectional that runs the perimeter of our ridiculously large living room in a wide crescent, and throw it at him. "Cover yourself, Jed. For the sake of the nation."

Jed sits down on the couch and wipes the crust out of his eyes while I gag inwardly at the thought of his naked ass on the mushroom-colored Italian leather. He crosses his legs and perches the pillow comically over his genitals, flashing me his trademark laid-back grin. Hope sniffs, audibly and with great inflection, before walking over to the window. Jed has made a lot of money, but Hope comes from money, which carries with it a distinctly different flavor. Having done neither, all I can do is sigh a this-is-my-life kind of sigh, resigned, but not without some trace of contentment. Jed is my best friend, and sometimes a bit of an asshole. Hope is my fiancée, and while I don't think she's a snob, I can see why Jed might. They are polar opposites, triangulated by my central presence between them. Physically, though, they could be siblings. Both are effortlessly beautiful, tall and lean, with thick hair and chiseled features. Jed's prominent forehead and thick nose lend him a vaguely European look, like a Calvin Klein model, and he cuts his hair short so he doesn't have to brush it. Hope's hair is thick, obedient, and often suspiciously similar to Gwyneth Paltrow's latest style, although she would never admit to such pedestrian influences. I stand between these two attractive people as something of an oddity, like the guy taking the light readings at a photo shoot, miraculously connected to both of them, conspicuously average; the man in the middle.

Jed and I met in Columbia and became roommates after we graduated, in a run-down junior four on 108th and Amsterdam. At the time, he was working as an analyst at Merrill Lynch and I was writing long, boring press releases full of disclaimers for a PR firm specializing in pharmaceuticals. Then Jed quit his job to join a hedge fund investing in Internet startups and, like everyone else except me, became a millionaire by the year 2000. By the time the bubble had burst, he'd already bought the brownstone, inviting me to move in with him, and sold enough stock before the fall to bank a healthy few million to boot. For a while he talked about going back to work in the financial sector or maybe starting his own hedge fund, but then our buddy Rael got killed and Jed pretty much forgot about all that, and announced that he was going to just stay home and watch television for a while. That was almost two years ago, and as far as I can tell, he seems to have found his true calling. The nudity is more of a hobby.

Rael, my best friend since the third grade, lost control of his BMW on his way home from a night of gambling in Atlantic City. The car swerved up an embankment on the Garden State Parkway and crashed through the woods before flipping over into a gully. It was two in the morning and the parkway was empty when it happened, so it took a while for help to show up, and by then he was dead. I doubt they could have saved him anyway, since his internal organs were pretty much crushed on impact when he was impaled on the steering wheel. It would be comforting to think he died instantly, but it actually took a while. I know, because I was sitting next to him.

"Did we really have an earthquake?" Hope says, sounding like a little girl as she peers out at Eighty-fifth and Broadway. Her whine is gone, and I love her again.

"So it would seem," Jed says.

He turns the television to one of the local channels while we gaze out the window, considering the possibility of terrorist actions. Since 9/11, we take nothing for granted. The din of the car alarms is starting to lessen, and a few hardy souls have ventured out onto the street to assess the situation. They're showing an old Clint Eastwood film on channel 55—urban Clint, as opposed to grizzled Western Clint—and after another minute, the crawl appears at the bottom of the screen confirming that yes, in fact, we did have a minor earthquake. No injuries or damages have been reported.

"Since when does Manhattan have earthquakes?" Hope says in a tone that suggests she's inclined to write a letter to someone's supervisor about this. "I've lived here my whole life, and I don't recall there ever being one before."

"Maybe not on the East Side," Jed says. "Here in the West, we get them all the time." He never misses a chance to needle Hope about her privileged roots. "Teach you to go slumming." He winks at me, a quick, effortless wink that I have fruitlessly tried to cultivate from time to time. My facial muscles apparently lack the required flexibility, and my cheek always manages to get dragged into the fray, lending the gesture a ticlike quality guaranteed not to impress.

Hope looks down her perfect nose at Jed. "You are an ass," she declares sincerely.

"No," he says, standing up briefly to bend over and flash her some moon. "This is an ass."

"Oh, for God's sake," she squeals exasperatedly, turning to me like it's my fault and flashing me her what-lovely-friends-you-have smirk. Her genteel origins did not prepare her for guys like Jed, or me for that matter, and I have to say that she's adjusted rather admirably in the name of love. "Let's go back to bed," I say, taking her hand. Jed plops back down on the couch, the leather farting as it scrapes against his skin, or else he's actually let one rip, which would hardly be out of character. We won't wait around to find out. He flips on the television, surfing aimlessly through the vast desert of late-night programming. "Night, Jed," I call to him from the stairs, but he's already gone, swallowed up in the numbing blue-green glow of the fifty-two-inch plasma screen, his true home for the last two years.

"*X-Files*," he announces exuberantly. "Damn. I saw this one." He'll sit there until morning, watching reruns and infomercials, effectively doubling his odds of encountering Chuck Norris. At some point he'll take a nap and a shower, order in some breakfast, and, thus replenished, resume his mindless vigil.

Back in my room, I try to capitalize on our unscheduled wakefulness and extract Hope from her pajamas, but although she lets my hands roam blissfully under her shirt, she obstinately refuses to relinquish it. "I have to be at work early," she says.

I gently rub her left breast in what's intended to be a seductive motion, running my hand across her nipple and down to where the softness disappears into her ribs and then back up again, her breast filling my palm, overflowing against my fingers like a rising cake when I press inward. Hope has the greatest body of anyone I've ever been allowed to touch. Her long, toned torso is crowned with two remarkably pert, grapefruit-size breasts whose tall, barrel-shaped nipples jump to attention at the slightest manipulation. Her legs are lean and toned from her thrice-weekly spinning workouts at the Reebok Club, and above them sits a Magritte apple of an ass, firm but deliciously yielding. "Come on," I say, already popping out of my Felix the Cat fly. "Earthquake sex."

She looks at me skeptically. "Earthquake sex?"

"Of course."

I am forever cataloging the vast cornucopia of the various kinds of sex there are to have. New Partner Sex (basic and always fun), Shower Sex (more technically difficult than it appears on Cinemax), Platonic Friends Dry Spell Sex (the sexual equivalent of emergency rations), Sloppy Drunk Sex (self-explanatory), Hotel Sex (make all the mess you want, since you won't have to clean it up), and Wake-Up Sex (absolutely no tongue kissing), to name a few. When it comes to sex, my inner teenager pretty much has the run of the place.

Hope remains unimpressed. "I've got a maritime auction tomorrow," she says, firmly removing my hand from under her pajamas.

"Do you realize what a rare opportunity this is?" I say. "What are the odds of another earthquake in Manhattan?"

"Only slightly better than the odds of your getting any right now," she says with a yawn, rolling over and closing her eyes.

"Come on, I'll be quick."

"Sorry. I need to sleep."

"But what about my needs?"

Hope opens one eye and rolls it at me. "We had sex three hours ago," she says.

"And wasn't it great?" I say.

The other eye opens. "The earth moved," she says, and

smiles lovingly, a rare smile devoid of her habitual irony. I love that smile, and how it feels to be both its cause and effect.

"There you have it, then," I say.

She leans over and gives me a quick peck on the lips. "Good night, Zack." Her tone leaves me no wiggle room. Not that I'm keeping count, but I suspect I've been getting a lot less sex since this whole engagement business started. I roll over painfully onto my vestigial erection, and then turn to watch her drift off to sleep. I love the way she folds her hands under her cheek, like a child pantomiming sleep, the way she rolls her knees up, curling herself into a compact ball. Hope at rest is a rare thing, and it gives me time to contemplate her beauty, to wonder, as I often do, at the dumb luck that has brought this angel into my bed. "Why do you love me?" I've asked her repeatedly.

"Because you have a big heart," she's told me. "Because you've spent your life taking care of your brothers, and you don't even understand the strength and love that that must take. Because you think you have to earn everything, that nothing is coming to you, which means, among other things, that you'll never take me for granted. Because," she has said, "every boyfriend I ever had loved me for my potential, for what they expected me to become once we were married, an accessory to affluence. But you have no great plans for me. You love me for who I am right now, which means you'll always love me, no matter what I become."

"Why do you love me?" I whisper to her now.

"Because I knew you were going to ask me that right now," she murmurs without opening her eyes.

When I fall asleep, I dream of Tamara.

• • •

Life, for the most part, inevitably becomes routine, the random confluence of timing and fortune that configures its components all but forgotten. But every so often, I catch a glimpse of my life out of the corner of my eye, and am rendered breathless by it. This is my own doing, this life, with my millionaire-playboy housemate and my stunning fiancée with blood as blue as the clear winter sky. I spend my days toiling in my office, and then come home to a spectacular brownstone where I hang with rock musicians and beautiful people. This is no accident. I made this happen. I had a plan.

I am about to fuck it all up in a spectacular fashion.

Morning. I don't have to open my eyes to know that Hope is long gone. She'll have awakened at six, preferring to shower and change in her own apartment before going to work. Hope works at Christie's, evaluating nineteenth-century paintings that will ultimately be auctioned off to the rich and stuffy, and although she won't come out and say it, she's mildly disgusted by my shower, with its gooey shampoo bottles, dented Irish Spring bars, scattered Q-tips, and disposable Bic razors planted strategically on every available surface. I've repeatedly offered to stock her Bumble and Bumble hair care products and Burberry body wash, but she blanches at the impropriety of the whole premarital bathroom thing. In truth, she's only recently begun sleeping over—mostly on weekends—a gracious concession to the diamond I recently, unbelievably, placed on her finger.

I roll over and survey my room lovingly, and with a touch of wonder, as I've done almost every morning for the last three years. It's a large, square room, about eighteen by eighteen feet.

I've furnished it sparingly to maintain the feeling of open space. It contains my queen-size bed, a small cherrywood desk from the Door Store upon which sit a black eighteen-inch flat-screen computer monitor, a cell phone charger, a cordless phone and charger, scattered pictures, receipts, dry-cleaning stubs, and approximately six months' worth of miscellaneous mail and papers that I fully intend to get to, although I probably never will. The floor-to-ceiling bookcases are crammed with an eclectic collection of trade paperbacks, contemporary fiction mostly, some of the classics for show, a handful of the better Star Trek novels, screenplays printed off the Internet, and three or four years' worth of *Esquire* and *Entertainment Weekly*. Opposite my bed is an entertainment center containing a thirty-two-inch Panasonic flat-screen with built-in DVD player, a VCR, and a Fisher stereo. The center of the room contains only an expanse of thick wine-colored carpeting that is more than occasionally littered with discarded clothing. On one wall hangs a framed, original *Rocky* movie poster on which a bloodied, pre-steroids Stallone collapses into Adrian's arms, and on the opposite, a well-known Kandinsky print, a gift from Hope. The door to the bathroom is between the bookcase and the desk. The bedroom in my last apartment was roughly the size of my bathroom.

On my way to the shower, I see that Hope's hung one of my suits on the bathroom doorknob with a yellow Post-it note in her elegant script. *Perfect for the party, but it needs to be dry-cleaned. Love you, H.* Her parents are throwing a party in our honor this coming Saturday night in their apartment, to officially announce our engagement. This despite their evident disappointment in their daughter's selection of a mate, although I think I'm starting to grow on her mother, Vivian, who finds my suburban middle-class sensibilities humorously quaint. I consider Hope's note and the somber dark suit she's selected, clearly having overlooked the Moe Ginsburg label or she'd have rejected it for sure. Today is Monday. "Fuck," I say for no readily apparent reason.

My bathroom is all done in a soothing gray, the tiles, the wallpaper, sink, bath, and toilet all peacefully monochromatic, contrasted nicely by the white towels that hang on the brushed chrome rack. It's like a halfway house between sleep and consciousness, muted, functional, and unchallenging to the eye.

While I'm taking a leak, I notice something disturbing. My piss, usually a vibrant Big Bird yellow in the morning, is colorless, except for what appears to be the occasional flash of a cola-colored thread within the stream. When I look into the bowl, the colors have separated and I see a small floating nebula, which is now an unmistakable blood red. I feel an icy sensation in my belly, a tremor in my bowels. I study myself in the mirror for a minute, my brow furrowed in consternation. "That can't be good," I say.

When I step into the shower, I find myself wistfully wondering what it could be, and if it might somehow get me out of the engagement party.

two two two two two two two two two two two two
two two two two two two two two two two two two
two two two two two two two two two two two two
two **two** two two two two two two two two two two
two two two two two two two two two two two two

My father has an erection. I haven't seen him in at least six or seven years, and he shows up on my doorstep at breakfast time with a hard-on that lifts his suit pants like a tent pole. "Hello, son," he says, like Pa Kent to my Clark. Fathers from New York generally refer to their sons by their proper names. "Son" definitely requires a sun-drenched cornfield in the background. And fathers all over the planet generally tend to maintain a substantial distance between their offspring and their erections.

"Norm."

"That's right," he says as if pleasantly surprised that I recognize him. "How are you, Zack?"

"I'm okay. How are you?"

He nods slowly. "Shipshape. Shipshape."

But seaworthy? I wonder. "You have a hard-on."

"Yeah," he says, looking down and shaking his head sheepishly. "I took some Viagra a little while ago, and it just won't quit."

"Of course," I say, like it makes all the sense in the world. "I always like to sport some wood when I visit the family."

My father grins, wide and devilish. "I had a sudden change of plans," he says by way of explanation.

"Well, I don't think all of you got the memo."

He smiles good-naturedly, his perfect teeth gleaming white like a toothpaste commercial. "Teeth and shoes," he used to say. "Teeth and shoes. You show up to a meeting with lousy teeth or shabby shoes, you've already made a bad impression, before you say word one." He's sporting a day or two's worth of stubble that's tellingly whiter than the ring of unkempt hair that encircles the radiant center of his balding head. He's allowed these few remaining strands to grow ridiculously long in the back, and the effect is kind of like Jack Nicholson playing Ben Franklin, which would actually be an inspired bit of casting, if you think about it. Despite Norm's pronounced gut, he's somehow smaller and altogether less substantial than in my memories. I don't keep any pictures of him around.

"I heard you're getting married," he says. "Heard she's a beautiful girl."

I don't know how he could have possibly heard about it, but I won't give him the satisfaction of asking. "She is," I say.

"Listen," he says. "Can I come in?"

"What for?" I say.

His smile falters. "I'd like to talk to you."

"I'm late for work."

"Have you been getting my messages?"

"Sure." He's been calling sporadically ever since the Twin

Towers came down, leaving long, rambling messages saying that the tragedy had made him realize what was truly important, and that we needed to get together and talk. It's typical of Norm to see the annihilation of some three thousand lives as an opportunity. I've taken to screening my calls.

"Well, I can certainly understand why you don't call back, but I am suggesting that I'm here in the interest of getting past all of that. I know I've let you down before. I've been a lousy father, no doubt about it. But I wanted to tell you, in person, that I'm sober now. Just hit my ninety-day mark—"

"So now you're an alcoholic?" I say skeptically.

"I am," he says with an air of practiced humility. "And I'm up to step nine of the twelve steps, which is making amends."

"Nice tactic, Norm," I say, unable to keep the sarcasm from creeping into my voice. "The nine-eleven thing didn't work, but who can say no to a recovering alcoholic, right? It's brilliant."

"Naturally, you have every right to doubt me."

"You think?"

He sighs. "Listen, I've been on my feet for a while already. Can I please just come in for a glass of water?"

I peer down at him, trying for a moment to look past all of my issues and his bullshit and just see him for who he truly is, but all I can see is a sixty-year-old con artist in a worn, wrinkled suit, down on his luck, with the bad sense to play the sympathy card while sporting a chemically induced erection. He looks dirty, decrepit almost, and even though I'm disgusted with myself for the sudden wave of sadness and pity that washes over me, I let him into the brownstone, and he waits in the living room while I fetch him a glass of water.

"Great place," he says, impressed. "You own, or are you renting, if you don't mind my asking?"

"It's Jed's," I say, handing him the glass. He drinks the water quickly, wiping his wet lips with his sleeve as he hands me back the cup.

"You feel that earthquake last night?" he asks me.

"Sure."

"You know, in ancient times, some cultures believed that earthquakes were occasions for intense introspection, the gods shaking up the fates, giving you the opportunity to change your destiny." He looks at me meaningfully.

"Or maybe it was just the gods gangbanging the thirteen-year-old virgin that had been sacrificed the night before," I say.

Norm grins ruefully. "Listen, Zack," he says. "All I'm asking for is a half hour, an hour at the most. I know you're angry, and I'm certainly deserving of your anger, but I'm still your father, and like it or not, I'm the only one you'll ever get."

I have no time for this. I'm still thinking disconcertedly about the blood in my piss, wondering if I should do anything about it. "I really have to get to work," I say.

He stares at me for a moment and then nods slowly. "Okay," he says. "Now's not a good time." He fishes into his suit pocket and hands me a bent business card. Few things are more pathetic than an unemployed man with a business card. "My cell," he says. "I'm headed down to Florida in a few days. A guy I know down there wants me to run his sporting goods store. But I came here first, because this is important. Please, Zack. I'm staying with some friends downtown. I'll stay a few days more if that's what it takes."

"I'll think about it," I say, ushering him toward the door.

"I am suggesting that that's really and truly all I could ask for," he says solemnly. Over the years, Norm's developed this odd manner of speech, his sentences festooned with flowery malapropisms that he thinks make him sound better educated, the distracting patter of a bad salesman. He extends his hand. I shake it, not because I want to but because what the hell else can you do when someone extends his hand. "It's great to see you, Zack. You look wonderful, really terrific."

I'm pissing blood. "Thanks," I say coldly.

He grins widely, as if he's achieved a minor victory. "How, then, is your mother?" he says.

I tell him that's none of his business, not because I care but because I want to see if I can wipe that shit-eating grin off his face.

I can.

As a young boy, I would wake up scared in the middle of the night, terrified that I'd been left alone in the house, and I would come running into my parents' room, always to his side of the bed. His large arms would hoist me up and onto him, where I would lie with my head pressed flat against him, listening to the beating of his heart through his soft, fleshy chest as he rubbed my back, pulling my pajama shirt up in the places where it clung to my small, sweating trunk. And then, as my staggered breaths became slower and deeper, he would sing to me, his voice hoarse and dulled with sleep.

Good night, sweet baby, good night
I'm right here to watch over you
And the moon, stars, and I
And this old lullaby
Will make all your sweet dreams come true

You can never totally hate someone who sang you to sleep like that, can you? Who calmed you down and eased your fears.

You can feel angry and betrayed, but some part of you will always love them for being there on those scary nights, for giving you a place to run to where your nightmares couldn't follow, the one place where you could descend finally into slumber knowing, at least for the time being, that you were completely safe.

three

my mother did all the household accounting, so when my father started sleeping with his secretary, Anna, he rightly worried that paying for motel rooms two or three times a week could lead to discovery. He decided the smarter move would be to simply bring Anna home during his lunch hour to fuck her in the familiar comfort of his own marital bed. While this precluded the possibility of a money trail, it nevertheless must have left some forensic traces, because when my mother finally stepped into the room to catch him in the act, she was prepared. Rather than get hysterical and throw things, she simply snapped some damning pictures with the Nikon she'd bought him as an anniversary gift a few years earlier, when he'd declared a newfound, if typically fleeting, passion for photography. As he and Anna scrambled for their clothing, my mother walked calmly down the stairs of our attached house and then three blocks over to the Ace Pharmacy, where she dropped off the film to be developed. The Nikon hanging from her shoulder irritated her, so she tossed it into a corner trash can, bought herself a diet soda, and took a long walk.

In the days that followed, an eerie calm beset our house, none of us willing to shatter the inscrutable, fragile truce that had somehow been forged in the aftermath of this event. My siblings and I were able to piece together what had happened, because the walls of our attached townhouse in Riverdale were paper thin, and my parents' whispered bedroom arguments, my father's desperate pleas and my mother's bitter recriminations, were easily discernible from the hall bathroom.

I was twelve years old, Pete nine, and Matt an already angry seven. We all knew this meant trouble. Even Pete, who was mildly retarded and didn't always catch on, knew some bad shit was afoot, but none of us really believed this might be the watershed event. It wasn't the first time this had happened. We all knew the drill, even Pete. Dad screwed up, things got tense for a while, and then Dad made up for it. He'd once even confided in me that when it came to him and my mother, he was the comeback king.

But there would be no comeback this time. A few weeks later my mother sent out her Jewish New Year cards, and instead of a family portrait, that year's picture was my father and Anna at the horrifying instant of their discovery. No airbrushing, no posing, just the raw, messy truth of middle-aged coupling captured from a blunt angle, anatomy as nature never intended it to be seen.

Norman King, my father, was a popular character in the neighborhood. He walked the streets like a politician, greeting everyone he passed by name, and if he didn't know your name, he'd either introduce himself or say, "Good morning, chief."

He was the sort of man who was on a first-name basis with all the shopkeepers, and knew to ask after their wives, children, or parents with perfect specificity. He would draw the men into lengthy discussions of their businesses, offering suggestions and tax-planning strategies. His job in the bookkeeping department of a large Manhattan corporation lent him the aura of white-collared big-business expertise, and he took great pains to burnish that image, not in the least because he believed in it, often throwing on a tie even just to run out to the grocery store for a carton of milk. He came across as a guy who knew how everything was wired, who had the inside track. His own slew of failed entrepreneurial ventures never seemed to diminish this perception, even to him. "Your failures are the foundation upon which your success is built," he would say grandly. Occasionally, as I grew older, it would occur to me to wonder what success, exactly, he was referring to, but he spoke with such assuredness that I instantly doubted my own doubts, and that, in actuality, was his greatest gift. He was the most believable bullshit artist I've ever known.

Norm was also abundantly chivalrous to the ladies, greeting them with a gallant flourish and flattery, always able to point out a new haircut or dress. He was on friendly terms with most of the women in our neighborhood, and if it ever seemed to me that there was an inappropriately sexual nature to some of these relationships, I dismissed the thought out of hand and chalked it up to my own immaturity, until he started getting caught. Mostly, I enjoyed walking the streets with him, basking in his popularity, feeling like the son of a king.

So it had to have been a devastating blow to Norm when my mother sent out those cards. It went well beyond the public documentation of his infidelity; it was a humiliation of the highest order, the emperor exposed, warts and all, in the unforgiving clarity of 200 ASA Kodacolor. She knew what she was doing, my mother. After years of silently suffering these betrayals, not only had she hatched a plan that trashed his reputation, shattering forever the carefully cultivated persona he'd been refining for years, but she was also forcing her own hand, making further reconciliation impossible. Because now, when she felt herself weakening and leaning toward her customary forgiveness, the pressure from the community would keep her from relenting. And even if she managed to overcome that, she knew that now Norm would never be able to stay in Riverdale.

We forgave my mother for this, and for failing to realize, in the haze of her flaming rage, that the inflammatory pictures she'd sent out to her friends would find their way into the hands of their children and ultimately into the halls of our elementary school, not only making a laughingstock of her sons but affording them the ineffaceable view of their father in mid-coitus, his hairy, dimpled ass, his guilty, shriveled penis, and the unrestrained rolls of his belly fat frozen for all posterity as he flung himself off Anna, who lay engorged and spread-eagled beneath him. I'm here to tell you, you don't forget something like that. Ever.

Until then, the only nudity I'd ever seen was in the *National Geographic* magazines my friends and I pored over in the public library, studying the oblong taffy breasts of aboriginal women, their square, sandpapery asses, so unlike what we thought an ass should be, what we imagined lurked like buried treasure beneath the skirts of the high school girls we jerked off to. Then I happened upon Mike Rochwager and Tommy Chiariello in the boys' bathroom, copiously examining the New Year's card purloined from Mike's parents' mail drawer. They wordlessly handed me the picture and watched me as I looked at it, my face carefully blank. Beneath the picture was calligraphy, in Hebrew and English, wishing the recipient a happy and sweet new year.

"Is that really your father?" Mike asked.

"Yeah."

"My dad says your mom's going to take him for every red cent he has."

"What's that supposed to mean?"

"You know," Mike said. "In the divorce."

"They're not getting divorced!" I shouted, tearing the photo in half.

"Hey, that's mine!" Mike yelled, pushing me against the wall, wresting the two halves of the picture from my fingers and handing them to Tommy for safekeeping.

"Give it back!" I screamed, lunging at Tommy, but he'd hit puberty in the fifth grade, and the head start put him a good head taller and twenty pounds heavier than me. He deflected me easily, holding the pictures above his head in one hand while shoving me to the sticky tiled floor with the other. I jumped up, fully prepared to get my ass kicked by Tommy, but at that moment the bathroom door swung open and Rael stepped in. He sized up the situation in an instant and quickly walked over to stand by my side. "Is that the picture?" he demanded. Rael wasn't quite as large as Tommy, but he was close, and his sharp fearlessness bridged the gap.

"It's mine," Mike whined, cowering behind Tommy.

Rael ignored him, his eyes never leaving Tommy's. After a few seconds, Tommy said, "Whatever," and tossed the two halves of the photo disgustedly to the floor. "Let's go," he said to Mike. "He probably wants to beat off to his father's whore."

After they were gone, Rael handed me the pieces with a

sympathetic frown, and then leaned against the door as I tore furiously at the photo until it was scattered like confetti at my feet, hot tears running down my face in a steady stream. Who the fuck said anything about a divorce?

This is what happens. Your father shreds the family with his repeated infidelities and then takes off for parts unknown, leaving you and your siblings to stumble into a new philosophy as to what life is all about. You're the oldest and therefore feel the greatest sense of betrayal as you witness the extinguished eyes of your mother, the sullen glare of your younger brother Matt, who denies that he's crying himself to sleep at night even though you can plainly hear him, and Pete, whose lack of comprehension should be viewed as a blessing in this instance, but in whose uncompromising, sweet demeanor you see only a reminder of the depth of your father's transgressions. You see the members of your family floating in their own separate orbits of misery, and you vow to replace your worthless father, to provide the strength and guidance your siblings need, to take what weight you can off your mother's shoulders so that maybe the light will return to her eyes, the easy laughter and affection you'd always taken for granted. Maybe Matt will start smiling again, and stop playing alone in his room with his action figures, and maybe it will feel like a family again, instead of an ongoing funeral. You're twelve years old, and you don't yet know that you don't know shit. You're just determined to be everything your father wasn't, for them and for yourself, and it takes a while for you to understand that it's not within your power to undo the damage that Norm did, that the injuries go much deeper. By then, your determination not to emulate him has become something of an obsession, and it's a point of pride whenever you can point to the ways in which you're avoiding your progenitor's defective character. *I'm not like him* becomes your mantra, and while you would never cop to it, it may very well have become your universal philosophy boiled down to its absolute essence.

four four four four four four four four four four
four four four four four four four four four four
four four four four four four four four four four
four **four** four four four four four four four four
four four four four four four four four four four

i ride the subway in misery, my thoughts condensed into a chain of four words repeated in an endless loop to the beat of the rhythmic drumming of the subway car. *Blood in my urine–blood in my urine–blood in my urine.* I disembark at Times Square and head east to Sixth Avenue, arriving at work only a half hour late, tense and distracted, the dash of crimson against white porcelain still haunting me. What does it mean?

I work for the Spandler Corporation. We are a three-hundred-million-dollar business, with offices in twelve states. We have over five hundred employees. We are known throughout the country as a leader in the industry. Our customers rely heavily on us. We produce nothing. We sell nothing. We buy nothing. If we didn't exist, Kafka would have to invent us.

We call ourselves supply-chain consultants. We call ourselves outsourcing specialists. But our true vocation can be summed up in one word. We are middlemen.

We service the world's largest companies in the overseas manufacturing of their products. We know where to go for everything you need. We have relationships with every possible type of manufacturing facility you can imagine, and many that would never occur to you. We might order ribbons from China, fabric from Italy to be upholstered in Canada on die-cut metal from Los Angeles, injected molded plastic tags from Korea, acrylic trays from Taiwan, brushed-aluminum signs from Providence, custom wooden hangers from Slovakia that will be silk-screened in Weehawken, New Jersey. We know who's reliable and who isn't, who's expensive and who's cheap. We know what to watch out for, the pitfalls to avoid. You can try to do it yourself, but if you want it brought in on time and under budget, you'd be well advised to call us.

I am a middleman. I hate my job.

I am the conduit between the client and the vast, stratified world of design and manufacturing. I translate abstract needs into reality, concept into construct. I am the voice of reason and experience. I bring to the vendor much-needed work, and to the client desperately sought product. I get yelled at a lot.

When you're a middleman, everything is always your fault.

My computer monitor tells me that I have fifty-seven new e-mails. I delete the spam and the forwarded jokes from associates with too much free time, and now I'm down to eighteen. I dash off a few quick reports to a handful of my clients, updating them on the progress of their ongoing projects, and then call some vendors to remind them of impending deadlines. At the Spandler Corporation, we spend our days making three kinds of phone calls. We call our vendors to hound them about schedules and late deliveries; we call our clients to reassure them that everything is on schedule or to get blamed because it isn't; and we call potential clients to kiss the asses of the people who will one day blame us for everything. When you're a middleman, the only good phone call is no phone call, and there are never no phone calls.

Craig Hodges, my contact at Nike, has already left me two urgent voice mails. I am manufacturing a quarter of a million acrylic versions of the Nike logo, referred to reverently as the "swoosh," that will be mounted on the top of a new sneaker rack Nike will be rolling out to shoe stores across the country. Craig had asked to see a preliminary sample before we shipped the order from China, so I had them FedEx him a boxful. According to his messages, something is wrong with the samples.

"The color is off," he tells me when I call him back.

"What do you mean?"

"I mean it's the wrong color," Craig says testily. "It's supposed to be blue, and these pieces are purple." Craig is a few years older than me, tall, angular, and uptight as all get-out. I took him out to dinner once, and he drank too much and told me how lonely he was. Nike has him doing the job of three men, and he always sounds inches away from shouting.

"Hang on a second," I say, leafing through my file. I find Craig's spec sheet, on which he's listed the PMS color, and then look up that number in my Pantone color chart. It's purple. I check again and am flooded with a sense of relief as it becomes apparent that the fuckup wasn't mine. "Craig," I say. "You specified PMS number 2597. According to my chart, that's purple."

"What are you talking about?" Craig says, his voice flying up a few notches on the hysteria meter. I hear the frantic shuffling of papers on his desk. "Holy crap," he finally says, having located his copy. "That's not the right number."

"It's the number you gave me."

"This won't work," he says. "The fixture is done in blue. The entire rollout is done in the blue. The swoosh has to be blue."

I remain silent as I check the ship date of the order. It's this coming Friday, which means a quarter of a million purple swooshes have already been produced in Qingdao, China, packed into custom cartons, and loaded into four containers, which may still be sitting on the factory grounds or may have already left by truck to the port. The fact that the order is on time would normally be great news, would be cause for goddamn celebration, but today it is nothing less than a catastrophe. Somewhere there will be a quarter of a million sneaker racks unable to ship because the crowning swooshes are the wrong color. Late racks mean no product in the stores, which means lost sales for Nike, which means Craig is fucked. There is ironclad documentation, in both hard copy and e-mail, that this is clearly not my fault, but now it's definitely my problem.

"Where are you in production?" Craig asks. It's a stupid question. We both know the order is scheduled to ship this week.

"I'll have to check with the vendor," I say. "But based on the ship date, I would have to say that they're either shipped or waiting to be processed at the port."

"Fuck." A silence grows between us and I can almost hear Craig's mind racing, not for a solution but simply to come up with a way to make the whole thing my fault. "You know," he says after a bit, and I can feel his sweat dripping through the phone, "the whole point of getting a sample is to be able to approve it before the production run. I never would have allowed production to go forward if I'd seen this earlier."

"You asked for an accelerated lead time," I say. "You got

your production sample less than two weeks after placing the order. That's standard. The only reason you can't make changes is that you moved your ship date up by three weeks."

Thrust and parry, but all very pointless. The middleman can never win these duels. If I stick to my guns, I'll never do business with Nike again.

"Zack," Craig says, adopting a false tone of rationality. "Get in touch with your vendor and see what you can do for me, okay? There's a lot more business behind this order, but the first one has to be a home run for me to keep you in the system here." Translation: Craig will blame this on me when he speaks to his bosses, I'll lose my largest account, and the Spandler Corporation will be blackballed.

I sigh. "I'll see what I can do."

"Thanks, man."

"Don't thank me yet."

"Thanks, man," Craig says firmly, and hangs up.

It's deep-fried fuckups like this that keep the burnout rate so high here. Just last week, Clay Matthews, who sat three cubicles down from me, became the latest casualty. First we all heard the screams. *Motherfucker! You fucking bastards! Will you just fucking die!* By the time we'd all gotten off our conference calls or e-mails, the demolition had begun. Clay's phone came flying out of his cubicle at a fearsome velocity, leaving a cone-shaped dent in the plasterboard wall before it hit the floor. Then he came charging into the hall, crazed and red-faced, his comb-over flapping maniacally behind him, stomped on the phone until it lay in barely connected pieces, and then kicked those pieces down the hall. If he noticed the lot of us rubbernecking, he didn't let on, but stormed back inside, yelling "Fuck!" at the top of his lungs. Who knew Clay had such range? He ran the office football pool with such calm efficiency. His computer monitor soon followed, and that made a hell of a noise, a small explosion really, when it hit the ground. Bill, our boss, was too economy minded to spring for flat-screens, so Clay had the full benefit of a forty-pound Dell monitor to punctuate his fury. When the HP LaserJet 2200d followed a few seconds later, the mild, crumpling sound it made as it hit the floor paled by comparison. After that, Clay disappeared into his cube for a bit, and all we could do was listen to the mayhem as he tore up files and threw framed pictures at the wall, kicking and overturning his furniture as he went. Finally, he stepped into the hall, sweat-stained shirt untucked, tie wildly askew, face dripping and throbbing, and sank down to the floor, leaning against the wall, head in hands, quietly sobbing. He had calmed down somewhat by the time security arrived to escort him from the building, and actually appeared happy and relaxed as they led him to the elevators, nodding his head as if he could give a shit.

Clay had it coming. He broke the 80/20 rule and he broke the lead-time rule. There are many principles we live by here at the Spandler Corporation, and you can maybe bend a few of them when the moment demands it, but there are some rules that can't be bent at the same time, or they'll bury you. Clay depended on less than twenty percent of his client base for over eighty percent of his revenue. He allowed his largest client to become his only client, and he compounded that error by allowing his client to pressure him into a lead time he couldn't live with. Poor schmuck was living on borrowed time.

I shook my head and pursed my lips solemnly like everyone else, but the truth was, I envied Clay. I envied him his violence, his release, and most of all his escape. He needed to get out, to alleviate the pressure that was closing in on him from all four sides, and goddamn if he didn't do just that. Clay lost it,

Clay was insane, Clay went postal, but the bottom line was this: Clay had stepped out of the middle. He was free.

I go through my papers and schedules in a futile attempt to come up with some miraculous solution to the Nike problem, but I already know the score. Craig fucked up, but I'm the one who's screwed. I can still see the expression on Clay's face as they led him away, surprised and unsure, but maybe a little exultant as well. When you start envying people their nervous breakdowns, it's probably time to start examining your own life a bit more closely.

Then this: I have to pee.

The light tickle in my bladder is no doubt the same as always, but now it's also a symptom of something as yet unidentified, filling me with dread even as it demands release. I distractedly navigate the maze of cubicles, the hushed sounds of commerce emanating from behind the upholstered walls buzzing in my ear like an insect, and enter the restroom, where I find the unfortunately named Bill Cockburn, our group manager, scrupulously scrubbing his hands, looking every inch the head honcho, in a blue striped oxford, burgundy tie, and matching suspenders. "Morning, Zack," he says crisply, eyeing me in the mirror.

"Morning," I say.

"How's it going?"

"Super."

The trick with Bill is to say as little as possible. He is notorious for his long-winded lectures on salesmanship, and you never know when a simple pleasantry might trigger a mini Dale Carnegie seminar. You know Bill. You've seen him on airplanes, speaking too loud to the poor bastard in the seat next to him about the stock market, or about the latest PDA applications, or the flaw in Amazon's business model, and you've thought to yourself, *If he's such hot shit, why is he flying coach?* In his mid-fifties, with a fleshy, mottled complexion and an erratically receding hairline, he believes there is no problem that can't be solved with a ten-minute PowerPoint presentation. Bill worships devotedly at the altar of corporate management, a firm believer in systems, an ardent user of buzzwords. He is forever "touching base," "making sure we're on the same page," and asking to be "kept in the loop." He is all about making the sale, closing the deal. Bill's system of management is to dispense the myriad inspirational truisms he's accumulated in his thirty years in the trenches, delivering these adages to us in the manner of a Zen master guiding us toward enlightenment. "Sell to the masses, eat with the classes," Bill says. "Don't lead with your chin," Bill says. "Measure twice, cut once," Bill says. "Sell yourself, then your product," Bill says. "The journey of a thousand miles begins with one step," Bill says.

Bill would be significantly more convincing if he weren't the oldest executive in middle management by at least ten years. He carries with him the smell of stale coffee and bad aftershave, and wears the haggard expression of a man struggling under the weight of his own mediocrity. He is a career middleman, and a stark reminder that I have to get the hell out of here before I become him.

"I see from your Open Order Report that you're shipping the Nike signage," he says, drying his hands painstakingly with a paper towel.

"That's right," I say. Bill might as well stay in the restroom, because he's going to shit a brick when he finds out what's going on with the Nike order.

"What's that, hot-stamped acrylic?"

"Silk-screened."

"Ah," he says, nodding sagely. Bill knows from silk-screening, the nod says.

"Congratulations, Zack," he says, grabbing another towel. "Reeling in Nike was a major coup. I'd watch that one carefully." He looks into the mirror and all but pulls out a compass and protractor to align his necktie.

"Thanks," I say, desperate for him to leave so that I can pee in private. The pink, virgin skin peeking out from underneath his deteriorating scalp is making me think of chemo and radiation, and the word "cancer" floats ominously across an LCD display in my brain.

Bill finally leaves me in an aphorismic cloud. He cautions me to stay on top of it. You have to crawl before you walk. You can never have too many caring eyes. And finally, stepping out of the men's room, he lobs back one of his favorites: You don't get a second chance to make a first impression.

I dash into a stall, unzipping as I go. My urine stream has returned to its customary vibrant yellow, and watching it, I feel my hopes soar, as I detect no traces of the faint rust coloring from this morning. I feel a smile forming in the corners of my mouth, and a great bubble of relief rises up in my chest as I zip up my fly. This morning was just a fluke, a mild physiological burp, and nothing more. But then, as I lean in to flush, my eye is caught by a tiny splash of color floating in the bowl, a red liquid nucleus with tentacles that swirl and fade into the dominating field of translucent yellow. Damn.

Washing my hands, I find myself wondering what a tumor actually looks like.

I spend the next hour scouring medical Web sites, searching for possible answers. The presence of blood in the urine is called hematuria. It may be caused by an injury to the urinary tract or by the passing of kidney stones, but my lack of pain seems to rule out those possibilities in favor of various vascular diseases, kidney ailments, tumors, and of course bladder cancer. My phone rings. I ignore it.

I retrieve my doctor's number from my PalmPilot and call his office. He's with a patient, I'm told by the receptionist. Would I care to hold? I would. I am treated to the Muzak version of the Stones' "Ruby Tuesday." *Ruby red,* I think, and we're back to the blood in my toilet.

"Hello, Zachary," Dr. Cleeman says. "How are you?"

In no mood to exchange pleasantries is how I am, so I dive right in and tell him. He asks me a few questions. Has it ever happened before? About how much blood? Was there any pain? He puts me on hold for a minute and comes back with the number and address of a urologist.

"Dr. Laurence Sanderson. He's on Park Avenue. Go see him as soon as you can."

"Do you think it's something serious?"

"Probably nothing," he says with less conviction than I'd like. "But you need to get it checked out. Tell Dr. Sanderson that I said he should see you today, okay?"

I hang up and quickly call the urologist. His receptionist grudgingly squeezes me in for a lunchtime appointment. "You might have to wait a little," she warns me in a clipped Russian accent before hanging up.

five five five five five five five five five five five five
five five five five five five five five five five five five
five five five five five five five five five five five five
five **five** five five five five five five five five five five
five five five five five five five five five five five five

five

Dr. Sanderson has salt-and-pepper hair, an impeccably trimmed beard, and sharp eyes behind gold-rimmed spectacles. He looks exactly like what you would want your doctor to look like, except that at thirty-two years old, you don't want your doctor to look like anything, really, because you shouldn't need a goddamn doctor, shouldn't have to attempt to articulate the sensations you may or may not have felt in your dick while you were pissing blood this morning.

"Has this ever happened before?" he asks me.

"No."

"Have you had any injuries recently, any trauma to your stomach or sides?"

"No."

"Any pain during urination?"

"No."

"Are you a smoker?"

"No," I say. "I mean, I was, back in college, but not anymore. I mean, not regularly. Sometimes, in bars, you know? When I'm having a few drinks."

"Would you characterize yourself as a heavy drinker?"

"No. That is, um, sometimes. Rarely." I have to remind myself that I'm not interviewing for a job.

"Do you jog?"

"No."

"Play any contact sports?"

"No."

"Are you on any pain medication?"

"Tylenol or Excedrin, sometimes, for headaches."

"Do you get a lot of headaches?"

I've got one right now. "Not really."

I wish he would just cut to the chase and look inside me already. I've already filled out enough forms in the waiting room to apply for a loan and, on the instructions of the pretty Hispanic physician's assistant, disrobed and donned a gown made out of the thinnest cotton known to man. I've done my part; now let's get on with it. Dr. Sanderson finally has me lie down on my side on the examination table and squeezes some clear gel onto my side and lower back. The gel is shockingly cold and my whole body clenches in surprise.

"I know. It's cold, isn't it?" he says.

"Yeah," I say. Fucking sadist probably refrigerates it to watch his patients squirm.

"What I'm doing is just a routine ultrasound, to get a look at your kidneys. Hematuria can be caused by any number of things, kidney stones, urinary tract infections, jarring physical activity. . . ." His voice trails off as he begins to rub the probe on me and a colorful image appears on the machine's small television screen. After a minute or so, he tells me to roll over onto my other side. It would be nice if he'd give some indication as to what he thought about the first kidney, but apparently he likes to take in the whole show before offering his review, and while I could ask him, I'm suddenly superstitious about upsetting his ritual, so I roll over silently, the gown sticking to me uncomfortably where the gel remains. He spends another minute or so examining my left kidney and then says, "Lie flat on your back, please."

The left kidney seems to take even less time than the right, which is probably a good sign, indicating that there was simply nothing to see. Unless the left kidney was so obviously cancer infested, just riddled with throbbing tumors, that it only took an instant for him to know that I'm totally fucked, and now he's having me lie on my back in case I pass out when he breaks the news to me. Or maybe the right kidney is the bad one, so all the left one required was a perfunctory check, because he's already ascertained that I'm totally fucked. I lie on my back, and now I'm sweating, can feel my heart accelerating in my chest. Forget the cancer—I'm going to die of a massive coronary right here.

He pulls up my gown like a perverted uncle and squirts some more of the cold gel all over my pelvis. I close my eyes and try to concentrate on nothing but moving the air in and out of my lungs. I do this for a while, until it occurs to me that he's been working down there for quite some time, rubbing the probe just off my pelvic bone and clicking his mouse repeatedly. I open my eyes and am instantly terrified by the furrow in his brow and the way his eyebrows seem to be raised. "What are you doing?" I ask him.

"I'm looking at your bladder," he tells me distractedly as

if he's forgotten there was a person attached to the lower half he was examining.

"Everything okay?"

"Hmm," he says.

You never, under any circumstances, want to hear your doctor say "Hmm." "Hmm" being medical jargon for "Holy shit." "What is it?" I say.

He turns the TV monitor toward me and I'm treated to the sight of the dark, quivering horror movie of my bladder wall. "There," he says, using a mouse to draw a small circle on the screen. "Do you see that?"

"What?"

"This brighter spot over here."

"Yeah," I say. "What is it?"

Dr. Sanderson peers intently at the screen, nodding slowly. "I'm not sure," he says, and just like that, everything changes.

I sit in a puddle of my own sweat, my gown pasted to my gel-splattered sides as my bladder pulsates grotesquely before me, and the room starts to spin. I stare at the little spot distorted into gray nothingness by the TV monitor, and say nothing. The doctor is telling me that it could be some aggregate capillaries, nothing to worry about, and I need to come back tomorrow for a cystoscopy so he can get a better look, just to be sure, but his voice is distant and hollow sounding. He may not know yet what that spot is, but I know what it is definitely not.

It's not nothing.

six six six six six six six six six six six six six six six six six six six six six six six six six six six six six six six six six six six six six six six six six six six six six six six six six six six six six six six six six six six six six six six six six six six six six six six

I leave the doctor's office in a haze, thoughts of cancer running rampant through my head. I won't make a good cancer patient; this much I know. I won't discover within me heretofore untapped reserves of strength, will not lift everyone else's spirits with my courage, will not be funny and frank about my illness and wear a clever hat when my hair falls out. I am just not movie-of-the-week material. Probably, I'll be a weeping, vomiting mess, will hide in my room, curled up pathetically in a self-pitying fetal ball as I fade into nothingness. I will be a big, fucking baby.

I want my mother.

My cell phone tells me that I have seven missed calls. The middleman must always be reachable. I resist the powerful, almost inborn instinct to check my voice mails. There's no way I can work with this hanging over me. I hold up the cell phone and just look at it, wondering what the hell to do. I should call Hope. That's what you do in these situations, right?

But when I finally make a call, it's Tamara's number that my fingers dial.

"Hey, it's me."

"Zack! What's up, babe?"

"You feel like a visit?"

"Sure. You coming for dinner?"

"I thought I'd blow off work and come now. Take Sophie to the park, hang out a little."

"You're going to blow off work?" she asks skeptically.

"I do it all the time," I say.

"Fine," Tamara says. "Except, no you don't. Not ever. So what's going on?"

"I'm just in a foul mood."

"So you figured you'd bring your coal to Newcastle."

"Misery loves company," I say.

"That it does," she says. "Come on over. I'll do my best to make your problems pale by comparison."

"I'm counting on it."

Tamara laughs. "What a team we make. You want me to pick you up from the train?"

"No. I'll take Jed's car. I'll see you in about an hour."

"Good. I'll wake the little monster up from her nap."

Jed keeps his car, a Lexus SC 430 convertible, in a garage around the corner from our apartment. The attendants know me by now, since, with both Tamara and my mother living in Riverdale, I tend to use the car a lot more than Jed, who never seems to go anywhere anymore. I often wonder why he bothers keeping the car at all, and paying the exorbitant monthly garage fees, but I suppose when money's no object, you're willing to pay just to have the option available to you, yet another case of his conspicuous consumption benefiting my freeloading ass. Before I go to get the car, though, I take a shower and touch up my shave. Tamara will kiss my cheek and give me a hug, and I want to smell good when she gets that close.

When Rael and Tamara got married, the plan had been to stay in Manhattan, but when Sophie was born, their studio apartment became too cramped, and they bought a small split-level in Riverdale, less than a mile away from where Rael and I grew up. Although he didn't like to admit it, Rael was thrilled to be back in Riverdale, saw symmetry in raising his daughter in his own hometown. But then he died, leaving Tamara a stranger in a strange town, with a daughter and a mortgage and no idea of where to go and what to do with herself.

Tamara's house. She's sitting cross-legged on the round kitchen table in shorts and a tank top, sipping at a Diet Coke, her long dark hair partially concealing her face as she intently reads a *People* magazine. She has no interest in celebrity divorces and red-carpet fashion faux pas. Without having to look, I know she's reading one of those tearjerkers about a child, the little girl who suffered burns on ninety percent of her body when her mother's car was struck by a drunk driver and exploded, the young boy being treated for an exotic form of leukemia, whose classmates all shaved their heads in solidarity, the teenager from Cambodia who received a kidney from a retired postal worker in Scranton, Pennsylvania. Since Rael's death, Tamara has cultivated an obsession with sick and dying children. She's all Sophie has now, and she's terrified that she's not up to the task.

Faster than a heartbeat, I take in Tamara's legs, which are pale and not particularly shapely, but always appear as if they would be satiny soft to the touch, the soft curves where her triceps meet her broad, athletic shoulders, and the buoyant presence of her breasts, somewhat obscured, but no less formidable under the tank top. With all beautiful women, there's always one feature that puts them over the top, and on Tamara it's her lips, which are full, and a deep crimson that no lipstick could ever hope to achieve. They seem to have been extruded like putty out of her face, pulling her porcelain skin taut into a robust, sensuous, and wholly unintentional pout. Sure, her emerald eyes, each set under a thick dark brow, would be captivating all on their own, but those lips are the kicker, and when you first see them, you have to remind yourself that you're not seeing her undressed, because for the first moment, that's always how it feels, and you suddenly understand what the Muslims were going on about when they invented the burka. Lips, done right, are as much a sex organ as any of the more obvious ones.

This is what it's come to, a secret, devoted inventory taken at light speed, like I'm guilty of some kind of perversion. The radio is playing loudly, and she hums along with an Eminem song as she reads. On the tiled floor, Sophie has spilled a carton of milk and is taking Cheerios out of a cup, one by one, dipping them into the milk puddle, and eating them. "Zap here!" she says when she sees me. She drops her cup of Cheerios and quickly gets to her feet, running up to my thighs, crunching Cheerios underfoot as she goes, her chubby hands already raised for me to pick her up. I do, kissing each of her soft apple cheeks. "Pok," she says urgently to me. "Zap tape Sophie pok."

"I told her you're taking her to the park," Tamara says, putting down the magazine and leaning past Sophie to kiss me on the cheek. I never react to these kisses given in greeting, but every time she gives me one, I realize I've been waiting for it, and it is received with a great deal more consciousness than I will ever admit to. These visits used to be innocent, I'm sure of it, weekly gestures of friendship and support, looking in on my best friend's widow and the baby he left behind. But somewhere along the line, something changed, and she became unbearably beautiful in her quiet grief, in the way she bravely embraced the new solitude of her life, in her serene acceptance of her own tragic circumstances, and something was born in me, something that comes alive only in her presence, that dreams unspeakable things and considers a wide range of absurd possibilities.

"You okay?" she asks me, her eyes demanding in their concern.

"I'm not sure."

"You want to tell me?"

"Later," I say. "Are you coming to the park?"

"Nah," Tamara says. "I'll clean the place up while you're gone."

"You smell something?"

Tamara nods. "She needs her diaper changed before she goes out."

"Zap change you," Sophie says.

"I guess you're elected," Tamara says, patting my arm with a smirk. She is not big on changing diapers, is not one of those mothers who lovingly bury their noses in their babies' behinds to determine, through the layers, if they've soiled their diapers. She steps over the spilled milk and pads down the hall, her bare feet barely making a sound on the floor. I watch her from behind, so strong and still so vulnerable, all at the same time. The rush of illicit affection is a hot, liquid burst in my chest, like inhaling in a steam room. In my arms, Sophie pulls herself into an upright position and farts into her diaper.

"Fart!" she says gleefully.

In the park, there are climbers and swingers. Sophie is a swinger. "Higher," she cries, not instructing but observing, and she laughs deliciously when I tickle her legs as I push. Her fine blond hair, so much like Rael's, falls in her eyes whenever she swings forward, lending her the illusion of an older girl being coy. My weekly trips to the park with her have become something larger to me, a stage on which I get to play myself in another life. We are surrounded by children and their mothers, with the occasional nanny thrown in for good measure, and as far as they're all concerned, I'm a devoted father taking time off work to play with my daughter. Or else I'm unemployed, which makes me somewhat pathetic. But maybe I'm just self-employed, an author or a musician, and thus able to put in this quality time on a regular basis. I wear no ring, so I'm divorced or maybe a widower, and either way that hikes up my appeal quotient.

Tamara didn't want children, but Rael wore her down. That was his specialty. He was the consummate salesman. Ice cubes to Eskimos and all that. So they had Sophie, and then Rael died, leaving Tamara alone with the lifetime commitment he'd talked her into. Since Sophie was only ten months old when he died, I am now the closest thing to a father figure that she has, and while that's tragic, I can't deny that I enjoy the sense of pride and possessiveness I have when it comes to her. When she finally acquiesces to being removed from the swing, she hugs me snugly, and I run my free hand along the soft, plump skin of her narrow, unformed shoulders. The aroma of baby shampoo and lotion fills my nostrils, and when she rests her cheek on my shoulder, it feels perfect, like each was designed specifically to fit the other, a matching set. Holding her like this, I feel trusted and reliable and altogether more useful than at any other time in my life.

"ABCDEFG," she sings into my ear, her voice high, sweet, and cutely off-key.

"How I wonder what you are," I sing back. It's our little game.

"QRSTUV," she sings.

"Like a diamond in the sky."

She laughs, from her belly, and it's more musical than her singing. "Zap funny."

Zap is funny. Zap has the hots for your mother, who, even if she weren't too wrapped up in the tragic clusterfuck of her own life to notice, would probably be out of his league anyway. And she's the wife of his best friend, which comes with a whole other set of complications, not to mention the minor fact that Zap is, in fact, engaged to another woman, and thus ineligible for competition to begin with. Zap has got himself caught in a theoretical love triangle, although it's really more like a love square, since Rael's presence can't be discounted, even in death. And just to spice things up further, to juice up the sitcom of his life for sweeps week, Zap may have a malignant tumor in his bladder, which, if true, will throw a colossal monkey wrench into the proceedings.

"Zap funny," Sophie says again, giggling tiredly and clutching my chin in her little fingers.

I grab her hand and press her palm against my cheek. "Yeah," I say. "Zap hysterical."

Later, Tamara and I sit outside, in the porch swing Rael ordered from a SkyMall catalog while on a business trip. We sit in the fading afternoon light, not because it's particularly scenic or to enjoy the weather, which is actually overcast and unseasonably muggy for October, but because Sophie fell asleep in the stroller on the walk home and she doesn't transfer well. If we attempt to move her to the crib, she'll wake up screaming and refuse to be put down for a half hour. I'd like to think that, like me, Tamara wants Sophie to keep sleeping because she cherishes our quiet time together, but the truth is, she just doesn't want to deal with a screaming baby. She knew in advance she wasn't mother material, but Rael assured her that she'd fall in love and that would all change. He was old-fashioned enough to think that all women are mothers waiting to emerge, and he didn't live long enough to be disabused of that notion. In actuality, Tamara dotes on Sophie, but she clings to the bad-mommy act as a way of dealing with her feelings of maternal inadequacy.

"So what's going on with you?" Tamara says.

I tell her about the blood in my piss and the bright spot on my ultrasound. "Tomorrow I have to go back for a cystoscopy," I tell her.

Hope would want to know the statistics, the odds. She would want me to run the scenarios, would talk about specialists and delve into family histories. Tamara just nods and says, "Are you scared?"

"Of cancer?"

"Of the procedure."

I think about it for a minute. "Yes," I say. "I guess I am."

"Do you want me to come with you?"

I do. Not because I need her to but because her offer underscores our closeness and, since I'm such a geek, this casual recognition thrills me even though I know it in no way validates my other, secret feelings. For a moment I can fantasize about living in a world where it would make sense that Tamara accompany me to the doctor. She has always been highly discerning, stingy even, in the doling out of her affections, which makes it doubly sweet to make it over the walls and through the gates into the fortress of her concern. But, of course, she can't come with me because of Hope. I love Hope and Hope loves me, and when I'm not in Riverdale, that arrangement suits me just fine. That's my reality. So what the hell is it about Tamara that challenges it all every time I see her?

"It's okay," I tell her. "I don't think it's the sort of thing I really want an audience for."

"I understand," she says.

Here's an interesting thing: by some tacit agreement, neither of us ever mentions Hope. No matter what the topic, we will phrase things in such a way so as to keep any trace of her out of our conversation. As far as Tamara knows, Hope may not even be aware of my weekly visits to her. And she's fine with that. It's as if we exist in our own little world, and we're reluctant to allow anyone else with any claim on either one of us into the circle. So we never mention Hope. Rael, who, being dead, is only slightly less of a threat, is most often referred to in the pronoun form. "Him" or "he." I know why I do it: because I'm a sick bastard who, for the brief moments I'm with Tamara, is preserving a fantasy that is highly inappropriate, at best. But why is she doing it? What secret agenda is she protecting?

For some reason this line of reasoning, obtuse and flawed though it may be, sends an exhilarated shiver up my spine. We sit there watching Sophie sleep, and I take in Tamara's scents, the slightly fruity bouquet of her shampoo and the scented moisturizer she uses. I imagine pulling back her wild dark hair and burying my face in the hollow of her neck, my lips on her skin, engulfing myself in her scents. Probably, it wouldn't go over too well.

"Look at her," Tamara says, staring lovingly at Sophie. "She looks like such an angel when she sleeps. You'd never know what a demon she is."

"She does have a lot of energy," I say.

"She's so demanding now. If she doesn't get her way, she cries in this really loud voice and just doesn't stop. I can understand those mothers who get arrested for throwing their babies against the wall." I give her a look. "I'm not saying I would do it. I'm just saying I understand the impulse. You just want to stop that damn noise."

"Maybe don't repeat that to anyone else," I say.

She laughs. "I know. I'm just thinking out loud."

My leg is our rudder, rocking us gently back and forth on the swing. "I get so mad at him sometimes," she says, "him" being Rael. "It's just so typical of him, to have this baby and then leave me with the mess. I mean, I love her to death, but how the hell am I supposed to get on with my life when I've got her? You know, if you're going to die on someone, you ought to leave her with no strings attached, so she can move on, start something new. Instead, I've got a daughter to take care of, and I've got his parents on my back every day checking up on me because they don't think I'm fit to be a mother. It's like he locked me into his world and then he got the hell out. And so I hate him, and then I feel guilty for hating him and I freak out about that for a while."

"You're doing okay," I say.

"I'm a shitty mother."

"It's pronounced 'single.' You're a single mother."

"I curse too much, I don't give her a schedule, I don't change her diaper nearly as often as I should, she eats whatever she wants, and I resent her for tying me down. What's going to happen when I start to date again?"

Alarm bells go off in my head. Warnings lights spin.

"Did someone ask you out?"

"Come on," she says. "Look at me. Who's going to want to date this?"

A powerful sense of relief courses through me when she says this, and with it the guilty realization that my own misdirected possessive feelings and Tamara's needs will soon be at cross-purposes.

"Who wouldn't?" I say, forcing myself to play the role that until recently I thought I'd been doing for real. I'm not really a concerned, platonic friend, but I play one on TV. "When the word gets out, you'll have more guys than you know what to do with."

She frowns. "I wouldn't know where to begin. Rael was the only guy I ever trusted. I never really had a serious relationship before him."

"There's no rush," I say. "You'll know when you're ready."

I'm picturing the men that Tamara will date. They will all be taller and broader than me, with perfect, low hairlines, the kind that come to a point in the middle of each temple, like arrows, forming a rectangular forehead under a muscular bush of thick dark hair. They will be thick-necked men of independent means who manage hedge funds and drive German sports cars. Men who can wear Armani suit jackets over dark silk T-shirts without seeming like hopeless poseurs and who will think nothing of inviting her for a weekend escape to wine country after only two or three dates. Men who will be conspicuously respectful of the role I've played for Tamara even as they propel me to the perimeter, marginalizing me with their condescending chumminess.

She leans her head against my shoulder and squeezes my arm. "You'll have to screen them for me," she says. "Anyone who wants a date will have to go through you."

If so, none will make the cut. I will lay down a perimeter of land mines and bear traps, the kind you have to gnaw your own leg off to get out of. Let's see how great you look in your Armani hopping around on one leg.

I pat her leg companionably and lean my head on hers. "You'll be fine," I tell her. "You're smart, beautiful, and compassionate. Any guy would kill to have you." *I would kill to have you.*

"Zack," she says softly, changing the subject.

"Yeah."

"Don't be sick. You're all I've got."

"I'll do what I can," I say.

"I mean, God's already screwed me. He wouldn't do it again so quickly. It would just be too much."

Tamara's theology is all over the map, from God to horoscopes, the one consistent thread being an uncompromising certainty that there are unseen forces at work shaping our fate and that every action has potentially cosmic consequences.

"Okay. Then I'll try not to let you down."

She gives me a gentle shove. "You know what I mean."

"I do," I say. "Thanks."

She looks up and gives my chin a quick, friendly kiss before settling back down on my shoulder. We sit on the swing in silence, rocking to the rhythm of Sophie's light snoring, and I'm thinking that I've mind-fucked myself something fierce here, and wondering how the hell I'm going to undo it.

seven seven seven seven seven seven seven seven
seven seven seven seven seven seven seven seven
seven seven seven seven seven seven seven seven
seven **seven** seven seven seven seven seven seven
seven seven seven seven seven seven seven seven

The day Rael died, he called me at work. "Vegas, baby," he said.

"What?"

"Let's go to Vegas."

"Okay," I said. "When do you want to go?"

"Tonight."

"Yeah," I said, absently responding to an e-mail. "That's not going to happen."

"Come on, Zack," he said. "Live a little. You're young and single."

"And you're old and married," I said. "I still can't go."

"Zacky."

"Raely."

"I've spent the better part of our lives talking you into enjoying yourself," Rael said. "You always say no, then I go to work on you, and in the end you agree and, nine times out of ten, end up having a better time than me. So why don't you save us both the time and pretend I've already spent a half hour talking you into it, and let's book our flights."

"Well," I said. "At least I can save you the half hour, because I can tell you that barring an act of God, there's no way in hell I can get on a plane to Vegas tonight. I'm working on about seven different deadlines, and I'm having dinner tomorrow night with Hope's parents."

"Fuck 'em," he said. "It's Vegas, baby."

"And I'll have to confiscate your copy of *Swingers*."

He sighed. "Zacky."

"Raely."

"I knew you were going to say no," he said.

"Good. You know how I hate to disappoint."

"And that's why we're going to the Borgata Hotel Casino and Spa in Atlantic City!" He delivers this last line as if I've just won a living room set on *Wheel of Fortune. Thanks a lot, Pat. I just wonder how the hell we're going to fit that into our trailer.*

"Are you serious?" I said.

"As a heart attack."

"I don't know."

"Come on. It'll be just like the old days."

"We didn't gamble in the old days."

"It will be the old days we should have had," he said.

"I hate gambling."

"It's not about gambling."

"Atlantic City is not about gambling?"

"It's about us, Zack. You and me on the open road. Hanging out, talking, listening to music, eating shitty rest-stop food, and staring at hot women we'll never sleep with."

"Did you ask Jed?"

"He's got a date."

"So you let him off the hook, and I get the hard sell."

"Jed's too much of a high roller, anyway. You know you want to come."

I sighed. Rael could go on like this all day. "Okay," I said.

"Great," he said. "I'll pick you up at seven."

"Raely."

"Zacky."

"What if I'd said yes to Vegas?"

Rael laughed. "Are you kidding? Tamara never would have gone for it."

The average man, when contemplating a trip to Atlantic City, pictures two things: money, and hotel sex with a stranger. There's absolutely no reason to believe he'll score in either category. On the contrary, the smart money has him dropping five hundred to a thousand dollars at the twenty-five-dollar blackjack tables, getting drunk on watered-down drinks, and ogling the desiccated cocktail waitresses through smoke-stung eyes as they scurry about in comically tailored uniforms that showcase raised, tired cleavages, legs clad in skin-hued panty hose to hide their varicose veins. And even after he's realistically adjusted his standards, he doesn't dare hit on them, because the carefully vacant look in their eyes seems to be a front for something infinitely more volatile, something that could spill over, in an instant, to a dangerous, man-hating rage, and if there's anything worse than rejection, it's loud, violent rejection involving security personnel. So instead he simply overtips, nonchalantly pressing his ten-dollar chip into her hand with a polite smile, as if in contrition for the brief but sordid fantasy of hotel sex in which he was engaged just moments before, because, honestly, he's not one of *those* guys. The average man will show up to work the next day throbbing, unsexed, and hungover, his throat scratchy from secondhand smoke, his wallet empty because he's never completely internalized when to and when not to double down. But ask him a few months later, and he'll be ready to go again, eyes glazing over at the prospect of the financial and sexual windfalls that await. I don't begin to understand this phenomenon, but someone in the marketing department somewhere deserves one hell of a raise.

The average man is an idiot to think that his night at Atlantic City will end with pornographic acts in a comped suite at the Borgata, but he's nonetheless justified in the presumption that he won't end the night suspended upside down in a demolished BMW, his chest crushed by the steering column, his vital organs pierced by his own splintered bones. I mean, what are the odds?

It's nice to think, in view of what happened, that Rael spent his last living hours living it up with his best friend. Nice, but not particularly true. I wish I could say otherwise. That we won big, or lost but laughed our way through it, or had some wildly memorable experiences along the way, that Rael was ebullient and talked about how happy he was to be married and have Sophie, that we bonded and reminisced and cracked inside jokes and bantered with sexy women and had a boisterous good time. That in his few remaining hours, he was bursting with the vim and vigor of life. But really, it was just your typical, average working stiff's ill-advised weeknight trip to Atlantic City, utterly forgettable were it not for its tragic conclusion. We dropped a few hundred at the blackjack tables in the first hour we were there, then set off on what would prove to be a fruitless search for cheaper tables. Rael grumbled about not being able to take full advantage of the free table drinks because he was going to have to drive home at some point, and I annoyingly pointed out that he should have thought of that before we left. We sat among the damaged and the elderly at the slot machines, our vision fuzzy from smoke and exhaustion. Tamara called his cell frequently—Sophie was giving her a hard time—and he would excuse himself to find a spot where he could hear her above the din of the machines. When we'd lost all that we were willing to lose, we found an ATM and lost a bit more, and then we found a nightclub to sit in, sipping cocktails and staring at women who didn't stare back. Both of us wanted to go home already, but neither wanted to be the one to suggest it, to put voice to the depressing mediocrity of the evening.

I don't remember leaving the casino. There are small chunks of time in there that are missing. It was around two a.m., and I know we stopped for gas and to stock up on Drake's Cakes and extra-large coffees for the ride home. I remember how the white powder from the doughnuts formed a thin Clark Gable mustache on Rael as he sang along to the Ramones, driving down the Garden State Parkway, one hand on the wheel, one hand clutching his 7-Eleven coffee cup. I even remember the song, "Bonzo Goes to Bitburg." A few months later that same song came over the radio in my office, and I spent the rest of the afternoon shaking and crying in the corner bathroom stall.

But that's all I remember, which means either I fell asleep in the passenger seat or else I've blocked it out. The next thing I can recall is the screaming of the BMW's tires chewing up the grassy embankment at high speed, the crumpling steel, so much louder than I ever would have imagined, the imploding windows showering us with glass, and the engine roaring like a wounded bear as the car corkscrewed into the forest that lined the parkway.

When I came to, we were upside-down.

Rael was unconscious, and appeared to be sitting in the backseat, except that didn't make any sense, since his head was hanging just inches from the steering wheel. He also seemed to be hanging in more of a reclining position, while I was hanging in a perfect, seated position.

"Rael," I said. It came out as a hoarse rasp, and my entire chest hurt from the effort. The seat belt was digging painfully into my chest and thighs, and I couldn't move at all. "Rael," I tried again. This time my voice came out stronger, but my ribs convulsed and I thought I might vomit. The silence in the car seemed starkly wrong after the deafening noise of the crash, but other than the occasional sound of a car speeding by on the parkway below us, and the odd, hissing sigh from the destroyed engine, I heard nothing at all. I realized that our accident might have actually gone unobserved, since the parkway was basically deserted at that hour, and that our wreckage might not be visible from the road. I craned my neck to get a better look at Rael. It was pretty dark, but the geometry of his body, and the car, for that matter, didn't look right to me. It was like the car had swallowed him, and I was seeing way too much cracked dashboard and not nearly enough Rael.

Then, with a jolt, he came to life, coughing and spitting out a horrifying amount of blood. "Zack," he gasped, the sound forcing itself through the liquid in his throat.

"Yeah," I said, my voice cracking with relief.

"I'm fucked up, man."

"I know. Me too."

"I can't really breathe."

"Just take it easy, man. Don't panic."

"It's hard," he wheezed.

"I can't find my cell phone," I said. "Where's yours?"

"On my belt."

"Do you think you can pass it to me?"

A strained, wet sob. "Zack."

"Yeah."

"I can't move my arms."

"It's okay," I said idiotically. "I'll try to reach it."

"I can't move my fucking arms, Zack. I'm fucking paralyzed."

"You're not paralyzed," I said, feeling around for the release on my seat belt. "You're just pinned by the car."

"I can't feel a fucking thing!" he shouted, his head writhing from side to side. "I can't feel my legs! I can't fucking move." He started to scream, but he was coughing up gobs of blood and the sound kept getting forced back down his throat and he started to bang his head against the steering wheel.

"Rael!" I screamed, my torso trembling in agony as the wind from my voice brushed past the raw edges of a thousand wounded muscles. "Calm down!" But by then he'd passed out again.

I don't know how long it took for me to get out of my seat belt. It might have been five minutes, it might have been a half hour. When I finally hit the clasp right, I fell headfirst onto the car roof, and when I rolled over, I vomited. As I lay there, involuntarily contorted into a ball, gagging on the stench of my own vomit, the temptation to go to sleep and let someone else sort out this mess was so great that I actually closed my eyes and took a little nap. Someone would find us, and take us out properly, on stretchers, with those yellow boards to immobilize our necks, and say comforting things to us in the ambulance as they hooked up our morphine drips. It might be a trick getting Rael out, but they'd use the Jaws of Life if they had to, right? I mean, this was clearly a job for the professionals, and I was supremely unqualified, would probably do more harm than good.

"Zack!"

"Yeah."

"Wake up, man."

I rolled over and sat up, the torn steel of the roof slicing painfully into both of my knees, and I had to fight the powerful urge to flee the claustrophobic confines of the ruined car. I crawled over to Rael, whose face, I now saw, was bloodied and swollen, and his chest, fuck, his chest was a mess, and I had to just look away, because if I looked at his broken body any more, I would just collapse into a weeping mess.

"Jesus, Rael," I said.

"I know," he said, his voice frighteningly calm, almost detached. "It's okay. I can't feel anything."

At some point I managed to reach around to where I thought his waist should be, my trembling fingers seeking out his cell phone. His sweater was soaked with blood and the heat was emanating from him in waves. It took the ambulance forever to show up, and in that time Rael drifted in and out of consciousness, and I did my best to support his suspended head by sitting cross-legged under him, placing my shoulder under his head like a table. I think I prayed a little.

"Tell Tamara I'm sorry," Rael said.

"Tell her yourself."

"Come on, Zack," he said. "Don't waste my time. Just tell her I love her, and I'm sorry. Will you do that for me?"

"You want me to call her right now?"

"No. I don't want her to hear me like this."

"Okay. I'll tell her." I was pretty sure he couldn't see the tears that had started to run down my face. He coughed up some more blood, which landed with a heavy thud, like it was something more solid than just blood.

"Zack."

"Yeah."

"I can feel myself dying. I can actually feel it."

"Just hang in there," I said. "They're on the way."

He shook his head. "I'm already gone."

"Fuck you! Just stay with me."

"Believe me," he said, his voice starting to get weaker. "I'd love to."

"We'll be hanging out in your house in a few weeks and you're going to feel really stupid about this."

"Tell Sophie about me," he whispered. "When she's older, I mean. Tell her what I was like, okay? Tell her she made me happier than I've ever been in my life."

"Okay," I said. "Just please, try to stay with me."

"I didn't see this coming," he said, more to himself than me. "I never would have guessed this."

"Please, Rael. For fuck's sake, just hang on." I was weeping audibly now. In the distance, I could hear the sirens. "You hear that?" I said to him. "They're here. Just stay awake!"

The sirens stopped and I pictured the paramedics grabbing their fat orange cases and heading urgently up the embankment to find us.

"Zacky."

"Raely."

He closed his eyes for the last time and smiled. "We should have gone to fucking Vegas."

eight eight eight eight eight eight eight eight
eight eight eight eight eight eight eight eight
eight eight eight eight eight eight eight eight
eight **eight** eight eight eight eight eight eight
eight eight eight eight eight eight eight eight

Usually, whenever I leave Tamara's house, I need Hope in the worst possible way. I run to her like a junkie to crystal meth, needing to believe that my reality is every bit as good as the insane fantasies I entertain in Tamara's universe. Even before I've started the car, I've got one hand on my cell phone, ready to flip it open and say her name, to hear the reassuring steadiness of her voice on the other end, so firmly grounded in reality that it leaves no room for doubt, and to be whole again. "Hope," I say at the voice prompt. I get her voice mail and leave her a message, not mentioning where I am, but telling her that I miss her and that she should call me. It's six thirty, and I know she's working late tonight.

This is what happens. You're in your car, driving slowly along the service road of the Henry Hudson Parkway as dusk turns into night and the headlights of passing cars are laying claim to the highway. (Ever since the accident, you will always choose service roads over highways.) You're thinking about one woman while trying to reach another, and despite this apparent abundance of women, you feel lonely and desolate as hell, and, almost unconsciously, you drive to the house of a third, and the third woman is your mother. It has to be unconscious, because conscious, you'd know right away that it's a big mistake. Somewhere, there's a therapist sitting alone in his office, staring wistfully at his door, wishing for a patient like you.

My mother and Peter live about a half mile away from Tamara, in the house I grew up in, the house from which Norm was ceremoniously ejected after the Anna incident. Said ceremony actually happened a few days after Norm was gone, when my mother brought the soiled linens from the crime scene down to the driveway and, using a can of lighter fluid, set them ablaze underneath our basketball hoop. The burn marks on the concrete became our foul line and out-of-bounds indicators.

Peter's on the front lawn raking leaves. When he sees me, his eyes light up and he waves with just enough abandon to reveal his condition. "Hey, Zack," he yells. "What's new and exciting?"

"Hey, Pete," I say, climbing out of the car. "How's it hanging?"

"A little to the left," he says with a giggle. "Sweet ride."

"You know it."

He drops the rake and runs down the small slope of lawn to greet me, his arms dangling behind him in the awkward body language of the mentally impaired. His kiss is wet on my cheek, and his stubble leaves a mild burn as it scrapes my skin. He's twenty-nine years old, short and stocky, bright in his own way, and as eager to please as a puppy. But no matter how happy Pete seems, no matter how well he lives in the aftermath of the chromosomal car wreck that took place during his creation, there's still an undeniable element of tragedy to his life. Every day, for him, is like trying to play the piano wearing oven mitts. "I missed you," he says, and I feel a stab of guilt and make a mental note to call him more and spend the random Sunday with him doing brotherly things. Loving the mentally challenged means never feeling completely guilt free.

"I missed you too," I tell him, throwing my arm around his shoulder as we walk back up the lawn. "That's why I came to see you."

"How's Hope?" he says.

"She's great. She said to say hi."

"Tell her I said hello."

"I will."

For just a moment, as I feel the cold, crisp air against my face, the wind against my brown suede jacket, the brittle multihued leaves being crushed under my rubber soles, I feel a surge of optimism, a sense of the wide range of possibilities. Autumn can do that to me.

My mother is in the kitchen, scrubbing dishes in the sink. She has a perfectly good dishwasher, but to use it would be less of a dramatic sacrifice on behalf of Peter, so it's not an option. Caring for Peter has never been enough for her. Over the years she's developed a finely honed martyr complex, and she isn't satisfied that her work is being done if some form of self-flagellation isn't stirred into the mix. I was too young at the time to know whether this trend developed before or after my father's final transgression, if it was an effect or a cause of their marital woes, but it's certainly the reason she's remained alone. Maybe it's a defense mechanism, or some misdirected Zen acceptance of her lot in life; I don't know. I'm the last one qualified to figure out someone else's psychoses. Suffice it to say that

Lela King, generally speaking, is no barrel of laughs. My brother Matt wrote a song about her called "Saint Mom."

From the back, with her trim figure, jeans, and bleached blond hair, she looks like a much younger person. But then she turns to face me, wearing her customary expression of weary martyrdom, and in an instant I take in the creases below her eyes, the slack jaw, and the now ingrained purse of her lips, and I want to hug her and say something that will make her smile even as I struggle to repress the urge to flee this dreary brown kitchen, still decorated in the avocado wallpaper of my childhood, and never come back. My mother can do that to me.

"Zack," she says.

"Hey, Ma."

She turns off the sink and holds her rubber-gloved hands theatrically away from me as I lean to kiss her cheek.

"What are you doing here?"

"I was just in the neighborhood," I say.

She gives me a stern look. "What's wrong?"

"Nothing."

"Don't give me nothing. What is it?"

Just so we're clear, my mother is not this bastion of maternal intuition, instantly gleaning, like a mother hen, that something's wrong in the universe of her eldest and, on the surface anyway, least screwed-up son. Her middle son was rendered brain damaged by a freak genetic mutation and her husband fucked his secretary on her side of the bed, and she lives every day with the unshakable, theistic conviction that God isn't through dicking with her. Some people say hello. Lela King says "What's wrong?"

"Everything's fine, Mom. I'm just passing by."

"Is it Hope?"

"Is what Hope?"

"You're not getting cold feet, are you? Because that's perfectly normal."

"Ma."

"I'm just saying." She shrugs and frowns. The Eskimos have a hundred words for snow; my mother has a thousand ways to shrug and frown. She could give seminars.

My impending wedding looms totemic in her mind. As far as I know, she doesn't have much of a social calendar, and the wedding has unaccountably stirred a long-dormant vanity in her. I know she's been clipping pages from fashion magazines on gowns, hair, and makeup, has been preparing a virtual folio of options for herself. She claims she doesn't want to embarrass me, but we both know that's a crock. Since my engagement, she's had her teeth professionally whitened, started wearing contact lenses again, and has been experimenting with different shades of blond hair coloring. I don't want to discuss my mother in sexual terms, but the fact is she's still a good-looking woman, slim and well proportioned, with soft skin and pale blue eyes, and your average sixty-year-old man wouldn't kick her out of bed for eating crackers. My mother wants to look beautiful at the wedding; she wants to dance and laugh and charm people as she once did, a lifetime ago. And the idea that those desires are still alive somewhere in her should thrill me, but instead it just makes me feel guilty and sad, because it's like she's allowing herself only the briefest visit to the life she might have been leading if she hadn't shut herself down so many years ago.

"You want something to eat?" she asks me.

"No, thanks," I say. I'm already eyeing the door, looking for my opportunity.

"We had spaghetti and meatballs," Pete informs me, plopping down into a kitchen chair.

"I've eaten already."

"You were at Tamara's?" she asks me.

"Yeah."

She is unable to conceal her disapproval. She finds it dangerously inappropriate for me to be spending time with Rael's widow, but thankfully, she's unwilling to navigate the terrain of his death with me, so she has no choice but to leave it alone.

"Tamara's a hottie," Pete says enthusiastically.

"Don't be fresh, Peter," she says.

"She is," he argues. "You could bounce a quarter off her ass."

"That's enough!" my mother snaps at him.

"Come on, Mom," I say. "He's just repeating something he heard. He doesn't even know what it means." But I do, and it takes me a moment or two to banish the image of Tamara's naked backside from my mind.

"It means she's tight," Pete says, and we both laugh while our mother sighs exasperatedly.

"Listen," I say. "I have to go."

"You just got here," Pete complains.

"Your brother's very busy." She says it to Peter, but it's aimed at me, right between the eyes.

"Matt's playing at Kenny's Castaways tonight," I say. "You want to come?" My invitation doesn't start out sincere, but suddenly it is, and I want badly for both of them to come, for Saint Mom to put on a dress and some makeup and for her and Peter to squeeze into Jed's tiny Lexus with me and come into the city, for us to be like a TV family. I'll put the top down, and Mom will laugh as her hair whips around her head, and Pete will close his eyes and plant his face in the wind, and we'll sing along to an oldies station, and with the speed of the car and the open air, I'll be able to love them without suffocating. But even as I think it, I know it will never happen. The last spontaneous thing my mother did was to set fire to her husband's bedspread almost twenty years ago, and Pete is scared of crowds and tends to act up.

"Tell Matt I said hi," Pete says.

"Will do," I say.

"I'll pack up some meatballs for Matt," my mother says. "He's really much too skinny."

As I kiss her good-bye, she pulls me close, gently grabbing a fistful of my hair. "You're not yourself," she says softly, looking me in the eye.

"Neither are you."

She nods, and offers up a wry, apologetic smile. "I've got my list of lame excuses," she says. "What's yours?"

I shake my head. "I'm fine, Ma, really," I say. "Don't worry."

She kisses my cheek and then lets go of me. "I have to," she says. "It's the only thing you'll let me do for you."

Pete steps out with me onto the darkness of the porch, and asks if he can drive the Lexus. I sit in the passenger seat as he pilots us slowly around the block, his hands at ten and two, signaling each left turn far in advance, his face a mask of rapturous concentration in the ambient glow of the dashboard. I'm filled with an unexpected wave of tenderness for him, and I resolve, as I do so often, to build a life for myself that will enable me to take care of Pete, to afford him all of the simple pleasures that, in his uncomplicated mind, make up the sum total of happiness. The advantage to Pete's kind of happiness, as opposed to the average man's, is that it's more easily quantifiable and therefore, in my mind, more easily attainable.

"Satch sometimes lets me drive his car."

"Satch Bowhan?"

"Yep."

"What are you doing hanging out with that asshole?"

Satch Bowhan, a year older than me, had been a holy terror when we were growing up, always getting suspended from high school for fighting or drugs, until he stopped going altogether. He always was strangely fascinated with Pete, and seemed to take a perverse pleasure in manipulating him in public, convincing him to drink from the toilet at the arcade or to pull down his pants and dance around the pizza store. Pete, always so eager to please, interpreted the attention as inclusion and was always more than happy to accommodate Satch, who called him his little buddy. I was in more than my share of fights defending Pete from the cruelty of our peers, but it was rumored that Satch carried a switchblade and had used it before, so whenever our confrontations started to verge on violence, I always backed down. When I was in college, I heard that he'd been arrested a few times and joined the Marines to avoid a jail sentence.

"Satch is a good guy."

"Pete," I say, turning to face him. "Satch is a lowlife. You should steer clear of him."

"He's my friend. He gives me a discount at the hardware store. And he lets me drive his car sometimes. That's all."

"He was always so mean to us when we were kids."

"Well," Pete says, "he's different now."

"Just promise me you won't let him take advantage of you."

Pete turns to me. "I may be retarded," he says. "But I'm not stupid."

"Eyes on the road," I say, pointing to the windshield. "I know you're not stupid, Pete. But I'm your older brother. It's my job to worry about you."

Without being told, Pete knows to park in front of the neighbor's house, to avoid discovery by our mother. "I know, Zack," he says. "I love you."

"I love you too, Pete," I say. He's the only man I've ever been able to say that to. "You can drive me anytime."

"On the highway?"

"Don't push it."

"Ha!" He laughs and bangs the steering wheel with his hand. I'm about to open the car door when he says, "You still sad about Rael?"

I lean back in my seat, looking at him inquisitively. "Yeah," I say. "Sometimes."

"Me too," he says. "He was always real nice to me, you know. He didn't act like I was retarded or anything."

"He loved you a lot."

"Tamara would make me cookies."

"She still will," I said. "She just doesn't feel like making cookies yet, you know?"

"I know," Pete says, staring down at his lap. "I used to wish that you and me would live with Rael and Tamara forever. The four of us, you know?"

I can feel a lump forming in my throat. "That would have been nice," I say, although his words hurt me in ways I can't begin to understand.

He looks up at me. "Tomorrow's inventory after work," he says brightly. "I make an extra thirty dollars."

"That's great." I've always envied Pete's ability to snap out of a funk at a moment's notice. He works in the stockroom at Bless My Soles, a children's shoe store on Johnson Avenue. "You've been working there awhile already, huh?"

"Four years," he says proudly. "Mr. Breece says I'm irreplaceable."

"That's why they pay you the big bucks."

"Ha!"

"I'll see you soon, okay, Pete?"

"On Saturday."

"Saturday?"

"Your engagement party, stupid."

"Oh. Right." For a moment there, I'd forgotten.

I watch Pete as he ambles awkwardly back up the lawn, my stomach churning with the pure, pained love reserved only for him, pulling away only when I feel the tears threatening.

I'm in the Sunoco station throwing the Tupperware of meatballs into the garbage when my cell phone rings. I can see on the caller ID that it's Craig Hodges, no doubt calling to find out if I've made any progress on the Nike debacle since this morning. He'll hound me until this thing gets resolved to his satisfaction. I have no further information for him, so I let the call go to my voice mail. If he thought about it, Craig would realize that I couldn't possibly have any news for him yet, since China is just waking up now, but Craig has no mind for the details. Like the rest of us, he just desperately wants to be told that come what may, everything's going to be all right.

nine nine nine nine nine nine nine nine nine nine nine nine nine nine nine nine nine nine nine nine nine nine nine nine nine nine nine nine nine nine nine **nine** nine nine nine nine nine nine nine nine nine nine nine nine nine nine nine nine nine nine

When the divorce started to get nasty, Lela's lawyer hired a private detective who secured testimony that Anna was not the first coworker Norm had slept with. This was supposed to somehow help Lela's case, but what it did instead was get Norm fired, and his subsequent inability to stay at any job thereafter would become something of a dour family legend, referenced sardonically by aunts and grandparents in hushed kitchen conferences during holiday gatherings as Lela bemoaned his frequent failure to pay child support. What really infuriated her was that in most cases, Norm wasn't being fired. He was quitting.

"What do you mean, you quit?" we heard her through the walls, wailing on the phone to him. "You can't afford to quit!"

But he did, repeatedly, always believing he was being

mistreated, or passed over, or disrespected, or, in one case, the target of a mob conspiracy.

During this time, his visits started to become more sporadic, and more often than not we would find ourselves on Sunday mornings, dressed and waiting in the living room, awkwardly avoiding eye contact with each other while, upstairs, Lela desperately worked the phone, trying in vain to track Norm down. Eventually, I stopped expecting him, and Pete, as usual, followed my lead. But for a long time, Matt would get dressed every Sunday and sit sullenly in the living room, his jacket beside him on the couch, staring out the picture window and flashing accusatory glances at us when we padded by in our pajamas to get breakfast, as if our diminished expectations were the cause and not the effect of Norm's negligence. He knew as well as we did that Norm wasn't coming, but something in him, some incipient masochism, compelled him to relive the disappointment anew every week, as if he were consciously building a case to support the budding anger that would one day blossom like a mushroom cloud within him. After the vandalism began, Lela put him in therapy, but that seemed to make him only more sullen, and she could hardly be shelling out seventy-five dollars a session for something that didn't seem to be having any effect.

A little while later, Norm announced that he had accepted a position with a firm in Boston and, with a flurry of promises of a better life to come for us all, packed all his possessions into the run-down Nova he was driving and headed north. It was a small pharmaceutical company, but they were poised to take off, and he was getting in on the ground floor. And he wasn't going to be an accountant; he was going to be a salesman—Massachusetts would be his territory initially—and it didn't matter that he'd never been in sales before, that he'd taken some liberties with his résumé, because sales was all about forging relationships, about looking people in the eye and letting them know they could count on you, and that was Norm's specialty. He was a people person, and who better than him to charm receptionists and lunch with doctors on the company dime? And after he'd proven himself in sales, he had his eye on a position with upper management. This was the start of a promising new career and the salve to all our financial woes. And we shouldn't worry, because Boston wasn't that far, really, and he would get a large apartment, the rents there were so much more reasonable than here, and we could come up for weekends, see the Red Sox and the Bruins play, and he would come down to see us as well, and maybe, once he'd accrued some vacation time, we could all go to Disney World.

And we smiled our forced smiles and nodded by rote while Lela looked on silently, eyes frosted over in icy detachment. She didn't have to say anything, because by that point we were already living with the painful consciousness of what he'd become, or what he'd always been that had been obscured by the veil of marriage and fatherhood. We knew that within a year, two at the most, he'd have been fired over some misunderstanding or another, or yet another inadvisable workplace tryst. Or he'd have quit because they were damn fools who didn't know what they were doing and who didn't appreciate the wisdom of his suggestions. But we listened as if we believed, exclaiming positively at all the right pauses. At some point in the disconnect, a role reversal had taken place, and we now humored him as if he were an errant son in constant need of stroking and encouragement.

So we hugged him good-bye and watched him go, hoping in the manner of children that despite all we knew, this time things might be different. And for the first few months, it seemed as though they might be. Norm called regularly, telling us about his fancy new office with a view of the Charles River, and relating amusing stories of the you-had-to-be-there variety about his new buddies and his life on the road. Every other weekend he would drive down to New York to visit us, handing Lela his child support checks with a beneficent expression that made the veins in her neck bulge. We were living on Lela's teaching salary, and the added money should have been a boon for us, but she resolutely banked the checks with a severe frugality, like a squirrel anticipating the inevitable frost of winter.

And after about a year the visits started becoming more sporadic, and Lela began having to fight for her checks, and one day I called Norm's apartment and the phone was disconnected. We heard nothing from him for a spell, during which time Lela assured us that Norm would resurface. "He's like a bad penny," she said. "He always turns up." I didn't know what that meant, but he did resurface five months later, living in London, of all places. I was eighteen, and a month away from my high school graduation. Although I didn't like to admit it, I'd been harboring hopes that he would attend, and see what a success I'd become in his absence. "I've met a wonderful woman," he told me, his voice distant and hollow over the long-distance connection. "Her name is Lily, and she's a singer. We're getting married and I'm going to manage her career."

"You're getting married?" I said. "When?"

"We haven't set a date yet," he said. "She's a real bohemian, so we'll probably just have some wacky private ceremony on the beach."

"I didn't think there were any beaches in London."

He laughed, too hard. "Yeah. Well, I guess you're right about that."

"I'm graduating next month," I said.

"I know," he said. "I feel terrible I can't be there. But this opportunity came up and I just couldn't pass it up. I hope you understand."

"It's okay," I said, because really, what the hell else was I going to say. I wished it was Matt and not me on the phone, because Matt would have simply cursed and hung up on him. But as soon as Matt had heard "London," he'd stormed upstairs and sequestered himself in his room, and I just didn't have it in me. I was the soft touch, and Norm knew it.

"Listen, we'll come stateside as soon as we can, okay? I'm dying for Lily to meet all of you. You're all I ever talk about."

"Why didn't you call to tell us you were leaving?"

He sighed. "Everything just happened so fast," he said. "I met Lily and then she was leaving, and I just couldn't let her disappear like that, so I flew with her, and the next thing you know, I'm living in England."

"Just like that," I said.

"Yeah," Norm said with a chuckle. "Just like that. Listen, give my love to the boys, okay? And tell your mother I'll send you all some money as soon as I get myself set up here, okay?"

I hung up in a daze, and Lela, who'd been listening from her chair in the kitchen, put down her crossword puzzle. "If there's one area in which your father is completely reliable, it's in being unreliable," she said.

"He's still my father," I said defensively.

"He's gravy," she said dismissively. "All flavor and fat. No meat. Expect nothing. Then you can appreciate him without letting him hurt you over and over again."

I nodded, struggling to swallow the lump in my throat as she stared at me, tasting the bile of her own resentment, her eyes daring me to cry.

ten

When we were kids, Matt had this cherubic face, spaghetti-straight blond hair, plump pink cheeks, and our mother's soft blue eyes. I would stand by his crib for long stretches of time, watching him sleep, relishing his baby smells, infatuated by the sheer perfection of his composition. Now his head is shaved, his arms heavily tattooed, his face gaunt and violated at various junctions with metal knobs and bands, and he storms angrily across the stage in torn cargo pants and a ratty Sex Pistols T-shirt, singing songs about masturbation and suicide pacts. I sit in the back at a merchandise table loaded with CDs and T-shirts, watching my little brother stomp like God as his band, Worried About the WENUS, plays through their scorching set at Kenny's Castaways.

Jed was sitting with me until about twenty minutes ago,

at which point he selected one of the young, barely dressed women dancing nearby, seemingly at random, bought her a few drinks, and eventually disappeared with her into the bathroom. He considers groupie sex a perk of his devoted service to the band. Worried About the WENUS plays mostly to college crowds, touring up and down the East Coast in search of a record deal, and Jed is a passionate fan of college girls. Or, at least, he used to be. Ever since Rael's death, the whole thing seems to have become a joyless affair for him. He still comes, still hooks up with these girls, but I get the feeling he's no longer fully inhabiting himself at these times, watching himself like he watches the television, waiting for something, the music or one of these young girls, to ignite something within him. You don't think of loud, shameless nihilism as a positive attribute, but since he abandoned it, Jed seems only half-alive, as if he's only coming here and getting laid out of force of habit, or nostalgia for when he gave a shit. Somehow, when we're in the apartment, his stupor is somewhat less obvious, or else I've just gotten too used to it to notice it, but when we go out to the WENUS gigs, and I see him charming and seducing these young girls from a mile away, sleepwalking through the motions, I have to fight the urge to grab him by the shoulders and scream at him to wake the hell up.

Instead, I sit at my little concession table, watching the crowd and getting hammered on free drinks—the other, less glamorous benefit of being with the band. Before Hope, I did hook up on occasion, but my success rate paled in comparison to Jed's, and I usually had to wait until he had already chosen his partner for the evening, since no one would give me a second glance while he was still there. Looks are a function of circumstance, and I become much better looking when Jed's not around.

Sure enough, within a few minutes, a girl with almond eyes and a dancer's body walks over and sits down in Jed's empty seat. Her straight shoulder-length hair is standard-issue blond, darker at the roots and parted in the middle. Her body is its own selling point, and her posture and the clinging halter top she wears indicate that she knows it. It's pathetic, really, but that's all it takes: nice eyes and lively breasts on a thin frame. Everything else is just icing on the cake. She's hot and flushed from dancing. "Hey," she says. "T-shirt man."

This is apparently a salutation, so I respond in kind. "Hey, sweaty girl." She throws back her head and laughs. I picture her in her dorm room, looking in the mirror as she rehearses this gesture, possibly picked up from a Sandra Bullock movie. "I know," she says. "I get a little carried away with the dancing. This is my third WENUS show this year." Her skin glows pink in the spotlighting of the club. She's pretty in an unsophisticated way, like a Midwestern farm girl, and you can see the wide-open prairies behind her, the blue-skied meadows in her eyes. As far as one-night stands go, I could do a lot worse. I know this because I have. "Can I ask you a question?" she says.

"Sure." We're both shouting to be heard above Matt, who has just launched into a thrashing cover of "Believe It or Not," the *Greatest American Hero* theme. I suggested it to him about a year ago, and it never fails as a crowd-pleaser. It occurs to me that the girl now sitting with me probably was in diapers during that show's brief run, and I feel ridiculously old.

"What does Worried About the WENUS actually mean?"

"Ah," I say. I get asked that question often. "Did you ever watch *Friends*?"

"Sure," she says. "In high school." She is leaning close to me to be heard, affording me a clear view down her flimsy shirt as her breath tickles my ear. The alcohol fumes mingling in the air from our collective breath could be ignited with the scrape of a match.

"It's an obscure reference to a particular episode."

She looks up at the band skeptically. "They were *Friends* fans?"

"It's a somewhat ironic reference," I admit.

There comes a point in every one of these types of conversations when you somehow know it's yours for the taking, and when she leans in to me and says, "I'm Jesse, by the way," I know I'm in.

"Zack," I say. We shake hands like idiots.

Later, after enough drinks to lose count, we slow dance in the back, right near my table, and if you need another confirmation that sex is in the offing, slow dancing to punk rock is usually a good sign. I am in that blissful state of drunkenness where your impaired senses are not yet aware of the frothing cauldron stirring in your guts, and you foolishly believe your buzz will simply taper off like smoke in the breeze, rather than end abruptly in the acidic violence of a late-night puke. Jesse presses her cheek to mine and I enjoy the feel of her spry bosom crushed against my chest. Soon we're making out, the deep, wet, wide-open kisses of horny strangers. She brushes her thigh blatantly against my crotch, her tongue flitting hungrily about my lips, the volume of the music somehow granting us license for this salacious behavior. On some distant plane of consciousness where the alcohol has not yet seeped, the guilt is percolating, but oddly enough, instead of seeing Hope's face there, I see Tamara's. My benumbed mind is not up to examining the complex stratification of this drunken betrayal, so I choose to forget about it. Consequences are a concept for the sober. My body feels weightless, suspended by the booze, by the deafening sound system, and by Jesse's arms, and as I close my eyes, I can feel myself sinking into a pleasant oblivion.

The band finishes their first set to a raucous round of applause, and I feel like a kid in a movie theater when the lights go up at the end. Fooling around with a stranger in public is somewhat more awkward without the comforting insulation of loud music and darkness. Jesse and I return to the table, where we quickly down a few more drinks in the hopes of sustaining the sexy mood through the jarring break while the band takes an intermission.

Jed comes back from the bathroom, rumpled and lipstick scarred, and nods knowingly at me when he sees Jesse leaning on me. He pulls over a chair for himself and one for his new friend, a tall brunette who looks like a poor man's Christy Turlington.

"And how are things on the O.C.?" I say.

"You're one to talk," he says, eyeing Jesse pointedly. He turns and theatrically offers her his hand. "I'm Jed, by the way."

Introductions are made all around and Jed calls for a pitcher. The waitress informs us that now that we have guests, we'll have to start paying for our drinks. "I left my wallet in the van," I say.

"It's okay," Jed says, discreetly pulling out a wad. "I got it."

Jesse flashes me a sly look. "You have a van?" she says.

This is what happens. The cold air hits your face like a slap as you stagger out of the club and down Bleecker Street to where the band's van is parked. You're thirty-two years old, with a fiancée to boot, and yet you find yourself climbing into the back of a van with a sweetly game college girl. She's ten years younger than you and finishing the last credits of her religion major, and she has about her a practiced air of seasoned sexuality. She will prefer to be on top—you know this instinctively—and will be unabashed in the pursuit of her own gratification. This is all wrong. Even if you weren't engaged, you'd be too old for her. But her skin is smooth and unblemished as fresh snowfall, and in the dim lighting, it has a satiny sheen, and you feel something apart from the guilt and self-pity that are growing like twin tumors in your belly, a sense of desperate longing to be that young and whole again.

Matt's van has only the two seats up front. The back is open and windowless, to facilitate the transport of the band's musical arsenal. Jesse climbs in and sits up against the wall. "Can you turn on the heat?" she says.

The engine coughs twice before turning over with a loud backfire, and the air whines through the vents like a dying animal. "Put on some music," she calls to me, shivering in the back. I fumble through the tapes scattered around the floor of the passenger seat. It's mostly punk, not exactly mood music. The cold air has sobered me somewhat, and it seems preposterous that I'm really going to have sex with a college girl in the back of a van. I finally find a battered Pink Floyd album and slide it into the tape deck.

In the back, Jesse's seated Indian-style on the corrugated metal floor, lighting up a joint. She offers me the roach clip and I take a long drag. It's been a few years since I smoked any weed, and it dries me out instantly. I feel a sting in my throat, a churning in my belly, and the rise of acid in the back of my mouth. I hand her back the joint and sit down across from her.

I don't want to cheat on Hope in the back of a van with some young stranger. I don't know what's going on with Tamara and me, but this feels like cheating on both Tamara and Hope, which makes no sense, again, but there it is. Also, no one's had van sex since the seventies. It's tacky. With the grandiose resolve of the inebriated, I decide that under no circumstances will I go through with this. Jesse carefully sets aside the roach and climbs onto my lap, straddling me as she starts to kiss me deeply. She tastes like strawberry lipstick, smoke, and tequila, and I celebrate my decision to not have sex with her by kissing her back. We do that for a little while, our tongues colliding in their sloppy explorations, and I guess the van's heating has finally kicked in, because she pulls off her flimsy top with her bra in one practiced motion and I'm suddenly face-to-face with her astounding breasts. I feel my drunken resolve crumbling in the face of her impressive nakedness. The fact is, I don't want to do this, but then again, I really, really do. Story of my life. Relief comes from my roiling stomach juices, which unite in revolt and rise up in a spastic convulsion. I manage to push Jesse off my lap just before I vomit prolifically all over the van.

"Oh, shit," Jesse shouts, throwing herself away from me and scrambling toward the back of the van on her ass. I open my mouth to apologize but instead just vomit some more. Jesse opens the rear door and scampers out of the van, only realizing afterward that she's not wearing a shirt. "Are you okay?" she says, climbing back in but leaving the door open.

I nod woozily and pass her shirt to her. She examines it hastily to make sure it's clean and then throws it on. Her bra has not met with the same good fortune and she discards it in the gutter with a shrug. "Listen," she says, stepping out of the van. "Do you need a hand?"

"I'll be okay," I say, climbing out of the van and wiping my mouth in the bend of my elbow. "I'm really sorry about that."

"Don't worry about it," she says, but she's already distracted, mildly repulsed, and looking to make a graceful exit.

"So, I'm going to head back inside," I say, to give her an out.

"I think I'll go home," she says, relieved.

I nod. "Well, it's been fun."

"Same here," she says with a wry smile. I have already faded into a one-dimensional memory, nothing more than a cautionary tale she'll relate to girlfriends in the years to come during the exchange of drinking horror stories. Realizing this makes me feel sadly unsubstantial as I make my way back into the club, light-headed and heavyhearted.

Jed is still in his seat, brooding over his kamikaze, and beside him is a new, equally fetching girl. The Gin Blossoms are being played too loudly over the amplifiers, and the houselights are still up, hurting my eyes. "What happened to you?" he says as I half slide, half fall into an empty seat.

"I got sick," I say.

"So I smell."

The new girl, a brunette with a pixie haircut and pierced eyebrows, fishes into her pocket and hands me a Certs with a smile. I pop it gratefully.

"And your friend?" Jed says.

"We grew apart."

"It happens." Then the girl's got her tongue in his ear and I don't exist, and she doesn't know it but neither does she, so, with nothing else to do, I head unsteadily backstage to tell Matt that I'll be leaving before the second set.

eleven

Sam, the bass player, and Otto, the drummer, are reclining on the stairs, still drenched in sweat from their performance, sipping at vodka shots and working out some details on the set list for the second half of the show. Matt's the songwriter and front man, but he leaves all other decisions in the hands of Sam and Otto, which probably explains why they're still playing the same clubs they were playing when they formed the band six years ago. They're fair musicians, but they're also potheads and overgrown frat boys, and their vague ambitions don't extend very far beyond playing gigs and laying groupies. Matt, on the other hand, wants to hit the big time, is counting on it more than he'll let on, but seems unable to break out of the career dead end in which Worried About the WENUS find themselves. Jed's been talking to Matt about coming on board as manager, and while the boys are wary of an outsider stepping in, I think Jed could bring some much-needed business acumen and funding to the band. But no one's asking me.

"Hey, Zack," Otto says. He's a short, overweight guy with thinning hair and comically thick-rimmed black glasses. Sam, emaciated and stoned, nods solemnly at me. The bass players are always the quiet ones, pissed at the world, convinced their contribution is being overlooked.

"Hey, boys," I say. "You guys are sounding great."

"We didn't suck," Otto says proudly.

"Matt's all freaked-out about something," Sam says dully as he scribbles a song list onto a napkin.

"What?"

"You'd have to ask him."

Otto nods agreeably. "Dude, you better go talk to him. He's acting weird."

I step into the dressing room to find Matt sitting on the vanity table, distractedly tuning his Gibson. There's a cute redhead curled into a ball on the couch behind him, chattering softly into a neon flashing cell phone. I always experience an acute sense of relief when I see Matt alone after he's been playing onstage, his face finally composed and at rest, no longer distorted by the angry scowl frozen in place when he performs. He plays with such rage and desolation that I fear one day I'll come backstage and find him a weeping, cursing mess with a gun in his mouth. Baby brothers and punk rock are a bad combination for a sentimental fart like me.

"Hey, Matt," I say, stepping into the room. "Great set."

"What the fuck, Zack?" Matt says.

"What?"

"What are you trying to do to me here?"

"What are you talking about?"

He studies my face a moment. "You don't know?"

"Know what?"

He hops off the table and puts down the guitar. "Come with me. You're not going to believe this." He hurriedly ushers me to the door, ignoring the girl when she asks where he's going. Matt leads me to the corner of the stage, just out of sight from the crowd below, and points to a table in the far back corner. "He showed up during the last song."

Even in the dim club lighting, Norm's stout profile is unmistakable. "Oh, shit," I say. He must have walked in while I was retching in the van.

"You don't sound surprised to see him," Matt says, his voice laden with a range of unformed accusations.

"I'm not. I mean, I knew he was in town, but I never thought he'd come here."

"What do you mean, you knew he was in town?"

"He came by my apartment yesterday."

Matt is stunned. "You invited that asshole over?"

"He just showed up."

"Bullshit."

"Why would I lie, Matt?" I say wearily. I can feel a major headache coming on. "Did you invite him here? No. He just showed up. Same shit, different venue, that's all."

"Well, you could have warned me," he said sulkily.

Matt, as the baby, and a burgeoning rock star, has the unfortunate tendency to believe that he's still the center of everyone else's universe, that I'm still standing quietly like a loyal sentry beside his crib, waiting for him to wake up so I can play with him. *I've got problems of my own,* I want to say. *I've been looking at crop shots of my bladder, at spots that shouldn't be there, fucking up million-dollar accounts at work, and falling in love with the last person on the planet I should.* But all I say is "Believe me, if I had any idea he was going to come here, I would have called."

Matt was only seven when Norm evacuated, which means it took him the longest to figure out how full of shit Norm really was, rebounding from every forgotten visit and broken promise to enthusiastically believe the next one. When he finally figured it out, he took it pretty hard. So where I contented myself, at least outwardly, with writing Norm off and cultivating a quiet, simmering bitterness over the long term, Matt went straight to an unmitigated hatred that never seemed to wane, just like, as a child, he'd continue to cry passionately, long after he'd forgotten why he was crying to begin with. Whenever he had downtime, he exacted minor vengeance with malicious little plots, tracking my father through means never fully revealed, taking out credit cards in his name and running up huge debts, calling up and canceling Norm's phone service, ordering expensive deliveries to his apartment, subscribing him to twenty magazines at a shot. Norm no doubt logged many hours on the phone with various customer service representatives, trying to untangle the web of consumerism Matt was constantly spinning around him.

Matt looks at me. "What, so are you two now, like, hanging out?"

"Oh, for Christ's sake," I say, heading back toward the dressing room.

"Well, why's he here?"

"I don't know. I guess he wants to see us."

"Is he dying or something?"

"I don't know. We didn't get that far."

Sam and Otto are waiting for us in the dressing room. "Everything copacetic?" Otto asks concernedly.

"Yo, man," Sam says. "We're on in ten and we have to go over the set list. I've made some changes."

"Fuck that," Matt says. "We're not going on. I can't play."

"What are you talking about?" Sam says. "Of course we're playing."

"I can't, man." He looks at me. "Not with him out there."

"Who?" Otto says. "Not with who out there?"

Matt shakes his head and collapses on the couch. The girl, now off her cell phone, puts her hand on his lap and looks at him inquisitively, but he keeps his eyes trained on me. He's been launching his stealthy offensives at Norm for years, and while he's surely envisioned an actual confrontation in some form, scripting and editing his invective just as I did for so many years, it's apparent to me that he never really believed it would happen, and now his eyes reflect the fear and vulnerability of a scared little boy.

"You want me to see if I can get him to go?" I say.

He nods.

"Get who to go?" Sam yells. "Who the fuck is here?"

"Chill out, Sam," the girl says.

"Shut your piehole, Yoko!" Sam snaps at her. "You don't belong here."

"Sam," Matt says, pained. "Just calm the fuck down."

"I'll see what I can do," I say, and leave the room.

"Hey, Zack," my father says, acting all nonchalant, like it was no trick at all to have tracked us down like this. He motions to the chair next to him. "Join me."

"No, thanks," I say. "What are you doing here?"

"I came to hear Matt play," he says, as if I should have expected no less. "And to tell you the truth, I didn't expect to like it as much as I do. It's a lot more melodic than I'd imagined, and the harmonies are actually quite sophisticated."

"I'm glad you approve," I say. "Now you have to leave."

"He was always so musical," Norm says, ignoring my entreaties completely. "I would play Sinatra on the stereo, and you and Pete would go about your business, but Matt, he would sit down on the floor, right by the speaker, eyes closed, and tap out the rhythm on his lap. He was so intense about it, so focused. I told your mother, more than once, that she should give the boy piano lessons. He could have been one of the greats. I don't know why she never gave him piano lessons."

"Money was tight."

He looks up at me and nods. "Point taken," he says with an affected gravity, clearly convinced that the concession itself is part of his absolution. I can see why he was drawn to AA. It's just too perfect for him. He can go through the motions of contrition, wearing his manufactured humility like a badge of armor, and even if we don't buy it, he ultimately gets to forgive himself and pat himself on the back for working the program and having the serenity to accept the things he can't change and the courage to change the things he can. And at the AA meetings, they'll probably shower him with congratulations and praise, and maybe even give him one of those commemorative chips for his efforts. And the bastard will sit there grandly accepting all this uninformed love and support, actually buying into it, thinking himself a hero for facing up to the revelation that he's done some bad things in the past. The really good liars, the true grandmasters of bullshit, are so damn convincing because they actually believe their own lies.

"You need to go," I say. "Matt's not up for this. You're going to make him mess up."

Norm takes an unhurried sip from his drink. "The hell I

will," he says. "The boy's a pro. Did you see the way he handles that guitar?"

"I thought you didn't drink anymore."

He raises the glass. "Club soda," he says. I resist the urge to grab the glass from his hand and verify the absence of gin. While our relationship may be a huge question mark, I don't like the intimacy that would be implied by random drink testing. "Although, while we're on the subject," Norm continues, looking me over. "You look like you've had a few too many yourself."

"Fuck off."

He raises his hands defensively. "You're right. Too soon. Sorry."

"Norm."

"Norm?" he says. "My friends call me Norm. You can call me Dad."

"Dad."

"Yes?"

"I will have you bounced."

Norm winces at my tone, his shoulders sag, and for the brief second that his expression wavers, I can see the pain and fear etched into his face, the tenuous resolve that's keeping him here. "Zack," he says just loud enough to be heard over the house music. "I know you boys have a lot to be angry about, and I'm sorrier than you'll ever know, than I can ever begin to express to you. But I have to start somewhere. If nothing else, when I'm dead, you'll remember that there was a point at which I came to understand the nature of my offenses, and I tried, maybe unsuccessfully, but tried nonetheless, to make amends. You're young yet, and you've got decades to waste on your anger. I'm older than I ever imagined I could get, and I am suggesting to you, the one thing I'm sure about, the one thing I can hang my hat on, is that there's no more time to wait it out, to come up with a plan. So I understand your attitude, but you need to understand mine." He takes a deep breath and I can see that his hands are actually shaking. "I came here to hear my son play. And that's what I'm going to do. If he doesn't play, that's too bad. But I will not go to sleep tonight knowing that I retreated at the first sign of resistance. So if you want to have Maurice throw me out, bring it on. I wasn't expecting this to be a cakewalk."

I stare at him, momentarily shocked by his little soliloquy. "How did you know the bouncer's name is Maurice?"

"I make friends easily."

"Are you dying?"

He sighs and studies his hands on the table. "We're all dying, Zack."

Oh, Jesus. I'm about to lash out at the obviousness of his platitude when the houselights come down and the band takes the stage to raucous screams and applause. "Well," Norm says, clapping enthusiastically and letting go with a shrill whistle. "I guess Matt's decided he's going to play after all."

Matt lashes on his guitar and steps up to the microphone. Behind him, Otto begins tapping out a slow, rolling beat on the snare, and my heart sinks as I recognize the introduction to "Saint Mom." Matt's apparently decided that having Norm in the audience is too good an opportunity to pass up. What's the point in writing a song excoriating your father if you never get to see the look on his face when he hears it? The audience, recognizing the slower beat of a ballad, takes their seats. As Matt strums the opening chords of the song, he looks over to my father's table, eyes on fire, a wicked smile playing across his face. "This is a song I wrote about my family," he says into the mike. There are some scattered cheers in the audience, maybe because some die-hard fans know which song he's about to play, or maybe just because people listening to rock bands will cheer just about anything the singer says. Either way, the place falls silent as Matt begins to sing.

Saint Mom remembers when her life was more than just laying down
Before Daddy broke his promises and Daddy fucked around
And all her children's broken dreams were scattered to the winds
And Mom climbed up upon her cross to die for Daddy's sins

Norm freezes like a corpse as the lyrics sink in and stares straight ahead, his countenance fiercely devoid of expression, and I don't need the houselights to know that all the color has been drained from his face. Matt briefly backs away from the microphone to play out the measure, and then steps back up for the second verse.

And what were we to do there, how did we survive
Remembering the light that used to shine in Mother's eyes
All I could do is lay in bed and watch the peeling paint
You'll never know what hell is till you try to love a saint

Then Sam and Otto start shouting, "Saint Mom," in two-part harmony into their mikes while Matt sings the chorus over their voices.

(Saint Mom)
If you're so good why does it hurt so much
(Saint Mom)

If you love me why can't I feel your touch
(Saint Mom)
Dad's love was a nuclear bomb
That blew your insides all to hell
Left nothing but the shell
Of Saint Mom

And now Matt's guitar is thrashing and wailing, and Otto's laying down the thunder with ferocious precision, and even though the song wasn't on the set list, the lighting guy has improvised well, suffusing the stage in a hellish amber glow, and the music unfurls like a flag in increasing sonic waves, growing louder with each undulation and practically throbbing with intensity, and Norm sits paralyzed in his chair like the Memorex man, buffeted and paralyzed by the music washing over him, and even though the whole thing shakes me to the core, watching Matt launch his pain out from the stage and watching my father absorb it, I still manage to think that this is what music, at its purest, is supposed to do, and goddamn it, Matt's good at it.

There's another verse to the song, but Matt doesn't sing it. Instead, he takes a scorching guitar break, his body bending and contorting as he coaxes higher and higher notes out of the Gibson, and then, just as he hits the climax of the guitar solo, he stops playing, and lets the guitar hang loose against his hips as he cradles the mike with both hands. Sam keeps the bass line going while Otto softens the beat, and Matt sings the chorus again with his eyes closed, this time slowly, his voice dripping with venom. When he's done, he steps back, out of the spotlight and into the shadows, leaving Sam and Otto to finish out the song with a slow fade. Then there's a moment, a crystalline instant of perfect silence, when the music has stopped and the audience hasn't reacted yet, and it feels like the entire club has been stunned into silence. And then, all at once, the applause comes, not mounting gradually, but already up there, a surging wave of clapping and cheering that reverberates through the room like a storm. And at the forefront of this wave of sound is Norm, who has gotten to his feet and is shouting and cheering as he claps demonstratively, almost comically, his arms sweeping widely as if he's trying to signal Matt, which of course he is. I wonder if it's actually possible that he's missed the point of the song, that he's obstinate enough to have willfully overlooked it, but then the sweeping stage lights flash into the audience and I can see that even as he hoots and claps, his face is unmistakably streaked with tears that continue to stream from his eyes even now. And when I see his tears, I can feel my own, hot against my flushed skin.

The applause lasts for well over a minute, and then Matt launches into "Bring Your Sister," a hard-rocking, up-tempo number about teenaged lovers that actually got some radio play on the college stations last year, and the audience jumps to their feet, clapping and dancing, pointed fingers and fists waving in the air, punctuating the music. Matt doesn't allow his glance to wander to our side of the room, and after a moment, Norm nods to himself, wipes his face with his sleeve, and turns to leave.

"I'll see you, Zack," he says, straining to be heard above the music.

"You're leaving now?" I say. As I look at him, I notice for the first time that his remaining strands of hair are grouped together in a symmetrical network of rows, like on a doll's head, the unmistakable grid of a failed hair transplant. That Norm went to extreme measures to try to reverse his baldness is hardly surprising, but it's the fact that I can look down at his scalp that throws me for a loop. I didn't notice before that I am actually taller than him. I wonder how old I might have been when that happened.

"I think I've seen what I came to see," he says.

"He's angry," I say, following him toward the exit, upset with myself, even as I say it, feeling the need to explain, or excuse Matt. "You had to know he'd be angry. That we'd all be."

"I knew," he says. He's still somewhat shell-shocked from the musical assault, and he's eyeing that exit door like a drowning man eyeing the distant shore. He takes a few more steps, and then turns to look back at the stage, the lights dancing in the wet flesh of his cheeks, and his moist eyes meet mine knowingly. "He's something else, though, isn't he?" he says.

I nod. "That he is."

"Goddamn," he says, shaking his head in wonder. "And how is he otherwise?"

I consider the question, wondering how much I want to share with him, how much he's entitled to know, and whether I want the information to hurt him or not. "Otherwise," I say, "he's a big, fucking mess."

Norm nods sadly as we step out of the club and onto the street. "Well, you tell him that I was proud of him tonight, okay? That I've never been prouder."

"I'm not sure that's what he wants to hear."

"Just tell him for me," Norm says. "Will you do that?"

Our eyes meet. "Sure," I say.

"Thanks, Zack."

I watch him as he walks down the street, head down, shoulders stooped against the cold, and I can feel things quivering inside me, emotions, as yet unrecognizable, messing with my blood, diving at random into the slipstream of my consciousness, fucking with me. It's been a long day; it feels like weeks ago that I woke up and pissed a red thread into the toilet. I can feel my last reserves of strength fading, but as I watch my father being swallowed up into the darkness of the Village, hunched over in his blazer for warmth, the strange thing is that despite my inability to discern how I feel about anything these days, I'm pretty sure that I'm sorry to see him go.

twelve

Only when I climb into the cab does it hit me that I've forgotten to tell Matt about vomiting in the van. I turn on my cell phone and dial Jed's, but even if his is still on, he'll never hear it ring in the club. Sure enough, I get his voice mail and hang up. My own voice mail icon is blinking, so I dial up my messages. There's only one, from Hope.

"Hi, Zack. Sorry I couldn't call you earlier. I was stuck in meetings until after nine. I did try you earlier in the day at work and then at your apartment. Where did you go? You're usually so reachable. I know you're at Matt's show now, so call me when you head home. I'll keep my ringer on, even if I'm sleeping, so I can at least say good night to you. I love you, babe, 'bye."

Her voice opens the floodgates, and the guilt comes pouring in like a tidal wave. What the hell is wrong with me? What is it that's driving me to screw up my relationship with this beautiful, bright, passionate woman who has defied the natural order of things by unaccountably falling for me? A few years ago I was your average single man, a jaded member of the Upper West Side infantry, hitting the bars in teams of two and three, scanning, scoping, and on occasion engaging. More often than not, I found myself targeting slightly flawed women, big boned or slightly pudgy, women with smaller chests or imperfect complexions. Basically, decently attractive women who wouldn't have that resigned look in their eye, that exhaustion born of being too beautiful and hit on too often. If the beautiful women didn't want the attention, then why did they come out to the bars? The inescapable conclusion, of course, was that they were looking to meet someone too. I just knew intuitively that that someone wasn't me. If a woman was too good-looking, I always felt that any approach was too obvious, that to concede my intentions would result in instantaneous rejection. And even with nothing to lose, I pathologically avoided that rejection, concealing my intentions by ignoring them, which worked great, except I didn't get laid very often at all.

Hope, though, is a once-in-a-lifetime score. She's the embodiment of that molten perfection I'd always viewed wistfully from afar, the kind of girl who, if anything, would want to be friends and talk to me about her boyfriends. And I would take that unintentional abuse, because there's a whole other kind of love out there exercised by the sexual middle class, guys like me who tolerate such one-sided relationships, because we're either blind optimists or merely idiots, needing to be close to that kind of woman, even platonically, to feed the ugly, deformed thing in us, the hunchback in our bell tower that lives to experience that beauty on any level we'll be allowed. But now I've lived the dream; I've risen above my sexual station and landed a woman just like that, who actually loves me back. I'd have to be certifiable to put it at risk.

I've always known that infidelity is in my blood, enmeshed somewhere in the strands of my DNA, and I've dedicated my life, more consciously than I would care to admit, to doing everything in my power to not be like Norm. Yet here I am, engaged to one woman, obsessing about another, and, for reasons still unclear to me, getting hot and tawdry with a college girl in the back of a van. It's as if his very proximity is accelerating the genetic fate I've been fighting my whole life.

I dial Hope on my cell. "Hey," she says, her voice husky with sleep, and I can picture her perfectly in her high four-poster bed, curled up under her floral-patterned comforter in a sheer nightshirt from Victoria's Secret, her fresh, cool linens smelling faintly of lilac, her face scrubbed and Ivory clean, her sandy-colored hair pulled back in a loose ponytail, her bare legs freshly shaved and moisturized, her body warm with sleep. I can feel myself growing stiff just thinking about it.

"Hey," I say.

"I miss you," she murmurs. "Where are you?"

"In a cab."

She yawns, and I can see the feline arc of her back as she stretches. "Mmm," she says. "I wish you were here with me now."

"I can tell the driver."

She giggles. "No. I need to sleep. I have an early meeting."

"Oh, well," I say.

"It's not that I don't want you in my bed, because I do."

"I know," I say. I can't get her bed out of my mind now, everything clean and smooth and fragrant. Ever since the first time I slept with Hope in her bed, the smell of freshly laundered sheets gets me aroused. "I love you, Hope."

"I love you too, babe," she whispers, and I can tell she's falling back asleep.

"I'm lucky to have you," I whisper, a bit self-conscious about the cabdriver, even though odds are he doesn't understand a word I'm saying.

"You're sweet," she says. "I think I'll keep you."

"I'll speak to you in the morning."

"Good night, babe."

I can fix this, I think desperately as I flip the phone closed. It's within my grasp. All I have to do is rededicate myself to Hope, establish some healthy distance from Tamara, and make sure I avoid any more unfortunate lapses like the one tonight. In other words, live my life the way it's set up to be lived. Be the anti-Norm.

But then I think of Tamara's wide, sensual eyes glistening with ethereal tenderness and understanding and wisdom and pain and—I'm pretty sure about this—passion. Not passion for me, of course, but for life, for love, for a party to be named later. And when I think of that party being anyone other than me, when I think of those lips, moist and plump as grapes, kissing someone other than me, of her leaning her head on anyone else's shoulder, of some other man's leg rocking her porch swing, things inside me start to wither and fall away.

I stare at myself in the taxi window, watching as the lighted signs from storefronts pass through the sad, amorphous ghost of my reflection, and the ghost makes me think about Rael, and I wonder if he's looking down at all of this, if he's concerned or pissed or just laughing his ass off because he knows now that none of it really matters anyway.

Outside, a woman walks a Labrador puppy, who tugs eagerly at his leash, tearing back and forth frenetically along the sidewalk, thrilled beyond measure to be a dog. As I watch the dog urinate into my reflection, I wonder how I can be in such an abject state of misery when just a few days ago everything was fine. It occurs to me, just before I pass out, that maybe I was miserable before, but things were going too well for me to notice it.

thirteen thirteen thirteen thirteen thirteen thirteen
thirteen thirteen thirteen thirteen thirteen thirteen
thirteen thirteen thirteen thirteen thirteen thirteen
thirteen **thirteen** thirteen thirteen thirteen thirteen
thirteen thirteen thirteen thirteen thirteen thirteen

thirteen

i wake up Tuesday morning with swollen eyes, my throat parched and sore, and a world-class hangover like a spike through my brain. I lie paralyzed, trying to slip under the radar of the spectacular pain in my head while disjointed images from last night flicker through my mind in reverse order. I vaguely recall the rough shoves and curry smell of the cabdriver, muttering at me in an indecipherable accent as he woke me up in the backseat, the ride uptown in semiconscious delirium, the taste and smell of the college girl in the van. Try as I might, I cannot remember paying the driver, making my way into the brownstone or up the stairs to my bedroom. Nor do I recall vomiting again, but the stinking evidence, hard and crusty on my chest and sheets, is indisputable. Daylight pours through my window, illuminating a galaxy of floating spores. In my stupor last night, I didn't think to lower the blinds, an omission that probably has cost me a few more hours of blessed oblivion. The light creeps up my bed like nuclear fallout, and when it reaches my face, my eyeballs throb like bruised testicles. The pain is a blanket, thick and suffocating.

This is what cancer feels like all the time, I think.

Gradually, I become aware of an insistent pulse in the depths of my groin, and even though I know it's just an overflowing bladder, I picture that little dark spot inside me, pulsating malevolently like a black heart, devouring and assimilating cells wantonly as it grows. I crawl to the bathroom and pee with my eyes closed, cradling my head in my hands. When I stumble back into bed, the blood-colored, oversized digits on my clock radio catch my eye, and I'm surprised to see that it's past nine. I should call the office, but I can't muster up the strength to find the phone. My cell phone lies on the floor near my bed, but to turn it on will be to unleash hell. I picture my empty cubicle, the e-mails stacking up like Tetris bricks on my monitor, my phone ringing off the wall, my voice mailbox filled with increasingly frantic messages from Craig Hodges about the impossibility of purple swooshes. I open my mouth and whisper the word "swoosh." The sound, blowing through my rubber cheeks, somehow soothes my headache, so I spend the next few minutes *swoosh*ing quietly. Eventually, I fall back asleep.

I wake up again, a little after ten, to the muffled sounds of enthusiastic sex coming through the ceiling above me. Apparently, Jed brought someone home from the club last night. I listen to them for a moment, the muted squeals of the anonymous girl, the rhythmic shifting and groaning of bedsprings, and the light banging of the headboard against the wall. From where I lie, it sounds awfully strenuous, and I can't imagine ever having the strength to have sex again.

My hangover seems to have been downgraded to a dull

headache, so I slowly get out of bed, pop too many Excedrins, and take a hot shower. I seem to be doing everything at half speed, as if rehearsing for the real thing. I find myself staring at the stream of my shower, the splay of my toes on the tiles, the little hairs on my stomach as I wash myself. I consider sweatpants, but then throw on some chinos and a sweater, a grudging acknowledgment that I'm not going to call in sick. I have to be downtown later for my cystoscopy anyway. It takes me over an hour from when I woke up until I head downstairs to hydrate myself.

"He's alive!" Jed declares as I come slowly down the stairs. He's on the living room floor in a pair of boxers and nothing else, doing crunches while he watches *Judge Judy.*

"Not so loud, please," I say with a groan.

"That bad, huh?" he says, sitting up and transferring himself to the couch.

"You have no idea." I go to the kitchen and fill a beer mug from the water cooler.

Jed nods and begins channel surfing. "Your boss called here looking for you."

"My boss?"

"Some guy named Bill?"

"That would be him," I say, a sinking feeling in my stomach. "What'd you tell him?"

"I told him there was a family situation."

"That's good," I say approvingly. "Do you think he bought it?"

Jed shrugs. "He might have. He didn't strike me as the sharpest crayon in the box. Either way, he'd like you to call him at your earliest convenience concerning an urgent and timely matter, and I believe those were his exact words."

It sounds like the Nike shit has hit the Spandler fan. I sip thoughtfully at my water, a palpable unease growing in my belly. "Speaking of family situations," Jed says. "That was your dad at the gig last night, huh?"

"Yeah."

"So, what's going on there?"

"Nothing. He's just a sad, lonely old man," I say, surprised at the harshness in my voice.

Jed studies my face for a moment. "No crime in that," he says.

The offices of the Spandler Corporation look exactly like the place where you will not write your award-winning screenplay should look. The walls are an off-white that looks old right out of the can, the carpets a defeatist shit brown to preempt the midtown dirt we track in every day. The account executives are all men in their late twenties or early thirties who wear cheap suits and brandish their PDAs, laptops, and cell phones ardently, in the fervent hope of being mistaken for investment bankers. There's not a whiff of creativity, a hint of color, to be found in these halls, only the base grit of commerce as it exists in its lowest incorporated form.

Rael and I had this great idea for a screenplay. But he was working as a salesman in his father's paper company and I was here, and even though we could talk our asses off about it, about characters and scenes and plot twists, there was no way it was going to happen. So we made a pact. We were going to wait until the end of the year, at which point we would quit our jobs, set up shop in the brownstone, and write the damn thing. Jed, who liked the idea but had no patience for writing, promised us he would take it upon himself to shop it around Hollywood when the time came, or else put up the money to produce it independently if it came to that. It was a great plan, and when the three of us got together, we spoke of little else. Even if we failed, Rael said, it would be a worthwhile exercise. But then he got himself killed, and, worthwhile or not, the dream seems to have died with him.

I sit down at my desk, banging a quick hello to Tommy Pender on the other side of my cubicle wall.

"King!" he yells from behind the wall.

"Pender!"

"Bill's in the production meeting. He wants you there."

"Swell."

My voice mail light is flashing, but I can't bring myself to play the messages. I have 130 new e-mails. At least half of them are nothing more than solicitations to buy toner, membership to various porn sites, or generic Viagra. I picture a gargantuan warehouse, somewhere in Middle America, stocked with nothing but ink cartridges, erection pills, and porn. The rest of the e-mails are primarily from clients, checking on projects, demanding updates, presuming that I have nothing else to worry about other than answering their petty inquiries, holding their hands, and letting them know everything's on time. How the hell have I done this for so long? It's just after noon, and my doctor's appointment isn't until four. I decide to skip the production meeting and see if I can make any headway on the Nike problem before I see Bill.

One of the drawbacks of doing your manufacturing in China is that because of the vast time difference, you can never get a quick answer. And today, for whatever reason, there is no response to the urgent e-mail I jotted off yesterday before I left. It hardly matters, though, since I know that everything's already been produced. Craig will accept nothing less than a new production run, which he has no intention of paying for. The first run will have to be scrapped, at a raw cost of approximately $120,000, which we'll have to eat. We will also have to pay for the second run, with a probable twenty percent surcharge for a quick lead time as well as expedited shipping to get it in by Nike's original deadline. I'd calculated the Spandler Corporation's commission on the order to be a whopping eighty thousand dollars, twelve thousand of which would have been mine. Now not only will there be no profit, but we stand to incur significant losses remanufacturing the order, even if I manage to get Craig to foot the bill for the expedited shipping, which isn't likely. The Spandler Corporation will write off the loss, effectively halving it, but I will see no such benefit in my own loss.

There is another option. I can go over Craig's head and present the documentation to his bosses. It was Nike's screwup, after all, and we've got the spec sheets to prove it. Nike would then pay for the first order and place a new order in the correct color, and I would magnanimously offer to drastically reduce our margins on both so that we only break even, as a gesture of goodwill. A hell of a lot of work for which we would not make a dime, but we help them through the crisis, proving to be partners rather than vendors, and they reward us with future business. Of course, this strategy presumes that Craig will be fired, because if he isn't, he'll be gunning for me and we'll never get a dime's worth of business from Nike again.

I stand between the money and the client, between Craig and his bosses at Nike. No matter how I act, there will be negative repercussions for me, and all because of someone else's screwup. The middleman wears a big fat bull's-eye on his shirt, our version of the Nike swoosh. And the worst part of this whole mess is that Bill will have to be in on it, and he'll find some way to turn this on me, just like Craig did. Regardless of the facts, there will be no getting out of being blamed for this. It always goes down this way, like a familiar refrain: Clowns to the left of me, jokers to the right, here I am, stuck in the middle . . .

And the thing of it is, today I can't bring myself to give a shit. Something in my internal processes has gone horribly awry, and there's this spot, this microscopic group of rebel cells breaking the rules and congregating where they shouldn't, smoking and drinking and getting tattoos, growing and mutating and fucking around with the system. My system. And I know it's probably nothing, but what if it isn't? Sanderson said it would be eminently treatable, but even so, if it came once, it can come again—statistically speaking, it most likely will—and I'll spend my life wondering when the other shoe is going to fall.

I stare blindly at the computer screen until my vision becomes pixilated, and then I give up. I'll be useless today. I pick up the phone and dial Hope's number, intending to tell her what's going on and ask her to meet me at the doctor this afternoon, but I hang up after the first ring, not ready to bear the added weight of her worry on top of my own.

My unwillingness to involve Hope flummoxes me. Am I really so concerned for her peace of mind? That damn spot has me so worried, I could use someone else to do some of the worrying for me. So why can't I bring myself to call her? Another, less altruistic reason occurs to me. Tamara knows. Hope doesn't. In some way, admittedly a petty, twisted one, this makes me closer to Tamara than to Hope, and to tell Hope would end that. Hope's genuine concern—she would, of course, insist on accompanying me to the doctor, would aggressively pepper him with questions in the nature of a concerned mate—would in effect nullify this new chunk of intimacy with Tamara, would reassert the reality that lately I seem to be bending where Tamara's concerned.

So, call Tamara, I tell myself. *Call somebody before you explode.* But I can't call Tamara either, because I belong to Hope, and my unwillingness to exercise my right to worry her in this manner makes calling Tamara seem like nothing better than a blatant substitution, underscoring my precariously ridiculous perch in the relationship universe at this juncture. It isn't lost on me that my waffling devotions, as secret and, so far, unrealized as they are, have nonetheless managed to thoroughly isolate me, leaving me to deal with this crisis on my own, and frankly, I'm not up to the task.

Bill has sent me a barrage of e-mails asking for a CSR on the Nike situation, and judging by the tone and frequency of the e-mails, all sent before I arrived at work, he's well aware that the status is fucked-up beyond salvage. Hodges, that prick, has gone over my head. Like many middle managers, Bill believes that control and efficiency are best achieved by inventing an infinite array of internal reports, to which he assigns acronyms to make them seem like sophisticated business tools rather than a direct manifestation of his compulsion to cover his corporate ass. A CSR is a Client Status Report, a one-page document reviewing all current activity on a particular account, to keep Bill up to date. We account execs are supposed to furnish him with one per client on a weekly basis, a mandate we ignore thoroughly. Bill himself forgets to ask for them, until something goes wrong, at which point he insists upon them, rather than a quick, verbal update, as if this clerical process itself will keep the chaos at bay. The more paperwork Bill can jam between himself and the clients, the happier he is. Bill is scared shitless of the clients.

I'm about to e-mail him a response when he rings my intercom.

"Zack."

"Hi, Bill."

"We're finishing up the production meeting in the conference room. I realize you came in a bit late today, but I figured you could join us now and bring us up to speed on the Nike problem. Maybe we can do some brainstorming."

I'm in no mood for Bill. To be fair, I'm never in the mood for Bill, but right now, Bill could put me over the edge. "I'm actually dealing with that as we speak," I say.

"Well, I think we should all put our heads together on it," Bill says. He's got me on the speakerphone, and in my head I can see all the other account execs staring at the voice box, faces determinedly straight, silently thanking God it's not them for whom the shit's creek bell tolls this time. "We have our Tuesday meetings for a reason, Zack, and whether you appreciate that or not, I still expect you to attend and participate."

I sigh. "I'll be right there."

There are sixteen account executives in the branded display and packaging division that Bill oversees, and twelve of them are seated around the conference table, shuffling files and doodling on Spandler Corp. pads or pecking away scrupulously at their wireless e-mail devices. I make thirteen; Len Schaktman and Mike Wharton are traveling, and Clay is God knows where, strolling through Central Park, enjoying a novel he'd always meant to read, scanning the classifieds, or sitting at his kitchen table staring at the wall, his hot, home-brewed coffee failing to warm the icy terror growing in his belly as he wonders what the hell comes next. Through the scattered morass of Starbucks cups, diet Cokes, and water bottles, Bill can be spotted at the head of the table, jotting notes onto his legal pad, his gold wire-rimmed glasses slipping precariously toward the tip of his patrician nose. The account execs all look up as one as I enter the room, gazes quickly and not so quickly averted, and you can smell the schadenfreude filling the air like excessive aftershave.

"Sorry I'm late," I say, hoping we can leave it at that, but alas, we cannot. Bill won't let such manifest disregard for his Tuesday Production Meeting go unchallenged.

"Zack," Bill says, still looking down at his notepad. "These are your colleagues. They're all very busy, as busy as you. And yet, they all take time out of their hectic schedules to attend the Tuesday meeting. Because it's important. And because, as their boss, I demand it. Updating each other, sharing our respective triumphs and challenges, transforms us from a group of disjointed entrepreneurs into a formidable team. Because our separate experiences become a greater whole, a collective memory upon which we can all draw when we go out into the field. Your colleagues have taken time out of their busy schedules to be here for you, and the least you could do, as a member of this team, is to return the favor. I think," Bill finishes, finally looking up from his pad, which creates the illusion that he's been reading this little speech, "that you owe us all an apology."

"Hence my opening statement 'Sorry I'm late,' " I say.

Bill frowns. "Very well, Zack. I'm not going to press the point, because I know you're under some pressure right now. Why don't you bring us up to speed on the Nike situation."

I tell the group about the wrong-colored swooshes, and Hodges's unwillingness to take the fall for his screwup, leaving out the fact that I've been avoiding Hodges's calls, since the middleman never lets a call go unreturned. There follows a brief question-and-answer session between Bill and me that feels like a skit at one of the Spandler Management Seminars the head office sends us to at Holiday Inns around the country, Crisis Management 101 over complimentary doughnuts and coffee.

"Who's the vendor?"

"Qingdao Target."

"What's our leverage? Anyone else here have major projects going at Qingdao?"

No one in the room does. I know all this already.

"What's our exposure if we make Hodges the hero?"

"All told, somewhere in the area of fifty grand," I say, "not including the expedited shipping costs."

"Has he projected any orders after this one?"

I sigh. "It's a test program."

"Damn." Bill is thoughtful for a moment. "Is Hodges a good guy to have in our corner?" No conversation with Bill is ever safe from the stray sports analogy.

"Hodges is an asshole."

Bill inhales sharply. "Come on, Zack," he chastises me in a hollow voice that suggests it isn't outside the realm of possibility that our offices might be bugged by the client, little ladybug-size transmitters with microscopic swooshes on their undersides.

"I'm sorry," I say exasperatedly. "But don't you ever get tired of bending over for the Craig Hodgeses of this world? You have this whole network of systems you've created—you've practically buried us in systems—all designed to avoid this very scenario, to make sure it never happens. So what the hell is the point of it all if we have to take the hit when it's someone else's fault?"

"I take issue with that, Zack," Bill says hotly. "I don't bend over for anybody. I'm just looking for the most fiscally responsible solution for us. That's my job. Our job. We are professionals. You don't piss away a major account because you happen to be of the opinion that your client contact is an asshole. In the grand scheme of things, fifty grand might be a drop in the bucket, a small price to pay for holding on to Nike. All I'm saying is, we don't want to be penny-wise and pound-foolish here."

"No, we certainly don't want that," I say with maybe just a soupçon more irony than I probably should.

"Zack," Bill says, slowly removing his glasses and assuming a deliberately false avuncular tone. "Do you have a problem?"

Every instinct tells me to back down. I should let him take me through this exercise, this middle-management masturbation, answer his questions, and quietly take his direction. I'm disrespecting him in front of his entire department, which he doesn't deserve and which will further compel him to assert his authority with force. A bad career move, any way you look at it. But today they're going to stick a tube through my dick and into my bladder, and while I've never had that done before, I'm fairly certain I'd prefer to have my eyeballs cattle branded, and that spot on my bladder wall may very well have some genuine life-changing implications, so sue me if I'm having a hard time thinking consequentially about much else. And he did ask, after all. "Yes, I do, Bill," I say, getting to my feet. "I have a big fucking problem. I am sick and tired of kissing the asses of poorly educated, lazy pencil pushers, of ignoring the principle and paying for the indolence and incompetence of others, all in the name of making the goddamn sale. When did being right become worthless, and being at fault irrelevant? We eat shit on a daily basis, and I worry about the long-term effects of so much fiber in my diet. I may be nothing more than a middleman, but goddamn it, I'm a professional middleman, and there should be a certain degree of dignity and fair play that goes along with that!"

My tirade is greeted with a stunned silence, and you can hear every molecule in the room look up to see how deeply I've put my foot into it this time. I certainly didn't mean for it to come out as a call to arms, but goddamn if the rest of the account execs aren't nodding in appreciation. There's even a faint smattering of applause, but Bill quashes that by bringing his fist down like a gavel on the table and getting slowly to his feet, and I can actually see him anxiously scanning his mental database of clichés to find one appropriate to this discussion. "Listen, Zack," he says, apparently giving up. "I don't know what's going on with you, and there might be a forum to debate our policies and strategies when it comes to issues like this, but this is not it. You need to calm yourself down and focus on the issue at hand. This is no time to take your eye off the ball." Sports analogy number two, if you're counting, which I am. "It's just business. You can't take it personally."

"Apparently, I can."

"Well, regardless of what you think of Hodges, he's still your client, the Spandler Corporation's client. Remember the rule of the three Cs. Crisis plus Communication equals Control. So be a professional and return the man's calls," Bill says sternly. "Work it out."

I sigh deeply, already regretting the whole conversation. They'll be talking about this all day now, exaggerating it to everyone else in the office, wondering if I'm poised to go postal like Clay. My standing in the burnout pool has no doubt just risen considerably. Come to think of it, I might want to take some of that action myself. "I'll call him," I say.

"And you touch base with me after you speak to him, okay?" Sports analogy number three, and we have a hat trick.

"Will do."

He starts to say something about there being no problems, only opportunities, but I walk out of the room before he can finish. I can hear him shouting angrily after me as I run down the hall, and I know I should have stayed, but I'm thinking that life is just too damn short to listen to any more of this crap.

fourteen

Dr. Sanderson holds up something that looks like a miniature plumber's snake and describes the horrific procedure he's about to perform. "It's called a cystoscopy," he says. "Basically, we enter the bladder through the urethra, and the camera here gives us a full view of what's going on in there."

I'm having trouble paying attention, because at the moment a young, dark-haired Hispanic woman is cradling my penis in her latex-gloved hands. She begins slathering something onto it, pulling slightly on me as she does so, and I am terrified at the possibility of an erection. If it can happen on the subway, or sitting innocently at my desk, why not here? I'm reclining on an examination table, legs splayed, completely naked but for the flimsy gown the physician's assistant handed me right before she began handling me. She is deft and professional, and I wonder what impact, if any, spending her days handling limp, cowering penises might have on her sex life. *Get that thing away from me, honey. I've had quite enough today, thank you very much!*

"That's a topical anesthetic," Dr. Sanderson continues. "Once it takes effect, Camille will administer a local and we'll do the procedure." He looks at me. "Are you feeling okay?"

"I usually get kissed first," I joke lamely.

Camille's smirk says tell me one I haven't heard.

Only once I've been laid fully back with my knees spread does it sink in that the cystoscope will be inserted into my tiniest of holes. A low terror starts to build in me, and I begin to tremble involuntarily. "Don't worry," Camille tells me unconcernedly. "You'll barely feel it," which is easy for her to say, since it's not her genitals into which she's poised to plunge a nasty-looking metallic syringe the length of a small baseball bat.

Dr. Sanderson finally steps in, and I lay my head back and squeeze my eyes shut. "I'll need you to relax," he says. If so, he's in for a disappointment. "Try to release your muscles, like you do when you urinate," he tells me. I take some deep breaths and suddenly feel a hot pinch. "Good," says the doctor. "We're in." My eyes remain resolutely shut. I am firmly committed to not seeing what's happening below. It's bad enough just hearing the sounds of his manipulations as he adjusts the cystoscope and flips on the TV monitor.

"I feel like I have to urinate," I say after a few minutes.

"I'm filling your bladder with water," he informs me. "I need to expand your bladder wall so that I can see everything."

"I'm not sure I'm going to be able to hold it," I say.

"Try," he advises me. "It'll only be for a little while."

After a few minutes, Dr. Sanderson nudges my leg and tells me to open my eyes. At some point while my eyes were closed, Camille took her leave, and it is now just the doctor and me. I become conscious of a puddle forming on the protective paper beneath me on the table. "Don't worry about that," the doctor says. "It's just excess water."

I have a glimpse into the continuous indignities of long-term medical care, the exposure, the clinical manipulation of your most intimate parts, the private by-products and secretions that will pour out, uninvited, for all to see. And all the while, the doctor looming above, unhurriedly doing his work, waiting until the last possible instant to share any findings with you.

"So," I say. "What do you see?"

Dr. Sanderson frowns. "Hard to say," he says. "There's definitely a small mass there, just off the bladder wall. I'd be surprised if it's cancerous, but still . . . We'll do a biopsy, just to rule it out."

And even though I'd been steeling myself for continued bad news, I realize at this moment that for the most part I hadn't really bought into the possibility. But now he's used the words "mass" and "biopsy," and I can feel an icy chill expanding upward from my hyper-clenched bowels. On the bright side, at least it's too late for me to wet myself.

I clear my throat. "When you say you want to rule it out, do you mean that in a 'we're living in litigious times and you need to cover your ass' kind of way, or is it more like a 'that mass looks like it may very well be a malignant tumor, and procedurally, a biopsy is the next step in diagnosis and treatment' kind of way?"

The doctor turns away from the screen to look at me. "Listen, Zack, I understand your concern. The odds are highly against someone your age, with your medical history, having bladder cancer. But what I see in your bladder is something that shouldn't normally be there. That concerns me, and we need to figure out what it is. I'm sorry I can't give you a more concrete answer right now. As hard as it is, you're going to have to just believe in the odds and wait to see what we find out."

"I understand all that," I say. "But off the record, what's your gut?"

"My gut?"

"You see this stuff all day. You must have a gut reaction."

Sanderson exhales slowly. "My gut is, I shouldn't be seeing something like that in someone your age and I'll feel better when I know what it is."

"Thanks," I say. "That wasn't remotely helpful."

"Even if it does turn out to be a cancerous or precancerous growth, you should be advised that in most cases it's highly treatable."

"Great." For a guy who's been doing this as long as he has, he is staggeringly clueless. I don't want to hear "treatable," because "treatable" means it's something, and even if it can be cured, or removed, or whatever the term is for cancer, it won't change the fact that it was there to begin with, that my body betrayed me by allowing this to happen, that I'll never feel safe in my own skin again. Where's the silver lining in that? I'm like Craig Hodges and his stupid purple swooshes, donning my blinders when it comes to reason and rationale, only interested in hearing that the problem isn't really a problem.

He performs the biopsy right through the scope, cuts a microscopic piece of tissue right out of me. I feel another hot pinch, this time in the depths of my belly, and the slightest convulsion, and then it's done. Now that the scope has been in me for a while, I'm dreading its removal, imagining the slow, sickening drag as he pulls it out, but the anesthetic is still working and I barely feel a thing. Afterward, I piss for what feels like five minutes, the stream vibrating oddly through my numb instrument. There's a lot more blood now, but I've been warned by the doctor to expect that for a day or two after the biopsy. I dry off with a towel and get dressed again. I examine my genitals carefully, but everything seems to be just as I left it. The doctor warns me that in addition to the blood, I might experience a mild burning sensation when I urinate over the next few days. If the pain or bleeding continues after that, I should give him a call. He'll have the results of the biopsy by Friday, and I should try not to worry about it. "Statistically speaking," he tells me again, "the odds of someone your age having bladder cancer are very slim."

Maybe so, I think as I ride down in the elevator. *But do those odds still apply once you've already established that there's a biopsy-worthy mass lurking in there?* Somehow, at this point I think we're dealing with a whole other set of stats, and while I'm not interested in hearing them, I'm fairly certain that they would be somewhat less encouraging.

The instant I turn my cell phone on, it starts to beep and flash the message icon. I have three urgent messages from clients who need to hear back from me first thing in the morning. When you're a middleman, everything is always an emergency. The last message is from Hope, wondering where I am. Since it's just about six, I decide to surprise her at her office. I cut over to Fifth Avenue and then downtown through the Fifties, to Rockefeller Center. The sidewalks are swarming with the after-work crowd, grimly staring ahead, talking on cell phones, or taking in the questionable merchandise in the hodgepodge windows of immigrant electronics shops.

I wait in the lobby at Rockefeller Plaza, leaning against the wall as I watch the exodus pour out of the elevators, the men in their upscale, corporate-casual outfits, the women looking as if they're all headed to an audition for *Sex and the City,* dressed to titillate in aggressively short skirts, expensive haircuts, and designer shoes that clack authoritatively against the marble floor.

After about fifteen minutes, Hope emerges with two women I don't know, the three of them immersed in laughing conversation. She looks magnificent as always, in dark dress slacks and a light, formfitting cardigan. I watch her for a few seconds, reveling in the grace of her walk, the swing of her hair, and the furtive and not-so-furtive glances she elicits from the men she passes. Observing her in this manner, I feel a rush of pride and inevitable skepticism. I still can't get over the fact that someone this beautiful would have any use for me. It occurs to me that Hope might have made plans, and will not appreciate my spontaneous arrival, but when she sees me, her face brightens gratifyingly, and she charges across the lobby to give me a kiss.

"What are you doing here?" she says happily.

"I had an appointment in the area," I say.

"Fantastic!" She kisses me again in a rare public display of affection.

"You're in a good mood," I say.

"And why shouldn't I be?"

I could give her a reason or two. At this point, she remembers her two friends, who are now hovering behind her with anticipatory so-this-is-him grins. "Oh, sorry," Hope says, stepping out of my embrace. "Zack, this is Dana and Jill."

Nice to meet you, heard so much about you, congratulations on the engagement, isn't it so exciting? Under Hope's watchful eye, I smile and charm to the best of my abilities, wishing that I were taller and better dressed, more for her sake than mine. After all, I've already gotten the girl.

As we walk uptown, I find out what has her so excited.

"I've been asked to help catalog a private collection for the nineteenth-century group," she tells me. "It's the first time they're sending me alone."

"That's great," I say. "Where's the collection?"

"In London."

"London, England?"

"The very same."

"When do you leave?"

"Tonight," Hope tells me animatedly. "I'm heading home right now to pack and get a cab to the airport. Isn't it insane?"

"Yeah," I say. "How long will you be gone?"

"I'll be back Friday evening. That will give me all day Saturday to rest up for the party."

Hope stops walking and looks at me. "What's with you?"

The anesthetic has now completely worn off, and it feels like someone jammed a knitting needle into my crotch. "I had a procedure done today," I tell her.

"What kind of procedure?" she asks, concerned. I tell her about the blood in my urine and the cystoscopy, but leave out the part about the biopsy. "Turns out it was nothing," I say offhandedly.

"Well, you needed to be sure."

"Yep."

Hope takes my hand and smiles. "Well, I was going to suggest a bon voyage quickie at my place, but it sounds like you're not up for it."

I nod, shuddering at the thought of intercourse in my current state. I suspect it would be something akin to putting my penis through a meat grinder. I think about my near infidelity at the WENUS gig, and thoughts of poetic justice and divine retribution run briefly through my head. "I'm not," I say. "Thanks for the thought, though."

"Why don't I get us a cab," she says. "You drop me off, then go home and rest."

"Okay."

In Manhattan's Darwinian traffic sprawl, only someone who looks like Hope can get a cab so quickly on Fifty-third and Park. I collapse into her on the seat, and she puts her arm around me, rubbing my back sympathetically, while her perfume puts up a valiant but futile struggle against the redolent stink of the driver's body odor.

As we ride uptown, I tell Hope about my father's return. "Why didn't you tell me sooner?" she demands.

"I don't know," I say. "It just didn't seem real."

"What's he like?"

"I don't know. Still a mess, I guess."

She nods. "Well, did you invite him to the party?"

"No."

"Are you going to?"

"He doesn't belong there."

"He *is* your father," she says. "Don't you think I should meet him?"

"Trust me, you don't want him there," I say.

Hope gives me a look, and seems poised to say something, but then doesn't, choosing instead to give me a soft kiss on my neck. "Well, you have a few days to think about it, I guess."

The cab drops her off in front of her building, on Eighty-ninth and Fifth. " 'Bye," she says, and gives me a long hard-lipped kiss. "You get some rest." She pats my crotch gently. "I expect the both of you to be in top form when I get back."

"We'll do our best."

"I'll call you from the airport."

I tell her I'll miss her, but by then she's gotten out, and the taxi door slams on me in midphrase. As the cab heads west through Central Park, I wonder whether I've done the right thing, not telling her about the biopsy. She was on such a high about the London trip, I didn't want to spoil her mood. She wouldn't have been able to go off to London knowing that I'm sitting here on pins and needles waiting for the results. Still, I feel bad that I didn't tell her. Or maybe I feel bad because I suspect she might have still gone anyway.

fifteen

this is what happens. You're out at a bar on a cold Friday night with your two best friends, feeling inferior and hopeless because one, Jed, is the indisputable stud and the other, Rael, is newly married and just along for nostalgia's sake, to bask in the utter irrelevance of it all. So one has nothing at stake and the other has nothing to prove and there you are in the middle, with plenty at stake and everything to prove, and no real prospects of success. It's been eight months since your last relationship, six months since you've had any kind of sex, and that was of the desperate, rebounding nature, and you're starting to feel invisible in the Big City, wishing you could go back home to your small town, where it was so much easier and the girls were so much more approachable, so much less jaded. Except that you don't come from a small town; you come from here, or, at best, a soulless suburb of here, and there's nowhere to go back to, so you're just going to have to soldier on, get over your fear of rejection, and find someone who will somehow recognize that thing in you, that thing you can't even recognize in yourself but you know is there, that will make you seem like a worthwhile investment, the thing that will somehow inspire a woman to take you home and exchange fluids and then stories and then secrets, in the hopes of finding a love that will fill you both up to the point where you can stop looking for it.

Who could blame you for being a little drunk?

Your crew is well positioned on three stools by a high table at the window, where you can watch the people come and go, and you're joking around rowdily with Jed and Rael, hoping you look like three guys who could care less if there are even any women in the room, feeling self-conscious even though you know there's no reason to, since no one's really checking you out.

And then you see her, standing with her girlfriend against the wall, holding her Coors bottle just a little too perfectly, not organically, not like someone who has a genuine relationship with longneck bottles. And she has this sweeping mane of sandy-colored hair and a square jaw that frames her features perfectly, features almost childlike in their delicacy, that bespeak a childhood of privilege and insulation. Her eyes are the blue of faded denim, her nose small and wide, like a kitten's, and her cheeks soft and ever so slightly plump, the cheeks of a nymphet. And you know, instinctively, that she hates those cheeks, that she habitually looks into mirrors when she's alone and sucks them in, and you want to tell her she shouldn't, because, set as they are atop her lean, gym-toned body, and under those mesmerizing blue eyes, they're two pockets of soft, flawless flesh that hold the infinite promise of untold pleasures, like the perfect ass above her lean, muscled legs, or the lovely, upturned breasts above the flat expanse of her abdomen. You know what it will feel like to brush those magnificent cheeks with your own, what those cheeks will look like from above with her eyes closed, lips parted, as you lie on top of her, lowering your head to kiss her open mouth.

And you're so caught up that you forget to man the controls of your disinterest, and she catches you staring at her, so there's nothing left to do but get off your stool and, drink in hand, walk over to where she's standing, and as you do, you feel an alien resolve clicking into place with the muted thunk of a luxury-car door, and since you're already committed, you decide there's nothing to lose.

"I'm Zack," you say, raising your voice to be heard above the din of the jukebox, the loud conversations going on around you, and the frenzied fluttering of the butterflies in your stomach.

"Hope," she says, extending her hand, and for the briefest instant you don't realize it's her name, but imagine that she's wisely identified the defining motivation that brought everyone in the place out tonight.

"There's no easy way to break this to you," you say, "so I'm just going to come right out with it. I'm here to hit on you."

Hope laughs, and it's a rich, musical laugh, unguarded and comfortable, like you're old friends. Not at all what you expected. "Well," she says. "I appreciate your candor."

"May I begin?"

"Go for it."

And what follows is two hours of perfect conversation, the kind you couldn't have scripted if you wanted to, the kind where it becomes instantly apparent that your sensibilities and wits jibe, and when the conversation turns to banter, it's easy and fun and never veers away from the substance of the discussion.

And she quickly becomes familiar, touching your wrist when she laughs, leaning in to you easily when the crowd jostles her. And after a while, you realize your friends have left, and her girlfriend is long gone, and it's with mixed feelings that you realize that they're ringing last call at the bar, because on the one hand, when was the last time you made it to last call, but on the other, what the hell do you do now? You've long ago determined that tonight will not be about sex (as if it were up to you anyway), not because you don't want it, God knows you do, but because you don't want to ruin this one with a crude one-night stand. But you don't want the night to end, either, even though it already has. So you offer to walk her home and she acquiesces, and that works out well because it's bitterly cold outside and she doesn't so much hold your arm as wrap herself around it, and the wind blows her hair into your face, drawing tears as it whips at your eyes, and there's intimacy in this, so much more so than with casual sex. Her building is one of those posh monoliths on Fifth Avenue, and you start to say good night, your voice hoarse from hours of shouting above the jukebox, but she pulls you past the doormen—*"Hi, Nick. Hi, Santos"*—and into the elevator. And before you can work up the nerve for a good-night kiss, she does it first, kissing you deeply, hungrily, backing you up against the elevator wall, the full length of her body pressed against you, making you wish to God you weren't both wearing thick coats. And this goes on for fifteen flights, and then a little bit more, since she doesn't stop when the door slides open on her floor. And then she steps back, breathless and windswept, deliciously disheveled, and says, "That was lovely." She pulls out a silver Cross pen from her bag and writes her name and number down on your hand, and under that she writes *To Be Continued,* and then she turns serious and says, "Listen, Zack. I'm not into games and I don't like players.

If you like me, call me, okay? There's no appropriate waiting period. If I don't hear from you tomorrow, I'll assume you're not interested."

"I passed interested about three hours ago," you say.

She smiles and kisses your nose. "Then I'll speak to you tomorrow." And then she ducks out and the door slides shut, and you fall to your knees, savoring the sweet pain of the unfulfilled erection shrinking in your pants, and offer a short prayer of thanksgiving as the elevator car slowly brings you back down to earth.

We began dating after that, intensely and exclusively, and I kept waiting for the bubble to burst, for Hope to look across the table at me and realize that somewhere, an error had been made, that she'd mistaken me for somebody else. But her smile always seemed utterly sincere, and she laughed at my jokes and returned my kisses with unchecked ardor, and when we walked, she always reached for my hand while I was still considering the implications of reaching for hers. That was pretty much how it went, Hope leading the way while I refrained from making any moves, terrified of calling any undue attention to myself that might cause her to reconsider my general worthiness. But it never happened, and three weeks into it, as we climbed into a cab after a late Friday-night movie, she interrupted me as I started to give the driver her address, and gave mine instead, smiling out the window as I trembled silently beside her. When we got home, I unwrapped her like a gift and we fell into bed, and at some point during that thrilling, sleepless weekend, I forgot to worry about it and just accepted that she was mine, that it could really be this easy, and the way she devoured me left no doubts that I was hers as well.

"Come and meet my parents," she said to me a few months later.

Her parents lived a few blocks over from her apartment on the Upper East Side. When I arrived, the uniformed doorman informed me that I was expected. "What floor?" I said.

"Fifteen."

"Fifteen what?"

He just smiled and pointed toward the elevator. "Just fifteen."

The elevator opened into a private vestibule with only one door, at which Hope was waiting, looking radiant in a white cashmere sweater and black stretch pants and boots. She led me into a gargantuan anteroom with a marble floor and a large diamond-shaped skylight cut into the high ceiling. There were doors at various intervals, leading deeper into the apartment, and at the far end of the room was a grand staircase that went up to the second floor. I'd heard about apartments like this, had seen them in movies, but I never really believed real people actually lived in them. "Nice place," I said.

"Don't let it freak you out," she said apologetically.

I shook my head. "It's beautiful."

Hope's father, Jack Seacord, had inherited his father's medical supply company and grown it into a publicly traded, multinational conglomerate, of which he was still majority owner and CEO. He was a large, athletic man in his late fifties whose small, commanding features were jammed between the jutting slabs of his prominent forehead and chin. His smile was plastic, like a politician's, and he had a quick, efficient manner about him, shaking my hand and sizing me up in the same instant. His lone displays of affection were reserved for Hope and seemed just a tad abnormal to me, his kisses landing squarely on her mouth, his hand resting casually on her backside, fingers stroking absently as he held her next to him.

Hope's mother, Vivian, was a stunning woman, a long-limbed brunette with a gleaming, Botox-smooth porcelain complexion, a pixie haircut, and a languid, feline expression, a cat in sultry repose. In her prime, she'd actually been a rated tennis player. Now she sat on the boards of various museums and philanthropic foundations, and had this whole down-to-earth vibe that usually seemed so contrived in obscenely wealthy women, but seemed completely genuine in her case.

He was unimpressed. She thought I was hilarious, and told me so repeatedly, her loud laughs reverberating off the ceilings. Neither thought I was good enough for Hope, but naturally they were too polite to say so. It was evident in the way Jack nodded seriously as I explained what I did for the Spandler Corporation, his seeming lack of condescension simply a highly stylized version of it. "I know the company," he said. "Great little outfit." Vivian found me to be refreshingly grounded, which was fine for passing the time, but in no way made me a suitable mate for Hope. Hope's only sibling, an older sister named Claire, was a militant lesbian living in LA, which Vivian mentioned with contrived pride at every possible opportunity, the word "lesbian" rolling off her lips with a practiced flourish. Claire's outing had left Hope as the sole remaining member of the Seacord progeny to bear the burden of her parents' dreams of succession, and that was a pretty tall order for a middleman to fill. So the dinner was a friendly affair, warm even, but there was a general undercurrent of shoulders being shrugged in the manner of the underwhelmed.

After dinner, Hope and I cuddled on a couch in one of the

many densely decorated dens scattered throughout the labyrinthine halls of the massive apartment. "So," she said, curling up into me. "What do you think?"

"They seemed great."

"Oh, come on," she said, hitting my chest lightly. "They were awful. But they mean well."

"I didn't say that."

"It's okay, Zack. I'm not blind."

"No. I meant the part about them meaning well. I didn't get that at all."

She giggled and kissed me.

"Your father seemed disappointed."

"He's just very protective."

That's because he's maybe a little too into you. "Yeah," I said. "I got that."

"Lucky for you, they don't get a vote."

"Really?"

"Really."

"They won't cut you off, or something?"

Hope laughed. "It doesn't work that way. Besides, as the straight daughter, the world is pretty much my oyster. I've got some leeway."

"So I guess I've got that going for me."

"You've got me going for you."

She kissed me and I kissed her and soon we were making out on the couch like a couple of teenagers. "Let's go to my room," she whispered.

"Are you serious? Your parents are sitting in the living room."

"I know," she said, tongue in my ear, hand in my pants. "Hurry."

sixteen

I stagger into the brownstone at around seven, to find Jed sprawled in his usual position on the couch, shoveling Cap'n Crunch into his mouth and watching *Entertainment Tonight*. Living with Jed is like having a puppy. No matter what time of day or night you come home, he'll be there to greet you. "Hey, man," he says with his mouth full, taking in my haggard appearance. "What happened to you?"

"I had a tube shoved up my dick," I say, plopping down next to him.

"A cystoscopy," he says knowledgeably.

"You've had one?"

"Hell no. But I watched one on the Learning Channel." Jed has become quite well-rounded since he took up television full-time. "Why'd you have it?"

"Blood in my urine."

"Hematuria," he says, nodding.

"Very impressive," I say.

"If it's out there"—he indicates the television and then points to his head—"it's in here."

"Well, do you think you can pry yourself away long enough to get me some Tylenol?"

"No need," Jed says, reaching into a crack of the sofa and feeling around. His hand emerges a moment later, clutching a bottle of Aleve. "Sometimes I get headaches from watching," he says in response to my incredulous look.

I down three pills with one of the many half-finished Coke cans that litter the coffee table.

"So, what's the verdict?" Jed says.

"They found a spot," I say.

Jed actually looks away from the television for a minute. "Oh, shit," he says worriedly.

"It's probably nothing."

He nods. "Probably. They do a biopsy?"

"Yeah."

"So when do you find out for sure?"

"Friday."

"What's today?"

"Tuesday."

"That sucks, man."

"Yeah."

We sit together in glum silence, watching Mary Hart feverishly discuss the latest celebrity pregnancy. I'm thinking that Mary ought to cut down a bit on the caffeine before taping. She's looking more and more like a *Saturday Night Live* sketch of herself.

"Oh, hey," Jed says after a few minutes. "Your dad's here."

"What?"

"He's in your room."

I look at Jed. "What's he doing there?"

Jed shrugs. "He was tired. Said he wanted to lie down."

"So you just let him go up into my room?"

"What's he going to do, rob you?"

I pull myself off the couch. "I can't believe you let him upstairs."

"That's right, Zack," Jed says, getting annoyed. "I had the gall to let an older man rest in his son's room."

"Don't get all righteous with me, Jed. You have no idea what he's like. What he did to us."

Jed nods. "You're right. Sorry. I didn't mean to come off like that." He looks up at me. "I can barely remember my dad, Zack. He died when I was seven. But I still miss having one, you know? Those years when my company took off, you know, when I was so successful, I always missed having a father to be proud of me. It made the whole thing feel, I don't know, hollow. And after Rael died, you know . . ."

"I know," I say softly.

"I mean, I'll get it together," he says, looking back at the television. "I'm not going to watch television forever. But I sometimes wish I had a father, you know? Someone to just look to in all of this, to tell me to get off my ass. To set me straight, I guess."

"Mine is not really the kind of father who sets people straight," I say.

"So he's a fuckup," Jed says with a shrug. "What are we? The point is, he's still here and you're still here, and as we both know, that's an equation that can change pretty quickly." This is far and away the closest Jed's ever come to discussing Rael's death.

"Jed," I say.

"Yeah."

"This is the first meaningful conversation we've had in over a year."

"You see, he's already having a positive effect," he says with a smirk, but his eyes dance purposefully away from mine, back to the television, and the moment is lost.

My room is engulfed in the twin odors of aftershave and flatulence, a noxious combination that actually stops me in my tracks for a minute. Norm is sitting at my desk, shoes off, belt undone, his belly bumping up against the desk like a docked dirigible. He's bent over a large, warped journal with frayed edges, scribbling copiously and humming atonally to himself. I watch him for a moment as he sits there unaware of me, trying to discern some hidden truth in his posture, trying to connect this bloated man with the version that was frozen in my head when I was twelve years old, trying to justify the intense longing and sadness I've always felt with respect to him. It's not happening, so I clear my throat. "Zack!" he says, closing the journal and spinning around on his chair. "Hello, son."

"Jesus," I say, stepping into the room and opening the window. "How can you stand to be around yourself?"

He smiles good-naturedly. "An unfortunate side effect of my Frappuccino habit."

"What are you doing here, Norm?"

"Oh," he says. "I hope you don't mind. I just figured I'd get some work done while I waited for you."

"For all you knew, I wasn't even coming home tonight."

My father flashes a simultaneously sad and defiant smile. "After all these years, do you think a few more hours are really going to make a difference to me?"

I don't want to sit down, because that will somehow ratify

his presence here, but a sitting position seems to be the only thing that soothes the fire burning in my crotch, so I sit down on the bed. “So, what’s up?” I say.

Norm stands, pulling up his pants, and starts tucking in his checkered button-down shirt. “I’m hungry,” he says. “Let’s go get some dinner. My treat.”

“No, thanks,” I say. “I just want to go to bed.”

“Come on, Zack, it’s just dinner. It’s no big deal.”

“Yes,” I say hotly, and you don’t think of your voice as coming from your groin, but when I raise it, I feel a sharp bolt of pain there. “It is a big deal. It’s a huge fucking deal. Because we don’t do that. Ever. We aren’t that father and son. We never have been. And you can’t just materialize, showing up at Matt’s gig, sitting in my room, at my desk, like it’s our fucking routine or something, as if you’ve been around for the last fifteen years, as if you gave a damn about us before today—” And then I have to stop, because goddamn if my voice isn’t breaking and I can feel the tears threatening, and I cannot, under any circumstances, give him that, because he’ll be fucking dancing in the streets over his breakthrough, will be celebrating the connection he thinks he’s made, will be so impressed with himself, thinking that he was right to come back and knew just what to do to reach out to me. I’ve had a shitty day, I’m on edge for a thousand different reasons, and the last thing I want to do is inadvertently validate this absurd notion he’s always subscribed to that a few grand gestures will accomplish what should take years of building or rebuilding.

“You’re right,” Norm says, standing awkwardly in front of the bed, nervously patting down the anorexic strands of his hair. “It is a big deal, and I in no way meant to minimize your feelings. I apologize.”

"Forget about it," I say, feeling nonplussed by my reaction and annoyed with his recovery speak.

"Zack," Norm says. "I've always prided myself on my ability to read people, and I'm going to tell you what I'm reading in you."

"Please don't."

"Obviously, there's a lot of hostility toward me."

"Wow. They should give you a talk show."

"I said it was obvious," he says. "But there's more. I've been disliked before—"

"Say it isn't so."

"—So I have a pretty good idea of what it feels like. But I am suggesting that what I'm getting from you is very scattered and unfocused. It's as if you're too distracted to hate me properly. I mean, look at Matt," he says admiringly. "Now, that boy can hate."

"You're criticizing the manner in which I dislike you?"

"No, I'm analyzing it. And what I come up with is that while you certainly do have your issues with me, as well you should, they're not foremost on your mind. You were drunk at Matt's show last night, not fun drunk, but desperately drunk, if you take my meaning. You looked to me like a man with way too much on his mind." He smiles at me. "You were always a worrier, even as a kid. Whenever there was a thunderstorm, you would always ask me for a flashlight. You were five years old and you were worried about blackouts. Do you remember that?"

"No," I lie.

"Well, anyway. It just seems to me that on the list of things that are troubling you, I'm nowhere near the top right now. I don't know if it's work, or your engagement, or what, but I just know this: it's not me."

"Don't sell yourself short," I say. "You're still way up there."

Norm lets out a bone-weary sigh and picks up his notebook, carefully organizing some of the tattered pages sticking out at various angles. "What is that, anyway?" I ask him.

"I'm writing my memoirs," he says without the faintest whiff of self-consciousness, and something about it just makes me laugh out loud. "What?" he says defensively.

"Your memoirs," I say, unable to hold back a laugh.

"That's right," he says defensively. "And I'll have you know that I've already shown them to a friend or two in the publishing game, and they're very interested."

"No doubt." I'm still smiling, and I can see it's aggravating him.

"Look," he says, annoyed. "Are we going to eat, or what?"

And maybe it's the insanity of the last twelve hours, maybe it's my current worries about my own mortality, maybe it's because I'm scared and I want a father, any father, or maybe it's just because this is the first time I can recall laughing in recent memory, but suddenly, I have no resistance left in me. "Fine," I say. "Let's go eat."

"Hallelujah," Norm says.

seventeen

We eat at Arnie's Deli, a small restaurant on Broadway with a deliberate coffee shop feel. "How are you guys doing?" the waitress says, handing us our menus. She's tall and slim, her hair, an unnatural platinum color, fed in a ponytail through the hole in the back of her baseball cap, and Norm is all over her in an instant, shamelessly looking her up and down with an appreciative grin.

"I'm just fine, Penny," he says, reading her name tag. "Thanks for asking. And how are you?"

"I'm good," she says with considerably less enthusiasm.

"You look beautiful this evening," Norm says.

"Well, thank you. And what can I get you tonight?"

"What's good?"

"I don't know. What are you in the mood for?"

"Well, I usually get to know a woman better before I answer that, but since you asked . . ." He laughs loudly at his little joke, nudging my arm to get me in on it, smiling at the other diners, the inadvertent beneficiaries of his sharp wit.

"Norm," I say quietly.

"Sorry," he says, not taking his eyes off her. "My son doesn't like to see his old man flirt."

"And you do it so well," Penny says. Oblivious to her sarcasm, Norm breaks into raucous laughter, as if she's bantering with him.

"Well, no one ever died from being told they were beautiful, did they?"

"I'm dying," I say, and Norm goes off again.

I catch Penny's eye and I want to explain everything to her, how I haven't seen him in years, how he coerced me into this, how sorry I am for the inconvenience. "We'll need a few minutes," I say ruefully.

"I'll be right back, then," she says with a grin, heading back to the counter, and I realize that I've overestimated her reaction to Norm.

"I'll watch you go," my father says, leaning out of his chair.

"You behave now, Norm," she says, casting a playful glance back at him.

"This is behaving," he calls after her, smiling around the diner at his unwitting audience, somehow seeing approval in their indifference. Then he casts one more longing look at Penny's ass before sitting back in his chair. "Now, that will keep you warm at night," he says appreciatively.

"Jesus, Norm," I say.

"What?"

"It's a shitty enough job without having to be hit on by dirty old men."

"She didn't seem to mind," Norm says.

"She was being polite, because this is her place of work, and if she tells you to fuck off, she could lose a tip or her job."

"And I think it's a long night, and a tough job, and maybe a little flirting breaks up the monotony and makes her feel good about herself. Besides, I think she liked me."

"What, you and her?" I say, inexplicably frustrated by his delusions. "Are you honestly telling me that you think you have a shot at getting a date with her?"

"Why not?" Norm says, perturbed. "What's wrong with me?"

"You think a twenty-year-old girl like her lies in bed at night dreaming of the fat, bald sixty-year-old man who's going to come into the restaurant and sweep her off her feet?"

The hurt in his eyes is instantaneous, the collapse of his smile, the sagging of his jowls, and I immediately regret the remark. "Listen, Norm, I didn't mean it like that. It's just, I live here, you know? I eat here all the time, and I was a little embarrassed."

"I'm sorry I embarrassed you," he says. "I'm an outgoing person. That's just the way I am. When I see a beautiful woman, I let her know she's beautiful. Once in a while, I'm lucky, and it leads somewhere. If not, I've at least paid her a compliment, brightened her day just a little bit. Either way, I'm not going to apologize for it."

"No one's asking you to," I say quickly, noting the waitress's approach and trying to end the conversation.

"You made up your minds yet?" she says.

"Is the minestrone soup any good?" Norm asks her.

"Sure is."

"I'll have that and the grilled cheese."

I order a salad and grilled cheese. "We always had the same taste in foods," Norm tells Penny with pride.

"So," I say brightly once she's gone. "What would you like to talk about?" I'm still feeling bad about shooting him down before, haunted by the acute sadness instantly readable behind his fallen smile. I realize that regardless of whether he truly believes in the appreciation of indifferent bystanders and the possibility of young waitresses, or it's just an attitude he's embraced as a survival mechanism, the behavior is symptomatic of a deeply ingrained loneliness that informs his every impulse.

"Just about you in general," he says, sitting back in his chair. "How are things at the Spandler Corporation?"

"How do you know where I work?"

"I looked through your desk while I was waiting in your room."

"Jesus," I say angrily. "You're a piece of work, you know that?"

"It looks like an impressive place. What do you do there?"

"I don't want to talk about work."

"So tell me about Hope."

"I don't want to talk about her either."

"Do you still think about writing screenplays?"

"Nah. That was never a serious thing."

Norm nods sadly. "Zack," he says. "A man's two great loves should be his woman and his work. You seem unwilling to talk about either one. Now, if I were a long-lost son whose no-good father showed up, I'd want him to see how well I'd made it without him. I'd take great pleasure in letting him know that I'd made a success out of my life, that I was doing well at work and I was in love with a great woman. It would be the most natural impulse in the world. And yet I can't get you to discuss either one with me. Why do you think that is?"

"You haven't given a shit about me for all these years," I say, my voice coming out louder than I'd intended, and I'm vaguely aware of the other diners pausing in their conversations and looking our way. "Don't you think it's a bit presumptuous to show up and think I'll share any details of my life with you? You're not a part of it, Norm. It's none of your fucking business, that's all. A man's two great loves should be his woman and his work? That's great, Norm, really brilliant. You cheated on your woman more times than I probably know, and unless things have changed dramatically in the last few years, you haven't ever held down a job for more than a year or two in your entire life. Maybe somewhere in there, one of your great loves should have been your children, don't you think? It would have been much harder to lose us, but I guess you managed to pull that one off too."

Norm stares straight at me, willfully absorbing my tirade, his face reddening from the effort of it. Then he nods, frowning slightly. "Everything you say is true," he says. "I'm not going to deny any of it. It's no great secret that I've made a colossal mess of my life. But just because all of that's true, it doesn't change my instincts that you are under a tremendous strain, and that all is not right with you. I'm worried about you, Zack."

"That's just self-serving bullshit," I practically scream at him. "You're worried because you want to be worried, because you want to feel like the father you never were."

"Nevertheless, I am."

"Well, there's no need. Believe me, I'm fine. Just fine, thank you very much."

Norm takes a sip from his water glass and flashes a small, wry grin. "You sound fine," he says.

Before I can respond, the waitress arrives, gingerly setting down Norm's soup and my salad with the posture of someone inching her head out of a hiding spot, ready to retreat in an instant. "Okay," she says nervously. "Let's all try to calm down a little. Family's family, right?"

"Penny," Norm says to her. "I want to apologize to you if any of the remarks I made earlier offended you. That was certainly not my intention."

"Don't be silly, Norm," she says, rubbing his shoulder. "You're a sweetheart."

We eat in an uncomfortable silence, the only sounds coming from Norm as he aggressively slurps his soup. After a while he looks up at me between mouthfuls. "How's Pete doing?"

"He's great."

"I send him a birthday card every year," Norm says.

"Well, that changes everything, then, doesn't it," I say.

Norm puts down his spoon and looks at me. His forehead is dappled with beads of sweat, either from the soup or from the strenuousness of making conversation with his bitter fuck of a firstborn son. "This isn't going very well," he says to me.

"No shit," I say wearily.

He wipes his sweating pate with a napkin, and then wipes his lips with the same one, and I wonder if he can taste his own sweat. "Listen," he says. "I am working under the assumption that there must be something we can talk about in a civilized manner for as long as it takes to eat a grilled cheese sandwich, something that won't get you angry. I've struck out so far, so why don't you give it a shot?"

I look at my father wiping his soup bowl clean in circular strokes with his onion roll before taking a messy bite out of the roll. I hate that he's right, that after all these years, he's just stepped back in and called it so accurately. How can someone so obtuse be so sharp? It's nothing more than a coincidence, my personal dramas coinciding with his delusion that he can still lay claim to the instincts of a true father. I'm loath to make it so easy for him, to concede that his blind shots have nonetheless hit their mark. There are crumbs on his shirt as well as a soup stain or two just above the upper swell of his belly. The limp dust-colored strands of his hair are askew from leaning over his bowl, and when he grabs another roll, I can see that his fingernails are jagged and bitten. Just like mine.

"I might have cancer," I say.

Somehow, in discussing the potential of death, I end up talking about my life, and within forty minutes or so, I've pretty much told him everything, about work, Hope, Tamara. And there they are, my deepest fears and secrets, spoken aloud, laid out before the least likely person to whom I'd ever imagined spilling my conflicted guts. The only part I leave out is my aborted infidelity last night at the WENUS gig. If Norm wants to feel kinship with me over grilled cheese, that's fine, but I will not let him have *that* in common with me. He listens attentively, his brow furrowed, chiming in only to offer some predictably worthless advice about my situation at work. When I'm done, we order some coffee and sip at it quietly for a while. "It's probably nothing," he finally says.

"Probably," I say.

"Listen, Zack," Norm says, putting down his mug with an air of finality. "I know I'm the last person you want to be hearing any advice from."

"Somehow," I say, "I suspect you're not going to let a minor detail like that stop you."

"I gotta be me," he says with a smile. I notice for the first time that he has Matt's smile, and maybe mine, for all I know. "I'm going to admit something to you that I never usually admit, even to myself. Letting my marriage to your mother fall apart was the biggest damn mistake I ever made in my life. I'm sixty years old now and I've got a boatload of mistakes to show for it, but they can all be traced back to that one, ultimate mistake. That's what sent my life down the course it took, and every bad thing that happened to me afterward was a consequence of that one mistake. I know you think you're in a bad place right now, but I would give anything to be standing in your shoes at this moment. Because you're still in the before. There are decisions to be made, but you haven't made them yet. You have an opportunity—one I blew—to do everything in your power to look into yourself, I mean, really look into your heart, and make the right one. You should embrace where you are now, see it for the blessing that it is. I've been in my after for almost twenty years, and I have to tell you, it has not been a picnic. I often think back to the times right before I destroyed my marriage, and I wish someone like me had shown up and pointed out to me that I was in my before. Maybe I would have pushed myself more, to understand myself and figure out what was really in my heart."

He sits back in his chair, somewhat breathless from the speech he's just given.

"Norm," I say.

"Yes."

"I'll keep that in mind. Thanks."

"Don't mention it," he says, beaming.

Before we leave the restaurant, Norm heads to the back to personally hand Penny her tip, clasping her hand in both of his. He whispers something to her, and, unbelievably, she leans forward and gives him a quick peck on his cheek, casting a meaningful look in my direction. In that instant I'm able to see him through her eyes, his handsome smile, his kind expression, and I realize that I've sold him a bit short. "Don't forget," he calls loudly to her as we head for the door. "Fat people try harder!" He pats his gut as his bellowing laugh rattles the windows.

We step wordlessly out onto Broadway, into a gusty autumn night. The days have been getting shorter for a while now, but the early onset of night is still unsettling to me. I just want everything to slow the hell down for a minute. Some kids in a tricked-out Hummer nod in time to the rap song playing through their speakers at full blast, and Norm briefly breaks into a little dance, shuffling his legs and snapping. His face is flushed from walking, and his hair is instantly blown wild by the wind and now sticks out in stiff, haphazard angles behind each ear. He walks the sidewalk like a dervish, openly ogling the women, nodding at strangers, and greeting doormen like he owns the block. When I was a kid, it really felt like he did, and now I wonder if he was the popular character I've remembered, or if he was as much of an oblivious ass then as he is now, and I was just unqualified to recognize it. I'm still reeling from our conversation. Opening up like that had not been on my agenda, and it's left me feeling vaguely disappointed. I always dreamed, or planned really, that he'd come back, broke and contrite, to find me having succeeded in all that he failed in. I'd be wealthy from my various entrepreneurial enterprises, happily married to a beautiful woman, and maybe even a young father in my own right. Despite my anger, I'd be forgiving, would write him a substantial check to help him out and savor the expression on his face when he saw the amount. And now he's finally arrived, as if on cue, and all I've done is show him what a mess I am. I don't know how he got me to talk, but no matter, the dream is dead. And as I watch him in my periphery, huffing proudly along the sidewalk like he's leading a marching band, no doubt thrilled that he's managed to pierce my defenses, I can feel the powerful resentment reasserting itself, filling me like mercury, and if he looks at me right now, if he dares shine the light of that shit-eating grin into the shadows of my cave, I know I'll cheerfully strangle him.

And let me tell you, that perennial erection of his is not helping his case any.

eighteen

morning. Dr. Sanderson warned me that I might experience some discomfort urinating in the days immediately following the procedure. It turns out the good doctor has understated things a bit. A hot, searing pain rips through me, like I'm pissing molten lead, and I let out an agonized cry as I double over in shock, splashing the floor and my legs in the process. What little urine has made it into the bowl is dark with blood. I stagger into the shower and finish there, groaning softly as my bladder empties. The final drops pass through me like shards of glass, and then, miraculously, the pain is gone. If I had to guess, I'd say that today is not going to be one of my better days.

This is what happens. You get to your office and everything looks different. Nothing is, of course, but the place feels suddenly alien, like it's been replaced with a perfect replica of itself. You say hello to your buddies, same as always, make your way through the honeycomb of partitions to the sanctuary of your cubicle, and drop into your worn, ergonomically correct, mesh-backed chair, a knockoff of a popular German design, looking around your office with a stupefied expression. There's your L-shaped workstation, your monitor and keyboard, a metal wire frame that holds your current files in graduated elevations, a Toshiba telephone, and a picture of Hope in the Crate and Barrel frame she supplied because no way was she going to have you pin her to the cubicle wall, to be lost amidst the various CAD renderings from the engineering department. This is it. This is the extent of the niche you've managed to carve out for yourself after almost a decade in the workforce. Your voice mail light blinks urgently; your computer emits a low chime heralding the arrival of each new e-mail with a disturbing frequency that borders on rhythmic. This is the job you're supposed to refer to in interviews with *Entertainment Weekly* as the soulless drudgery you engaged in before you realized your dream of becoming a screenwriter. Beyond that, of what use can it possibly be?

The dull clatter of my coworkers' scurrying fades to white noise and I stare at my walls, locked in a state of suspended animation, waiting for something, some cosmic intervention, to push me in one direction or another. My eye falls on the snapshot of Rael, Jed, and me dressed in black tie and leaning against the bar at Rael and Tamara's wedding: Rael in the middle, looking flushed, happy, and only a little drunk; Jed on one side, looking customarily dapper, a young James Bond; and me on the other side, distinguishable from the waitstaff only due to the shredded boutonniere pinned to my lapel.

Hey, Rael. What the fuck do I do now?

Between my cancer fears and thoughts of a meaningful

career in something, I find myself completely unable to focus on anything. I am filled with an intense nervous energy that shakes my legs and makes me drum my fingers ceaselessly on the laminated surface of my desk. I'm thinking I don't want to end up like Clay, driven to madness by a nebulous career in a nonexistent field. I want to do something I care about. I sit twitching at my desk, staring into nothingness, while something undefined broils ominously inside me. My brain seems too big for my head, my organs pressed against the sides of my body. The upholstered walls of my cubicle suddenly seem claustrophobic to me, and I know I have to get out of here.

Tamara calls me on my cell phone. "My Zack alarm was going off," she says.

"Your timing is impeccable."

"What's up?"

"I'm going a little crazy," I say.

"I'm downstairs."

"Thank God."

Tamara's in the lobby, dressed in jeans, a long, belted sweater coat, and boots that add a good two inches to her height. I practically dive into her hug. Lately, I've noticed that the nature of our hugs is changing. Where we used to simply hug and separate, we now cling for a few extra moments, and there's significantly more body contact. And then there's the way her cheek rests against mine, and the way her arm wraps itself over my shoulders so that she can curl her fingers around my neck, which seems somewhat telling and, I don't know, just a tad naughty. These hugs have become something else, a nonverbal expression of an unspoken feeling of . . . what, exactly? I don't know, but the fact that she hugs me like this is terrifying and thrilling, and though we've never discussed it, not once, it's become an integral part of our ritual. These hugs are no accident. They're neither a greeting nor a farewell, but a destination all their own.

"So, how'd it go?" she asks me.

"That's still unclear," I say. "They might have found something."

Something petty and needy in me shivers gleefully as her expression falters. "What?" she says softly.

I tell her about the spot and the biopsy, leaving out the gory details of the procedure. "So it's still probably nothing," she says.

"The statistics are in my favor," I say.

"You say that like it's a bad thing."

I look at her. "I went there to hear that it was nothing. Statistically speaking, that would be a lot better, wouldn't you say?"

"I see your point," she says, grinning lightly. For some reason, I am uncharacteristically transfixed by her today, dwelling on all of her individual features instead of the whole person. "What?" she says self-consciously. "Do I have something in my teeth?"

"No," I say. "It's just, you look very pretty today."

She breaks into a full, surprised smile. "You're just saying that because it's true," she says, blushing.

My phone rings. I let it go to voice mail. "You're screening?" she asks, raising her eyebrows. Screening is the universal marker of an embattled middleman.

"I'm just not in the mood today."

Tamara grabs my arm and steers me toward the door. "You need Bloomingdale's," she declares.

• • •

Tamara tears expertly through the labyrinth of racks in the evening wear department at Bloomingdale's, pulling dresses off and folding them over her arm, handing them to me when her pile threatens to become unmanageable, all the while insisting that the odds are still in my favor. "It could be anything," she says. "A kidney stone, a muscle tear, or a million other things that mean nothing."

Although she's shed it for the most part, the trained ear can still occasionally pick up the last vestiges of Tamara's suburban New Jersey accent, the softer *r*'s and stretched vowels betraying an adolescence of food courts, big hair, and Bon Jovi albums. The accent becomes more pronounced whenever she's speaking forcefully, whether in anger or, as is now the case, stern, maternal tones, and I always take a secret pleasure in hearing the unpolished syllables roll off her tongue, a vocal intimacy to which few are privy.

"I know," I say.

"Just don't jump to conclusions," she says. "You'll make yourself crazy."

"I just can't shake this feeling that it might be something serious. Things have been going too well for me lately. I feel like I have some bad karma headed my way."

Tamara frowns at me as she leads me toward the dressing rooms. "That's a pretty dire outlook on life," she says. "What's the point in working to be happy if you're going to be constantly looking over your shoulder, wondering when it's time to pay the bill?"

"What are we shopping for?" I ask her through the dressing room door, trying not to think about what she looks like slipping in and out of dresses on the other side.

"A dress for your thing."

"What thing?"

The door swings open and she steps out, making minor adjustments to a snug black cocktail dress. "Your engagement party? This Saturday?"

"Oh," I say. "Right."

"You forgot your own engagement party?"

"Just for a second."

She looks at me inquisitively, seems about to say something, and then flashes a wry grin. "She's a lucky girl, Zack."

She steps back into the changing room and within seconds the dress is flung half over the door. What technique does she employ, I wonder, that enables her to doff it so quickly? "Come in and zip me," she says.

Christ.

I step into the stall and she turns her back to me, staring critically at her dress in the mirror. When I pull on the zipper, the dress moves ever so slightly back, giving me an accidental view of the spot where her spine descends into her backside, and I am afforded an inadvertent glimpse of the twin uppermost curves of her bottom, just below the waistband of her thong. As I move the zipper up past the creamy expanse of her back and the soft curves of her scapulae, I can feel my hand starting to tremble. When I'm done, I look up to find her staring back at me from the mirror, a strange expression on her face. We stand like that for a few seconds, daring each other's reflection, and then she turns around to face me. "So," she says, banishing the moment with her bright tone. "What do you think? A little too slutty?"

I step back and affect a critical pose. "Just slutty enough, I should think."

"Just slutty enough," she repeats delightedly. "That's exactly the look I was going for."

It's close to noon when she's done shopping. We step out

of the store into midtown, a cold October wind battering our cheeks as we walk downtown, toward my office. The sidewalks are teeming with the professional lunch crowd racing to and from lunches, grimly purposeful, looking up only to invoke their right of way against turning cabs at crosswalks. "Listen," Tamara says, looking at her watch. "I have to get home. Celia's babysitting, and I told her I'd be home by twelve."

"Where are you parked?"

"Around the corner from your office."

"You're going to be late."

"I always am. Just ask her."

"Don't you two get along?"

"As well as anyone can get along with the overbearing mother of her dead husband," she says.

"So, no," I say.

"I guess not. She and Paul are constantly checking on Sophie, like there's no way I could be taking care of her properly without Rael there to help me. And I don't know if I'm projecting this or it's real, but I feel like I'm not allowed to seem happy around them. Like, how can I be happy when Rael's dead, you know?"

"Are you ever?"

"What?"

"Happy."

She sighs. "I have my moments."

It's begun raining by the time we reach the Spandler building, just a faint mist, and Sixth Avenue is chilly and gray. Tamara isn't wearing a coat, so she stands shivering under the building's awning, hugging her arms to her sides for warmth, her shopping bag between her knees. I look into the lobby uncertainly.

"What are you thinking?" Tamara says.

"I'm thinking I can't go back up there," I say.

"You're worried about the biopsy."

"Of course I'm worried. I don't want to die."

She reaches forward and grabs my forearm. "Zack. You're not going to die."

I nod. "Suddenly, nothing in my life seems right."

"What do you mean?"

"I don't know," I say. "My life, this job, getting married. I feel like none of it makes sense to me."

"You were just saying how well things were going," Tamara points out.

"That was what I thought," I say. "But now everything makes no sense. There are so many things I want to do with my life that I'm not doing. If I did die, I would die never having done them."

"So what are you going to do?"

"I don't know," I say. "I think I just need to get out of here for a few days, to do some thinking."

"You're going to just sit in your room until Friday, waiting to hear the results of your test?" she says. "You'll go crazy."

"I'm going crazy here," I say. "If I stick around, I'll be climbing the walls."

Tamara takes my hands and centers herself in front of me. "Zack," she says softly. "Is it possible that you're overreacting a little?"

I look at her dark, wide eyes and the soft lines of her lips. I wonder why I'm finding her so utterly captivating today. "I'm beginning to suspect that I've been underreacting for some time now."

Her smile conveys perfect understanding. "It's going to be okay," she says. "I know it."

"Maybe," I say. "But until it is, I just don't want to be here."

"Okay, then," she says. Her face is burnished pink from the drizzle, and she looks adorable bouncing in place lightly to keep warm.

"Tamara," I say, a powerful rush of warmth vibrating in my chest. "You're the greatest."

She smiles, and steps forward and there we are again, in one of our patented hugs. I inhale the clean aroma of almond shampoo and scented soap. "It'll be okay," she whispers in my ear, giving me a light kiss on my temple. And then, without any warning, I pull back and plant a kiss on her lips. It's a medium-length kiss, openmouthed, with only the incidental contact of tongue, and maybe it could have been explained away later as an accident, except that while I'm kissing her, my hand comes up to brush the cool, damp skin of her cheek. Her lips are amazingly yielding, built for kissing, and seem to absorb mine automatically, ready for them, even though I'm not sure she's actually kissing me back. The rhythmic patter of the rain is all around us, punctuated by the swishing sound of taxi tires rolling through puddles, and when I finally pull away, her eyes are wide and questioning, her lips still in the half-opened position of a kiss.

We look at each other for a long moment, my lips still reeling from the sense memory of hers. She nods slowly, as if to register the kiss in some internal log, and then flashes a bemused smile and says, "What was that?" There is no anger in her voice, nor even surprise, for that matter. Her tone is inquisitive and even mildly amused.

"I have no idea," I said. "It just seemed like the thing to do at the time."

"Well," she says. "You certainly did it."

"I'm sorry—"

"Don't." She waves her hand to cut me off. "Don't apologize. You'll just make it weirder."

"Okay."

She leans forward to hug me again, and gives me a light kiss on the cheek, as if to undo the first one. "Call me tomorrow, okay?"

"Okay."

She smiles at me and heads uptown, toward her garage. I watch her walk away until she rounds the corner, and then pull up the collar of my jacket and head west, toward the subway, feeling strangely uprooted; a spectator to my own inconceivable actions. I cross Broadway to Seventh Avenue and the 1 and 9 trains, struggling to quell the powerful urge to run back upstairs to my office and reclaim the normalcy of my life. I can still feel Tamara's lips, still taste her on my tongue, and it brings a crazy smile to my rain-soaked face. My cell phone vibrates and I instinctively lift it to glance at the screen. Six messages. Without removing it from my coat pocket, I know my Blackberry is heavy with unreturned e-mails. I turn the phone off in midring and jam it into a coat pocket, a move that feels every bit as reckless as kissing Tamara.

Clay threw office equipment and kicked the walls, but I'm thinking that maybe there are other, quieter ways of losing your mind.

nineteen nineteen nineteen nineteen nineteen
nineteen nineteen nineteen nineteen nineteen
nineteen nineteen nineteen nineteen nineteen
nineteen **nineteen** nineteen nineteen nineteen
nineteen nineteen nineteen nineteen nineteen

nineteen

Rael and Tamara's wedding. Jed, Rael, and I were leaning against the bar, drunkenly toasting our friendship, while Tamara and her bridesmaids posed for some impromptu photos on the dance floor. Jed caught me watching them and said, "Oh, no," waving his hand in front of my eyes as if to break a trance. "Don't do it, man."

"Do what?" I said, still staring across the room.

Jed put down his gin and tonic and turned to face me, grinding an ice cube between his teeth. "I have one rule about dating," he said.

"No you don't," I said.

"But I do."

"This from the man who lost his virginity to his aunt," Rael said, snickering.

"Ex-aunt," Jed clarified. "She was already divorced from Uncle Phil."

"Oh, well, then that's okay."

"Listen," Jed said. "It's a good rule."

"Fine," I said. "Do tell."

Jed leaned back and took another sip from his drink. "Let me start by saying that rules for dating are like rules for being mugged at gunpoint. The very concept is flawed, since it flies in the face of one simple fact: you're not in control."

I leaned back and sipped at my own drink, a whiskey sour. "And yet, you have a rule."

"Five words," Jed said. He placed his drink on the bar, fixed me with a somber look, and paused for dramatic effect. "Don't date the fucking bridesmaids."

Rael and I nodded sagely. "Wow," Rael said.

"Brilliant," I concurred.

"Go ahead, make your jokes," Jed said, shaking his head sadly. "But remember this moment, because one day you'll be sorry you didn't take heed."

"Explain," I said.

"Bridesmaids are an optical illusion, aglow with excitement and ripe with sexual promise, an idealized version of the true woman beneath. It's false advertising. Their hair and makeup are professionally done. Those gowns are designed to accentuate the positive, while any flaws are hidden beneath all that puffy crinoline. How else can you explain why they look so good in such ridiculous dresses? Plus"—he paused and held up his empty glass demonstratively—"you're probably drunk."

Rael and I looked at each other and laughed.

"I'm serious," Jed insisted. "You get them out of that getup and it's all there: the bad skin, the sagging breasts, and an ass that has somehow, magically doubled in size. And the tragedy is, if you'd met her like this to begin with, you might still have been interested, but the contrast to her idealized self is simply too much to overcome."

"Tamara was a bridesmaid when I met her," Rael said with a grin.

"The exception that proves the rule," Jed said dismissively.

But Jed had it wrong. It wasn't the bridesmaids at whom I'd been staring. It was the bride, smiling as she came toward us at that moment, her hair pinned back to expose the graceful descent of her cheekbones, her tan skin luminescent above the scooped neck of her dress. In the year or so that she'd been dating Rael, I'd grown close to Tamara, and I was certainly aware of her beauty on an instinctive, male level, but she was my best friend's fiancée, and I'd never taken it personally before. All through the ceremony, I'd been too wrapped up in my duties as best man to really pay her much attention. Now, though, I couldn't take my eyes off her. "So, Zack," she said, grabbing me by the arm. "You going to dance with me or what?"

"Go ahead," Rael said, leaning against Jed. "I'm just catching my breath."

The song was "Wonderful Tonight," and as we danced, reflections from the ballroom chandelier sparkled like Roman candles in her eyes. "Rael told me about Lisa," she said.

Lisa, whom I'd been dating for the last few months, had broken up with me last week because, as she put it, we'd "maxed out our emotional connection." I didn't disagree, but I'd been hoping we'd last a little while longer, so that at least I'd have a date for the wedding.

"I'm over it," I said with a shrug.

Tamara fixed me with a look. "Why didn't you tell me?"

"I told Rael."

She stopped moving and looked up at me, eyes wide and

demanding. "Zack," she said. "Rael and I are married. We haven't merged into one being. After all the long nights I put in talking to you about your love life while Rael was snoring away, I would hope that you'd look at me as a true friend, and not simply an extension of Rael."

"Point taken," I said. "I guess with the wedding only a few days away, I didn't want to rain on your parade."

She nodded, mollified, and gave me a soft kiss on the cheek. "You're too sweet, Zack," she said, resting her head on my shoulder as we finished the dance. "Lisa didn't deserve you."

"Who does?" I said.

"I don't know. But she's out there. And we're going to find her."

"We?"

"Damn right, we," she said, pulling back to look at me. "You're my best man too, and that makes you my responsibility. Now, dip."

"What?"

"It's the end of the song," she said. "Dip me."

And so I dipped her, taking in the triangle of soft flesh beneath her upturned chin as she threw her head back, and when I pulled her back up, Rael was there to dance with his bride. "I'll take it from here," he said, grinning at me.

"She's all yours," I said, and then watched as he led her away from me, vaguely troubled by the intense feeling of loss that momentarily came over me. But then Jed stepped up behind me and threw his arm over my shoulder, and the feeling disappeared as suddenly as it had come on. "And then there were two," he intoned gravely, steering me toward a group of women in lavender taffeta congregating near the bandstand.

"Don't date the bridesmaids," I said dully.

"Don't date the *fucking* bridesmaids," Jed corrected me, maintaining our course.

"The swear is integral?"

"Imperative."

"Why's that?"

Jed sighed and downed the rest of his drink in one savage gulp. "Because we never fucking learn."

twenty twenty twenty twenty twenty twenty twenty
twenty twenty twenty twenty twenty twenty twenty
twenty twenty twenty twenty twenty twenty twenty
twenty **twenty** twenty twenty twenty twenty twenty
twenty twenty twenty twenty twenty twenty twenty

i get off the train at Eighty-sixth, but rather than go home, I walk slowly toward Central Park, relishing the cold sensation of the rain soaking my skin through my clothes. Wet weather has always seemed to me to be an invitation to extreme action, and, having just behaved extremely, the stinging spray is a welcome, retroactive justification. Leaving work in the middle of the day is erratic behavior, to be sure, but nothing that can't be explained away. Kissing Tamara, on the other hand, was just plain reckless, and it leaves me feeling perplexed, ashamed, and undeniably excited. I want to take it back and do it again, all at the same time. I think of Hope in London, sifting through recondite paintings in a musty basement, dust mites collecting on her designer clothing, and I feel a deep pang of guilt. I think of Tamara and wonder what she's thinking about me, if she's reliving that kiss over and over again the way I am. Best not to think about that too much. But still . . .

I step into the living room an hour later, teeth chattering, to find Matt and Jed napping in front of the television, Matt sprawled on the floor and Jed on the couch. A romantic comedy plays itself out on cable; a mistaken identity has been perpetrated by the woman in the name of unrequited love, but the deception will ultimately be forgiven, since both parties are just so good-looking and because only a fool would overlook the soundtrack and lighting cues that make it clear where the happy ending lies. A worn copy of Nabokov's *Laughter in the Dark* lies face-down on Matt's chest. Despite the tattoos, earrings, and other assorted accoutrements of his trade, Matt's not at all what you'd expect from a punk rocker. He's passionate about literature, is majoring in it on his protracted route through college, which explains the Nabokov and why, mixed in with songs like "Bring Your Sister" and "Jerk-Off Jimmy," you'll also find ones like "Vonnegut's Weed" and "Mr. Palomar" in his body of work.

I tiptoe upstairs to my room, peeling off my wet clothes as I go. As I rub the rain out of my hair with a towel still damp from this morning's shower, I enter into a staring match with the toilet. I've managed to avoid it all day, since this morning's agonizing unpleasantness, but the telltale throbbing in my groin says that I can run, but I can't hide. I decide to go sitting down. My piss is razor sharp, and in the mirror over the sink, I catch a glimpse of my face contorted in pain, the cords of my neck standing out in protest as I gasp through the stream. But then it's over, and in retrospect, it wasn't as bad as this morning, although I don't know if that's actually the case, or if I've only taken the element of surprise out of it. There's definitely less blood than this morning, although that's hardly a cause for celebration.

There's a message on my machine from Hope, telling me that she's arrived safely in London. She sounds somewhat put off, no doubt wondering why I didn't call to check on her and why I'm not at work and not answering my cell in the middle of the day. She leaves me the number at her hotel, says she loves me, and hangs up. I should call her right now. I really should.

Matt stirs when he hears me come into the living room, and then sits up with a grunt. "Hey, man," he says groggily.

"Hey," I say, pulling on a sweatshirt.

"You puked in our van."

"Yeah. Sorry about that."

He shrugs, a seasoned veteran of wayward regurgitation. "It's raining out?"

"Yep."

"What time is it?" he says, sitting up slowly, groaning at the stiffness in his ribs.

"It's one thirty," I tell him. As he turns to face me, I can see the dark shadows under his bloodshot eyes, the gaunt lines of his face. Not for the first time, it occurs to me that my little brother is slipping away, being slowly devoured by the anger that propels him. The healing bruises from a loan shark beating he suffered a few months ago form a crescent-shaped penumbra from the corner of his ear to his temple. Yes, my little brother's been into some shit: drugs, debt, dealing. If it involves any form of self-destruction, Matt will usually be up for it. Sitting on the floor, he looks so small and wasted, and I just want to throw my arms around him, like when we were little kids, and feel like I can protect him, tell him that it's okay to let go and get some rest, that I'll be here to watch over him. "You look like shit," I say.

"It's only rock and roll," he says with a smirk, his tongue

darting out to lick his desiccated lips. "But I like it. What are you doing here?"

"I actually live here."

He nods. "I mean now, in the middle of the day."

I sit down on the floor, my back against the couch. "I am either on the cusp of what may very well be a grand epiphany or else a minor nervous breakdown."

He looks up at me appraisingly and nods his head, his brief smile revealing the jagged line of his cigarette-stained teeth. "Zack, my brother," he says with a yawn. "Welcome to the monkey house."

By the time Norm shows up later, the three of us are good and stoned on some stale joints Matt produced from the depths of his cargo pants, watching *The Terminator* on the Sci Fi network, while Jed passionately holds forth on the inherent contradictions and liabilities of fucking with the space-time continuum. When Norm walks into the room, a wet duffel bag slung over his shoulder like Santa Claus, we all stare up at him as if he might be a clever group hallucination.

"Hello, boys," Norm says, dropping his duffel onto the carpet with a thud. He's wearing jeans and a faded red sweatshirt, his hair plastered against his scalp from the rain.

"Hey, Norm," Jed says agreeably.

"What are you doing here?" I say, too stoned to get up.

"The door was open." He looks over to Matt, who is sitting cross-legged on the floor in front of the television, his bent silhouette framed by the large screen. "Hello, Matt," he says formally.

"Norm," Matt says with an exaggeratedly formal nod.

"Great show the other night," Norm addresses him gingerly. "I was really very proud of you."

"Thank you, Norm," Matt says, staggering to his feet. "That makes it all worthwhile."

Norm nods and looks at me. "Why aren't you at work?"

"I'm taking some time off," I say. "A mental health day."

"And you're accomplishing that by getting high?"

"Don't knock it till you've tried it."

"Where are you going?" Norm says to Matt, who is making a show of throwing on his worn jacket.

"I've got somewhere I need to be."

"Where's that?"

"Anywhere but here."

"Can't we just talk, son?" Norm says plaintively.

Matt stares at him, eyes wide and angry, then storms over to him with so much force that for an instant I'm certain he's going to hit him. Instead, he stops right in front of him, fists clenched at his sides, his face contorted in rage. "Fuck you, Norm," Matt spits at him. "Fuck you. My life is shit and it's your fault. It's your fault I had to deal drugs to buy a goddamn guitar, it's your fault I can't keep a girlfriend for more than a month, it's your fault I can't look people in the eye or say what I really feel."

"Matt," I say.

"Shut up, Zack. You know I'm right."

"I'm still the only father you'll ever have," Norm says weakly, holding his hands up defensively.

Matt's smile cuts his face like a razor. "You're just the sperm donor, Norm," he says, heading for the door. "That's all you were ever good for. Fucking sperm."

Matt storms out the door and Norm looks at us, red-faced with chagrin. "Jesus," he says. "If I'd have known I was going to get beat up on like this, I would have worn a helmet." He looks at the door and makes a snap decision. "Matt!" he calls, and tears out the door after him. We listen to the two sets of footsteps running down the stairs, and then Jed leans back on the couch, craning his neck to see out the window. "Wow," he says to me, collapsing back on the couch. "For a heavy guy, your old man sure can move."

"I wouldn't know," I say, heaving myself off the floor and heading for the stairs. I'm still woozy from Matt's stale ganja, and when I trip over my father's discarded duffel bag, it's all I can do to keep from falling on my face.

It's eight p.m., which means it's one a.m. in England, a fact that only occurs to me after they've put me through to Hope's hotel room. "Hey, baby," I say.

"Zack?" she says, her voice groggy and slurred. "What the hell?"

"Did I wake you?"

"Of course you woke me," she grumbles. "It's the middle of the night."

"Sorry about that," I say. "I thought you might be jet-lagged."

"What's wrong?" she demands.

"Nothing. I just missed you."

That pisses her off. "You had plenty of time to call me earlier, if you missed me so much. Why weren't you at work?" She has not fully committed to consciousness yet, and her voice is muted and irregular as she slides in and out her slumber.

I almost tell her about having walked out of work. About how empty and demeaned I've been feeling there, and about wanting to do something that will actually mean something to me, that will actually make it worth answering when people ask me what I do. Hope will be sympathetic, I have no doubt about that, but she won't appreciate the timing of my vocational crisis, coming as it has in the midst of our engagement, at the merging of our lives. She'll worry about my potential future earnings, about my abilities as a long-term provider, about our chances for a *New York Times* wedding announcement. She'll talk around it for a while, but ultimately, the need to help me fix things will get the best of her. She'll insist I meet with her father, and next thing you know, I'll be a Vice President of Bedpans, walking the carpeted halls of Seacord International in suits and braces under the watchful, controlling glare of my father-in-law, bearing the hateful mark of nepotism upon my forehead, disregarded out of hand as the old man's loser son-in-law.

"I'm just a little under the weather," I say.

I can hear the rustling of sheets, the drag of the telephone on the nightstand. "Zack, is everything okay?"

I sigh. "It's just been a little crazy here, with my father and all."

"Have you been spending some time with him?"

"A little."

"That's nice," she says through a long yawn. "I'm going back to sleep now, okay?"

"How's London?" I ask, suddenly lonely.

"Call me when I'm awake and I'll tell you."

"Okay."

"Good night, babe."

I crawl under the covers much too early, flipping between various news programs and movie channels. There are brush fires in Los Angeles, car bombs in Iraq, and USA is showing a made-for-TV movie in which a lousy actress from a popular sitcom has lost her memory and is being chased through the woods by a masked assassin. Somewhere in all the excitement, I doze off.

Tamara's voice on my answering machine awakens me an indeterminate amount of time later. I open my eyes, disoriented by the darkness that arrived unannounced during my unplanned nap. "Anyway," Tamara's saying. "I'm worried about you. So give me a call if you get a chance, okay?" It's strange to hear her voice in the confines of my bedroom. I almost always speak to her from the office or on my cell. My hands search for the cordless, which is buried somewhere in the folds of my comforter. "You can call till whenever," she continues. "I turn off the ringer when I go to sleep." There's a momentary pause. "Whatever," she continues awkwardly. "I just wanted to let you know I'm thinking about you, okay? That's all, folks. 'Bye."

My hands locate the phone just as she hangs up. I start to dial her number, but then stop. We're still suspended in the postkiss ether and if I call her we'll either discuss the kiss or pretend it never happened, and either option will bring us crashing back down to reality, which isn't an acceptable scenario to me right now. USA is now showing an old James Bond film, Connery speeding in his convertible past laughably false backdrops. I flip absently through the movie channels, waiting for something to grab me, but every movie seems to star Freddie Prinze, Jr., leading me to wonder, not for the first time, why I bother paying for premium channels. I go to the bathroom. This time there's less pain and considerably less blood. Still, I pop three preemptive Tylenols before getting back into bed.

I lie in the dark, my thoughts flitting erratically between Hope and Tamara and my father, before settling with a thud on the dark spot on my bladder. I see it every time I close my eyes and I wonder if it's growing inside me the way it is in my mind. I address a few tentative words to God, offering up an array of incentives for him to keep me in good health. It's a few hours before I fall back asleep. When I do, I dream of Camille, the dark-haired physician's assistant, once again handling my privates, but this time under considerably friendlier circumstances.

twenty-one

"Don't ask," my mother says in a controlled hysteria. I haven't, but that's not really the point. "Peter bought a car."

It's eight o'clock on Thursday morning, and her call has jolted me out of one of those sweaty dreams where it's cocktail hour and everyone you ever knew in your whole life is there, and you're searching in vain for a hiding place before they all notice that you're not wearing any pants.

It takes me a minute to wrap my brain around what she's just said. "What?"

"You heard me."

"Who would sell Pete a car?" I say angrily. A good part of my childhood was spent watching out for Pete, and I still get the same instinctive surge of fury whenever someone mistreats him.

"That Bowhan character," my mother says tiredly. "Satch. Who names their kid Satch, anyway?"

"Does he realize that Pete doesn't drive?"

"Of course he does. He had the car delivered to our driveway this afternoon."

"I'll come out there today," I say.

"I'm sorry to have to ask." There is a lifetime of quiet pain in my mother's voice. Someone has taken advantage of her baby, and she wasn't there to stop it. You would never send your five-year-old out into the world unprotected, but having a grown, mentally retarded child feels like that every day.

"How did he pay for it?" I ask.

"He wrote a check."

"Peter has a checking account?"

"He makes money," my mother says defensively. "Why shouldn't he have a checking account?"

"No," I say. "You're right."

"Anyway," she says. "I don't want to talk about it anymore. It makes me sad. How are things with you?"

"Fine." I'm wondering if I should mention Norm's resurfacing.

"You didn't look so good the other day," she says.

"Gee, thanks."

"I'm just saying."

"What, Mom?" I say, irked. "What are you just saying?"

"Nothing," she says tiredly. "I'm sorry. I don't mean to give you a hard time."

"No, I'm sorry," I say. "I didn't mean to snap at you."

"Peter wants to talk to you."

There's a whine of static and then Pete comes on the phone. "Hey, Zack," he says. Pete has overactive salivary glands, and whenever he talks on the phone, he sucks up the excess saliva in the back of his throat. I got used to it a long time ago, but over the phone it's more pronounced.

"Hey, Pete, what's up?"

"I got a car."

"So I hear," I say, grinning. "What kind?"

"A '95 Ford Mustang. Red. I got a great deal, a thousand bucks. It's only got a hundred and sixty thousand miles on it. But Mom says I have to give it back."

"Well, do you have a driver's license?"

"Nope."

"What's the point of having a car like that without a license?"

Pete says, "Chicks," and then convulses into a fit of hoarse, snorting laughter. I laugh along with him.

"Pete," I say. "You don't need a car to get chicks."

"It helps," he says.

"Look at me," I say. "I don't have a car."

"Number one," Pete says. "You don't need to get chicks, because you're engaged to Hope." Pete debates in number form, and I can picture him standing there, with the phone tucked into his ear, ticking off the count on his hands. "And number two," he says, and then pauses.

"Yeah?" I say.

"You're not a retard."

Norm is in the kitchen, in boxers and a wifebeater, scrambling eggs when I come downstairs. "Hey, Zack," he says, full of urgent cheer. "I made you some breakfast."

"Did you sleep here?" I ask incredulously.

"Onions and tomatoes, just like when you were a kid," he says proudly, expertly sliding a heaping mound of eggs from the frying pan onto a waiting plate. "You still like it like that?"

"Can you answer my question?"

He looks at me. "I crashed on the couch. Jed said it would be fine. I wanted to clear it with you, but you were already sleeping."

"So, what?" I say. "You're moving in here now?"

"It's just for a few days," he says apologetically, placing the plate in front of me.

"I thought you were staying with friends."

He shrugs. "I think I might have overstayed my welcome."

"Go figure."

He greets my sarcasm with the same nullifying smile he always uses, like he's in on the joke rather than the butt of it. "So," he says. "When do you leave for work?"

"I'm not going to work today," I say. That raises his eyebrows, and I quickly lift my hand to shush him as he's about to speak. "And if I were you," I continue quickly, "I would carefully consider whatever it was you were about to say. It could mean the difference between your being welcome to stay here or not."

He looks at me for a long moment, then nods his head with a small grin. "I was just going to ask if the eggs need any more salt."

I take a forkful into my mouth and chew it thoughtfully. "They do," I say. "Thanks."

He slides the saltshaker across the table. "Don't mention it."

"Did you catch up to Matt yesterday?" I ask.

"I did."

"And?"

"I told him his father wasn't perfect."

"I hope he was sitting down when you dropped that bomb."

Norm shrugs. "He wasn't listening anyway." He drops the

pan into the sink, and then, as he's turning, his erection inadvertently pops through the fly of his boxers and there I am, face-to-face with the instrument of my own humble origins, Norm's purple, nascent member.

"And we're done with breakfast," I say, disgustedly pushing my plate across the table.

"Sorry about that," he says, grinning sheepishly, but not without pride, as he tucks it back into his shorts.

"Okay," I say. "I'll ask. What is it with you and the Viagra?"

Norm sits down across from me. "I'm trying to condition myself."

"Condition yourself."

He nods and leans back in his chair. "When I was your age, it didn't take very much to get me going. See a nice rack on someone, a good, firm ass, and I'd get so hard I could write my name with it, hang a towel on it, you know? But I'm sixty now, and my dick has let me down on more than one occasion. You wait until you're my age—you'll see. It's not that easy. So what I'm doing is, I'm programming my body to believe that erections are a normal, everyday function again. This way, when the occasion does arise, then by God, so will I."

"I see," I say, much the way I would if I were talking to a rational person. "And you're doing this under medical supervision?"

"Nah. It's my own idea," he says proudly.

"And you don't see anything wrong with walking around all day with a hard-on?"

"On the contrary. It makes me feel young again. Alive."

"I'm young," I say. "I don't walk around with a hard-on all day."

He flashes his trademark grin. "You don't know what you're missing."

Hope calls, still irked about my waking her up last night, but more concerned about my not being on the way to work already. "Why are you still home?" she says.

"My father dropped by," I say.

"Oh. But you're going to work today, right?"

"I'm not sure. I'm still feeling a little out of it."

There's a pregnant pause on the other end of the line as Hope considers her options. "Zack," she says softly. "What's going on? Do I need to come home early?"

"Of course not," I say. "Everything's fine. I'm just not feeling too well, that's all."

"What are your symptoms?"

"General malaise."

"What does that mean, exactly?"

"I don't know. I'm just feeling somewhat run-down."

"Does this have anything to do with that procedure you had?"

"No."

"You're making me very nervous." In the background, I can hear the discreet clatter of a keyboard abruptly stop as Hope quits multitasking.

"Why?"

"I don't know. You're acting strange. You don't call me all day yesterday; then you wake me up sounding drunk, or stoned, or something. And now you're skipping work for the second day in a row when there doesn't seem to be anything wrong with you. I mean, none of this is normal behavior for you. Are you having doubts about us? Because if you are, you should just come out and say so."

"It's nothing like that," I say. "Jesus. Can't a guy have an off day without the whole world coming down on him?"

"I'm not the whole world. I am your fiancée," Hope says in a thin, icy voice that can go either way. She might burst into tears, or she might coldly eviscerate me.

"I know. I'm sorry."

Our frustrated silence is punctuated by the twelve-cents-a-minute overseas static.

"Have you seen Tamara?" she finally asks me.

"What?"

"Tamara. I was just wondering if you've gone out to see her and Sophie lately."

This is a trap, a trick question, and I don't know the right answer. But waiting too long will be an automatic disqualification, so I have no choice but to hazard a guess. "I did," I say. "On Monday."

"You left work early?"

"Yeah."

"You didn't mention it."

"It wasn't a big deal. Tamara was going a little stir-crazy, so I took Sophie to the park for a few hours."

Hope is aware that I check in with Tamara and Sophie from time to time. She's less than thrilled with my retained connection to my best friend's widow, but she's never said anything about it, too proud to be unfairly cast in the role of the insensitive jealous girlfriend while Tamara and I nobly grapple with the larger, universally sympathetic themes of death and grief. And while this delicate dynamic grants me license, I make sure to keep the frequency of my calls and visits with Tamara a secret, because if Hope knew how often we speak and how much time we spend together, her instinct for self-preservation would override her pride, which would lead to a final, tearfully angry ultimatum. So I carry on my relationship with Tamara according to a nebulous formula being constantly recalculated to indicate the minimum amount of disclosure necessary to cover my ass while continuing the charade. Hope sees only the tip of the Tamara iceberg, its mammoth, faceted walls spreading out below the churning surface, lying in silent, deadly wait.

"It's not a big deal at all," Hope says. "I'm glad you're able to help her out. I'm just wondering why you didn't mention it."

"I don't know," I say. "That night was Matt's show and Jed and I got kind of drunk, and then my father showed up and I guess, in all the excitement, I forgot about it."

"Fair enough," Hope says, but her tone remains unconvinced. "Listen, I have to go into a meeting. I love you and I don't want to be a nag, so I'm just going to ask you one last time, is everything okay? With you, with us, with work. Everything."

I choose my words carefully. "Everything's fine, Hope. Really. I'm just feeling exhausted, the kind of exhausted that movie stars get when they check into hospitals and their reps announce to everyone that they're suffering from exhaustion. That kind of exhausted. Except I don't have reps, so I'm just laying low for a day or two so that I can be well rested and happy at our engagement party. That's all. Okay?"

"Okay," she says, mollified by my reference to the party. "I love you, babe. Call me later."

"I will."

Hanging up feels portentous, the powerful sense of an opportunity missed, although I have no idea what that might have been.

• • •

The phone rings again a few minutes later, and, thinking it might be Hope, I pick it up.

"Where the hell are you?" Bill shouts hysterically into the phone.

Fuck. "I'm calling in sick," I say.

"You can't disappear for a day and then call in sick!" Bill protests. "Hodges is on the warpath!"

"Tell him I'm working on it," I say. "As soon as I know something, I'll call him."

"I'm not your goddamn secretary!" he screams at me. "You call him right now, Zack. I mean it. I don't know what's gotten into you, but if you blow this, you're finished here. Do you read me?"

"I'm already finished," I say.

"Excuse me?"

"Okay," I say, and hang up the phone. I'm thinking it might not be a bad idea to leave my cell phone home today.

twenty-two twenty-two twenty-two twenty-two
twenty-two twenty-two twenty-two twenty-two
twenty-two twenty-two twenty-two twenty-two
twenty-two **twenty-two** twenty-two twenty-two
twenty-two twenty-two twenty-two twenty-two

It's unseasonably warm for October and there I am, in the middle of the working day, cruising down Houston in a Lexus convertible, top town, blasting Elvis Costello through the Bose speakers, looking every inch like someone who has his shit together. I catch a glimpse of myself reflected in the window of an electronics shop and, for a moment there, I almost fool myself.

Matt's waiting for me on the stoop of his Lower East Side building, dressed in jeans and a torn roll-neck sweater, his version of presentable, smoking a cigarette and fiddling with his iPod. "Hey," he says, ambling over to the car.

"Where's Elton?"

"Fuck."

He runs back upstairs and returns a minute later carrying a small brown shopping bag. "Elton," he says with a smirk, tossing the bag into the backseat.

The first time our mother saw Matt's shaved head, she cried for days, telling him that nothing in her life had ever made her sadder than seeing her baby's head like that. "Your husband cheated on you," he pointed out. "Your sister died of breast cancer."

"This is worse," she insisted through her tears.

Matt shaved his head as a concession to his receding hairline, unbecoming for the front man of a punk pop band, and he refused to grow it back. But every time Lela saw him, she'd cry inconsolably. Matt's girlfriend at the time worked in the costume department of *Saturday Night Live,* and in a moment of inspiration she brought home a wig created for an Elton John sketch that was bumped at the last minute. It was a near-perfect fit, and from then on, Matt would wear the wig when he went to visit Lela. They never discussed it, but somehow the Elton John hair was an acceptable surrogate and the issue was thus wordlessly resolved.

We hit the FDR at top speed and it feels good, two brothers on a midday road trip, the wind flowing over the windshield to kiss the tops of our heads, the sun-dappled surface of the East River shining like sequins, and it's so easy to imagine us in another life, one in which we're both successful and better adjusted, able to positively impact ourselves and each other, our ambitions and desires manifest, and not muted by the restive inner monologue of discontent that is our birthright.

Matt names the bridges under his breath. The Brooklyn Bridge, the Queensboro, the Triboro, and, off in the distance, the Whitestone and the Throgs Neck. That was what Pete always did when we were kids in the back of Norm's LeSabre, returning on Sunday evenings from visiting our grandmother in Brooklyn, heads on shoulders in the backseat, Norm and Lela singing along to Simon and Garfunkel and Frank Sinatra on

WPAT-FM 93, the rhythmic bumping of the highway seams lulling us to sleep. It's one of the only lingering memories I have of us as a family, of feeling insulated and complete.

We're driving along the service road in Riverdale when Matt suddenly sits up in his seat. "I don't believe it," he says.

"What?"

He points. "Look."

And there's Norm, trudging up the service road, duffel bag over his shoulder, face flushed, panting lightly from his exertions. I slow down and we watch Norm from behind.

"For an absentee father," Matt says, "he sure is around a lot."

"He is rather ubiquitous," I agree.

"It's like he thinks everything can be fixed through sheer omnipresence," Matt says.

"Like his erections," I say. "He thinks he can condition us into accepting a new standard."

Matt looks at me like a small, perfectly formed flower just sprouted from my nose. "Okay," he says slowly. "I don't know what you're talking about, but you need to come up with a better analogy, preferably one that doesn't involve Dad's schlong."

"You just called him 'Dad,' " I say.

"No I didn't."

"Sure you did. You said 'Dad's schlong.' You see. His diabolical plan is succeeding."

"It was contextual."

I grin. "Whatever, man."

"Fuck you. It was."

I pull up alongside Norm, keeping pace with his trudging gait. He's completely focused on his walking, eyes straight ahead, head bowed into the wind, and it takes a minute for him to realize he has company. "Hello, boys," he says, beaming at us as he sucks wind. "Great to see you."

"What are you doing here?" I say.

"I thought you might need a little backup."

"What are you talking about, Norm?"

He steps off the sidewalk to lean forward over Matt's door. He's sweating in his decades-old Members Only windbreaker, and underneath it I can see the same red sweatshirt he wore yesterday. "I'm here to help you get Peter's money back."

"How do you even know about that?" I say.

"Now, don't overreact to this," he says. "I heard you on the phone with your mom."

"I was upstairs in bed. How could you have heard anything?"

"He's staying with you now?" Matt says incredulously.

I shush him. "Not now."

"I listened in on the downstairs phone," Norm says.

"You're a guest in my house and you're eavesdropping on my phone calls?" I say, furious.

"So he is staying with you," Matt says huffily.

"I just wanted to hear her voice again."

"Then you should have called her," I say. "Jesus Christ! You're out of control, Norm."

"Let's not overlook the larger issue here," Norm says.

"Oh. And what's that?"

"Someone screwed Peter."

"Fuck off, Norm. Someone's always screwing Peter," Matt says. "And we'll handle it, like we've always handled it. Without you."

Norm stands up straight and looks down at us. "Boys," he says. "I'm sure it hasn't escaped your attention that I didn't ask your permission to come with you today. The reason for that, in case you were wondering, is that I don't need it. I'll bottom-line it for you: it's not your call. I took a subway and two buses to get here." He leans all the way forward now, forearms pressed against the car door, his head hovering directly over Matt's, his expression stark and determined. "I'm not turning back," he declares emphatically. "So, having freed the two of you from the onus of that decision, you should now be able to make the one decision concerning me that you are, in fact, in the position to make."

Matt looks at me, his eyes wide and smoldering with indignation. *No fucking way,* he mouths to me. I look at Norm, peaked and flushed from his walking, his features contorted into a rictus of grim purpose. I sigh. "Hop in."

"I don't fucking believe you," Matt mutters to me.

Norm can't fit in the Lexus's backseat, so he sits up on the seat back like a returning hero at his parade, face turned pleasurably into the midday sun like a dog, while Matt slinks down in his seat sulking, and in this unsightly manner we leave the service road and navigate gracelessly through the business district of our old neighborhood, toward our childhood home.

twenty-three twenty-three twenty-three twenty-three
twenty-three twenty-three twenty-three twenty-three
twenty-three twenty-three twenty-three twenty-three
twenty-three

twenty-three

twenty-three twenty-three
twenty-three twenty-three twenty-three twenty-three

Pete gets off at two on Thursdays, so the plan is to stop at the house to say hello, then pick up the Mustang and drive it over to the Diamond Hardware store that Satch runs. At that point, I'll explain the situation to Satch, who, I'm hoping, is open to reason and is not as prone to violence as he was when we were kids. In the meantime, Matt will stand in the background with his game face on, flash his tattoos, and look menacing. There's no obvious role for Norm, who was a last-minute addition to the roster, but I will discourage any ad-libbing. Beyond that, I have nothing concrete in mind, except the notion that it seemed like a much better plan on the drive up.

Before any of this can happen, though, there's the matter of Norm's reunion with Lela and Pete, which is something I'd pay good money to not be present for, but I can't see any way out. I'd love to wait in the car, but we can't just spring Norm on Lela, even though that would surely be his preferred modus operandi, given the choice.

"What the hell is that?" Norm asks as Matt throws on the Elton John wig.

Matt flashes me a look that says he will not abide any remarks from Norm on the subject. "Just go with us on this one, Norm, okay?" I say.

"You look ridiculous," Norm says, prompting me to wonder, not for the first time, how he's made it to the ripe old age of sixty without getting the shit beat out of him repeatedly. The man has no filter.

"People in glass houses," Matt says venomously, "should shut the fuck up."

Norm defensively rubs the pitiful remnants of his failed hair transplant, but refrains from any further comments.

"Now, just stay in the car," I say. "Matt and I need to tell her you're here."

"Got it," says Norm, checking his teeth and patting down his pate in the rearview mirror.

Matt and I deliberately crowd the door frame when Lela opens the door. She's in sweatpants, a white blouse with a faded floral pattern, and an apron, and I instinctively know she will consider this the worst outfit possible for facing her ex-husband again, but there's nothing we can do about it now.

"Hi, Mom," I say. "There's something we need to tell you."

"My Lord," she whispers, looking past us to the car. "Is that Norman?"

"Yes."

Her breath catches in her throat and she leans against the door frame for support. "What's he doing here?"

"He just kind of showed up," I say.

"We can't seem to get rid of him," Matt adds.

Lela's hands operate on instinct. One flies up to gingerly assess her hair, combing it desperately with her fingers, tucking loose ends behind her ears, while the other absently pulls at her apron, smoothing out her blouse underneath it. "He's so . . . old," she says, her fingers now worrying the weathered contours of her own face self-consciously.

Behind us, the car door slams. Norm has apparently done all the sitting still he's capable of, and he now exits the car and comes up the walk, his face hyperbolically solemn, his gait slow and formal, milking the gravity of this summit meeting. A peculiar half smile twists at Lela's thin lips, her brows arched, her eyelids at half-mast. The alien expression transforms her, and I realize I'm seeing, for the first time, a side of my mother that has nothing to do with being a mother, the part of her that was all of her before she and Norm procreated and, ultimately, destroyed each other.

"Hello, Lela," Norm says somberly. "You look wonderful."

"Hi, Norm," she says, her voice stronger and steadier than I would have thought possible. "It's been a long time."

He nods, but before the scene can play itself out any further, there's a loud whoop from inside the house and Pete bursts through the front door in nothing but his underpants, eyes wide, tongue hanging out of his gaping mouth, and, leaping down the porch stairs in one bound, throws himself into Norm's arms. "Daddy!" he shouts, hugging Norm fiercely. "I knew you'd come back! I missed you. Look, Mom. It's Daddy. He came back."

"Hello, son," Norm says in a choked voice as he hugs Pete and pats his shoulders. "I missed you too." He holds Pete at arm's length to look at him, shaking his head back and forth, and suddenly his eyes are brimming with tears. And then he lowers his head and emits a high, strangled wail that seems to suck the energy out of his body, and he collapses against Pete, who isn't prepared for Norm's full weight, so they fall to their knees, locked in their embrace, Norm sobbing profusely into the hollow of Pete's neck, Pete looking concerned, rubbing Norm's shoulders and saying, "Don't cry, Daddy. It's okay. Don't cry." And on the porch next to me, my mother says, "I'll get some coffee," and then bursts loudly into tears.

Later, Pete, Matt, and I throw a baseball around outside while Norm and Lela speak in hushed tones about God knows what on the living room couch. She's not necessarily happy to see him, but there's no trace of the antagonism and bitterness I would have expected from her. And rather than being pleased with this unforeseen turn of events, I find myself taking offense at the way she's let him in so easily, while I've been struggling, for her sake, to keep Norm at bay. After years of indirectly nurturing the anger in me, she has wordlessly invalidated my acrimony by effortlessly letting go of her own. Having been anchored in her rage for my entire adult life, I am suddenly cast adrift, with no idea of what to do with my own ingrained resentments. And I know these are all selfish and petty emotions, so on top of everything else, I get to feel like an asshole.

"What do you make of that?" I ask Matt, lobbing him the ball.

"It's fucked," Matt says, his tone indicating that I'll get no more from him. He leans back and tosses Pete a high fly.

"Jeter's under it," Pete announces, exaggeratedly squatting to catch the ball. "And . . . he's got it, and that will retire the side." Pete has adjusted instantly to Norm's return, like it's been days, not years, since he saw him last.

Lela steps out into the front yard while Norm uses the bathroom. "I don't trust him," she says to me.

"You two seemed pretty chummy in there."

"I was being civil, Zack, that's all," she says wearily. "When you have children in common, there's really no choice in the matter."

"If you say so."

"He looks awful," she says.

"He could lose a few pounds," I say. "What do you mean you don't trust him?"

"There's something ragged about him, a desperate look in his eyes. He's up to something."

I shrug. "He wants us to forgive him."

She shakes her head, watching as Matt playfully tackles Pete to the ground, Pete's ungoverned laughter ringing loudly across the yard. "It can't be that simple. He's got something up his sleeve. He wants something else."

"How do you know that?"

"Because with Norm, there's always something else," she sighs. "Peter!"

"Yes, Mom."

"You're wagging your tongue again."

"Sorry, Mom."

"You're a boy, not a dog."

"I'm not a boy—I'm a man."

She nods, a fond smile tugging at the corners of her mouth. "I stand corrected."

Pete laughs and tosses me the ball, drawing me back into his and Matt's game of catch. "Throw a pop fly," he says.

Norm steps out onto the porch, surveying the scene with unconcealed glee. "So," he says. "Let's go see a man about a car." He's so goddamn proud of himself, so transparent in his glee and determined to view this quotidian tableau as a personal triumph, and only a great measure of restraint stops me from trying to split his face open with a well-aimed hardball.

Satch's family owns the hardware store, and one would have hoped that a local merchant would have a greater sense of civic responsibility than to sell a car to Pete. In my memory, Satch is tall and beefy, with unruly dark hair and a threatening frown. In reality, the man finishing his cigarette underneath the store's green awning is balding and dull faced and a good heel shy of six feet, but the hairy arms protruding from the rolled sleeves of his flannel shirt are corded with a telling topography of vein and sinew, and his Semper Fi tattoo pretty much nullifies whatever threat we may have imagined Matt's scrawny, overly inked arms suggested. His remaining hair is crew-cut close, emphasizing his anvil of a head, his roughly hewn cheekbones suggesting that it would hurt just as much to hit him as to be hit by him.

"Hey, Satch," I say.

"Zack, how are you," he says, shaking my hand. "Long time." His tone seems to indicate he's been expecting me. "Listen," he says, eyeing Matt and Norm leaning against the car in question, which Norm has parked illegally at the bus stop in front of the store. "Pete's a good kid. Not for nothing, I even make a point to buy my shoes from him. I had the 'for sale' sign in that car for two weeks, and every day he would walk by and ask me to sell it to him, and I would laugh him off. But one day he comes in here with a check already made out to me, and he's dead serious. Tells me he's going to get his driver's license. I mean, the kid can work in the shoe store, so why not a driver's license, right? What do I know? Not for nothing, but I made sure he understood there would be no refunds."

I hate people who start sentences with "not for nothing." What does that actually mean, anyway?

"I hear you," I say agreeably. "That's why I made a point of coming up in person to speak with you. Pete speaks very highly of you. He's very bright, in his own way, and I understand that he might have convinced you that a driver's license was a possibility for him. But it isn't, and he has absolutely no use for the car, so what we'd like to do is just give it back and chalk it up to a friendly misunderstanding."

Satch appears to be lost in thought for a moment, mulling over the situation. "If you want me to try to sell it for him, I guess I could help him out like that," he says.

"We didn't come here to ask you to sell it," I say. "We came here to return a car that should never have been sold to him in the first place."

"I'm sorry," he says with a frown. "I made the terms very clear to Pete, and I can't just take it back."

"Not for nothing, Satch," Matt chimes in sarcastically. "But we're not here to ask. The car is already back. Now we want Pete's money."

"Shut up, Matt," I say, spinning quickly on him. "We're going to work this out." I turn back to Satch with a conciliatory grin. This is all a negotiation, and if there's one thing I can do, it's negotiate from the middle. "Now, Satch, I understand that the car has been off the market for two days, and that it's possible you've missed some other selling opportunities. So how about we knock fifty bucks off the top for your trouble. I think that's a pretty fair compromise, no?"

A small grin appears and then fades on Satch's face. He

sees the game I've started and is ready to play. "I'll take it back for five hundred," he says, nodding.

"Fuck that," Matt says.

"Nine hundred," I say.

"Five-fifty."

"You had no business selling that car to him in the first place," I say. "Eight-fifty, and that's my final offer."

"Six hundred," Satch says. "Who the hell gives a retard a checking account anyway?"

"That's it!" Norm yells, stepping forward, eyeballing Satch with disgust. "I can't listen to this anymore. It's bad enough that you took advantage of a mentally impaired man. But I'm not going to sit here and let you disparage him on top of that. You not only owe us a thousand bucks, you owe us an apology. Now, I'll live without the apology, considering the source, but you damn well better believe that I'm not leaving here without that money. So we can do this quick, or we can drag it out. I've got nowhere I need to be."

Satch makes a show of walking right up to Norm to stand in his face. "And who the fuck are you?"

"I'm Pete's father," Norm says. "And I know your father, George. I helped him board up that window right there when the store was vandalized in the seventies. I'm sure he would agree with me that this is something that needs to be undone."

"Well, Pete's father," Satch says. "George is my grandfather, not my father, and you could go visit him in the nursing home to discuss it with him, except that he might not have time, what with his busy schedule of shitting his pants and asking what his name is."

"I'm sorry to hear that," Norm says respectfully. Then he steps right into Satch's face, his belly brushing up against the younger man's belt, and stares unwaveringly into his eyes. "Now,

I'm through talking about this, so please, would you just give me my son's money."

"Jesus Christ," Satch says, taking a step back. "What are you, getting hard on my leg?" And sure enough, there it is, the unmistakable protuberance in Norm's pants. "You crazy faggot!"

"That's right," Norm shouts, eyes suddenly bulging, teeth bared. "I'm a crazy faggot. I get off on this shit. And there's nothing I like better than ass-fucking jarheads, so you'd better get me that goddamn money now."

"You sick fuck!" Satch says, roughly shoving Norm, who loses his balance and falls on his ass.

"Don't you touch him!" Matt howls, and launches himself onto Satch's back, throwing his arms around his neck, and the situation has officially gone to hell. Matt gets off two or three glancing blows to the side of Satch's head before the larger man lurches back sharply, ramming Matt's head into the brick face of the storefront. Then he grabs behind him for Matt's head, but comes away grasping only the Elton John wig as Matt falls to the floor. "What the fuck?" Satch says, staring in abject horror at the wig and then at Matt's bald head. The distraction provides me with a momentary opening for a football kick, which, though poorly executed, nevertheless connects solidly with the underside of Satch's crotch. Satch spins around to face me, but then sinks to his knees in pain, and a second kick to the chest puts him on the ground. And then I'm on top of him, holding his shirt with one hand and pounding his face with the other. And the thing of it is, I can't seem to stop, even after I feel his nose break on the third or fourth punch, even as I taste the copper salt of his blood flying into my mouth, which is open in an endless, primitive scream, even as the bones in my hand feel like they're being shattered against his skull and his arms stop coming up in defense. Because somewhere beneath the pain and horror of it all, it feels good, a golden release, the first, greedy lungful of air after emerging desperately from dark, watery depths, and it doesn't stop feeling like that, even after Matt and Norm pull me off, even as I'm vomiting onto the sidewalk, even as the police show up, sirens blaring, and lead us all, cuffed and panting, to the backseats of the waiting squad cars.

twenty-four twenty-four twenty-four twenty-four
twenty-four twenty-four twenty-four twenty-four
twenty-four twenty-four twenty-four twenty-four
twenty-four **twenty-four** twenty-four twenty-four
twenty-four twenty-four twenty-four twenty-four

twenty-four

Mom and Pete come to pick us up from the precinct in her Honda Civic, and I don't know if it's coincidence or the ghost of an old habit, but Norm gets into the front seat, while Matt and I join Pete in the back. And there we are, the family King, on a typical outing, except that the ice packs aren't for a picnic of luncheon meats and potato salad, but for my throbbing, swollen fist and the purple lump on the side of Matt's head. A few hours earlier I watched transfixed as a paramedic excavated a fragment of tooth that was buried in the flesh between two of my bloody knuckles, before closing the wound with three stitches and a Band-Aid. Matt's having a hell of a time keeping on the Elton John wig while icing a contusion the size of a golf ball under it, but the good news is, all charges have been dropped.

Norm, in typical fashion, jocularly introduced himself to our arresting officer, Jim Sheehan, from the backseat of the squad car as if they were sharing a cab, and in doing so learned that he used to carpool with the officer's father years ago when he still lived in Riverdale. It turned out that Mr. Sheehan senior had passed away in the last year, and Norm's fond memories of the man seemed to move his son. After hearing Norm's version of the events in question, Sheehan left us in an interrogation room and went to have a word with Satch, who was being treated at a nearby emergency room. Two hours later, Sheehan returned, having successfully brokered a compromise wherein Satch would agree not to press charges if we would agree to keep the Mustang and be done with him. I got the feeling, from the way Officer Sheehan explained it, that he'd leaned a bit on Satch in pressing our case. "Not for nothing," he said to Norm as we left the station, "but he was a real son of a bitch to sell your son that car. He deserves more of a beating than he got."

So there we sit, a fractured family temporarily fused in the confines of Lela's Honda with no idea how to be mended, what shape it is we're supposed to take, or whether we even want to try. An awkward silence envelops us, so Lela turns on the radio and Pete sings along to Dave Matthews with reckless abandon. I direct my mother back to Johnson Avenue, where I parked Jed's car. We all stand around for a moment, unsure of who will go with whom and who belongs to whom. Finally, Norm suggests we all go out to dinner, but that's more than I can bear right now; my innards are still trembling as my mind replays my earlier violence in a continuous, unedited loop. I say I have to get back to the city, and Matt's got a gig, so Norm decides he'll follow Lela and Pete home in the Mustang and have dinner with them. First, though, he thanks Matt and me for "having my back" in the altercation with Satch. "What a team!" he declares, swelling with macho pride. "The Fighting Kings!"

That's us. The Fighting Kings. What we lack in brawn we make up for in bizarre diversion, the strategically placed erection here, the surprise bald head there, and while your focus is shattered by the freak show that we are, we'll use the opportunity to bash your head in. Norm revels in our superficial wounds, somehow forgetting the fact that we were fighting for Pete and not for him and that we altogether failed in our mission to get our brother's money back. As always, Norm is judging success solely on the level of drama generated, rather than the actual result. I guess I really shouldn't expect anything more from someone for whom the traveling has always been famously better than the arrival.

Matt and I stand on the curb, licking our wounds as we watch our parents drive away, a view that would have been inconceivable as recently as this morning, even. Norm showed up only a few days ago with plans for instant rapprochement that bordered on delusional, and yet here he is, effortlessly enmeshed in the family dynamic as if he's never left. *Can it really be that simple?* I wonder. Can you just blow past the hurts and defenses of people, the transgressions of your past, and just steamroll your way into a new situation, one that works better for you? There's something appealing in the idea, something that makes me stop and consider my own pathetic situation. Maybe a little delusional bullheadedness is what's called for here. Yesterday I wouldn't have thought myself capable of it, but today feels different. Today I'm a guy who fights in the streets, who rides cuffed in police cars, who has to have teeth removed from his knuckles by paramedics.

For now, though, I can't stop shaking.

"Listen," I say to Matt, who has pulled off the Elton John wig and is gingerly rubbing his bruised temple. "Why don't you take the car back to the city? There's something I need to do."

"Here?" Matt says incredulously.

"I want to look in on Tamara and Sophie."

He takes the car keys from me and presses a button. Lights flash and locks click as the Lexus snaps to attention. "How's she doing?" he says.

"Who?"

"Who are we talking about?"

"She's doing fine," I say.

He gives me a funny look imbued with understanding. "And how are you doing?"

"I'll live," I say, shaking my sore fist.

"That's not what I meant."

I meet his gaze, allowing with my eyes what I can't seem to say out loud. "I know," I say.

"When's Hope due back?"

"Tomorrow afternoon."

"Oh." His eyes are open and sympathetic, inviting me to bare my soul, and it would be so good to say something out loud, to make everything a little more real, a little more possible, but it's just not happening.

"Can I get a lift?" I say instead.

He holds my look for a moment and then shrugs. "Sure thing."

Matt drives the Lexus much too fast for my taste, accelerating on the straightaways, taking the corners at high speed. "Some day, huh?" I say, to fill the vacuum of my unspoken confession as we pull up to Tamara's house. He looks curiously up the walk as I step out of the car, then nods, offering me a rare full-blown little-brother smile as he throws the car into drive. "It's not over yet," he says before tearing away from the curb and disappearing into the gathering twilight.

twenty-five

"I have the same dream at least once a week," Tamara says. "I walk into the bathroom in the middle of the night and realize that I forgot to take Sophie out of the bath. When I turn on the light, there she is, lying faceup under the water. She's been there for hours, and I yank her out and try to wake her up, but the whole time I'm shaking her and giving her mouth-to-mouth, she's cold and much too heavy, like she's waterlogged, and I already know she's dead, and that it's my fault."

We're sitting on the blue tiled floor of the bathroom while Sophie splashes around in the tub. Tamara has my wrecked hand on her lap and is holding a Ziploc sandwich bag of ice on it. Next to us, Sophie splashes happily in the bathtub, her light hair so much darker plastered to her wet scalp, her chubby cheeks glistening as she sings to herself. "Winnie the Pooh, Winnie the Pooh, willy nilly silly ole bear."

"And the thing of it is," Tamara continues, "no matter how many times I have the dream, I'm always shocked and horrified, and this little part of me, the part that's conscious of the dream, wonders how the hell I could have let it happen again, when I already know the dream." She looks at me with a self-deprecating smile even as her eyes grow misty at the thought. "Even in my dreams I'm a bad mother."

"Those dreams represent your fear of being a bad mother," I say. "And bad mothers aren't afraid of being bad mothers. So you see, it actually proves that you're a good mother."

Tamara smiles warmly at me. "Where would I be without you, Zack?"

"I honestly don't know," I say, but I'm thinking, *Happily married to a living husband?* Because without me, maybe Rael never would have gone to Atlantic City, or maybe if I'd said no he would have prevailed upon Jed, who would have driven the Lexus, or a million other ever-so-slightly divergent scenarios that would have had nothing in common other than they didn't end in a fatal car wreck. Tamara seems to read my thoughts, and looks away sadly for a moment to leave me with them.

There's nothing cleaner than a two-year-old in the bathtub. Sophie sits up on her knees, pulling herself up to peer over the edge of the tub at my hand and, in doing so, sends a mild spray of water cascading onto the floor, getting Tamara's shorts wet. "Zap have a boo-boo?" she says.

"Yes," Tamara says. "Zap has a big boo-boo."

"I kiss it."

I hate the thought of my ragged hand, now deformed with purple swelling and caked with dried blood around the stitches, coming into contact with Sophie's perfect pink, embryonic mouth, but Tamara's grin urges me on, so I extend my hand, angling it to keep the most ravaged sections away from her. Sophie takes my hand in both of her little wet ones, and peers intently at the damage. "Oh," she says with admiration. "Zap have big boo-boo." I'm sitting on the wet floor, knee to knee with Tamara, and when Sophie leans over and starts purposefully kissing my hand, it's all I can do to keep from bursting into tears. There's a wholeness here, a perfection, in Tamara's face and posture, in Sophie's dimpled flesh and innocent eyes. Their entire universe is contained in this little bathroom, and I want more than anything to join it, to be a part of the uncomplicated solitude of their life here. I can love Tamara and raise Sophie with her, move in with them and leave my old, middling life behind. At this moment, it seems so eminently possible, so within my grasp, and I feel like if I could just stay here indefinitely and never leave, everything else would sort itself out.

"Zack?"

Tamara is looking concernedly at me, and I realize that my face might be revealing more than I thought. I attempt a smile that I know comes out looking like an attempted smile, and retrieve my hand from Sophie. I lean back against the wall, and into Tamara, who wraps her arm around me. "I'm having a rough day," I say.

"Mommy kiss it," Sophie says.

Tamara smiles as she lifts my hand to her mouth. "There," she whispers, pressing her lips against my knuckles. "All better."

Sophie stands in the crib in the corner of her blue room, directing me in all the proper protocols for putting her to bed. When Tamara was pregnant, she didn't want to know if it was a boy or a girl. She was very superstitious about exposing the baby to the evil eye of fate. She adamantly refused to shop for supplies or to outfit the nursery until the baby had been safely delivered, feeling that any premature acknowledgment was opening the door to certain doom. But Rael couldn't be contained. The sonogram seemed to indicate a boy, and so Rael, in typical fashion, had the bedroom carpeted in a deep blue, with matching shades and baseball-themed crib bumpers. When Sophie was born, Tamara shrugged and said it served him right, hoping that his errant decorating would be appeasement enough to the evil eye. Consequently, Sophie's bedroom is missing the softer, pink hues of a little girl's room, which Tamara has ameliorated with pastel crib linens and quilted balloons on the walls.

"Sippy cup," Sophie demands, sticking her hand out. I hand her the cup, and she takes a pro forma drink before placing it carefully against the bumper of her crib. "My peppy," she says, and I hand her the pacifier, which she pops into her mouth before dropping easily onto her pillow. "Pooh banket." I pull the Winnie-the-Pooh quilt over her and tuck her into it. She rolls onto her side, her tiny, plump arm stretched out in a proprietary fashion across her pillow. "Zap rub my back?" she says. I rub concentric circles on the back of her terry pajamas and she closes her eyes. Sophie's face in repose is a study in circles; her round cheek, her closed eye, her puckered mouth. Effortless, rounded perfection, unmarred by a single worry or impure thought. Looking down at her, I can feel the violence in my belly start to abate, and I'm overwhelmed by a rush of love that causes me to brush her cheek softly with my fingers. "I love you, kiddo," I say softly. Her breathing has changed already, slowing down as she drifts into warm, liquid sleep. I get down on my knees to listen to her breathe, and I can feel my own breath catch in my throat as the surprised tears well up in my eyes, the overflow running down my cheeks and landing in little dark spots on the blue carpet. "What am I going to do?" I whisper to her in the dim silence of the bedroom. I watch her sleep through the vertical slats of the crib, like a prisoner staring through a tiny cell window for his only glimpse of the sun. She's the only perfect thing in my life, and she's not even mine.

Tamara calls over a neighbor's kid to babysit so she can drive me home. I sit in the passenger seat, watching the animated shadows from passing highway lights play across the delicate features of her face.

"What?" she says, self-consciously running her fingers through her hair.

"What?"

"What are you looking at?"

If I could tell her the truth, I would say I'm looking for flaws. Because that's what you do when you're in love with someone you don't want to be in love with. You look for imperfections in their skin, oddities in their features. You picture how they will age, where time will tarnish them. You try to catch them at harsh angles, discern some measure of awkwardness where their limbs connect to their trunks. You search for these deficiencies with an air of desperation, ready to lay claim to whatever you find, to inflate it grotesquely in your mind, and in doing so set yourself free.

I would say that I'm paralyzed, that I see things I can't reach for, have itches I can't scratch. And then there are the parts of me that I can't feel anymore at all. That my days are filled with a quiet dread that has as much to do with her, or at least the potential of her, as it does with that foreign mass trespassing in my bladder. That I'm so in love with her that I can't breathe, and that it's become the only color in my universe, a deep blood-red, rendering everything and everyone else in black-and-white, and that I don't want to live in black-and-white, but I'm terrified that it's where I'll end up anyway.

I would tell her that I love her from the core of my being, that she answers yearnings in me I never knew I had.

I would insist that none of this can be trusted. Because she's a mess and I'm a mess and she's alone and shaken and I might be sick, and after all she's been through, how could I do that to her, and there are so many ways for this to be a disaster, for it to be all wrong and make no sense. That it may be nothing more than a colossal accident of convenience and transference, a subtle transposition of fears and wants, the random synthesis of a savior complex and desperate grief, wrapped up in loneliness and tied with a thick red bow of unmitigated lust.

And I would tell her that even though it can't be trusted, I do anyway.

I want to tell her. Because she already knows. If she had any doubts, that insane kiss yesterday should have put them to bed. So if she knows, why the hell can't I say it? Probably, I think, because raw acknowledgment would compel us to address it, and doing so would hurl us headlong back into our separate realities. I can't be hers, and even if I could, she's not ready to be mine, and what if she was and I went ahead and got married anyway, or I could be hers and she wasn't up for it. Somehow, discussing it would turn it into a promise, broken before it was even made, and after a disappointment like that we could never go back to the sweet, untouchable love that now courses through our collective veins.

So I say nothing. And she takes her hand off the gearshift and places it on my arm, just like that, and we ride the rest of the way in a complex but uncomplicated silence, the atmosphere in her Volvo thick with forbidden thoughts. She double-parks in front of the brownstone and we sit together for a moment, looking out our respective windows at the night.

"I'm scared," I tell her.

"It's going to be okay," she says.

"Not just about the biopsy."

"What, then?"

I look straight into her lily pad eyes. "Everything."

She looks right back at me and smiles. "Everything will be okay too."

"How do you know?"

"It has no choice," she says.

"Sometimes it feels like I can't even breathe," I say.

"I get that too."

"What do you do?"

"I call you," she says. "You're my oxygen."

When I get out of the car, she climbs out too, to give me one of our borderline illegal hugs in the xenon glow of the Volvo's low beams. The cold has developed an edge, winter taking an early first bite out of autumn, and I shiver involuntarily in Tamara's embrace. "You're mine," I say.

She looks up at me, confused. "What?"

"Oxygen."

"Oh."

She kisses my cheek. We stand there, foreheads pressed together, looking at each other with weary smiles. Her lips float tantalizing inches away from mine, but I know it would be a mistake. After a moment, she kisses my jaw and climbs back into her car, and I wonder if she was waiting for me to kiss her. "Call me tomorrow," she says. I tell her I will and step back and watch her drive off. When I turn around to walk up the brownstone stairs, I'm startled to find Jed, standing bare chested in the living room window, staring down at me in dark, angry judgment.

"Was that Tamara?" he asks me when I come through the door. He's back on the couch, watching *CSI,* looking vexed.

"She gave me a ride," I say.

"That was nice of her."

"What's with you?" I say.

"Nothing."

"She just gave me a lift home."

He raises his hand to silence me, his eyes resolutely glued to the screen. "Not my business, man," he says.

twenty-six

by ten thirty Friday morning, I'm bouncing off the walls. I'm supposed to hear from Dr. Sanderson today with my biopsy results. So why the hell hasn't he called? If it were good news, I would think he'd have called already, only too happy to release me from the purgatory of my suspense. Bad news, though, he might wait to tell me, wait until he had a chunk of free time so as to answer my questions and discuss treatment. No one likes to deliver bad news. Maybe over the years he's developed a routine wherein he makes all his happy calls immediately and leaves the tough ones for the end of the day, after he's seen all his patients. Only then does he plop down into the rich leather chair behind his mahogany desk, take a measured shot from the bottle of single malt discreetly stored in a file drawer to bolster his resolve, and begin making the bad calls. He's a middleman too, all that stands between the lab results and the patient, and even though it's not his fault, it's still his problem. We're always quick to make the good calls, to tell a client his goods have shipped ahead of schedule, or that we were able to work out a production issue. But when it comes to bad news, we'll procrastinate as long as possible and then hope like hell to get their voice mail. I am Sanderson's Craig Hodges, my cancerous cells the wrong-colored swooshes, and even though it's not his fault, he still knows it won't be a pleasant conversation.

Fuck. I have cancer. I know it.

I've already dialed the doctor's office a half dozen times, only to hang up before the first ring. I am terrified of upsetting some delicate cosmic balance, as if the act of calling itself might somehow influence the outcome. No. The thing to do is to wait here, all Zen-like, remain calm, and wait for the call to come. But my sweaty back, my clammy hands, and my shaking legs are the antithesis of Zen, so I get out of bed and head for the shower. Under the insulating spray, I run the scenarios, scripting conversations with Hope and Tamara in which I reveal my illness to them. Hope cries and hugs me, and then gets on the phone with her family, pausing for a brief, heartfelt cry with her mother before getting down to business, insisting that her father locate the top specialists in the field and use his connections to get us seen immediately, her chin bravely set as she takes charge. Tamara fights back tears and then throws herself into my arms, releasing all of her pent-up passion in an endless kiss, and then wordlessly leads me to her bedroom with no greater agenda than to consummate our unspoken emotions in the face of my impending life-and-death struggle. And then, only after an hour or two of sweetly urgent lovemaking, does she let the tears come, burying her face in my chest as we lie hopelessly entangled in a damp, naked embrace.

And the thought of it arouses me in a way that no subsequent thoughts can diminish, and what the hell, I do have to kill time, right? *Either way,* I say to myself as I step out of the shower a few minutes later, *you are one sick fuck.*

At eleven thirty, I cave and call the doctor's office from the kitchen. Jed and Norm are in the living room, watching CNN. "Hello," I say pleasantly to the receptionist, as if her goodwill might help my case. "Can I speak with Dr. Sanderson?"

"Who is this calling, please?" She speaks in a deep voice with a Russian accent, her words formed with the careful precision of a neophyte.

"This is Zachary King. I was in earlier this week for a cystoscopy."

"The doctor is not available now," she says.

"Can you tell me when he will be?"

"Monday."

"Monday?" I say. "I'm supposed to speak to him today."

"He is not in today."

"Well, is he at the hospital or something? Can we page him?"

"The doctor is off for the weekend," she says. "Dr. Post is on call. Would you like I should page Dr. Post?"

I can feel the seeds of panic germinating in my belly. "Listen," I say. "What's your name?"

The receptionist is taken aback. "Irina," she says.

"Irina," I say. "The results of my biopsy are supposed to be in today. I don't know if I was supposed to call him or he was supposed to call me, but I'm supposed to hear today. Will those results be sent to Dr. Post?"

"No," Irina says. "They come here."

"Do you know if they've come in yet?"

"Only the doctor opens the lab results."

"Which is why I would really appreciate it if you would page Dr. Sanderson."

"He has no pager," she says. "He is not on call this weekend."

"Surely, though, you must know how to get in touch with him."

"He is out until Monday," she says firmly.

"Let me be clear on this," I say. "You're telling me that I have to sit here all weekend and wonder if I have cancer because you won't make a simple phone call?"

"The doctor will call you the moment he has your test results."

"But the test results are there," I practically shout at her. "Someone just needs to call the lab, or open the envelope, or something."

"I'm sorry, Mr. King. There is nothing I can do."

I bang the phone down and let out a frustrated scream. "Zack?" Norm calls from the living room. "You okay?"

I join him and Jed on the couch and tell them what's going on. "That's bullshit," Norm says, instantly getting to his feet. "Let's go."

"Where?" I say.

"To the doctor's office."

"What for?"

"I'm much more persuasive in person," Norm says, tucking in his shirt.

"What are you going to do?"

"What I always do," he says. "Kick ass and take names."

I open my mouth to object, only to realize that I have no objection to offer. Norm's blind obstinacy has proven to be highly effective over the last few days, and I can't really see a downside to harnessing that energy to work on my behalf. I can sit back and let him take care of things. I've heard stories where fathers actually do that for their sons as a matter of course.

We're almost at the door when we hear the television go off. I turn around to find Jed climbing off the couch. He shrugs self-consciously, then grins at me, last night's awkward encounter forgotten for the time being. "Just give me a minute to get dressed," he says.

The three of us walk into the grim, leaden silence indigenous to waiting rooms, not one silence but a collection of separate silences, the patients there to see other doctors in the practice peering discreetly over their *Newsweek*s and *People*s to charily mark our arrival before retreating back into their contrived oblivion. Irina turns out to be a large, middle-aged woman with sad Slavic eyes, a bearded mole on her leathery cheek, and a fierce expression etched into her features, maybe from years of squinting into the stinging wind of bitter Soviet winters. But nothing in Irina's considerable experience has prepared her for the likes of Norm, who shatters the quiet of the reception area like a boulder dropped into a pond, spouting nonsensical legal jargon with a convincing ferocity.

"The doctor is off until Monday," Irina tells him, raising her unibrow menacingly. Her desk is festooned with photos and crayon tracings of little hands from grandchildren who are probably scared to death of her.

"Listen to me carefully," he says, leaning over the large desk to get in her face. "If you can't get Dr. Sanderson on the phone in the next five minutes, there will be severe legal ramifications. Do you want to be responsible for that?"

"Move back from the desk, please," Irina says, standing up irately.

Norm looks her right in the eye and lowers his voice. "Your personal space is not what's important right now. Dr. Sanderson's weekend is not what's important right now. You see this man over here?" He points to me, and I nod a sheepish greeting, self-conscious about my role in what is certain to escalate into another Norm-produced freak show. "This man hasn't slept in a week because he's waiting for test results, results that he was promised today. If he has to spend one more night than necessary under this severe emotional distress because Dr. Sanderson dropped the ball, we will consider it to be gross negligence on the part of this office. Do you understand where I'm going with this?"

"This is not for me!" Irina hisses back to him. "I cannot help you."

"Then pick up the phone and call someone who can," Norm says sternly.

"You must stop making this disturbance!"

"Sweetheart, this is nothing," Norm says in grave, confidential tones. "I'm just getting warmed up."

"I cannot to reach him," Irina insists agitatedly.

In the hallway behind the reception desk, a door opens and Camille, the PA who handled me on my last visit, emerges from one of the examination rooms. She peers out to see the cause of the ruckus and then, seeing Norm and Irina locked in battle, frowns slightly before heading back down the hall. "Hello," says Jed quietly. "Who's that?"

"It's the PA," I tell him.

"She's a cutie."

"Go for it," I say sarcastically.

"Do you remember her name?"

I flash him an incredulous look. "What?" he says defensively.

"Nothing," I say. "Camille."

"Camille," he repeats. "Thanks. Now, can you create a diversion?"

I look pointedly at Norm, who has managed to yank the telephone receiver off Irina's desk and is holding it out of her reach so that she can't answer the incoming calls that are ringing on two or three different lines. She's leaning over the desk, cursing in her native tongue as she grabs desperately for the receiver, but he spins in a lazy circle, holding the phone over his head while entangling himself in the cord as the waiting patients look on in horror at the unfolding drama. "Done," I say.

In a flash, Jed disappears down the hall, leaving me to stand alone in the center of the waiting room. "Norm," I say, stepping in like a referee. "Give her back the phone."

"I'll give it back," he says, unwilling to break eye contact with the receptionist. "As soon as she tells me she's going to call the doctor."

They stare at each other for a long moment while the phone lines continue to ring, and then Irina collapses back into her chair, breathing heavily. "You are crazy, fat man," she says, shaking her head in disbelief.

"I'm just a concerned father," Norm says proudly.

A door opens behind her and a tall, bearish man in a white doctor's coat emerges, looking annoyed. "Irina, why are all the phones ringing?"

"This crazy man won't let me answer," Irina says.

The doctor fixes us with an angry stare. "What the hell is going on here?" he demands in a booming voice.

Norm holds his ground. "It's imperative that we get in touch with Dr. Sanderson immediately."

"He's off today. Irina can leave a message with his service."

"I'm afraid that won't be good enough."

"Well, it's going to have to be," the doctor says threateningly. He's an imposing man in a Paul Bunyan sort of way, thick necked and broad shouldered, with ruddy, freckled skin that glows red beneath his beard as his ire is raised.

"Can we speak privately?" Norm says, switching tacks.

"Do you have an appointment?"

"It's okay, Norm," I say, embarrassed. "Let's just leave a message and get out of here."

Norm turns around and faces the waiting patients. "My son Zack is supposed to receive the results of his biopsy today," he announces to them. "As you might imagine, this has been a very tense week for all of us." The doctor steps forward and lunges for Norm's shoulder, but Norm spins away from him and steps into the center of the room. "But his doctor took the day off, and so we'll have to spend all weekend wondering whether or not Zack might have bladder cancer. Can you imagine that? And all because no one in this office has the common decency to break protocol and make a simple phone call on our behalf."

The patients look down into their laps, chagrined at being dragged out of their waiting cocoons and into this unseemly drama. The doctor's face is now crimson, his fists clenched at his sides, and he looks ready to doff his white coat and jump Norm. For a moment, it truly appears as if the whole absurd situation is about to descend into actual violence, when Jed emerges from the inner offices.

"Forget it, Norm," he calls out from behind the reception desk. "Let's go."

"What the hell are you doing back there?" the doctor sputters, spinning violently to face Jed.

"It's okay, Doc," Jed says. "Everything's under control."

"Who are you?"

Unlike Norm, Jed is as tall as the doctor and he steps right into his face, meeting his glare with a breezy indifference. "I'm the guy who's going to make this problem go away."

The doctor backs off and we head for the door, stopping only to yank Norm along with us when he launches into what sounds like the preamble to a lengthy apology to the waiting patients. On the elevator ride down, Jed proudly shows us a piece of paper torn off a prescription pad, on which Camille has scribbled the name of the country club in Westchester where, she is quite certain, Dr. Sanderson is trying to squeeze in as many rounds of golf as possible before winter.

"The Larchmont Country Club," Norm reads. "I know the place."

"Couldn't we just call him?" I say, cringing at the thought of another incursion with Norm.

"She didn't know his cell number," Jed says.

"So what's that?"

"Oh. That's Camille's number."

"I thought it might be something important, the way she underlined it twice like that."

Jed smiles and folds the paper into his pocket. "You see the things I do for you?"

twenty-seven twenty-seven twenty-seven twenty-seven twenty-seven twenty-seven twenty-seven twenty-seven twenty-seven twenty-seven twenty-seven twenty-seven

twenty-seven

twenty-seven twenty-seven twenty-seven twenty-seven twenty-seven twenty

i fold myself into the minuscule backseat of Jed's convertible and Norm rides shotgun, which is unfortunate, because he somehow mistakes this necessary accommodation as an invitation to take Jed under his wing.

"What'd this car run you, sixty grand?" he asks.

"Norm," I say.

"What? I'm just asking. He doesn't have to answer."

"It's rude."

"Why? We're among friends."

"Sixty-three," Jed says, grinning at me in the rearview mirror.

Norm nods, affirmed. "And you haven't worked in a few years, so my guess is you have more than a few million sitting in the bank."

"I'm okay."

"Okay," Norm says. "So you're a rich, good-looking guy, in the prime of your life. You can be doing anything you want, literally anything."

Jed nods, no longer smiling.

"So why the hell are you sitting in your apartment all day watching television?"

"Norm!" I say. "Leave him alone."

"If Jed wants me to shut up, all he has to do is say shut up, Norm."

"Shut up, Norm," Jed says.

"Oh, come on!" Norm says exasperatedly. "We're men. We're supposed to speak our minds. What's with all the tiptoeing around here? You two amaze me with all this evasion and sensitivity, like a couple of uptight women. You want to know what I see?"

"No," Jed and I say in unison.

"I see two young men living in the most exciting city in the world. Your prospects are literally infinite, and yet you choose to sulk around in your million-dollar apartment, you frying your brain with television like it's heroin, and you"—he points a thumb back at me—"perfecting the art of general discontentment, too scared to take any positive steps to change anything. I've never seen a sorrier sight than the two of you. It's a goddamn waste, is what it is. You think you'll be this age forever? Let me tell you something, old age is coming faster than you think. It's a fucking locomotive, gathering speed."

"I'm regrouping," Jed says.

"You're hiding," Norm says, not unkindly. "Both of you are scared of I don't know what. Your friend died, and that's certainly tragic, but along with mourning him, you should have come to appreciate what a precious gift life is and what a crime it is to be wasting it. I mean, look at me, for Christ's sake. My family despises me, I'm a drunk, I've worked over fifteen jobs in my life, and I've got less than ten grand in the bank to show for it. If anyone should be scared to live, it's me. But I'm out there every day, suiting up and showing up, doing my best. Some days I might get somewhere and some days I might not, but I go to sleep every night knowing that tomorrow is another chance for my life to get better. And you know what? I sleep just fine. Like a fucking baby. I might need a pill to make my dick stand up, but the two of you need a pill for your souls." Norm nods, pleased with his analogy. "Yep, that's what this is. Erectile dysfunction of the soul." He opens up the glove compartment and rummages through it. "You have a pen in here? I want to write that down. That was pretty damn good. I should trademark it or something."

"Norm," I say. "You're one arrogant son of a bitch."

"It's okay," Jed says thoughtfully. "He's right."

"No," I say, overcome with a rage that materializes like a sudden storm. "Where do you get off, waltzing into people's lives and psychoanalyzing them? If you're such a wise man, why is your life such a wreck, huh?"

"It's okay, Zack," Jed says. "Leave him alone."

"Come on, Norm," I say, ignoring Jed. "How can you think you have any credibility at all? It's just amazing to me that someone who has fucked up his life as thoroughly as you feels he can give any advice at all about living."

Norm turns in his seat to face me. "Sometimes it takes a blind man to teach you how to see."

"Oh my God!" I scream into the wind. "You and these fortune cookie expressions. That doesn't even mean anything!"

"Cool it, Zack!" Jed says. On some level, it registers in me that the Lexus is picking up speed.

"It means that you can learn from my mistakes," Norm

says hotly. "The reason wisdom is meant to be imparted is because you acquire it only after it's too late to apply to yourself."

"That's pretty fucking convenient," I say. "You're sixty years old without a damn thing to show for it, but it hasn't been a thorough waste of life, because you've got your *wisdom.*"

"My life will never be a waste, Zack, thanks to my wonderful kids."

"And has it ever occurred to you that your wonderful kids are all hopelessly fucked-up because of you?"

Norm nods somberly, his hair flapping crazily in the wind. "Not all," he says mysteriously. "Not yet. That's why I'm here."

"To save us with your wisdom."

"Shut up, Zack!" Jed shouts above the engine. I peer over his shoulder and see that we're doing ninety-five on the West Side Highway.

"Slow down, Jed," I say. But instead, he accelerates and starts weaving through cars on the parkway.

"Whoa," Norm says, turning back to sit straight in his seat.

"Both of you need to shut the fuck up," Jed says grimly. He pulls past an SUV and comes within inches of rear-ending a gray BMW before swerving onto the shoulder to pass it, the warning grooves deafeningly masticating the convertible's tires. "Jed!" I scream.

"We're here to help Zack find his doctor. So leave the other stuff alone for now, okay? You're depressing the shit out of me."

"Okay," Norm says.

"Fine," I say. "Just slow down, okay?"

Jed swerves off the shoulder and back onto the highway. The speedometer needle holds steady at one hundred miles per hour as we tear through the traffic, passing cars that appear parked as we flash by them. But instead of asking him to slow down again, we just sit back and give in to the speed, melding into our seats to become one with it. We barrel up the highway like a bullet, the engine's howl drowned out by the screaming wind crashing over the windshield and battering our bodies as we cut through the atmosphere, three lost men allowing the cacophony of velocity to drown out, at least temporarily, the wounded raging of our own heads.

twenty-eight

The Larchmont Country Club's main building is a red brick Colonial mansion with high white columns that sits on Westlake Avenue, a major thoroughfare. To establish distance, there are thick, eight-foot-high hedges, and then an expansive parking lot. To maintain exclusivity, there is a guard booth and motorized gate at the foot of the driveway.

"This place is restricted," Norm says, shaking his head disgustedly. Norm is one of those Jews who only embrace their Judaism when it can be done heroically in the face of anti-Semitism. He gazes at the building suspiciously, envisioning all manner of Aryan rituals and high-level racist meetings taking place behind closed doors in plush conference rooms. "Fucking Nazis."

"How do you know?" I say.

"I know," Norm says enigmatically, his tone reflecting some

past trauma that, like his supposed alcoholism, probably bears a highly tenuous relationship with reality.

"Well, with two Jews like you, we'll never get through the front door," Jed says, pulling away from the curb. He's joking, but Norm nods somberly, as if they really might have Jew detectors in the lobby.

Restricted or not, it's easier to sneak into a country club than you might think. The key is the golf course, whose porous borders extend into the residential neighborhood, abutting the backyards of the massive Tudors and Colonials of Larchmont Estates. Jed takes the first right past the club, surveying the houses we pass, peering intently down their driveways and into their yards until he finds one that suits our purpose, and then parks the Lexus. "When I was a kid," he says, leading us authoritatively down the driveway of an impressive Dutch Colonial, white as a wedding cake, and up the stone stairs to the backyard, "we used to sneak onto the golf courses to steal the balls. Then we'd stand down the block and sell them for half price."

Behind the shrubbery of the yard is a five-foot-high chain-link fence, easily scaled, and beyond that is the open green expanse of the golf course, glowing emerald beneath the early-afternoon sun.

"You see," Norm says appreciatively. "Even as a kid, you were an entrepreneur."

"And a thief," I point out.

Norm shakes his head. "That's just a technicality. He identified a need in the marketplace, and figured out how to become the low-cost provider."

"We didn't make any money," Jed says, flipping himself easily over the fence. "We were just fucking around."

"Are you sure about this?" I say to him, hesitantly brushing the fence with my fingers. His brazen manner is making me nervous. "It's trespassing."

"You're already trespassing," he points out to me, turning to scan the golf course. "Come on. It's a victimless crime."

I give Norm a boost and Jed helps him down on the other side. Then I climb over. As I land, I feel Norm's hands on my back, unnecessarily assuring my upright landing, and it triggers a faded memory in me, something sweet and nebulous, from a time when I still thought of him as my father, and my legs go weak for a moment. "You okay?" Norm says, steadying me.

I shake my head and shrug. "Just got a little dizzy. I'm fine."

"Okay, kid."

Daddy.

We've come in at the third hole, and the fairway is empty, so we walk up the sloping hill to the next tee. It's a clear, gusty day, and we close our jackets against the chilly wind blowing in loud waves across the lawn, scattering dead, washed-out leaves in its wake. The grass, still wet from a recent watering, clings in a slippery layer to my soles, the wetness darkening the tips of my suede shoes. I exhale into my jacket, tasting the metal of my zipper, feeling cold and acutely alone, wondering what the hell I'm doing here at all. At the top, the course takes a sharp left, and from our vantage point we can see a handful of fairways. There are scattered golfers and golf carts visible now. As we head down the fairway toward them, something occurs to me. "They're all wearing white sweatshirts," I say. "And slacks."

Jed nods. "Club dress code."

Jed and I are dressed in jeans and leather jackets, and Norm's got his ridiculous red sweatshirt on. "We're going to stand out," I say.

Norm shrugs, already panting from the walk. "We would have stood out anyway."

"Just act like you belong," Jed says.

"That's going to be a bit of a stretch," I grumble.

We are now coming within range of the first foursome, two middle-aged men and their wives. "See anyone you know?" Jed says.

"I hope you'll recognize him," Norm says.

"The man stuck a tube up my dick," I say. "You never forget your first."

The golfers stop to look at us. The women are slim, coiffed, and unnaturally tanned, their discreet jewelry shimmering in the sun when they move. The men are potbellied and silver haired, with gold diver's watches and scrawny, bowed legs. Jed waves and Norm says good afternoon. They nod back in greeting and then, as we pass, hold a muted conference about us. A cell phone is produced. "And . . . we're screwed," Jed pronounces, although he doesn't seem terribly concerned. "Let's split up," he says.

"I'll go this way," Norm says, heading down the paved golf cart path that disappears behind some trees. "I'll call you if I find him."

Jed and I continue past the green of the third hole and across the lawn to the fourth tee. "Nice day," he observes exactly as if we're not about to be busted for trespassing on the grounds of an exclusive country club. It's quite a gift, I think, to be so comfortable anywhere you are, so unconcerned about the outcome. "What is it that you and Norm have that I don't?" I say. "The two of you never seem to worry about consequences."

"What sort of consequences?"

"I don't know, the consequences that come from disregarding basic social boundaries. Norm makes a scene at the doctor's office; you run into the back hall like you own the place. Now we're sneaking into a private club, and you know we're going to get caught."

"I'm still not hearing any dire consequences," Jed says.

"We could be arrested," I say.

Jed shrugs. "You got arrested yesterday, didn't you? And here you are today, consequence free."

"That was a fluke."

"Really, Zack," he says. "What's the worst that can happen? You get arrested, issued a summons, pay a fine, maybe. Either way, the sun goes down with you still sleeping in your own bed."

I nod, agreeing. "And yet, I'm nervous, and you guys are fearless."

"I'm fearless," Jed says, smiling bitterly. "That probably explains why I haven't left my apartment in almost two years."

"Hey, don't let Norm get to you."

He waves away my remark and turns to face me, scratching his chin thoughtfully. "You know what Norm and I have that you don't have?" he says. "Nothing. And like the song goes, when you ain't got nothing, you've got nothing to lose. No job, no girlfriend, no circle of friends. We're both alone, and so maybe what you consider fearlessness is actually just an expert level of loneliness."

"You're alone by choice," I say.

"It doesn't feel that way."

"And maybe I actually do need to lose something."

He looks at me and grins, nodding his head. "The grass is always greener."

We begin making our way down the next fairway, which descends away from us in a set of graduated slopes, and in the distance we can make out another group of golfers congregating on the green.

"You see him down there?" Jed says.

I cup my hand over my eyes to block out the sun and peer at the figures on the green below. They're four men, but at this distance, it's impossible to make out any details. "I don't know. Could be."

We're about to continue down the hill when we hear the rumble of an engine, and a gas-powered golf cart with a flashing yellow light emerges from behind the tree line to the rear of the green, heading up the hill in our direction. From our vantage point, we can make out the two men in their gray-and-blue uniforms, the driver watching us intently as his partner talks into the radio clipped to his shoulder.

"Uh-oh," I say.

"That was quick," Jed says.

"Should we run for it?"

Jed shakes his head. "Never make it. They're only rent-a-cops. Maybe we can bribe them."

The cart arrives and parks a few feet in front of us. The guards step out and approach us cautiously, game faces on, hands resting threateningly on the billy clubs dangling from their belts. The driver is tall and fair, with a lean, athletic build, while his partner is rotund, with a frowning, dimpled baby face. "Are you gentlemen members of the club?" asks the driver.

"Not exactly," I say.

"You're trespassing on private property," Baby-Face says. "How'd you get in here?"

"You fellows want to make some money?" Jed says, pulling out his wallet.

"Excuse me?"

Jed counts the bills in his wallet. "It'll be the easiest three hundred and sixty-three bucks you ever made."

The driver takes an angry step in Jed's direction. "I know you didn't just offer me a bribe."

"We need to find someone," Jed says, ignoring him and proffering the cash to Baby-Face. "He's golfing here now."

Below us on the green, the four golfers are still putting away, oblivious to the action developing up the hill. Even if it is Dr. Sanderson down there, the idea of approaching him under these conditions now seems iffy, at best.

Baby-Face eyes the cash and looks at his partner uncertainly, but the larger man's scowl ends the discussion before it can start. The driver pulls his radio off his shoulder and points it at Jed like a weapon. "These are your choices," he says. "You can get in the cart and be peacefully escorted off the premises, or you can resist, in which case we will radio the police and then forcibly restrain you until they come."

"Why don't we all just relax for a second," Jed says, holding out his hands in a placating manner. "Take it down a notch."

"Choice two, then," says the driver, reaching for the handcuffs on his belt.

"Holy shit!" says Baby-Face, staring up the hill behind us, causing us all to turn around. And here comes Norm, tearing red-faced down the hill toward us in his undershirt, eyes crazed, hands flailing, with two security guards running behind him. One of the guards is clutching Norm's red sweatshirt, which flaps in the wind behind him like a cavalry flag.

"Let's get him," the driver says, and the two guards step into Norm's path, bracing themselves to grab him. This is probably the perfect time for Jed and me to make a run for it, but the sight of Norm racing down the hill at high speed is mesmerizing, like a rare natural phenomenon, and we stand there transfixed as he collides with the guards like a charging bull, and the three of them go down, sliding a good fifteen feet in the wet grass before friction finally stops them just a few feet from us.

"Now, that is something you don't see every day," Jed says.

Norm is the first to his feet, looking like a swamp creature, his arms and shoulders caked with mud and wet mown grass. "Run for it!" he shouts hysterically before taking off down the hill again with all four guards in hot pursuit. "Holy shit!" I say as Jed and I belatedly run down the hill after them.

He almost makes it to the green. The four golfers on the green stand frozen in place, staring upward at the approaching melee with mouths agape, forgotten clubs limp against their legs. The guards catch up as Norm hits level ground, and it takes three of them to bring him down. As before, they slide appreciably in the wet grass, a rolling tumbleweed of arms and legs. As Jed and I come flying down the hill, I can see the billy clubs come out, pointed briefly skyward before coming down on Norm's prone, wriggling form, so there's nothing to do but launch ourselves head-on into the fray, sliding across the green with the guards, trying our best to grab at their swinging arms, slimy with grass, to divert their blows. A slippery scuffle ensues, mostly a lot of grappling on the ground, since the slick grass makes standing up a great disadvantage. At some point, dialogue is reinstated as the guards shout at us to stop resisting while we scream at them about brutality and lawsuits. Jed and I are each faced off with one guard, while two of them are standing on either side of Norm, who is on one knee between them, his breath labored, his face flushed and splattered with mud. Something seems wrong with his posture, his head lolling uncharacteristically on his shoulders, eyelids fluttering spasmodically. "Norm!" I shout to him, tearing away from my guard. "Are you okay?"

The guard makes a grab for me but then, seeing Norm, releases me. The guards back away from him, allowing me access. "Norm!" I call to him again. "Dad!"

He looks up at me, and his expression momentarily clarifies as our eyes meet. "It's okay," he gasps, his voice nothing more than a rasp of empty wind. "I just need to catch my breath." Then he grins at me, his eyes rolling up into his head, and says, "Fucking Nazis," before collapsing onto the grass.

twenty-nine twenty-nine twenty-nine twenty-nine
twenty-nine twenty-nine twenty-nine twenty-nine
twenty-nine twenty-nine twenty-nine twenty-nine
twenty-nine **twenty-nine** twenty-nine twenty-nine
twenty-nine twenty-nine twenty-nine twenty-nine

twenty-nine

They take Norm to the infirmary, where Jed and I watch as the skinny black nurse helps him pull off his undershirt so that she can apply her stethoscope. There's a long, raised scar down the center of his heaving chest, pink and cylindrical, ending just below his sternum. "You've had open-heart surgery," the nurse says.

"Eight years ago," Norm says, still concentrating on his measured breathing, which he's been doing ever since he regained consciousness as we were loading him into the golf cart. His belly is scraped up and grass stained from his fall, his skin crusted with grass and muck.

"What medications are you on?" she asks him.

"Lipitor and Toprol," he answers.

"No nitroglycerin tablets?"

"I don't get chest pains."

"You're not having any chest pains now?" she asks skeptically.

"I'm just a little winded," Norm says.

"They said you were running pretty fast," the nurse says, pointedly eyeing his naked paunch. "You don't look like someone accustomed to running."

"That's true."

"Maybe not such a good idea for someone with your medical history."

"You're making me miss my mother," Norm says with a weak grin. The nurse isn't amused.

"I think I should call you an ambulance."

"I'd rather you just called my doctor. His name is Larry Sanderson, and he's a member here. He's actually somewhere on the golf course."

"He's here today?"

"That's right."

The nurse quickly excuses herself, and as soon as she steps out of the room, Norm's face brightens and he smiles at us. "You see," he says. "There's a method to my madness."

"I don't believe it!" Jed says, shaking his head and laughing. "You faked the whole thing?"

"Always have a backup plan," Norm says.

I'm not amused. "That's not a fake scar on your chest," I said.

"No," he says, looking down at it. "That's the genuine article."

"What happened?"

"I had a heart attack. Passed out during a business lunch. Ended up having triple bypass surgery." He pulls himself off the table and pulls on his sweatshirt.

"You had open-heart surgery and you never thought of calling me," I say. "Didn't you think maybe you need your family around at a time like that?"

Norm looks at me, his expression grave. "I was dying to call you. I was terrified of dying, of never having the chance to make things right with my family again. Believe me, it's all I thought about."

"So why didn't you call?"

He looks at the floor, frowning and shaking his head. "I had no right," he says, his words thick and weighted with untold anguish. "Let me tell you, there's nothing in the world that compares to waking up in post-op with no one waiting to see that you've made it. You feel like you don't matter, like you don't even exist. I could have died that day, and no one would have missed me. The doctors were all congratulating me, and I was just wishing I'd died on the table." He clears his throat, wiping at a possible tear with the back of his mud-stained hand. "The worst day of my life was the day I came through that surgery," he says. "And that's coming from someone with more than a few bad days to choose from."

"You should have called me," I say.

"Shoulda, coulda, woulda."

"You're an asshole, Norm."

He looks up at me. "Tell me something I don't know."

Our conversation is interrupted as the door swings open and the nurse returns, leading Dr. Sanderson into the room. His presence here, after the day's misadventures, is so shockingly surreal, so out of context, that I'm rendered speechless. He looks the same, maybe a little wider in hip and thigh without the benefit of his doctor's coat. He's dressed like the other golfers, in a white club sweatshirt and brown chinos, and his expression is singularly perturbed as he takes in our mud-soiled clothing and splattered faces. "I'm sorry," he addresses Norm curtly. "Do I know you?"

"You know my son," Norm says, pointing to me.

"Hi," I say stupidly. "I'm Zachary King. I'm a patient of yours."

"I remember you," he says, the creases in his brow deepening as he struggles to assemble the facts in an order that will make sense. "What the hell is going on here?"

"I was supposed to get my biopsy results today," I say. "But you weren't there, and no one else could tell me."

His eyes widen as realization sets in. "Wait a minute. You came here to see me?"

I nod. "I just need to know."

The purple vein in Sanderson's temple throbs, and his jaw muscle flexes mechanically in his cheek as he stares at me. "This is absolutely unheard-of," he says angrily. "It's unacceptable."

He turns abruptly on his heel, but Jed has anticipated him and steps forward to block the door. "Listen," he says. "Mistakes happen. I'm sure you would never consciously leave someone to sweat out biopsy results for an extra three days if he didn't have to. I know you're upset, but there are larger issues here, don't you think?" He pulls his cell phone off his belt and extends it to the doctor. "Make the call, okay?"

Sanderson stares at Jed for a second, and then pulls out his own cell phone, walking into a corner of the room to speak in privacy. My heart pounds out a patter of distressed Morse code against my chest and the air becomes oppressively thick, like I'm inhaling syrup, as I wait for the doctor to get off the phone. I try to form an instant prayer, a single coherent message with impact, but when I think of God, I picture this book about creation and the Garden of Eden I had when I was a kid, where Adam had dark eyes and reddish hair and Eve was a brunette with cherry-red lips and these wide blue eyes that looked so naïve that even as a kid, you wanted to just shake her and tell her that any fool could see the serpent was up to no good. God was presented as a ray of tapered light beams emerging from the clouds like a special effect, but the kid I was didn't get that. Instead, I associated the picture of Adam with God, and at this very moment I realize that the image of God I've been carrying around since childhood is actually the crudely rendered drawing of Adam, complete with his fig leaf briefs, and that's who I've been praying to on those rare occasions that it's occurred to me to pray, and the implications of this case of mistaken identity are briefly staggering from a theological point of view.

Sanderson flips his phone shut and comes over to face me, his expression utterly inscrutable. He will speak in the next moment, but this one seems to be frozen, we can't get out of it, and I can see the dark pores in his nose as if I'm looking through a magnifying glass, the round follicles of his beard, the scattered razor nicks around his Adam's apple. There's time to follow each individual wrinkle in his skin and to discern the cracks just forming beneath the surface, the tentacles of a burst capillary in his left eye.

"Your biopsy was negative."

Norm throws his arms around the doctor in a bear hug, lifting him off his feet, while Jed lets out a strangled whoop and pounds my back. Inside me, doors open and close, armies advance and retreat, and as relief floods the streets, my vital organs vibrate, morphing and reorganizing, adapting to the new reality. "What a team!" Norm says exuberantly, leaving the doctor's reluctant embrace and throwing his arms around Jed and me. "Are we good or what?"

"We came, we saw, we got our asses kicked!" Jed says, laughing along with Norm.

Sanderson nods at me. "It's most likely just some aggregate blood vessels," he tells me. "If the hematuria continues, we can remove them, but it will probably just resolve itself."

"Okay," I say. "Thank you very much."

"You're welcome," he says. "Now, why don't you guys go home and get cleaned up." He offers up a small smile as he leaves, proving that even uptight pricks like him aren't immune to the pleasures of bearing good news.

The nurse procures three club sweatshirts and orders us to exchange them for our wet shirts, an act of hospitality that seems incongruous until an officer of the club steps into the room with three liability waivers for us to sign. Norm makes a show of scrupulous perusal that causes the officer to shuffle his feet nervously, but ultimately we sign the waivers and leave the club, this time through the front door.

"You see?" Jed says, throwing his arm around my neck as we walk back to the car. "No cops, no cancer. It's all good."

I smile and nod, all the while wondering why it doesn't feel that way at all.

thirty

I don't get it," Jed says to me. "You just found out you don't have cancer. So why do you seem less than thrilled?"

We're having a late celebratory lunch at Cafe Luxembourg. Norm, exhausted from the day's prior excitement, asked to be dropped off at the brownstone for a shower and a nap, instructing us to bring home a doggy bag.

"Of course I'm thrilled," I say.

"You look thrilled," Jed says sarcastically. "You haven't even called Hope to tell her the good news."

"Hope isn't aware that there's a need for good news."

His arched eyebrows are two question marks. "You never told Hope about the biopsy?"

"Nope."

Jed doodles shapes into his ketchup with the blackened

tip of a burned french fry. "So," he says, "what's up with you and Tamara?"

"Nothing," I say automatically, but Jed's uncompromising stare forces me down a new path. "Except I think I'm in love with her."

He sits back in his chair, staring down at his plate. "Are you fucking her?"

"Jesus, Jed!" I say. "It's not like that."

"What is it like, then?"

I sigh, leaning back in my chair. "It's like a big, fucking mess," I say. "I love Hope, and I know she loves me. But I could have been anyone, really. She had this checklist of requirements and I filled some and she figures I can be molded to fit the rest. We got along, we were attracted to each other, so we decided to fall in love. It's different with Tamara. We understand each other without having to explain. It's not something we decided on; it was already there all by itself, waiting for us. It's like this pure love, and it feels the way I always thought it was supposed to until I decided I was being unrealistic and gave up on it." I pause to catch my breath. "Turns out, maybe I gave up a little too soon."

"And it probably doesn't hurt that she's a little hottie," Jed says with a frown.

"I'm not going to pretend there isn't a strong physical attraction."

"Fuck, Zack. This is Rael's wife you're talking about!"

"No," I say. "It's Rael's widow."

"You're unbelievable," he says, getting angrily to his feet. "She's grieving and lonely and you're her white knight, riding in to rescue her. That's not love; it's a fucking Band-Aid. Hope can't compete with that, because she only loves you; she doesn't need you. Tamara's hurting and scared, and instead of being a friend, you're taking advantage of it because it makes you feel like a hero."

"Rael's been dead for almost two years!" I say, standing up to face him. "You don't need to keep reminding me, because I was there. I watched him die. And it's killing you that Tamara and I are moving on with our lives, because for whatever reason, you can't seem to do it. You're still hiding behind your grief, only it isn't even that anymore. It's like some sick, narcissistic tribute to your grief. Rael's dead. Get over it, and while you're at it, get over yourself."

We stare at each other for a few seconds, the air between us electrically charged. "You know what the saddest part of this conversation is?" Jed says.

"What's that?"

"It's that we're both right. But you know what? That doesn't make you any less wrong." He grabs some bills from his pocket and throws them onto the table. "Congratulations on being cancer free," he says with a nod. "If you even care." And with that, he grabs his jacket and storms out of the restaurant.

I sit back down and sip at my drink, waiting for the acid rage in my stomach to simmer down. I am cancer free, and that's great news, but what Jed would never understand is that the cancer—or, rather, the threat of it—was like a free pass to initiate drastic change. No one questions the actions of someone with cancer. It's like diplomatic immunity. While I was worried about it, I became a more daring version of myself. I told my boss to fuck off. I got into a fistfight. I kissed the girl. I'm relieved beyond measure to be healthy, but I could have used the threat of it for a little while longer. Now I'm left here wondering what my excuse will be.

thirty-one

hope returns from London with sex on her brain. She's waiting for me in her apartment in violet mesh lingerie, and throws me roughly against the door to kiss me when I step in. "Miss me?"

"You know it."

She leads me through the darkened apartment to her candlelit bedroom, where she starts kissing me again, her tongue pushing aggressively past closed lips and teeth to wrap itself around my own, her fingers tucked possessively into the waistband of my pants. "How was your trip?" I say.

"Less talking, more undressing," she says, breathing heavily as she tears open my shirt. My hands find her ass out of habit as I return her kiss, but I can feel myself not responding. She's only been gone three days, but it feels like I've been on a much longer trip, and the shock of being yanked back into her reality is disorienting. She goes down on her knees to take off my pants, her tongue on my lower belly as she pulls them down. Her fingers encircle me, coaxing me to stiffness, but even as she stands back up to kiss me, I can already feel myself softening. I may have only kissed Tamara once, but the damage has been done, because now, as I stand naked in Hope's writhing embrace, I feel like I'm cheating on both of them simultaneously. Nothing like a guilty conscience to hamstring the anatomy.

She pushes me down onto her four-poster bed and climbs on top of me, kissing me with liquid urgency, her fingers kneading and stroking me all the while, trying to resuscitate me below. "I want your cock in me," she moans into my ear. Hope has a number of sexual personas, and this one likes to talk dirty, which, I'll admit, was a turn-on when we first started dating, but now never fails to make me feel self-conscious, like we're filming an amateur porno film. "Put your cock in me," she whispers, grinding her wetness against me to no avail.

"What's wrong?" she says, momentarily breaking from character.

"Nothing," I say, trying to hide behind another kiss.

"Are you still sore down there?"

"No. I just need a little time."

But Hope will not be so easily dissuaded. Sex, to her, is another arena in which to excel, and she has worked energetically to cultivate this particular skill set, so failure is not an option. She tears into me, bringing to bear the full weight of her work ethic, sucking, licking, stroking, and pulling, and after a while she stumbles upon the right combination and the stalemate is broken. She pulls me into her, her nails digging sharply into my ass, throwing her head back to cry out as our pelvises meet. We couple fiercely, with great concentration, and it's like an athletic event, complete with grunts, sweat, and the very real risk of a groin injury. When she finally comes, her pleasured cries are tinged with the relish of sweet victory. Afterward, she lies on her back, reveling in the satisfaction of a job well done, while I lie in the jumble of my own contradictions, having compounded my crimes, a feckless spectator to the growing farce of my own life. So much for the afterglow.

Hope talks to me, about London and our engagement, about wedding halls, bridesmaids' gifts, and guest lists, and this is my Hope, beautiful, animated, and ever so slightly anal, unabashed in the unrelenting pursuit of her agenda. I listen with an impending sense of dread, peering out from behind the veil of my secret thoughts while she rambles on, oblivious to the growing distance between us. I'm terrified that despite everything, I'll still go through with it, and yet I'm equally afraid of losing her, a middleman through and through, waiting for nothing less than an act of God to move me one way or another, to unseat the incumbent inertia.

She turns over and grabs my hand, and I wince involuntarily at the pain. "Oh my God!" she says, studying the colorful damage. "What happened to you?"

"I got into a fight," I say as if it happens all the time.

"What do you mean, you got into a fight?"

And so I tell her about Pete's Mustang and our encounter with Satch, as well as our subsequent arrest and release. I get so absorbed in the telling that I almost start to include today's excitement, but then catch myself, remembering that she knows nothing of the biopsy. "You know," she says when I'm done, "I thought it was a good thing that you were spending time with your father. Now I'm not so sure."

"What are you talking about?" I say. "Norm didn't start the fight."

"I just don't think he's a good influence."

"I haven't been influenced by him in twenty years. Why would I start now?"

"Oh, please. Here or not, he's been influencing you your whole life." She sits up in the bed, pulling a sheet up in the name of modesty, a funny switch for the woman passionately demanding cock just a few minutes ago. "And you can't deny that you've been acting very strange since he got here."

"Define strange."

"Did you go to work today?"

"No."

"Okay, so that's what, three days you've skipped work for no apparent reason. And with all that free time, you couldn't be bothered to call me in London. No, wait, you did call me once, and you were stoned at the time. And now you're getting into fistfights."

"It's got nothing to do with Norm," I say defensively. "It's just been a crazy week."

She frowns and looks away. "What's going on with you, Zack?"

This is my chance. The critical moment is sitting there, ready and waiting to be seized, but somehow, lying in the wet spot with my thighs still sticky from our dried juices doesn't seem like the right time to be confessing my sins and doubts. "I may have quit my job," I say.

"What do you mean, you may have?"

"I left on Tuesday and I haven't been back. I haven't answered my cell, checked my e-mails, nothing."

"Why the hell would you do that?" she demands, the plucked tips of her eyebrows almost touching underneath her angrily furrowed brow.

"It's a shitty job."

Hope shakes her head exasperatedly. "Don't you think we should have discussed it first?"

"I wasn't under the impression I needed your permission."

Hope's eyes well up as if she's been slapped. "Oh, for God's sake!" She rolls off the bed and throws on a short satin robe. "It's bad enough that you didn't think to call me while I was away. You were obviously too busy smoking dope and getting into fights. But you made a major decision, one that affects me too, whether you like it or not, and you didn't call me to discuss it." She's in tears now, her mouth quivering as she speaks. "What could you possibly have been thinking?"

"You would have told me to stay."

"I would have helped you make a plan."

"I don't want a plan!" I shout at her, shocking us both with my vehemence. "I'm tired of having a plan. I've been planning my whole life, and it isn't working. I just want to sit back and breathe for a minute, figure out who the hell I am."

Hope stands stock-still, head cocked, aghast at my juvenile outburst. I steel myself for her response, but none is immediately forthcoming. She just nods her head slowly, wiping the tears off her face with the knuckles of her open hand. And looking into her moist eyes, it suddenly becomes clear to me that Hope gets it, that despite all the things I'm not saying, she's registered my festering ambivalence along with my inability to change course. But even though she sees it, she's not going to be the one who derails things, and she'll back down every time if that's what it takes. She understands that this will be a battle of attrition, and she has no intention of losing. "I already know who you are," she says softly. "I love who you are. I don't want to fight about this."

"Me neither," I say, feeling like an asshole.

I watch her as she walks into her bathroom to wash her face. From my vantage point I can see the smooth backs of her long legs, the soft curve of her behind peeking out from under her robe as she leans over the sink, and I can see her face in the mirror, red, wet, and resolved. She doesn't deserve this, and I feel terrible for her that I'm not working out according to plan. Up until a few weeks ago, I'd shown so much promise.

In the middle of the night, she wakes me up to make love again, and we do so wordlessly, in that ethereal state where sleep and consciousness dance. Only as we finish, and I taste the wet salt of her cheek on my tongue, do I realize that she's been crying again.

thirty-two

What are you doing?" Norm says to me in my room as I'm dressing for the engagement party.

"Hope wants me there early," I say.

He shakes his head. "I mean, why are you doing this? You don't want to marry her."

I look at him. "Of course I want to marry her."

"What about Tamara?"

"Tamara's a friend."

"That's not how you explained it to me a few days ago."

I start knotting my Burberry tie, a gift from Hope. "Forget about that," I say. "I was all messed up about the cancer thing. I wasn't thinking straight."

"Cancer or not, I think you're still messed up, and that's no way to go into a marriage."

"Now you're a marriage expert?"

"I'm an expert on failed marriages, and I can see yours coming from a mile away."

My tie knot skews to the left, and I undo it to start again. "I'm fine, Norm."

"Here, let me." He steps in front of me and starts fussing with the tie. "When I married your mother, I didn't have a doubt in the world that she was my soul mate. I went in with no reservations, not a single one."

"And we all know how that worked out."

He keeps his eyes fixed resolutely on the tie as he adjusts the knot, his forehead furrowed with concentration. "That's my point," he says. "I was as sure as I could humanly be, and still, I failed. So what do you think your chances are if you've already got serious doubts?"

"You're forgetting something."

"What's that?" he says, looking up at me.

"I'm not you."

He meets my gaze, nodding sadly. "That's right, Zack. You're not me. You're all about responsibility. You'll stay at the same cruddy job for, what is it, eight years? Because you're not like your flaky father. And you'll stay with your woman even while you know, in your gut, that maybe you'll never love her the way you could love someone else. Because you've made your commitment, and that's what matters."

"What do you want me to do, Norm?" I say, my voice shaking. "You want me to be like you, is that it, a chip off the old block? You figure if I fuck this up it will be one more thing we can have in common, like grilled cheese sandwiches? You've never lived up to a commitment in your life. You were always sure there was something better out there for you. Maybe there is something better out there, and maybe there isn't, but I'm not going to end up broke and alone when I'm sixty because I never saw the value in what I had right in front of me until it was gone."

He pulls back, stepping away from me to study my face. "You think I don't know what I've lost?" he says. "You think I don't lose it again, every day?"

I shake my head at him. "We loved you, Norm. We were your kids, your family. And you tossed us away like we were nothing. What did you think was out there that could be better than your own sons?"

I can see his face twitching, under his eyes and at the corners of his mouth, ancient hurts hurtling up to the surface, only to be batted down at the last second like insects by the sheer force of his will. Finally, with great effort he looks back at the tie and steps forward to put the finishing touches on my knot. "There," he says, stepping away from me to admire his work. "Perfect every time." He turns me to see it in the mirror. "You know what I worry about, Zack?"

"What?" I say, fingering the knot.

"I worry that trying not to become me, while certainly a worthwhile pursuit in its own right, has prevented you from actually becoming yourself."

"Well, maybe this is just who I am," I say weakly, sitting down on the bed and burying my head in my hands.

"I don't think so. There's something in you, something stronger and better than me. I think you're just scared."

"Of what?"

"Of disappointing people, like I did." He sits down on the bed beside me. "Listen, Zack, I know you think you're already committed, but you're not. You haven't taken those vows yet. If you're not sure this is the right thing for you, you need to stop it, as soon as possible. The hurt you may cause now is nothing compared to what it will be like if it happens after you're married."

I collapse back on the bed with a groan, covering my eyes. "What's wrong?" Norm says.

"I have a splitting headache."

"Why don't you take something?"

"I took some Aleve a little while ago."

"Wait a minute," he says. "Did you get them from the medicine chest in your bathroom?"

"Yeah. Why?"

Norm sighs. "Those are my Viagras."

I sit up, eyes wide. "What are you talking about?"

"The bottle was practically empty, so I figured I'd use it."

"Jesus, Norm! My party's in an hour!"

"Then you'd better find some aspirin, because if you think you've got a headache now, the Viagra's going to bury you."

"I can't walk around my party with a hard-on."

"Just don't think any sexual thoughts. The drug works in conjunction with arousal."

"But you're hard all the time when you take it."

Norm grins. "I'm just a dirty old man."

thirty-three thirty-three thirty-three thirty-three
thirty-three thirty-three thirty-three thirty-three
thirty-three thirty-three thirty-three thirty-three
thirty-three **thirty-three** thirty-three thirty-three
thirty-three thirty-three thirty-three thirty-three

The Seacords have transformed the main hall of their penthouse into a party room with a harvest motif. Rust, gold, crimson, and brown banners descend in long arcs from the chandelier to the four corners of the room, creating a tented effect. Carving stations featuring all manner of meats have been set up along the far wall behind the staircase, while lighter fare like pasta and sushi is served from behind crescent-shaped tables scattered along the perimeter of the room. A circular wet bar manned by two bartenders has been established in the center of the room, between two large potted trees with multihued leaves. Tuxedoed waiters stand ready to circulate hot appetizers on polished silver trays. On the first landing of the staircase, members of the four-man band have finished setting up their instruments, and are now hanging out in the loose manner of musicians as they fasten their ratty cummerbunds and clip-on bow ties. The grand double doors on both sides of the anteroom have been opened, allowing access to the living room and dining room respectively. As with their lesbian daughter, Hope's parents are compensating for their disapproval with an extravagant demonstration of acceptance, and into the chaos of this charade I stride, with the mother of all headaches throbbing in my temples.

"Hello, Zack," says Vivian, her lips like dry tissue paper against my cheek. "What do you think?" Her hair and makeup are done, but she's overseeing the final preparations in her bathrobe.

"It looks amazing," I say.

"The banners aren't draping the way they were meant to, but there's nothing to be done about it now, I suppose. They've already dismantled the scaffolding."

"I think they look great," I say. "And the trees are a very nice touch."

"Aren't they? They were trucked down from a nursery in Vermont."

"Where's Hope?"

"She's in her room, touching up. She asked me to send you up when you got here."

I find Hope sitting in front of her vanity, blotting her lipstick, her hair done up in a French braid to show off the graceful lines of her neck. "Hey there," she says to my reflection. "You look sharp."

"Thanks," I say, straightening my tie in the mirror. I walk up behind her and place my hands on her shoulders, studying our reflection in the mirror. There we are, the happy couple, ever after, till death do us part. The bride glowing, the groom blushing, either from excitement or from the inadvertent Viagra dose that even now renders the skin of his face hot and prickly, like a sunburn. I have somehow pulled this off, landed this gorgeous, vibrant woman, and there is a whole life out there waiting for us. There will be travel, and children, and ultimately a house of our own. We can have a room for Pete, who will be an adored uncle and who will probably come to stay for longer intervals as Lela gets older. We'll make friends in the neighborhood, become active in the school, immerse ourselves in the wonder of our growing family, and through it all I'll wake up every morning to the flawless beauty of Hope's face, go to bed at night enveloped in the soft warmth of her naked embrace. All I have to do is dismiss the delusion of a higher love with Tamara; this ephemeral fantasy triggered by nothing more than an untimely attraction and sublimated fears.

Hope meets my gaze in the mirror, her eyes questioning and kind. "You ready for this?"

I nod and lie. "You bet."

An hour later, the place is hopping. I am introduced to couple after couple of her parents' friends, and after my third drink or so, they all merge into the same couple, silver, tanned, and expensively preserved, and I stop feeling the need to impress. Norm and Lela arrive together, which is a whole ball of weird all its own, Lela glammed up in a regal black gown and borrowed jewelry, Norm looking uncharacteristically dapper in a dark suit and a water-stained tie. Pete follows behind them, looking scrubbed and spiffy in a new black suit and tie, his curly hair gelled into temporary submission.

Norm pulls Hope into a bear hug, kissing her cheek on the way in and then again as he releases her. "We finally meet," he says, grinning broadly, steadying her by holding on to her arms just above the elbows.

"I'm so glad you could come," Hope says, a little shaken, but smiling nonetheless.

"You, my dear, are positively breathtaking," he says, shaking his head in wonder, still holding on to her arms.

"Thank you," Hope says, embarrassed.

"Stunning. Absolutely stunning." He winks at her. "Just remember, if things don't work out, I'm always available." He leans in to kiss her cheek one more time. "I taught him everything he knows."

Hope laughs. "I'll keep it in mind."

"You didn't tell me he was such a flirt," Hope whispers to me, still blushing, after Norm lets go of her to meet Jack and Vivian.

"Is that what that was? I thought it was more like mauling."

"Oh, come on," she says, giving me a light shove. "He's very charming, in his own way."

"I will never understand women," I say. Hope squeezes my hand.

"This place is something else," Norm tells Jack, shaking his hand and nodding appreciatively as he surveys the apartment. "What is it, twelve thousand square feet?"

"I don't know exactly," Jack says, looking somewhere over Norm's shoulder.

"I can see where Hope gets her beauty from," Norm says, taking Vivian's hand in both of his.

"Thank you," Vivian says graciously.

"Thank *you,*" Norm says flirtatiously, raising her hand to his lips. Vivian laughs nervously and seems relieved when her hand is released.

Lela is altogether more reserved, greeting the Seacords with a stiff, rehearsed elegance. "Your house is lovely," she says.

I introduce Pete to the Seacords, who both shake his hand obsequiously, but when he launches himself at Hope for a long hug, Jack looks agitated, wondering if he'll need to call security. Pete has brought a little address book, and he asks Hope for her number, which he scribbles into it. "I'll see you later," he says to me before wandering into the crowd. We watch him approach one woman and then another, asking for their numbers and e-mail addresses.

"What's he doing?" Hope asks me.

"It's okay," I say. "It's how he deals with crowds. He collects numbers from all the women."

"Does he ever call them?" Vivian asks, prepared to be mortified.

"No. He can't read his own handwriting."

"Oh. Okay, then."

When he gets comfortable, if he follows his usual MO, he'll start asking the women to kiss him, but I don't see any reason to worry Vivian with that information.

We're interrupted by the arrival of a gaggle of Hope's girlfriends, who descend upon us in a flurry of shrieks and kisses. In the confusion, Lela slips away to keep an eye on Pete while Norm attacks the buffet. He doesn't take a plate, but simply picks pieces of food off the platters with his hand and places them into his mouth whole, working his way down the table, to the guarded consternation of the other guests. Hope frowns as she watches him, then, when she sees me watching her, shrugs and offers a wan smile.

"Charming," I say.

"In his own way," Hope says.

"I could use another drink."

"I think we both could."

I take the scenic route to the bar, stopping in the guest

lavatory to splash some water on my face, which feels hot to the touch. I realize that I didn't think to ask Norm about drinking alcohol while on Viagra. Too late now, I suppose. I get an apricot sour for Hope and another rum and Coke for myself, leaning against the bar for support. The bartender, a girl in her mid-twenties with intelligent eyes and a diamond stud in her nose, hands me the drinks with a smile. "It's your party, right?"

"And I'll cry if I want to," I say. She laughs, and I immediately envy her the presumed simplicity of her own life. She'll go home after this, to her apartment downtown, maybe to a boyfriend or maybe to a cat and a DVD, will lie back on her couch with a mug of tea and phone a girlfriend, talking lazily as they make plans for a late brunch. I want to cut out with her, find a nearby bar, and tell her my whole, sad story, see if she can help me figure things out. I'm sure she'll understand.

"Congratulations," she says, handing me the drinks.

"Thanks."

I turn around just in time to see Tamara tentatively enter the room, dressed in the little black dress she bought on our Bloomingdale's outing, her hair blow-dried straight, her face uncharacteristically made up with lipstick and blush. Standing slightly pigeon-toed in her heels, eyes casting about nervously in search of a friendly face, she looks exposed and vulnerable, and I have to forcibly restrain the impulse to charge over to her and throw my arms around her. Instead, I chug my drink—my fourth or fifth of the evening—in four quick swallows and ask the bartender for another. I watch as Hope greets Tamara, the two women smiling and speaking animatedly to each other, and suddenly I'm missing Rael so intensely that it stops me in my tracks, overwhelming me with a momentary vision of where life was headed before the accident sent it careening in a new direction. Rael is right there, walking in with Tamara, giving Hope a congratulatory kiss on the cheek before heading into the crowd to find Jed and me and hit the bar. Tamara is nothing more or less than my best friend's wife, my feelings toward Hope are pure and uncomplicated, I'm celebrating with my two best friends, and it feels like I have the universe wired, like I'm exactly where I was always meant to be. Instead, Rael's dead, Jed's pissed and probably won't even show up, and I'm staring at Tamara with a mixture of longing and dread so potent that it burns my eyes.

Then she sees me, and her face lights up with a smile, warm and knowing, as she makes her way across the room to me. Her kiss is soft and chaste on my cheek, and the familiar scent of her shampoo, slightly cooked by her blow-dryer, fills my nostrils and then, it seems, the rest of me. "Hey," she says.

"Hey."

"You look like you got some color."

I hold up the glasses. "Just a lot of drinks."

She looks at me. "You'd better pace yourself. The night's young."

I nod and look at her, wondering what the hell I'm going to say. "Thanks for coming."

"Sophie made you a card," she says, reaching into her bag and pulling out a piece of pink construction paper decorated with jagged crayon streaks. On the bottom, written in crayon, it says, *I love You Zack.*

"I didn't know Sophie could write."

"I wrote that part."

I nod and she looks away. "I love you too," I say.

Tamara laughs, like I'm joking, and starts to fold the paper. "You've got your hands full," she says. "I'll hold on to this for you."

"No," I say, putting my drinks down on the bar. "I want

it." I take the picture from her, fold it once more, and put it in my inner jacket pocket. Over Tamara's shoulder, I can see Hope watching me. "Listen," I say. "I have to go for a second. Why don't you get something to eat, and I'll find you in a few minutes, okay?"

"Don't worry about me," she says. "You've got to meet and greet. Press the flesh. I'll be fine. Is Jed around?"

"I haven't seen him yet."

"Oh, well. I'll amuse myself, then."

She wanders over to the smorgasbord, and I head back up to Hope, who takes my drink and kisses my cheek. "It was so nice of her to come," she says, her eyes following Tamara around the room. "Who's babysitting?"

"Rael's folks, I would imagine."

"She looks great, doesn't she?" Hope's feminine survival instincts, exacerbated by the overt sexiness of Tamara's dress, are in conflict with her natural generosity, and the tension adds a complex texture to her remark, which manages to extend goodwill and cloaked scorn simultaneously.

My response must be seamless, or she'll sense something. "She looks good," I say.

"I hope I can wear a dress like that after I have a baby."

It's a backhanded compliment, launched like praise but falling on the ear with a calibrated disdain.

"Dance with me," Hope says. We walk across the room and join the handful of couples dancing in the clearing right below the band, which is playing a slow, bare-bones version of "The Long and Winding Road." I can feel the eyes of the crowd on us as we sway to the music, Hope smiling grandly as her eyes dart around the room, while I cling to her, dizzy and flushed, wishing we could just disappear. As we turn, I catch a glimpse of Tamara standing in the living room doorway, drink in hand, watching us dance. Our eyes meet and she offers a bittersweet smile, lifting her drink in my direction. The milling guests crisscross between us, blocking my view, and when I can see her spot again, she's not there.

"You feel hot," Hope whispers, her cheek against mine.

"I'm okay."

"You're sweating."

The band segues into Gershwin, and no one under sixty can dance to Gershwin, so we stand there awkwardly until Jack steps over and says, "Can I cut in?"

"Be my guest," I say, but by then they've spun away from me and I'm talking to myself.

Matt arrives, dressed in leather pants, a pin-striped suit jacket, and his Elton John wig. He's standing by the vegetable table, dipping celery stalks and carrots into the hummus with the regularity of a machine, tapping his foot to the band as he surveys the scene.

"Matt."

"There he is," he says, stepping forward to give me a quick hug. His jacket carries the unmistakable whiff of marijuana. "Sorry I'm late."

"You didn't miss anything."

"Mom's here?"

"With Dad."

"Is he behaving?"

"He hasn't been asked to leave yet."

"Well, thank God for small favors," Matt says, eyeing the dance floor. "Is that Hope dancing?"

"Yep."

"Who's the guy grabbing her ass?"

"That's her father."

"Yikes," he snickers.

"So it's not just me?"

He shrugs. "What do we know about fathers, right?"

Later, the band falls silent and the singer speaks into the mike. "Ladies and gentlemen, may I have your attention, please? The father of the bride would like to offer a toast in honor of Hope and Zack."

Applause all around as Jack steps up to the makeshift bandstand, glass in hand, and the grand foyer fills as everyone surges forward from the ancillary rooms to hear what he has to say. "Where's Viv?" he asks into the microphone. A small commotion ensues as Vivian is coaxed to join him on the stairs.

"Good evening, everyone. On behalf of Viv and myself, I'd like to thank you all for coming tonight. It means a lot to us to be able to celebrate this occasion with you." His voice is calm and assured, the voice of a man accustomed to commanding the attention of large groups. "Hope," he says, turning to look at us. "It seems like only yesterday that you were this little, chubby baby, crawling around the apartment with that ratty teddy bear you took everywhere with you. You were always so precocious, such a determined little girl. I remember the first time I brought you with me to the office. . . ."

Jack tells his stories slowly, with great detail, and the crowd listens with rapt attention, laughing at all the right spots, while, beside me, Hope beams with pleasure. I'm so engrossed in his toast that I fail to see Norm slowly maneuvering his way through the crowd until he's made it to the side of the stairs and is whispering something into the bandleader's ear, and by then it's too late. Jack ends his toast, glass raised. "May you both enjoy a long and happy life together, filled with love and joy, and success in all of your endeavors." The crowd applauds as Jack sips regally from his drink, and it's at that point that Norm steps up to the bandstand, still clapping, smiling out at the crowd. Jack seems surprised, but he shakes Norm's outstretched hand and yields his position as Norm moves in front of the mike.

"Thank you, Jack," he says, addressing the crowd. "For those beautiful words, and for this beautiful celebration. You too, Vivian. You folks certainly know how to throw a party." He claps and nods to the crowd, encouraging them to join him in a round of applause, which, when it finally does come, is delayed and disjointed.

"Holy fuck," Matt says incredulously.

"What's he doing?" I hiss through my smile to Lela.

"He's being Norm," she says mutely, looking pale and resigned.

"Can you stop him?"

"When could I ever stop him?"

"Why?" Hope says, alarmed. "What's he going to do?"

"God only knows."

"But it won't end well," Matt says.

"Just keep an eye on the nearest exit," Lela advises from between clenched teeth.

"The majority of people in this room are friends of the Seacords," Norm is saying. "So I just wanted to take a minute to thank all of you, on behalf of the King family, for welcoming our Zack into your midst." He pauses to wipe the sweat off his brow with a napkin, leaving a trail of white particles stuck to his forehead. "You know," he continues, "Zack and Hope are in love, and that's wonderful. That's a little miracle right there. It's the God in your blood, the angel in your soul. But love is just the beginning. It takes so much more than that to make a marriage work. Just ask my ex-wives, God bless them." He guffaws loudly at his own joke, his laughs reverberating against the silence, while Lela looks ready to dissolve into a puddle of her own embarrassment. "Any moron can get married. Look at me. I did it a few times."

The crowd laughs uncertainly, and I wonder what a few times means. Were there others we never heard about?

"Jesus Christ," Matt says. "He's got a boner."

"Oh, shit. You're right."

"But seriously," Norm says. "Zack and Hope, I point this out only to serve as a reminder to you. I am suggesting that love isn't the destination. It's just the beginning of a long and sometimes perilous journey, and you must never forget, for even one moment, to take care of each other and this thing you've created. There will certainly be great joy along the way, but there will be hardship too, and that's why you can never take your marriage, or each other, for granted. Because the minute you do"—he grips the microphone stand for emphasis—"complacency will set in. And complacency is like a virus. It just grows and mutates until it takes over, and the next thing you know, you're a stranger in your own life, and you're living with this person you barely recognize, and when you look in the mirror, you barely recognize yourself. . . ."

His voice trails off for a moment, and the silence in the room is something more than silence; it's gravity, weighing us all down, locking us into place to witness the charred and twisted wreckage of his derailed train of thought. In the meantime, Norm suddenly becomes aware of the telltale bulge in his suit pants, and attempts to make an adjustment through his pocket, which serves only to call attention to it, and Vivian, standing on the steps in front of him, lets out an involuntary gasp as she takes in his profile. The noise seems to shake him from his stupor, and he flashes her a proud smirk before leaning back into the mike. "So, I guess, what I'm trying to say is this: Take care of each other. Treat your love like the amazing, fragile gift it is. Be protective of it. Vigilant, even. Make love often, whenever you get the urge, wherever you are. But don't forget to have plenty of sex too. They're two different things, and a good marriage should have both in good measure. Doubles our chances for grandchildren, hey, Jack?" he says, cracking himself up as he turns to Jack, who is staring intently into his empty drink glass, trying to will himself a refill. "Anyway," Norm says, wrapping it up. "You're a great kid, Zack. Your mother and I are very proud of you, and I, personally, feel blessed beyond words to have you in my life again." He chokes up at that last part, his eyes filling with tears as he nods to emphasize what he's just said. "Thank you, everybody. Have a good night."

In the ensuing, awkward applause, my mother, Matt, and I make a tight beeline for the bar.

thirty-four

I go to the bathroom, where I splash some more water on my sweaty face and stare myself down in the mirror for a good five minutes, peering into my own blank eyes for an answer that isn't there. "Just do something," I say, utterly disgusted with myself. I collapse against the wall, sliding down until I'm sitting on the floor with my head between my knees, eyes closed, waiting for the room to stop spinning.

A few minutes later, looking for a place to hide, I walk through the kitchen and duck into Jack's study, where I find Tamara perched on his desk in the dark, legs crossed, sipping at a martini and staring out the window at Central Park. She looks up, alarmed, as the light from the open doorway falls across her, but then relaxes when she sees it's only me. "Hey," she says.

"Hey."

"How are you doing?"

"I'm a little drunker than I meant to be," I say, closing the door behind me.

"I know why I'm drinking," she says. "This is the first time I've been out in almost two years, and I'm scared of everybody. What's your excuse?"

"Did you happen to catch Norm's little toast?"

"Enough said."

"Hey, I meant to call you. Turns out I don't have cancer."

"You got your biopsy back?"

"Yeah. Funny story, actually . . ."

But I won't get to tell it, because the force and speed with which she throws her arms around me knocks all the breath out of me, her tears wet against my neck as she whispers, "I knew you'd be okay."

Once, as a kid in summer camp, I broke curfew to sneak into the boathouse with Beth Wallen, where we made out in the deep blackness of the country night and held whispered conversations about everything that mattered in the hushed silence of the sleeping camp, the intimacy enhanced by the covert nature of our rendezvous, the palpable risk of discovery. Finding Tamara in the darkened study feels a little bit like that, and I hold on to her, my lips resting on her head, unwilling to let go. After a while, she leans back, resting her forehead against mine. "Okay," she says wryly, sniffling slightly, "I guess I was a little worried."

I take her head in my hands, softly wiping the tears from her cheeks with my thumbs even as I can feel my own coming, and she wipes mine away in the same manner. We stand like that for a few moments, cradling each other's head in our hands, a closed circuit of sad affection.

"What are you doing here?" I ask her after a bit.

"Thinking."

"About what?"

"About all the things we never talk about."

"What things?"

The room is dark, but I don't need light to reveal the impatient expression with which she's regarding me. She steps out of our embrace and leans against the desk. "Okay," I say, walking over and leaning against the desk beside her. "I know what you mean."

She considers me briefly, over the rim of her martini glass. "I'm sure it won't come as a shock to you if I tell you that I almost didn't come tonight."

"I can imagine."

She nods. "But you're my favorite person in the world, and I love you, and whatever other things may or may not be happening between us, the fact is that you've been my lifeline for the last two years, and there was no way I couldn't be here for you, one way or the other. You saved my life, Zack. You really did. I don't know what I would have done without you. And I want you to know that no matter what happens, I will never stop loving you for that."

I lean over and kiss her cheek. "Thanks," I say. "That means a lot to me."

"So, as long as I took the trouble to be here for you," she says, taking a dramatically deep breath, "I might as well tell you that I don't think you should marry Hope."

"What?"

She looks away from me. "If you had any idea how hard it was for me to say that, you would never ask me to repeat it."

"I'm sorry," I say. "I meant, why do you think that?"

She turns back to me, frowning uncertainly. "I've been struggling for months with whether to say something or not.

It's so hard to tell if saying something is the right thing to do, and you have to believe me, I only want to do what's right for you. If you think I'm wrong, please disregard everything, but just don't hate me for saying it. Okay? Because I don't think I could stand that."

I place my hand on hers, and it's impossible to tell where the trembling is coming from, her hand or mine. "That will never happen," I say.

"Okay," she says. "Here's the thing. I don't think you're in love with her, not all the way. If you were, I think you would seem more certain about it. More jazzed. You wouldn't hug me the way we hug, and say the things you say to me. You definitely wouldn't have kissed me the other day the way you did. I'm not saying you're in love with me. I'm just saying that whatever this thing is you feel toward me, this thing we're both too scared to mention, I don't think it could exist if you were head over heels in love with Hope. And if that's the case, if you're not head over heels in love with her, you shouldn't marry her."

I nod slowly, my chest fluttering with nervous excitement. There are many ways to respond to this, truthfully even, without getting into the thorny undergrowth of my feelings for Tamara. But it's dark, and I'm drunk at my own engagement party, and there's a potency to Tamara's directness, a hidden power lurking behind her words, and if I can match it with some directness of my own, who knows what cosmic forces might be unleashed? "So what do you think it is, this thing between us?"

"That's not what matters," she says, removing her hand from under mine. "We're not talking about me. What we're talking about here is whether you belong with Hope or not."

"I understand that," I say. "But as long as we're doing

this, let's do it completely. I need to know—do you think you might have stronger feelings for me than just friendship?"

"No way, Zack," she says, launching herself off the desk and stepping away from me. "I'm not going to let you do that to me. I'm not going to bear this responsibility for you. I've got my own problems, and besides, I need you too much to trust anything else I might feel. Either you believe, in your heart, that you belong with Hope, or you don't. I'm not a factor."

"But you are," I say miserably. "Because I love you, and I can't stop thinking about you, and it's fucking me up like you wouldn't believe. When I kissed you that day, it took every last bit of my willpower to stop. And that's how it is whenever I'm with you. I'm constantly holding myself back from letting you see how I really feel."

"Stop it," she snaps at me, and while I can't see them yet, I can hear the tears in her voice. "Just stop it. You can't say that to me."

"I'm sorry," I say. "I didn't want this. I was all set to get married and be happy. But when I'm with you, I feel like I could never be happy with anyone else. And I know it's wrong, I know you're in no position to return those feelings, and I'm certainly in no position to be having these feelings, but between you and me, that's how I really feel."

She stares at me, her eyes wide, tears streaming down her face. "I shouldn't have said anything," she says. "This was a mistake." She picks up her glass and heads for the door.

"Wait," I say. "You can't leave. Please. We're finally talking about it."

She turns around at the door. "I have to leave, Zack—don't you see that? You need to work this out for yourself, and I can't be a part of it."

"Just stay there," I plead, moving toward her in the dark. "Just wait a minute, please." I find her near the door and put my hands on her shoulders. "Please don't leave me here."

Her hands come up to rest on mine, and somehow, despite the darkness, we're able to see each other's face, and we stand there like that, looking into each other's eyes, and we're vibrating like electricity, and then she says, "Just one," and when our lips touch, hers open almost instantly, granting me entry as she steps into my embrace, pressing her body into mine like I've been molded to take her shape, and her fingers are like roots in my scalp, pressing into my head as she pulls me closer, our tongues pulling and probing with naked desperation. "I love you," I gasp, panting slightly, my lips still grazing hers.

"I know," she whispers back.

"No, I mean, I really love you."

She nods. "I know." And then we're kissing again, fiercely and recklessly, and her hand finds its way under my shirt, her fingers urgently pressing and stroking at my chest, and I've pulled her dress up above her waist to feel the hot skin of her lower back, and the Viagra has kicked in like gangbusters, but she doesn't shy away from it, pressing up against me with a low moan, her leg coming up to wrap around my thigh, her tongue like candy on my lips.

This is what happens. You're in the dark, kissing a woman you've been dying to kiss for as long as you can remember, and it feels just as you always imagined it would; her taste is exactly what you've extrapolated from your past, minimal contact. And maybe it's the ecstasy of discovery, the immense relief of the release of the hot torrent of feelings and yearnings that have been building up in you for so long, or maybe it's the booze and drugs still dancing like twin demons through your blood, but for the first time in memory you're not fearing the consequences, not thinking about the inevitable complications, and you're floating, suspended in this perfect, translucent moment where nothing else exists. So it's not surprising, really, that you don't hear the door open, don't sense your future father-in-law's arrival as he steps into the room, don't react immediately when the lights come on. After all, your eyes are closed, your universe reduced to the sweet vortex of your conjoined mouths, your diminished senses focused only on the wet sphere of her soft, open lips. And by the time you stumble back, eyes blinking in the harsh chaos of the light as, too late, you pull down your bunched-up shirt, he's already on top of you.

Jack moves fast for an older guy, barreling into me before I can get my bearings. "You scumbag!" he roars as he propels us across the floor. "I'll kill you!" We crash into his desk, then fall on top of it, Jack peppering me with glancing punches to my chest and face as papers and desk accessories scatter in our wake. The desk lamp goes over, landing without breaking, bathing the room in a skewed green glow. "Wait!" I gasp, but Jack's having none of it, his fist knocking my jaw as I speak, and now I can taste the metallic tang of blood on my tongue. "I'll kill you!" he screams again. Somewhere in the chaos, I register Tamara's panicked screams as she flees the room. Jack continues to swing away at me, but in his ardor he pays no attention to leverage, and I manage to roll onto my side, dumping him off me and onto the floor. I make a mad dash for the door, and then rush through the kitchen, stopping for a second to comb my hair with my hands and tuck in my shirt before stepping back into the main hall.

Fuck, fuck, fuck.

The party is still in full swing, and rejoining it is like stepping into a dream, all of the guests oblivious to the imminent shitstorm. Everything seems to be happening in slow motion, except for the spasms in my churning stomach as I make my way desperately through the crowd. *Fuck, fuck, fuck.* I figure I have anywhere from thirty to sixty seconds to find Hope and disappear with her, to explain things on my own terms and avoid a major public spectacle. As I make my way across the floor, I see that Matt's commandeered the band and drawn a crowd as he furiously abuses a borrowed guitar, cranking up the distortion as he leads the musicians through "Blitzkrieg Bop." *Hey! Ho! Let's go! Hey! Ho! Let's go!* The steady throbbing of the bass line pulsates up and down along my nervous system, keeping pace with my frantic heartbeat. *Fuck, fuck, fuck.* I spin around as my panic builds to a crescendo, scanning the room fruitlessly for Hope. My chest feels primed to explode like a bomb, spewing blood and tissue across the room onto the unsuspecting revelers.

And then, finally, I find her standing beside the bar, chatting breezily with a girlfriend. And I know it isn't actually happening like this, but it feels as if the crowd is parting on cue to give me a clear path to her. And as I approach, she becomes aware of me, and I can see her expression as it changes, from distraction to consternation, and then outright alarm, and I realize that I must be more of a mess than I thought. The noise of the party retreats like I've gone deaf, and all I can hear is the blood rushing in my ears as I reach out to her. And there's time to register the growing awareness of the people around me, and the horrified look in her girlfriend's eyes as she fades into the background. Hope takes a step toward me, and she really is so beautiful—even at this moment I can see that—and I feel a pang, like a hand closing around my heart, a lightning-fast preview of the pain to come. "Zack," she says, and before I can answer her, a fist hits the side of my head and I go down hard onto the bar, scattering glasses and bottles as I crumple to the floor.

"I'll kill you, you bastard!" Jack screams, sinking his knees into my stomach as he lands on top of me, knocking the wind out of me as he pummels from above. The sound has come back, but now there's nothing to hear other than the breaking glasses and Jack's incensed shouts. And then he's got a large champagne bottle in his fist, seemingly snatched from the air itself like in a cartoon, and he's wielding it by its foiled neck like a club, and I know instantly that it will crack my skull if he makes contact. I manage to free one of my pinned arms to desperately deflect his swing, and the bottle hits the floor with a heavy thud. I try to sit up, but he's got position on me, and I catch a forearm in the face as he lifts the bottle for a second swing. This time timing and momentum are on his side, and I know the bottle will hit dead center, shattering my teeth as it goes, the crazed look in his eye confirming that he will bludgeon me to death if he's able. Death by Moët & Chandon, a fitting end for the man found kissing the wrong woman at his own engagement party. Jack raises the bottle above his head and has just started his downward swing when another arm grabs his, stopping its descent. And then, impossibly, Jack is off me, thrown across the room like a laundry sack, where he collides noisily with a buffet table, sending breads and sauces flying through the air.

"Zack!" Jed says, pulling me to my feet. "You okay?"

"I didn't think you were coming," I mutter, trying to catch my breath.

"I'll bet you're glad I did, though," he says with a grin, straightening out my shirt and jacket. "Who is that guy?"

"Hope's father."

Jed stares as Hope and Vivian kneel on the floor beside Jack. "You're shitting me."

Four of the larger men in the crowd, corporate underlings of Jack's, start closing in on us in a small circle, not quite sure what's called for, but ready to go to battle if their CEO demands it, and at first we appear to be outnumbered, but then Matt pushes through the crowd, brandishing the guitar like a battering ram, the Elton John wig wildly askew on his head. "Everyone just back off!" he commands, planting himself in a defensive position in front of me, guitar poised on his shoulder like a baseball bat. "You okay, Zack?"

"I'm fine," I say.

"What the hell is wrong with you!" comes Norm's ragged, booming voice as he bursts out of the onlookers, charging at Jack with his fists raised. The men converge on Norm, grabbing his arms and hustling him roughly away from Jack as he writhes madly in their grasp, his face knotted with rage. "Don't you touch my son, you fucking animal. I'll bury you—you hear me? I'll bury you!"

Hope and Vivian help a dazed Jack to his feet and usher him gingerly toward the kitchen. "He was kissing that girl," he mutters dazedly to no one in particular. "Right in my study." Just before they disappear, Hope turns to look at me, and her eyes are like lasers, cutting through flesh and bone to pierce me at my core, her expression of bewildered devastation branding itself into my brain as it burns through my eyes. I stagger slightly, and start to fall as the room spins, but then I feel myself righted as a soft hand slips into mine, squeezing my fingers. "Okay, then," says Lela, her voice loud and authoritative. "Matt?"

"What, Mom?"

"It's time to go."

And so, with Matt leading the way, and Norm and Pete bringing up the rear, and a swath of angry destruction in our wake, the Fighting Kings make good their exit.

thirty-five thirty-five thirty-five thirty-five thirty-five
thirty-five thirty-five thirty-five thirty-five thirty-five
thirty-five thirty-five thirty-five thirty-five thirty-five
thirty-five

thirty-five

thirty-five thirty-five thirty-five
thirty-five thirty-five thirty-five thirty-five thirty-five

Something happens to me in the elevator, some final synthesis of the drinks, the Viagra, and the trauma of the last few minutes, and I leave my body to hover above us as we descend, taking in everyone else's shifting postures as their combined adrenaline dissipates in the air like smoke: Norm leaning against the back wall, red faced and disheveled, still catching his breath; Matt rubbing his neck thoughtfully; Jed tucking his shirt in—it came undone when he hurled Jack across the room—Pete humming nervously as he studies my own blank expression, worried about me; and Lela still firmly clutching my hand protectively. Her expression, an amalgam of concern and grim determination, would certainly move me to tears if I were in there to cry them.

We step out into the chilly night, and arrangements are

made, logistics confirmed, but I'm still floating, so it all happens beneath me. The sky is clear, but the glow of Manhattan makes it hard to see any stars, and I want to float higher until I can see them, but I seem limited to this lower level of flight, just a few feet above my own bowed head. Jed gives me a pat on the back and tells me he'll talk to me tomorrow, and I feel a rush of gratitude and want to hug him, but by the time I think of it, he's gone, and then I'm in the backseat of Lela's Honda with Pete and Matt, Norm riding shotgun as she pilots her way toward the Harlem River Drive. We head north toward home, exactly how we might have done a lifetime ago, before we had any concept of how far we would all drift. I lean my head against the window, the vibrations from the glass rattling my teeth, and this sensation proves to be the lone thread that pulls me back into my body, where a bone-deep exhaustion mercifully takes the bite out of what little awareness is there to begin with.

Lela takes charge when we get home, making tea for everyone as we sit, shell-shocked, in the living room, an ice pack pressed firmly to my temple, which is swollen from Jack's assault. Norm and Matt engage in the inevitable play-by-play, reconstructing the events from their separate perspectives, until, finally, Norm asks me, "What the hell happened back there?"

And so I tell them, and they nod, not terribly surprised, and somehow, talking about it makes it seem more pedestrian, less calamitous, so I find myself describing the scene in detail, my own editorialized version of my encounter with Jack. It's understood that we will not tackle the hairier issue of why, exactly, I was kissing Tamara to begin with, but keep the focus squarely on the violence, breaking it down, establishing an exact chronology, like athletes reliving a recent victory on the field. Pete sits next to me, his head on my shoulder, tired and confused, but not willing to miss out on this rare family time. And there is an undeniable warmth permeating the room as the five of us sit sipping at our teas, a tangible intimacy in which we're all reveling, and it occurs to me that it's something we've all been missing for some time now. We'll all sleep in the beds of our youth tonight, except for Norm, who refuses an offer to bunk with me, choosing instead to sleep on the sofa bed in the basement, and I intuit from the way he avoids looking at the stairs leading up that he's unwilling to get that close to the epicenter of his former life, the scene of the crime that led to our dissolution.

When we finally get up from the couches to go to sleep, Matt forgets himself, wearily pulling off the Elton John wig, and upon seeing his bald head, Lela's eyes fill with tears, and her hand goes to her mouth to stifle a sob. "Shit, Mom, I'm sorry," Matt says. "I forgot."

"It's okay," she says, wiping away her tears with the back of her wrist. "I don't even know why it makes me so sad."

"I can put it back on."

"No," she says, walking over to him and gingerly tracing the lines of his skull with her fingers. "You were my baby," she says, and then turns to look at Pete and me. "You're all my babies. And sometimes I just miss it so much, taking care of you."

"You take care of me," Pete says, alarmed by her tears.

She smiles at him. "I know, pumpkin. And you take care of me. God sent you so that I'd never feel worthless."

Being the oldest, I had my own room, while Matt and Peter shared. I don't remember it ever being a sore point. The linens on my bed are the same ones I slept in when I lived here, and it's as if Lela wanted to keep everything exactly as it was, so that it would all feel right to me in the unlikely event I ever came back. Climbing into bed, I take in the familiar scents of the house, the cone-shaped shadow on the ceiling cast by the streetlight outside, absently running the back of my hand along the textured wallpaper, which is how I used to lull myself to sleep as a kid. I nod off briefly, and then wake up with a start to find Lela sitting on the edge of the bed, the light from the hallway illuminating her in her nightgown as she gently rubs my legs through the blanket. "Mom," I say.

"Sorry," she says. "I didn't mean to wake you."

"Why aren't you sleeping?" I roll onto my back to look at her.

"I just like having you here," she says. "I can't remember the last time everyone was home, sleeping in their beds. The house feels alive again."

I nod, yawning as I stretch my arms. The evening's earlier debacle cannot penetrate the protective walls of my childhood bedroom, and I feel myself at a calming distance from the fiasco of my real life. "It's good to be here," I say.

She smiles tenderly at me, and I notice that the wrinkles around her eyes are starting to deepen, and beneath her jawline hang discreet pockets of looser flesh, the crumbling chin of an elderly woman. I feel a raw panic in my throat, a visceral sense of the inevitable mutability of everything, the wasted time and the losses to come, and I want to be a little boy again, safe in her uncomplicated embrace, with no notion of the future. "It's going to be okay, Zack—you know that, right?"

"I've got my doubts."

She nods. "Well, whatever it is that happened tonight—and God knows I don't know what it was—you have to believe it happened for a reason."

"The reason," I say, "is that I'm an idiot."

She laughs softly and leans forward to kiss my forehead. "You get some sleep, and we'll talk in the morning, okay?"

I grab her arm. "Thanks, Mom," I say. "For getting me out of there, and for bringing me here."

"You're welcome," she says softly. "That's your bed, Zack, and as far as I'm concerned, it always will be. And we are your family and you will always have us"—she grins—"no matter what kind of idiot you are."

She kisses me again, letting her lips linger on my cheek for an extra beat. "Get some sleep, baby."

But after she leaves, I roll around, unable to get comfortable. The clock radio on my dresser tells me it's past two in the morning, and even though my eyes are burning with acid fatigue, my heart pounds out a hip-hop beat, fast and insistent in my chest, my limbs pulsing with nervous energy. The first prickly hints of my incoming hangover are flitting about like insects in the front of my skull, looking for a nice, warm spot to land and dig in for the long haul. I roll out of bed and pad down the hall in my borrowed boxers and T-shirt, tiptoeing downstairs to get a drink of water. In the living room, I sip at my glass while flipping through old photo albums, from the days before Norm left. He'd been the photographer, always determined to capture our essences for posterity. Afterward, Lela was never big on pictures, possibly due to negative associations with cameras from the time she'd snapped Norm and Anna in her bed. As I look through photos of my siblings and me, a pattern emerges: Matt's always facing the camera full-on, smiling or being a ham, while I always seem to be corralling Pete, directing him to look at the camera, and thus, am never fully smiling myself. The effect is one disjointed picture after another, three boys out of sync, as if cut and pasted from separate photos altogether. The only pictures that seem composed at all are the ones with Norm in them, taken by Lela, his anchoring presence somehow fusing us, bringing us into focus together.

The stairs creak under my bare feet as I wander back upstairs to stand at the doorway to Matt and Pete's room. Matt's sleeping in his clothes, curled up in a fetal position on top of his comforter, his face less than an inch from the wall. Pete is flat on his back under the covers, snoring loudly, his mouth, even at rest, in a slight, smiling crescent. The articulated desk lamp is extended to its fullest height on the desk between them, watching over them like a sentry, the effect completed by the Elton John wig Matt's placed over it for safekeeping. On the desk is a picture of a three-year-old me holding an infant Pete, my eyes wide as I look down at him.

"What are you doing, Zack?" Pete whispers to me from his bed.

"Nothing," I say. "I can't sleep."

"You want to bunk with us?"

"Sure."

He climbs out of bed, still half-asleep, and expertly pulls out and raises the high-riser from beneath his bed, carefully arranging it so that the two beds are perfectly lined up, and throws one of his two pillows on it. "Get in," he says. There's no extra blanket in his room, but he moves to the edge of his bed to share his with me. "You're not going to marry Hope, huh?"

"It doesn't look good," I say.

"You going to marry Tamara?"

"I don't think I'm getting married anytime soon, Pete."

He lies back in his bed thoughtfully. "Women," he says. "You can't live with them, you can't live without them."

"Amen to that, buddy."

He laughs. "I like it when you sleep here."

"I know," I say. "I should do it more often."

He rolls onto his side, yawning. "I love you, Zack."

"I love you too, Pete."

I lie awake between my sleeping brothers, and I can feel the consciousness slowly bleed out of me as the soft, rhythmic sounds of their slumber lull me into a black, dreamless sleep.

thirty-six

Sunday is dead on arrival. I spend most of it slipping in and out of a sweaty, strenuous sleep, suffering through lurid, dizzying dreams in which I'm invariably running too slow from something or sliding too fast toward something, unable to stop myself. In the rare moments that I do wake up, either bolting from a nightmare or just to urinate, I'm listless and hungover, my eyes throbbing, my breath hot and rancid. It's past three in the afternoon when I finally drag myself to the shower, and only then, as lucidity claims me for the first time in almost twenty hours, do I feel the gaping hole in my belly where Hope used to be.

No one is home. I stand looking out the living room picture window, dressed in my suit pants and the T-shirt I slept in, with nowhere to go, feeling a dull resentment at my family for abandoning me like this in my hour of need, and even though I know at least some of them will be home soon, I can't face the suffocating emptiness of the house. There are no cars in the driveway, so I throw on my suit jacket and start walking. It's a bright, blustery day, warm enough in the sun, but the wind is laced with ice, and it blows right through my suit jacket, freezing me beneath my T-shirt. Still, I'm too lazy to go back to the house to rummage for an old coat. I fold my hands over my chest and turn my face into the sun, trying not to think about where it is that I know I'm headed.

Riverdale Avenue is alive with the buzz of late-afternoon traffic, drivers swerving around double-parked cars, waiting for parking spots, honking impatiently at crosswalks. The neighborhood is infamous for its dearth of parking, and Norm once tried to put together an investment group to build a parking tower, but by the time the project made it to the zoning board, he'd lost interest, moved on to the equally ill-fated possibility of a modern multiplex in the shopping center. Norm's short attention span and the municipality's elderly predisposition toward immutability had proven to be a lethal combination. The avenue is a congested hive of activity, mothers dragging children by the hand or pushing them in strollers, teenaged boys in baggy surfer pants plugged into MP3 players, young girls laughing into cell phones lit up like Christmas trees. I walk among them all like the undead, observing unseen from my timeless hell while their lives move innocently forward, crossing the street to avoid the hardware store, lest Satch catch sight of me and attempt to incite a rematch.

Ten minutes later I'm at Tamara's front door, trying to work up the nerve to knock, when she pulls it open, looking drawn and on edge. I want to step right into her, to fold her around me and kiss her for an hour, until all the madness recedes and we can just be ourselves again, figure out the next move together. And I would do it, if it weren't for this nagging fear that as soon as my lips got within striking distance, she might start to scream. We look at each other, each of us trying to determine where we fit into this new reality.

"Hey," she says.

"Hey."

"Oh my God, look at your face." She reaches out to touch the welt on my cheek, an imprint of Jack's diamond pinky ring, but retracts her hand before it can make contact, as if unsure whether she's allowed to touch me anymore.

"I had it coming."

"You're shivering," she says. "Do you want to come in?"

I step inside and we sit down on the couch. "Where's Sophie?"

"She's watching *Annie* in the den."

I nod, all out of small talk. "I need to ask you something."

She closes her eyes. "Don't, Zack. Please."

"You don't even know what it is."

"Yes, I do," she says, her voice cracking. "I know because I know you, better than anyone. Like I know myself. And I know I can't give you the answer you want."

Suddenly, I'm finding it hard to breathe. "Why?" I say, and it comes out in a broken whisper.

She knots her hair behind her head nervously. "It's not your fault, Zack. I knew where things were heading with us, just like you. I'm not innocent here. And I hate that now I'm cast in the role of the other woman. That's not who I am. I've only ever been the one."

"Listen," I say. "You've never been the other woman, and I've never been the kind of guy who cheats. Our timing was terrible; I'll give you that. But you were never the other woman. When I fell in love with you, Hope became the other woman. I'm not proud of that, but it's the truth."

She shakes her head resolutely even as the tears come. "It doesn't matter," she says.

"I don't understand," I say. "How can it not matter? Last night, that wasn't just me. I know you were feeling it too."

She looks up at me, her eyes wide and stricken. "You didn't choose me," she says softly. "You felt this way all this time, and you didn't choose me. And if we hadn't gotten caught the way we did, you'd still be with Hope. And I can't be the consolation prize, Zack. I might be lonely, and I might love you, but I will not start the rest of my life as anyone's backup plan. Not even yours."

"Tamara . . ." I say, but after that, I've got nothing.

"You didn't choose me," she says again. "And you know what the worst part is?"

"What's that?" I say.

"Now I lose my best friend too."

I grab her hands. "You don't have to," I say, pleading with her. "Just keep me."

She presses her forehead against mine, eyes closed. "I can't," she whispers.

After a moment, she gets up and runs upstairs. I walk into the den, where I find Sophie sitting on the couch, stroking a stuffed dog as she watches *Annie*. "Look, Zap," she says, pointing to the screen. She seems utterly unsurprised to see me, as if I'm always here. As if I live here too. "*Annie.*"

I sit down next to her and pull her onto my lap. She settles right in, clutching my fingers in her little fists. "What are they singing?" I say.

"Hard-Knock Life."

Her favorite part. She sings along phonetically in her thin, high voice while I bounce her on my knees. When I start to sing along with her, she says, "No Zap sing."

"Why not?"

"Only Sophie."

"No fair," I say, making a sad face.

She laughs. "No fair," she repeats gleefully. I can feel the laugh through her round belly, the way it spreads through her insides like running water, filling her.

"I love you, Sophie," I say.

"No fair," she says, and laughs again.

I leave Sophie to her video and step back into the front hall. Tamara is sitting on the steps, wiping her nose with a tissue. "You going?" she says.

"I guess so," I say. "Can I still come by to see you guys?"

She frowns. "No. Not for a while, I think."

"Well, can I call you?"

"Zack, please," she says, standing up. "I'm hanging on by a thread here. Don't make it harder."

She steps forward and puts her arms around me, resting her head on my shoulder for a moment. It's by far the saddest, lamest hug we've ever shared, a poor facsimile of a hug, at best. My fingers come up to disappear into her hair one last time. "I love you, Tamara," I say. "Whatever that means to you, it means to you. But I know what it means to me."

For the briefest instant, her grip on me tightens, and then she stiffens again. When she pulls back, she's crying again. "I'm sorry," she says. She pulls my head down to kiss the center of my forehead. Then she whispers, "Now go."

• • •

That night, back in my apartment, I dream of the car crash again, of Rael hanging upside down as his life bleeds away, only this time I'm trapped as well, my unfeeling legs disappearing into the twisted wreckage of the engine. When I try to free myself, my legs twist off like torn licorice as I fall to the ground. The me in the dream seems to accept this horrifying development as a matter of fact, is poised and stoic, walking through the inverted car on my hands as if I'd been doing it for years. But at some point the dreaming me catches on and I wake up with a gasp, my hands falling instantly to my legs, confirming their solid presence beneath my covers, shaking perceptibly even as the dream recedes. I roll out of bed to walk around my bedroom, needing empirical evidence of nonmutilation, and wander downstairs to get a drink.

This is what happens. You piss blood one day and it somehow makes you think that maybe your life isn't taking shape the way it's meant to and, at thirty-two years old, if you're going to be making any changes, you had best make them quick. So you give it a whirl, and it's like trying to make a ninety-degree turn in a speeding boat, and the whole thing just flips over, and you're submerged in the frigid, churning waters, bobbing roughly in your own broken wake. And no matter which way you turn your desperate gaze, there's absolutely no land in sight, which is strange, because you didn't think you'd gone out that far to begin with.

thirty-seven thirty-seven thirty-seven thirty-seven
thirty-seven thirty-seven thirty-seven thirty-seven
thirty-seven thirty-seven thirty-seven thirty-seven
thirty-seven **thirty-seven** thirty-seven thirty-seven
thirty-seven thirty-seven thirty-seven thirty-seven

thirty-seven

a few days later, the sheer emptiness of my life is staggering, an emptiness that is not simply the absence of things but an actual, weighted thing all its own lodged somewhere behind my throat, where my spine meets my skull. There's a certain type of person, a person with access to vast inner resources, who would view my situation as a grand opportunity, a chance to rebuild my life, bringing to bear all the wisdom from my past mistakes to create something vibrant and new, a streamlined life that will allow for only the most honest of relationships, the truest of motivations. I am not that guy. I'm more like the guy who makes it necessary to train lifeguards in the art of underwater self-defense, the guy who will thrash violently in his panic, unable to discern peril from salvation. I've got nowhere to go, nothing to do, and no one to see. I've become a cipher, and the only proof I have that I haven't disappeared is that if I had, I probably wouldn't be feeling this shitty.

For the last three days, I've been alternately writing and deleting the opening pages of the screenplay that I am now pretty confident I will never write. I can see the movie in my head, the characters, the conflict, the story arc, and I can even construct funny and authentic dialogue, pages of it, actually. But I'm missing something vital, the binding ingredient that moves the story along, and my pages are like fully formed bones without the requisite sinew and tissue to hold them together, let alone move them. Every few hours I take a break to dial Hope's number at work, then hang up before it can ring and register on her caller ID. My line is blocked, but she'll know it's me anyway.

I miss Tamara.

I think about Hope. Stupid things. Did she go back to work on Monday, or is she taking some time to get over the whole thing, torturously reviewing the past few months to discern all the signals she'd missed, berating herself even as she burns me in effigy? No doubt she'll recover quickly, hitting the dating scene with a renewed sense of purpose, undeterred by this tragic detour from her life's greater plan. I give it three months until she has another boyfriend, some tall, athletic MBA with thick hair and cut abs, a long-distance runner who reads *The Wall Street Journal* and fucks like a porn star. And as they lie glistening in the sweaty afterglow, she'll tell him about me, pleading temporary insanity, and he'll listen sympathetically, agreeing with her that I'm a total asshole, saying he'd love to track me down and beat the shit out of me, all the while caressing her breast with one hand, keeping the fire stoked so that as soon as she's done talking, he can pull her on top of him to watch the way she throws her head back, eyes closed, as he slides into her for the third time that night, his head on the pillow where mine used to be, his hands grabbing the soft flesh of her ass where mine used to, as he thrusts deeply, driving any lingering thoughts of me out of her mind once and for all. God, I miss the way her room smelled in the aftermath of our lovemaking, a complex amalgam of sweat, sex, and her perfumed linens. You never know when it might be the last time you'll ever make love to someone. If you did, you'd pay more attention.

On Wednesday, I ride the elevator up with the morning crowd, same as always, everyone staring in silence at the brushed-steel doors, the scent of freshly brewed coffee and feminine perfumes filling the air. I've always wondered why no one sells advertising space in corporate elevators. People will look at anything to not have to look at each other. I get out and swipe my magnetic Spandler ID card at the electronic doorplate. I don't know what I'm expecting, flashing lights and alarms, armed guards maybe, but there's a mechanical click and the door swings open, same as always. I walk unmolested through the halls, since everyone's in a sales meeting, and make my way to my cubicle, where I slide into my chair and log on to my computer. Three hundred some-odd e-mails fill my in-box, frantically jockeying for position on the screen. Riding to work, I didn't know whether I was coming here to save my job or to gather my belongings. But now, as I scroll through the angry minutiae of the communications, the drab details of my chosen profession, a certain calm comes over me, and I shade the e-mails in blue and bulk delete them in one fell swoop, and then conduct similar electronic genocides on my cell phone and BlackBerry, feeling a confounding mixture of terror and jubilation, like an alcoholic pouring the last remnants of his stashed bottle into the toilet. It's counterintuitive, but on a deeper level, I know there's a greater good behind it, and for the moment, I've somehow amassed the will to back it up.

Bill's door is partially closed, and I can hear him on the phone discussing critical competencies and supply-chain solutions. Bill is all about the jargon. I don't know if I've been fired or not. I suppose I should find out, because there are ramifications as far as unemployment and severance. The right thing to do would be to step in there and let him vent a little before terminating me or, failing that, formally present him with my somewhat belated notice. Go out like a professional. But even as I hear him pontificating on the merits of outsourcing (flexible access to assets without capital investment), I can feel the walls closing in, and I know I have to get out of there before I lose my nerve and start begging for my job back. I toss my ID card into the mail slot on his door, and by the time I reach the elevators, I'm actually running. Toward what, I have no idea.

Hope doesn't notice me right away. She steps out of her office lobby, dressed conservatively in a long black skirt and a faded orange blouse, her hair tied back in a modest ponytail. She's just turned to head east when she sees me leaning uncertainly against a building across the street, one leg up as if I've been standing there all day, which isn't true. It's only been about two hours. I wanted to catch her if she happened to leave early.

I debated long and hard over whether to come and see her. Maybe she would welcome the closure of seeing me one last time, to spit in my face and tell me what a pathetic excuse for a man I am. But it's equally possible that she's already written me off, accepting the admittedly less satisfying option of venting her pain through other channels in favor of never having to cast eyes upon me again. In that case, seeing her now could be detrimental, might set her back, but on the other hand, not seeing her might be unintentionally compounding the hurt, leaving her with the notion that I didn't even care enough for her as a person to call and apologize. Not that an apology would be worth anything to her at this point, but I at least owe her an explanation, the only problem being that I don't really have one other than the obvious, that I've failed her and betrayed her, and she hardly needs me to point that out.

And so, with no clear direction in sight, what it came down to was this: I simply had nowhere else to go.

So here I am, waving tentatively from across the street, and where I expect her eyes to narrow into baleful slits, they grow wide, her hand flying up involuntarily to her lips, which are parted in surprise, and by the time I manage to traverse the busy street, she's wiping her running mascara with a tissue from her purse. "I'm shaking," she says.

"I'm sorry. I didn't mean to take you by surprise," I say, even though I suppose I probably did.

"It's okay," she says. "Why are you here?"

"I don't know. I needed to see you. To tell you how sorry I am about everything. I still can't believe this all happened."

"Trust me, it did," she says, but strangely, without any malice. "It's still happening."

"I know. I'm sorry."

She looks at the bruise on my face, grimacing sympathetically, without a hint of the satisfaction I might have expected. "Daddy really clocked you, didn't he?"

I'm staring at the graceful architecture of her face, always so miraculous to me, and only at this moment does the full impact of losing her, of the death of us, finally hit me, and it's like watching helplessly as your home goes up in flames, with a lifetime's accumulation of memories inside. "Hope," I say forlornly.

"I know," she says. "Just tell me. Are you with her now?"

I shake my head. "I'm not with anyone."

"Was it going on for a while?"

"No. That night was the first time."

She nods, her eyes once again brimming with tears. "You know what I keep thinking?" she says.

"What?"

"I keep thinking that whatever happened was just this terrible, momentary lapse, a single instant of insanity because you were scared and anxious. And if my father hadn't walked in when he did, you would have felt awful about it but ultimately gotten over it, and I never would have known, and we'd have been just fine. And I lie in bed at night, and instead of hating you, I hate my father for walking in like that, for ruining everything. Isn't that crazy?"

"I'm so sorry, Hope."

She opens up her purse and pulls out a little ring box. "Look," she says, showing me the ring. "I've been carrying it in my bag. And every so often I just slip it back on my finger, and wonder if we haven't lost all perspective, if this wasn't just a small incident that got blown out of proportion by all the drama. I mean, imagine if you'd kissed her somewhere else, and then you confessed it to me. I'd be furious, certainly, but I think we'd have gotten past it. So what makes this any different?"

I can see the desperate invitation in her wet eyes, the burning need for me to breathe life into the idea. I can feel my belly shudder at the possibility that what I'd thought was irretrievably lost might unbelievably be within my grasp, that I might end this day back in her arms, the terrifying desolation of our current circumstances already retreating into the past, shrinking until it disappears.

"I can't," I hear myself say sadly, and Hope looks as surprised as I am. I never trusted that she could love me completely, and only now, as I irrevocably finish us off, does the reality of her love become clear to me, and it feels like I've lost her all over again. "I can't," I say again, my voice thick with emotion, the light around us swirling madly through the prism of our tears. People brush past us on the street in endless waves, leaving somewhere, headed somewhere else, laughing, smoking, speaking into cell phones, completely oblivious to the holocaust of an entire world casually imploding in their midst.

thirty-eight

I get back to the brownstone just in time to see a cherry-red Mitsubishi sports car pull over to double-park in front. A tall, striking woman with a long mane of wavy black hair emerges, dressed in spandex leggings that stop midcalf, exposing a rose tattoo just above her ankle, and a short, zip-up sweatshirt worn deliberately high so as to showcase her notable assets, both in front and behind, to great advantage. She opens the back door and pulls out a little boy about five years old, with a shock of curly blond hair and wide, thoughtful eyes that seem more suited to a man than a little boy. Holding his hand, she carries herself up the stairs with the practiced air of someone whose innate physical attributes are never far from her own consciousness.

"Can I help you?" I say, coming up the stairs behind her.

She and the boy turn to face me. Her skin is dark and

clear, her nails painted a garish red with white tips. The boy is holding a toy in his free hand, a small blue train with a smiling face. "Is Norman King staying here?" she demands of me in a slightly hoarse smoker's voice.

"He was," I say cautiously, instinctively knowing that a woman like this looking for Norm can only mean trouble.

"I'm Delia," she says, as if I should have known. "Are you Zack?"

The boy looks up at me when she says my name, and then quickly back to his toy train. "Yes," I say. "What can I do for you?"

"Norm said to call you if anything happened to him," Delia says.

"Okay."

"I've left you half a dozen messages."

"Sorry," I say. "I haven't had my cell phone on me the last few days."

She nods. "So," she says. "Has it?"

"Has what?"

"Has anything happened to him?"

"Norm's fine," I say.

"Then he's a fucking asshole," Delia declares, and then winces, belatedly throwing her hands over the boy's ears. "Shit. Sorry, Henry. Don't listen to me."

"Okay," Henry says.

"Why don't you sit on the steps and play with Thomas while Delia talks to the nice man."

Henry wordlessly lets go of her and sits down on the stairs. He pushes a button on the train and watches it roll slowly across the length of the stair. When it hits the wall, he turns it around to go the other way.

"Your son?" I say.

"No way!" she says, horrified at the notion, and something in me shudders, some organ that understands what's unfolding here before the rest of me does. "He's Norm's kid."

"What?"

"Listen," Delia says. "Norm paid me five hundred bucks to watch his kid for two days, three tops. It's been over a week now, and I can't get ahold of him. Now I know why he left me your number. Between the two of you, I can't get a goddamn callback. I dance nights and I've had to bring Henry to the club with me every night for the last week, and it's not exactly Disney World, if you know what I mean."

I lean against the banister, staring at the little boy as her words sink in. "Norm has a son," I say.

"Right," she says, speaking to me as if I'm a little kid. "I thought we covered this already."

I nod, swallowing. The boy looks down, watching his train with a focused intensity. "Where's his mother?"

"How the hell should I know?" Delia says, growing impatient. "All I know is, a deal's a deal. He's a great kid and all, but he's not mine, and I need my life back. Now, do you know where to find him or not?"

"I can find him," I say, my eyes glued to the little boy. "Do you want to hang out for a while?"

"I can't," she says. "I've got to drive back to Atlantic City. I'm on at nine."

"You work in Atlantic City?"

She fumbles through her purse and pulls out a bent business card that has an artful rendering of a nude woman bending over, and her name and a phone number in large print. Below that, it says, *Exotic Dancer. Bachelor Parties / Private Shows / Satisfaction Guaranteed.* "Satisfaction" is underlined.

"That's my cell. You tell Norm that if I don't hear from him by tonight, I'm calling the police. He's a sweet kid and I don't want to do it, but maybe I should, you know? I mean, what kind of father leaves his kid with a dancer, anyway?"

"Why don't you leave him with me," I say. "I'll be seeing Norm soon."

She raises her eyebrows, momentarily intrigued, but then shakes her head. "I don't know you, and I'm not leaving him with someone I don't know. I'm responsible for him, and you could be a pervert, for all I know. No offense."

"None taken," I say. "Norm's my father."

That surprises her. "You're shitting me."

"It's the truth."

She looks down at Henry, her expression softening. "That makes Henry your stepbrother or something, right?"

"My half brother," I say quietly. Henry looks up at me, and then quickly down to his train. When it hits the wall, he makes the sound of an explosion.

"And you didn't know?"

"Nope."

Delia considers me for a long moment. "I'd better not," she finally says. "I don't know who anyone is in this mess. I just know I don't belong in the middle of it." She bends down and grabs Henry's hand. "Come on, sweetie," she says, helping him to his feet. "You just find Norm, okay?"

"I will," I say.

I crouch down to look at Henry better. "Hi," I say. "I'm Zack." Henry hides his face behind one of Delia's toned thighs.

"You guys should go on *Oprah* or something," Delia says, leading Henry down the stairs.

"Wait," I say as she's helping Henry into the backseat. I

come down the stairs, reaching for my wallet as I go, pulling out a wad of bills. "There's about two hundred dollars there," I say.

She eyes the proffered cash suspiciously. "I already told you I'm not leaving him with you."

"I understand," I say. "Just don't call the police. I'll get this sorted out, okay?"

She sizes me up, a woman not unaccustomed to spontaneous negotiations over a fistful of cash. Then she takes the money, unzipping her sweatshirt slightly to tuck it into a red satin bra. "I'll give you one more day," she says.

"That's all I'm asking."

As she drives away, I see Henry's hand come up in the rear window, waving to me, and even though he's too small to look above the bench and see me waving back, I do it anyway.

"Who was that?" Jed says when I come in. He's sitting at the desk behind the couch, uncharacteristically dressed as he works on the computer.

"That was Delia."

"So we're dating strippers now?"

"How'd you know she was a stripper?"

He taps his temple. "It's like a sixth sense."

"Did you see the boy?"

"Yeah."

"That's Norm's son."

"Norm and her?" he says skeptically.

I shake my head. "It's complicated."

He turns away from the desk. "Explain it to me, then."

"I will," I say, collapsing onto the couch. "As soon as someone explains it to me."

"You had no idea, huh?"

I shake my head. "I don't know if I'm still surprised, or just surprised that I'm surprised."

He comes over to sit with me. "Did you see Hope?"

"Yeah."

"You okay?"

I think about it. It's been one thing on top of another today, and I'm having trouble matching up the corresponding emotions and phenomena. "I don't know. Ask me in a few weeks."

"Deal," Jed says.

"Can I borrow your car?" I say. "I need to go to Riverdale."

"I've got a date," Jed says. "I'll drive you."

"Thanks."

We sit on the couch in companionable silence for a few seconds. "Hey," I say. "Where's the television?"

"Yeah," Jed says, rubbing his chin self-consciously. "I got rid of it this morning."

"You got rid of it."

"I brought it down to the curb. Didn't even take twenty minutes. Some guy rigged up a dolly with some Rollerblades and a board."

I turn to look at him. "What are you going to do now?"

He nods, having expected the question. "I don't know," he says. "Ask me again in a few weeks."

thirty-nine

When I returned to the city, Norm chose to stay in Riverdale to spend some quality time with Pete. It seemed innocent enough at the time, but I should have known by now that everything Norm does has a back end, which, in this case, was avoiding the babysitting stripper with whom he'd left my name as an emergency contact. I walk into the house now to find Norm watching a video on the couch with Lela and Pete, just a puppy short of a Rockwell painting, and I want to pull him up by his shirt and hurl him out the front door on his ass.

"Hey, Zack," Pete says. "We're watching Indiana Jones."

"Zack," Norm says, pleased to see me. "What brings you here?"

I stand in front of the television and slap Delia's card onto the coffee table. Norm picks it up and I watch the trajectory of his reaction, from curious to surprised to comprehending to defensive. "Why don't we step outside," he says somberly.

"Why don't we stay right here," I say.

"What's going on?" Lela says.

"You're blocking the TV," Pete complains, craning his neck to see around me.

"When were you going to tell us?" I demand.

"Tell you what?" Lela says.

"That he's got another son."

Lela inhales sharply. "What?"

Norm closes his eyes. "I wanted to tell you," he says to me. "I was waiting for the right moment."

"Which, I guess, you were hoping would come some time before Delia managed to track me down."

"Delia's the mother?" Lela says.

"Delia's a stripper," I say.

"She's a dancer," Norm mumbles defensively.

"I'm confused," Lela says, standing up, and somewhere in the part of my brain that isn't on fire, it registers that she was sitting extremely close to him, practically spooning, and that there might have been something more intimate than I thought in the atmosphere I shattered with my arrival. She looks at Norm expectantly. "Is Delia the mother? Are you married?"

Pete looks around, belatedly realizing that something of significance is happening, and grudgingly pauses the video. "This is the best part," he grumbles softly.

"I'm not married," Norm says emphatically to Lela, and there it is again, a separate message woven into his words on a private frequency, and now I'm fairly certain that Norm's quality time has not necessarily been restricted to Pete. Maybe I'm imagining it, or maybe I was naïve not to have expected it from the start, two lonely former lovers, one of them hopped-up on Viagra, sleeping in separate beds under the same roof for four nights running now. Either way, I'll never ask, and they'll never tell. "Susan died about seven months ago," Norm continues.

"And who was Susan?" I say.

"She was my wife."

"So you're a widower?"

"Technically, no," he admits reluctantly.

"Let me guess."

He nods. "We were divorced two years or so before she died."

"When Henry was about two."

"I guess so, yes."

"Henry's your son?" Lela says.

"What's going on?" Pete says, squinting as he tries to follow the conversation.

"Go to your room, Peter."

"What for?"

"We need to have a private talk."

"But the video," he protests.

"We'll finish it in a little while."

"This sucks," Pete says, but he pulls himself off the couch and heads dejectedly upstairs, wondering how it all went so wrong so fast.

"So basically," I say once Pete's gone, "you got married again, had a kid, got divorced, again, and were off doing your whole deadbeat father thing, again, when your ex-wife dropped dead, leaving you suddenly in charge of a four-year-old boy you barely knew."

"I took care of her while she was sick," Norm says defensively. "She had no one."

"She had you, but then, I guess no one ever really has you, do they, Norm?"

Norm's head sags like I just kicked him in the crotch, his hands clasped tightly in front of him, trembling in his lap. "I thought we were past all this," he groans.

"Me too. Turns out we're not."

"Zack," Lela says softly.

"No, Mom. He's been lying to us the whole time."

"He had trouble telling us something," she says. "You're not so different yourself. How long did it take you to tell Hope you didn't want to marry her?"

"That's not the point," I say, turning to face Norm. "He could have brought Henry with him. It would have been perfect, introducing us to our half brother. It's got all the drama you could ask for, and we all know that Norm can't resist drama. Instead, he comes on his own, leaving his son with a stripper, for Christ's sake, and for much longer than he agreed. It just doesn't make sense, even for a shitty father like him. So I have to ask you, Norm, what did you really come back here for? Because I don't think anymore that it was just to make amends."

A thin ring of sweat has broken out on Norm's forehead, his face is deathly pale, and his breath is becoming labored to the point that I'm scared he might start hyperventilating. "Norm," Lela says. "Are you okay?"

He nods to her, taking a few deep breaths. "Sit down for a moment," he says to me, his voice thin and raspy.

"I'll stand."

"Please," he says, his eyes beseeching me from the couch. After a few seconds I relent and take a seat on an ottoman.

"You came here to dump your kid on us, didn't you?" I say.

Norm shakes his head. "I came here to see if I had what it takes to be a father again." He runs his arm across his face, and I can see that his eyes are watering. "I looked at that little boy depending on me to take care of him, and all I could think about was you and your brothers, how I'd failed so miserably with you. Some men just don't have it in them. That's something I resigned myself to a long time ago. My father didn't. I didn't either."

"Didn't stop you from having another one, though, did it?"

"Nothing ever stops me," he says, shaking his head miserably. "I'm the king of 'this time.' This time is always going to be different. Except it never is. And it was fine when I knew Henry had Susan. But when I became his sole guardian, I was terrified. I love him, but I loved you and your brothers too, and that didn't keep me from losing all of you. I came here to see my sons, to see how badly I'd messed up, and to see if you could forgive me. I know it's stupid, but I somehow thought that if I could be a part of my sons' lives again, it would give me the confidence to think things could be different this time around."

"So it was never about us," I say bitterly. "We're just the scene of the crime."

Norm looks at Lela, and then back at me, frowning. "I'm old, Zack. You have no idea how fucking old I am."

"Just say it."

"What?"

"You want us to do it for you."

Norm sniffs, unable to meet my gaze. "I just need help."

"Bullshit. You want out, like you always do."

"I want the best for Henry," Norm says, tears running down his face. "I'm sixty years old and I don't expect to see seventy. I've got a bad heart and no bypasses left to do. And I look at Henry, and he's so beautiful, so absolutely perfect, and I don't want to fuck him up too."

My rage is electric, coursing madly through my veins, igniting my blood as it goes. "Fuck you, Norm. You had no right."

"I'm sorry, Zack." He reaches out for me and I pull away as if repulsed.

"Fuck you."

He reaches for me again, and this time his weight shifts and he tumbles forward onto the glass coffee table, which cracks under his weight, sending him falling on his knees onto the jagged shards. He sits still in the wreckage, sobbing silently into his hands, until Lela sits down beside him, pulling his head into her chest and rocking him slowly back and forth, the way she used to hold me in my bed when I cried at night, empty and aching for something that I am only now beginning to get through my thick skull had never existed to begin with.

I hang out in Pete's room for a bit, while Norm and Lela hold a whispered conversation below. Pete has trouble understanding the concept of a half brother.

"He has a different mother?" he asks me for the third time.

"That's right," I say.

"But if he's our brother, how come we didn't have him before?"

"He's only five years old."

"I'm too old to have a five-year-old brother."

"No," I say. "You're not."

He thinks about it for a moment. "What's his name?"

"Henry."

"Henry," he says thoughtfully. "What does he like?"

"What do you mean?"

"Does he like ice cream? Which flavor?"

"I don't know."

"What's his favorite show?"

"I don't know anything about him, Pete," I say. "I just found out about him myself."

"Will he think I'm stupid?"

"You're not stupid."

"Maybe a five-year-old would think I'm stupid."

"I don't think anyone would think you're stupid."

"You're just saying that because you're my brother," he says, punching me lightly in the arm.

"Well, so is he," I say.

"Oh, yeah," Pete says, nodding. "I keep forgetting."

When I come downstairs, Lela is sitting in the dark, sipping at a tea glass, looking into space. "Where is he?" I say.

"You were hard on him."

"He lied to us."

She looks up at me, shaking her head. "You know, Zack, even when someone is deserving of your anger, they're still deserving of compassion. It's hard to pull off, believe me—no one knows that more than me. And if you're only going to pull it off a handful of times in your life, why not for family?"

"He's not your family," I say.

"You and your brothers make him my family."

I head down the stairs to the basement, where Norm is asleep on the pullout couch, still wearing his shirt, his belly rising and falling with his loud snores. Without the benefit of its usual, exaggerated animation, I can, for the first time, actually study his face, the lines of his jaw beneath his retreating jowls, the droop of his nose, the humorless set of his thin lips, almost a grimace. His face in repose is the face of a stranger. Holding my breath, I sit down at the edge of the bed, wincing as the springs groan and pop under my added weight. When the bed has settled, I stare at his face in the weak light from the upstairs hall, trying to feel some kind of connection to this unfathomable man. I lie down on my back, my head just inches from his heaving middle, looking at the speckled, water-stained drop ceiling. Matt, Pete, and I used to take the cushions off the couch down here and line them up, performing flips and somersaults while Norm sat at his desk in the far corner, scribbling a numeric score on his pad after each leap, then holding it up solemnly for us to see. He dubbed it the Basement Olympics, and in between scoring, he was also the announcer, assigning ridiculous names to our stunts, like the Triple Toilet Spin, or the Reverse Headbanger. Over time, we figured out that he scored higher for relative risk, regardless of execution, and Matt and I would try anything outrageous in our quest for second place. Pete always came in first.

"Remember the Basement Olympics, Dad?" I say. He doesn't respond. "I haven't thought about that in forever." I talk to his sleeping form for a while, recalling events from my childhood, telling him secrets I could never tell him if he were awake, until I feel my eyes growing heavy, my breath hollow and coming from far away. "We'll talk in the morning, Dad," I say. "We'll work it out."

But we won't. Because in the morning, Norm is gone with all of his stuff, and I find a note taped to the bathroom mirror. *Please take care of him. His birthday is February 19, and he loves soft ice cream (chocolate) and the Justice League of America. I'm sorry. If all it took was the love in my heart, I'd be father of the year.* I study my reaction aggressively in the mirror above the note. Under no circumstances should I be surprised. Then, leaving the note where it is, like a valuable clue that shouldn't be touched, I head upstairs, figuring I'll give him a few hours to change his mind before I call Matt.

forty

i knew there had to be a hidden agenda," Matt says. He's sitting on the couch, leaning forward on his knees, fidgeting agitatedly with the zipper on the pocket of his worn cargo pants. "Son of a bitch," he says. "If there was ever someone not qualified to have another kid . . ." His voice trails off. It's about three in the afternoon. It took me the better part of the day to track Matt down, as his cell phone service was recently suspended for lack of payment. Ultimately, I located Otto and enlisted him to go out on foot and find him, implying a dire family emergency.

"He's our brother," Pete informs Matt solemnly, for approximately the fifth time. "Our half brother. We all have the same father."

"I get it, Pete," Matt says testily, then quickly shakes Pete's knee on the couch beside him. "I'm sorry. I'm just a little shocked."

The three of us are sitting in the living room in the waning hours of the afternoon, discussing the situation, while Lela noisily stores fresh groceries in the kitchen. She made it clear that this was strictly a brothers' meeting and, having thus ousted herself, strains to eavesdrop effectively from behind the swinging door.

"Any idea where Norm went?" Matt says.

"Nope," I say. "A while back he mentioned some business in Florida, which might have been true, or might have been another lie."

"Part of the whole grand scheme," Matt says, nodding thoughtfully. I'd expected anger and recrimination, furious rants against Norm, and self-flagellation for our having put ourselves in the position, once again, to be abandoned. But Matt sits quietly, I would almost say serenely, were it not for the constant, nervous fidgeting of his hands. "You saw him?" Matt says.

"Last night," I say. "I was somewhat hard on him."

"Not Norm," Matt says, shaking his head. "The kid. Henry." I realize that Matt's not at all interested in Norm, that he's, in fact, written him off. Or maybe, unlike me, he'd never actually written him back in to begin with.

"Yeah," I say. "I saw him yesterday."

"How'd he look?"

"Yeah, how'd he look?" Pete says. There's an age-old familiar rhythm to this conversation, Matt asking the questions and processing the information for him and Pete, Pete participating by echoing Matt, while I try to play the role of the answer man for both of them.

"I don't know," I say. I think about it for a moment. "He looked serious. A little lonely."

Matt's nodding has become quick and exaggerated, out of

proportion to the conversation, his lips quivering with unbridled emotion. "So," he says. "When do we go get him?"

"Yeah, when do we get him?" Pete repeats.

We haven't discussed this part yet, the thorny issues of responsibility and guardianship, of lifestyles and lives interrupted. But looking at Matt, I can see that at least for now, such talk is unwarranted, and I feel a rush of affection toward him and Pete, the love of a brother, and some measure of paternal pride as well. "I figured we'd leave first thing in the morning," I say.

"Yeah," Matt says with a nod, getting to his feet and wiping at his eyes with his cuff. "Let's go now."

We'll take Pete's Mustang and there's a poetry to this, the car one brother never should have had being used to fetch the brother we never knew we had. As we're climbing in, Lela comes running down the stairs, carrying an old child safety seat in her arms, and a large shopping bag clutched in her fingers. "If he's under forty pounds, he has to sit in a booster seat," she says. "You just put it on the backseat, not in the middle, and use the regular seat belt."

We look at her. "Okay, Mom," I say. "Thanks."

She extends the bag. "Some sandwiches and snacks," she says. "It's a long drive. He'll probably get hungry."

Matt takes the bag. "Thanks, Mom."

She looks us over critically, slightly out of breath from her last-minute preparations, face flushed, eyes moist, wisps of her frizzed hair floating animatedly around her face. Then she steps forward and pulls off Matt's Elton John wig. "You'll freak him out," she says, rolling up the wig in her hands.

"Okay," Matt says, offering her a small, boyish grin.

We're all staring at her, surprised, expectant, depending on her. "What?" she says. "Norm might be an ass, but I've spent my life loving his children." She steps forward and gives us each a quick kiss on the cheek. "Now go get him."

Pete wants to drive, so after we get across the George Washington Bridge, I switch seats with him. Matt coaches him softly while I dial Delia's cell phone number in the backseat. "Hello," I say. "It's Zachary King."

"Who?"

"Henry's brother."

"Oh, yeah. Did you find Norm?"

"I did," I say.

"And?"

"Norm's gone AWOL."

"That bastard. I don't believe it."

"We're kind of used to it."

"Well, what the hell am I supposed to do now?"

"We're on our way to pick up Henry," I say, hoping I sound authoritative enough.

"Who's we?" she says, instantly suspicious.

"I've got two brothers."

There's a pause on the other end of the phone. "I don't know you any better than I did yesterday."

"Listen," I say. "He's our brother and we're coming to get him. When you meet my brothers, you'll see that we're the real deal. We all look alike. My brother Matt looks just like Norm."

"Fuck you," Matt says from the front seat. "I do not."

"I have to be at work in an hour," she says uncertainly.

"Perfect," I say. "Where's work?"

• • •

We pull into the parking lot of Tommyknockers, a self-proclaimed "upscale gentlemen's club," as the last light of day is fading over the forlorn Jersey shore. Nothing in Pete's experience has prepared him for the topless women cavorting on the runway, sliding on poles, and lying on their backs to perform splits to old Guns N' Roses songs. His mouth drops in a comical approximation of awe, and he looks absolutely terrified when one of the circulating strippers invites him into the back for a private dance. "No, thanks," Matt says while Pete giggles uncontrollably. "We're looking for Delia."

"You have to speak to Dave," she says.

"Who's Dave?"

"The owner." She points past the small round tables to the long bar that sits against the far wall. The bar is empty, save for one stool on the far left, upon which sits a large potbellied man with thinning steel wool hair and a beard that seems to have been trimmed specifically to show off the triple chin hanging like a rucksack beneath it. "That him?" I say.

"In the flesh," she says before wandering off to peddle some more of her own.

"Excuse me," I say to the man. "Dave?"

"If you're asking, then you already know," he says, sipping at his drink. He looks like someone who might have wrestled professionally in another life.

"We need to see Delia."

He turns on his stool to look me over. "You here about the kid?"

"That's right."

He looks at his watch and frowns. "She's on in ten minutes."

"Then we'd better be quick."

Dave frowns as he pulls himself off his stool and leads us

through a door to the right of the runway, down a hall, and into the dressing room. A handful of naked women sit at a bank of mirrors, adjusting their makeup, emptying out industrial-size aerosol cans into their hair, and dispassionately propping up their synthetic breasts in lacy undergarments. Other women strut back and forth in dangerously high heels and little else, hurriedly pulling on and off minuscule spandex skirts or tube tops, conversing easily with each other as they prepare to go on. Henry is sitting on the floor in the corner, oblivious to the writhing jungle of long legs and thonged asses that surrounds him. He has his Thomas the Tank Engine train clutched in one hand while the other is busy with a crayon, coloring in a flyer with the club logo, an outline of two naked women bending over in opposite directions.

"Henry," I call to him. I can tell by his expression that he recognizes me. "Do you remember me?"

He nods, pulling the train against his chest. I can feel Matt and Pete behind me, staring at him. Before we can get any closer, Delia steps away from a full-length mirror and positions herself between us. She's dressed in a sequined bra and panties, her face so garishly made-up that she looks like a marionette. "Hey," she says. "Zack."

"Yeah."

"They're here for the boy," Dave says.

"I know what they're here for," Delia says, looking over Matt and Pete. "You have some way of proving your identity?"

Matt and I produce our driver's licenses, which she expertly peruses before handing them over to Dave. "What do you think?" she asks him.

Dave gives her back the licenses without looking at them. "I think this is a business, not a day care center. If they're here for the boy, settle up with them and get your ass out there."

I kneel down in front of Henry, who is following the action with wide, intelligent eyes. "Henry," I say. "Do you know who I am?"

He nods. "Zack," he says.

"That's right," I say. "And these are my brothers, Matt and Pete."

Henry nods, reaches into his pants pocket, and hands me a bent and weathered photo. I open it to find a picture of Matt, Pete, and me on a fishing boat in Miami. Lela had gone down to see her mother through some back surgery, and I'd used the opportunity to treat my brothers to a small vacation. It was about six years ago, and I have no idea how the picture wound up in Norm's possession. "That's right," I say. "That's me and that's Matt and that's Pete." I look at Henry. "You're our brother too."

"I know," Henry says.

"How would you like to come and live with us?"

Henry considers the invitation with the air of someone for whom drastic changes in living arrangements are nothing out of the ordinary. "My mom died," he says matter-of-factly.

"I know," I say. "I'm sorry."

"Do you know where my dad is?"

"He's gone away for a while."

Henry nods, looking down at his Thomas train. "He always goes away."

"I know. He's my father too. That's why it's good to have three other brothers, right? This way, you'll never be alone."

Pete comes over and crouches down to join us. "I have trains too," he says. "Lots of them. And tracks and a bridge and a service depot."

"Do they have batteries?" Henry says.

"Some."

Henry nods and sticks out his hand. "Can I have my picture back?"

I hand him the picture, and the way he folds it like a talisman, with loving precision along its creases, before depositing it back in his pocket brings a lump to my throat.

"Fine," Delia says. "Just give me another thousand dollars and we'll call it even."

"What the hell are you talking about?" Matt says.

"I gave you two hundred yesterday," I say.

"And that bought you one more day," Delia retorts. "I've had the kid for over a week. I've had to feed him and clothe him, not to mention all the work I missed."

"Your deal was with Norm," I tell her. "Not us."

"Listen," Dave says. "Both parties had better come to an understanding immediately, because I need her ass on that stage in two minutes or my business starts to be affected, and you do not want to start affecting my business. Do you get me?"

"Fuck this," Matt says to me. "Let's get him out of here."

"She's entitled to something for her trouble," Dave says, planting himself in front of the door.

"Okay, fine," I say, pulling out my wallet and going through my bills. "I've got one hundred and eighty-three dollars on me. Matt, what do you have?"

Matt flashes me a look that says *Be real.*

"That's not acceptable," Dave says. Apparently, he's taken over the negotiations for Delia.

"I'm not a charity," Delia says. "I'm a businesswoman."

"You get paid to show your tits," Matt says hotly.

"Fuck you, you little punk!"

A shouting match erupts between Matt, Delia, and Dave, but I'm watching Henry, who has backed up to the wall, frightened by all the yelling. He stares at me for a few seconds, eyes wide with fear, and then, with no warning, he suddenly runs at me and jumps into my arms, burrowing his face into my shoulder as if he's done it a million times before. And as I wrap my arms around him for the first time, stroking his back as his curly hair tickles the underside of my jaw, there's something viscerally familiar about it, like a memory of the future. The argument dies down as Matt and Delia turn to stare at us, and suddenly the room is preternaturally silent.

"Please," I say, looking straight at Delia. "Let us take him home."

Delia looks at me for a long moment, then shakes her head and grabs the cash out of my fist. "Fine," she says, and then surprises me by leaning over to plant a kiss on the back of Henry's head. "Take good care of him." I turn to Dave, and after a tense few seconds, he yields his position and we exit the dressing room. Matt and Pete flank me like blockers as I walk through the club carrying Henry, who doesn't lift his head from my shoulder, holding my neck in a death grip until we make it to the parking lot.

We're passing Egg Harbor, about a half hour out of Atlantic City. I'm sitting in the back with Henry, who's fallen asleep in the booster seat, his head against my shoulder, when I suddenly lean forward and hit Matt's shoulder.

"Stop the car!"

"What?"

"Just pull over," I say. "Now!"

"What the fuck?" he says, pulling onto the shoulder.

"Shh!" Pete says to him, indicating Henry's sleeping form. "No curse words."

"Sorry."

I step into the chilly night, staring intently into the woods off the shoulder. I climb the grassy slope, moving diagonally forward, toward a large radio tower. This is the place, I'm certain. I haven't been back this way since, but I remember that tower rising up over the trees like a dragon against the night sky as they carried me away from the wreck. I move urgently through the trees, looking for broken branches or mangled auto parts, anything to pinpoint the exact location, but in the darkness there's nothing to be found. Then, in a small clearing, I come upon a tree trunk stripped of its bark at the bottom, the pearl flesh of the tree showing through like an exposed wound. I search the ground around the tree, but there's nothing there, the woods having expelled or swallowed up any last remnants of the wreckage. I sit down with my back against the tree and look out at the surrounding woods. There's a rustle to my left, and a rabbit ventures out from the undergrowth, trembling on its haunches as it surveys the area nervously. Its eyes lock on mine, and we stare at each other for a long moment, each of us contemplating issues of survival in the manner of our respective species. I pull my cell phone off my belt, flipping it open to search through the memory until it comes to Rael's cell phone number, which I could never bring myself to delete. Still watching the rabbit, I push Send, an eerie breeze blowing through my gut. The display indicates no active cells, but after a few seconds the phone rings. *This is Miguel. I'm not available right now. Please leave a message and I'll get back to you when I can. Adiós.*

"Hi, Miguel," I say. "This used to be my buddy's phone number. He died in a car crash about two years ago. You'd think I would have erased his number by now, but there it is. I guess I was kind of hoping that maybe, if I pressed the button at just the right time, I might have gotten him, but I guess not. Anyway, I hope things are fine with you, and that the number's working out for you. His name was Rael, by the way. Whatever. I'm sure you've got your own problems. I'll let you go. 'Bye."

I look down at the glowing screen and hit the requisite buttons to delete Rael's number. *Are you sure you want to delete Rael's cell?* the phone asks me. I click Delete again, and the number disappears. The next number that comes up is Rael's home. Tamara picks up on the second ring. "Hey," I say, but it's one of those one-way connections where I can hear her, but she can't hear me. "Hello?" she says. "Hello?" I say hello back, but she doesn't hear me, so all I can do is listen to her say hello a few more times, sounding mildly irked, before she hangs up, which is fine, because I don't know what I would have said to her even if she could hear me.

forty-one

Matt is in the living room, covering *Sesame Street* songs on his electric guitar, putting some punk into them, while Henry, dressed in a Buzz Lightyear costume, sits on the floor, laughing hysterically. They stop to look me over when I enter the room, dressed in an old monk's habit and a rubber goblin mask. Henry looks a bit nervous about the mask, so I pull it off, my hair tingling with static electricity. "It's just me," I say sheepishly.

"I knew it was you," he says, but he still looks relieved.

Matt plays a distorted version of "Elmo's World" on his guitar.

"You ready?" I say to Henry.

He stands up. "Don't wear the mask."

"Deal."

Matt gives Henry a kiss on the top of his head as he gets

off the couch. "Gotta go," he says. "We're playing the Halloween Ball at Irving Plaza tonight."

"That's a step up," I say, impressed.

"There was a last-minute cancellation," Matt says with a shrug. "Jed knew a guy."

"Good luck."

"Don't need it." He throws his guitar over his shoulder and heads for the door, stopping to point an admonishing finger at Henry. "No drugs and no underage women, you hear me?"

Henry nods seriously, in a way that makes us smile.

The streets are filled with roving gangs of pint-size trick-or-treaters and their accompanying chaperons. Henry holds my hand tightly, stopping every so often to marvel at the ghosts, monsters, 'droids, and hobbits moving past us on the street in the dim glow of the porch lights. After only two weeks, his trust in me is absolute, like a longtime burden he's finally found a safe place to deposit. For probably the thousandth time since we picked him up from Tommyknockers, I silently vow that I will be worthy. Making this vow in the dark, in my hooded monk's attire, seems to lend it some added weight.

"Why didn't Pete come?" Henry asks me.

"He likes to stay home and scare the trick-or-treaters."

"Oh."

We brought Henry directly back to Lela's house and turned my old room into his. We still haven't figured out exactly how we're going to configure everything, but in the interim, the prevailing idea is to surround Henry with family at all times. I've been staying there, sleeping downstairs on the sofa bed recently evacuated by Norm, and Matt comes by pretty much every day as well. A few days ago, Jed arrived in a rented van, introduced himself solemnly to Henry as Uncle Jed, and then proceeded to unload what appeared to be the entire inventory of the local Toys "R" Us while Henry looked on with unconcealed glee.

We left Henry and Pete to sift through the toys, and joined Matt, who was smoking a cigarette out in the backyard. "Hey, Matt," Jed said. "Did you tell Zack about my vision?"

"No," Matt said, stubbing out his cigarette. He'd announced his intention to quit in Henry's honor, but so far it hadn't been going well. "I figured I'd leave that to you."

Jed nodded and turned to me. "I was shopping for some new guitars with Matt, when I had a vision."

In the aftermath of what will forever be referred to by my family simply as Zack's Party, Matt and Jed reached some convoluted arrangement wherein Jed would serve as manager for Worried About the WENUS, booking their gigs and lining up a solid producer for their first demo. His first move was to buy the band all new equipment.

"You're having visions now?" I said.

"He's definitely onto something," Matt said.

"Or just on something."

"It's kind of like a musicians' superstore," Jed plowed on, ignoring my wisecrack. "A fully stocked, full-service musical equipment store with recording studios in the back for bands to cut demos, and a café with a stage to showcase local bands."

I nodded, thinking about it. "Interesting."

"The opportunities for cross-promotion are endless," he continued excitedly. "You've got four or five converging revenue streams under one roof: the café, the instruments, the recording studios, and the concerts. You host events to showcase new talent, and they come in and buy gear as well. We'll help bands make demos, and offer discounts on studio time when they buy equipment from us. And we can negotiate with the instrument vendors to underwrite the studio time in exchange for in-store advertising and advantageous brand placement. I've got a few VC guys I know who will be all over this. I'm putting the finishing touches on the business plan—oh, and once we have the prototype done, we can expand to other cities."

"It's going to be awesome," Matt said enthusiastically as he fired up another cigarette, already banking on his freebies.

There was a time, I recalled, when Jed used to sound like that all the time, animatedly pontificating on the latest company his hedge fund had discovered, why their product would revolutionize a particular industry, what his end would be. I didn't realize how much I'd missed it until that very moment, and I wanted to hug him and welcome him back to the living. Instead I just said, "Sounds great."

"I'll finish the plan and raise the money," Jed continued. "You'll negotiate the lease and handle all the vendor contracts."

"Oh, so I'm a part of this?"

He gave me a serious look. "You have something better to do?"

I grinned. "Count me in."

"Good," Jed said, shaking my hand. "Because we're turning your room into our office."

After an hour or so of trick-or-treating, Henry's bag is bulging with hard candies and chocolates, as well as the toothpaste and toothbrush set self-righteously presented by one well-meaning party pooper. A group of little kids race past us, laughing as one of their fathers sprays Crazy String all over them. Henry stops where he is, watching the kids with a happy smile, enjoying their antics, and it makes me wonder how often he got to play with other kids over the last year with Norm. I make a mental note to find him some friends in the neighborhood.

Back at the house, Dracula opens the door and growls savagely at us even as he throws Milky Ways into Henry's bag. "Hi, Pete," Henry says.

"Hi, Henry," he says. "Looks like you got a load of candy."

Henry nods, holding up his bag for Pete to inspect. "I got so much," he says enthusiastically.

"We still have one more stop to make," I say. "We just need your car keys."

"You can have them. But first," Pete says, grabbing Henry and hoisting him up into the air. "I'm going to suck your blood!"

"Dracula," I say. "Have a heart."

"Don't mind if I do!" Pete yells in his best Transylvanian accent, burying his masked face into Henry's chest while Henry convulses with laughter.

"Whose house is this?" Henry asks me from the backseat.

"They give good candy here."

"Oh," he says, nodding.

With Henry's permission, I am once again wearing the goblin mask underneath the monk's hood. Tamara answers the door in jeans and a cable sweater, her hair pulled haphazardly out of her face with some randomly placed plastic clips. "Buzz Lightyear!" Tamara says, kneeling down to examine Henry's costume. He nods, smiling shyly at her. I watch Tamara through my mask, the rubber, slick with my saliva, sticking to my face. It's a strangely disembodied feeling, being so close to her again while she has no idea. I'm dying to reach out and touch her face, to bury my hands in the thick rings of her hair, but she would no doubt find the advances of a satanic monk alarming, so I stand quietly, impotent in my disguise.

"What's your name?"

"Henry."

"Here you go, Henry," she says, tossing some Hershey's Miniatures into his bag. She looks up at me as she does, and I'm suddenly positive she can see me, right through the mask. But if that were true, she'd be angry, wouldn't she, at this violation? And the expression spreading across her face is anything but angry. Suddenly, impossibly, she steps forward and hugs me. I hug her back, too shocked to say anything. After a few seconds, she whispers into my rubber ear. "Please, just tell me it's you."

"I just figured this is how you treat all the grown-ups," I say, my voice muffled under the mask.

"Thank God," she says with a laugh, hugging me tighter.

"How did you know?" I say, spreading my fingers out across her back.

I can feel her trembling in my arms. "My Zack alarm was going off."

Finally, we separate. "So, what?" she says, stepping back as I pull off the mask. "Did you actually rent a kid for this little stunt?"

"This is Henry King," I say, brushing the sweaty hair out of my face while Henry clings to my leg. "My brother."

Tamara looks at me, nodding slowly as she figures it out. "Wow," she says. "I guess you've had an exciting few weeks, huh?"

"Never a dull moment. Where's Sophie?"

"Sleeping. Can you stay awhile?"

"I would, but I have to get Henry home. It's past his bedtime already."

She hugs me again and it's one of our originals, a no-holds-barred, full-on, cut-through-the-crap embrace, and only her arms stop me from crumpling like a rag doll. Sometimes you don't need to talk things out. Sometimes, with the right person, things just need some time to percolate on their own, without the messy lunge and parry of discussion to hinder them. "Come back later," Tamara says meaningfully, her eyes wide and deep, her voice borne on the currents of the unspecified promise in which we're suddenly, inexplicably floating.

Henry and I step outside into the starry night and, pagan holiday or not, I would swear I can see heaven up there.

Henry must be put to bed with two books, which, after being read to him, have to be left on the bed within arm's reach as he falls asleep. The closet light is left on with the door ajar, casting a long rhombus of light onto his bed, his Thomas train clutched tightly in his fist, the creased photo of his lost and found brothers folded squarely and tucked under his pillow. He is a boy of careful ritual, given to creating order and predictability in whatever small ways he can, having found the greater world around him sorely lacking in this department. Only once all of these safeguards are in place do I kiss him good night and leave the room, making sure not to leave the door halfway open.

My mother is sitting in the dark on the top stair, pairing little white socks from an ancient laundry bin. "You're very good with him," she says to me.

"Thanks."

"You know, I'm too old to raise another child."

I sit down next to her on the stairs and pick a batch of socks out of the laundry bin. "I know, Mom," I say.

Our elbows connect softly as we work, sparking with static electricity from the carpet. "He's a sweet boy," she says.

"And I'm here to help, but I'm too old to be his mother. He should have a normal life, maybe the first King boy in three generations to have a positive male role model."

She puts her head on my shoulder as I line up two white socks and roll them together into a tight ball, tossing them lightly into the bin. "I know, Mom," I say.

forty-two

Tamara hugs me fiercely when I step through the door, and we stand like that in her foyer for a long while, rocking slowly back and forth while things inside me twist and rotate on their axes like lock tumblers clicking into place.

"I did choose you," I tell her.

"I know," she says, smiling. "I've missed you so much, and I just decided that if you hadn't chosen me, you never would have made such a mess of things."

I stare at her incredulously. "If you felt that way, why didn't you call me?"

She shakes her head, leaning in to hug me again. "I knew that if I was right, you'd come on your own."

"There's so much I have to tell you," I say, my chest quivering, my voice soft and unsteady. She pulls back to look at me, smiling as she turns up to kiss me. "Later," she whispers, pulling me toward the stairs.

Afterward, I lie between her legs, still ensconced firmly inside her, as we hold whispered conversations that she punctuates with soft, lingering kisses on my chin and lower lip. "I have an idea," I say.

"Tell me."

"Let's skip the part where we have to feel each other out, trying to determine where the boundaries are, and who's feeling it more than the other and all that. Let's just agree that we're in love and take it on faith that there are no trapdoors."

Tamara runs a lone finger down my spine, and I shiver against her, moving my hands to where her breasts merge into my chest. "That's probably easier said than done," she murmurs, tickling the sweat off my neck with the tip of her tongue.

"Nothing has been easy for us yet," I point out even as I feel myself growing aroused inside of her again. "I figure we're due."

Tamara closes her eyes, arching her back up beneath me, chin to the ceiling, eyes at half-mast as she pulls me farther inside her. Her expression is one of pleasurable effort, and even though this is the first time we've been here like this, I know it's the expression that I'll forever associate with our lovemaking, that will appear unbidden behind my closed eyes whenever we're apart. "So, what do you say?" I whisper, stretching out over her.

"I say we give it a shot," she says in the last instant before her lips part to devour mine.

While Tamara sleeps, I tiptoe into Sophie's room to kiss her in her crib. She rolls over as I do, opening her eyes to stare up at me, instantly awake. "Zap here," she whispers, her voice hoarse with sleep.

"I missed you, Sophie," I say.

"Zap came back."

"That's right. Zap came back."

"The *Annie* DVD broke," she informs me.

"Should we go to the store and buy you a new one?"

"Yes, buy you a new one," she says, rolling sleepily onto her side. "Where I going tomorrow?"

"I don't know," I whisper to her. "Wherever you want."

"Where Zap going?"

I rub her back softly. "Zap's not going anywhere," I say.

As much as I'd like to, I can't spend the night. Henry has been waking up crying in the early-morning hours, tearing down the stairs to find me, terrified that I've left him. No matter how much I reassure him during his waking hours, his subconscious remains unconvinced. I'm hoping that it's just a matter of time, that unlike the rest of us, Henry is young enough to have escaped any lasting psychological damage from Norm's particular brand of neglect. I think about maybe getting him some professional help, but I don't want to be one of those people who send their kids to a different therapist for every little ailment. On the other hand, I don't want to be the kind of person who denies his child the benefits of therapy on principle, either. I discussed it briefly with Lela, who certainly knows a thing or two about screwed-up kids, but she just said welcome to parenthood, where the only certainty is uncertainty. Maybe so, but when I see the terror swimming in Henry's wide, red-rimmed eyes, his mouth opened in a petrified scream as I wipe the tears off his face, I'm fairly certain that I hate Norm with a passion that threatens to overwhelm.

But at other times, when Henry's playing peacefully with his trains or sitting on my lap as I read to him, his fingers absently, possessively pulling at the hairs on my wrist, I find myself thinking wistfully about Norm, grateful for his having brought Henry to me, and I wonder whether we'll ever hear from him again. In the short while he was here, his presence was so overpowering that it seems impossible that he's gone, that he was ever really gone. I realize that while I thought I understood him, he was more of a stranger than I'd ever imagined. To have wormed his way back into the relatively good graces of his family, only to abscond with our forgiveness once again, seems indicative of an inherent defect of the soul that goes much deeper than pathological irresponsibility. And, oddly enough, that very realization seems to facilitate a new acceptance, a willingness to meet him on his terms. At some point I'll have to discuss all of this with Henry, try to help him understand his father in as painless a way as possible, but that point is not now. He's nowhere near ready, and I know I'm not, either. But I'm hoping that perhaps, without the burden of expectations, Henry can grow to feel good about Norm, maybe even get to know him a little. And, I guess, maybe I can too.

But as I crawl into bed, my limbs deliciously weary from the past few hours with Tamara, I consider another, equally likely possibility, that someday in the not-too-distant future, the phone will ring, and it will be a police officer, maybe a Florida state trooper, calling to tell me that they found Norm dead in his room in some low-rent efficiency hotel in a crummy neighborhood, that his heart gave out while he slept, and I'll think bitterly, at that moment, that it served him right, that there was no other end for him but to die alone. But I know that somewhere in me will be the grief, already forming now, that every son has for his father, and I hope I'm smart enough by then to give voice to it and let it be heard, if not for my sake, then for Henry's.

And here comes Henry, like clockwork, tearing down the stairs, Thomas train gripped, as always, in his right hand, his frightened wail shattering the quiet stillness of our house, waking me up from the sleep I didn't even realize I'd slipped into. I sit up in my bed, arms open wide, and he performs a running leap, clearing the top of the bed to land squarely at my side, his arms flying around my neck even as the sobs wrack his body. And as much as I want him to get over this, I also know I'm thrilled to be the one he seeks out in his dread, the lone person who can right his world. I feel love in places I never knew existed within me. I hold him tightly, rocking back and forth as my whispered assurances gradually penetrate the somnambulant haze of his nightmare. Once he's calmed down, he kisses my cheek and curls up beside me under the comforter, nestling his butt against my chest like a sleeping puppy as I sing to him.

Good night, sweet baby, good night
I'm right here to watch over you
And the moon, stars, and I
And this old lullaby
Will make all your sweet dreams come true

I'm still not sure what I want for myself, but I know what I want for Henry, and that will be my guide. I will love him, and I will love Tamara and Sophie, and it occurs to me, as Henry snuggles easily against me, that there are better things than plans upon which to build your life, and by some miracle, in my flailing about, I seem to have stumbled upon them. Tomorrow I'll start looking for a place in Riverdale, close enough so that Lela can help out with the babysitting as my work schedule fills up. There will be schooling to determine, legalities of guardianship to address, and no doubt a host of complications I have yet to discover. The future is suddenly terrifyingly and magnificently uncertain, but tonight, as I lie fully awake in the dark, there is only now, the sound of Henry's slow, even breaths filling the room, and the electrified beating of my own racing heart.

about the author

JONATHAN TROPPER lives with his wife and two children in Westchester, New York. He is the author of two previous novels, *Plan B* and *The Book of Joe,* which is currently being developed as a motion picture by Warner Bros. Studios. *Everything Changes* is currently in development at Sony Pictures. Jonathan can be contacted through his website at www.jonathantropper.com.